DEDICATION

For my husband, Paul, whom I adore more than words.
For the good and the bad times that we've seen together, where you've been right
at my side and never faltered.
This is for you.
Always, D x

EVACUATION

KENDRO MOVED NEARER HIS OPEN office window, once again watching their dying sun setting for the night, too tired even to think—three days too tired. Rubbing his eyes, he stroked down the sides of his temple. A blue tinge of Croex energy from his fingers lit his royal birthmark in a rainbow of colours, the energy not reaching his weary mind. His broad shoulders seemed to have shrunk over the past three days.

Three tiers up in the royal palace, he glanced at the view below, making out soldiers in their dark uniforms as they loaded belongings onto shuttles in the growing twilight. The sight weighed upon his soul. He turned, regarding his empty office stripped of everything, but the desk and two chairs. *Best to do what work I can, before they come for these, too.*

Work didn't come for him. He stared at the portable screen, blank, seeing only his reflection, his handmade uniform, a bright blue in the glass. "You think you've won?" With a headshake, wiping away tears with the back of his meaty hand, Kendro flung his reader at a wall where it shattered. "Never!"

Resting his head on his desk, he paused for a brief moment. His breathing slowed, shaking himself awake. For almost three days now…with barely any rest since he ordered their planet's evacuation, within every tightening muscle and sinew, Kendro felt the strain.

"Kendro?"

His attention turned to his wife, Mika, standing in his open doorway. After stepping lightly over the wreckage of the smashed reader, she quickened her stride with a look of anxiety; the swish from her silken robes the only sound as she approached.

Drinking in her essence, Kendro's spirit lifted. Glorious, three

1

months pregnant, yet no one knew. The traditional, one-sleeved satin gown she wore allowed everyone to see the croex she contained. *Her energy shines brightly,* Kendro thought. The gown's figure-hugging material accentuated every growing curve. "You are beautiful."

Mika smiled. Her birthmark smaller than her husband's, it flickered red as emotion rushed to its surface, spreading down her neck and shoulder, onto her bare arm, igniting around her every finger. *Perfect.*

"You thought changing houses was bad when we were first mated." Standing, he reached for her. *Can I shield this dread much longer?* "Solar systems are so much harder. Exhausting."

A frown settled on Mika's lips. She looked into his darkening face. "You don't look so good," she said as she prodded him back into his seat so she could stand and ruffle his hair.

"I know," Kendro replied hearing her every thought, connected with not only his wife, but with all of his species.

Stepping behind him, Mika placed both hands on his shoulders kneading them with her small, neat fingers. "We'll be all right. Not only do I have faith in you, but so do our people."

Mika moved around, sitting before him, elegantly crossing her legs. "And you are biased. I'm getting bigger," she said, patting her stomach. "It won't be long—they'll wonder soon."

"I'm hoping we can feign an illness for you once we're on board the *Sol'Ishar.*"

Kendro felt the silvery strands of another vision tighten around his consciousness. Shaking it away, he focussed on Mika's lazy caress. Would he be able to save the little one, already named Taliri, as well?

Mika stared at him. "Do I need to know what your latest visions entail?"

Reaching out, Kendro took her face in his hands, sorrow humming through his fingertips. "If you tell, then our unborn son's life could be forfeited."

A sharp wind blew over Mika's bare arms, goose bumps rippling across her skin. She stood, lowering her face, tears forming at Kendro's admonition.

As Kendro expected, Mika's tone changed. "I'm excited." She pouted, rubbing her stomach, protective, fearful of his words. "Why not tell our people?"

"We can't." Kendro held out a hand for her. "All right?"

Taking her husband's hand, Mika kissed it. "I promise. Not a soul."

"If word gets out, it would take only one angry person to hurt you— I'd never forgive myself."

"I trust you." Mika backed away. "With my life. And with the life of our son."

2

A knock at the door wrenched Kendro's attention away. This wasn't what he needed right now. He knew who stood waiting for entry. *I need peace.*

"It's all right." Mika stood, her expression shifted, defeated. "I'll be waiting."

Mika palmed open the panel door, which lay flush with the nondescript wall. Wez stood silently. His eyes roamed the bare walls as his long, greying hair lifted in the breeze from the open window.

Glancing from Mika to Kendro, Wez lowered his head, both viewing his balding crown. "I am sorry, Your Highness." He fiddled with the hem of his sleeve knowing he wasn't welcome. "Shall I come back at another time?"

Stepping around him, Mika's smile was more of a grimace. "Don't worry, I'm leaving."

Kendro waved Wez inside. He would appease his irritated wife later. "Please, have a seat."

Even at eighty-four, Wez's graceful movement hid the pain and suffering he fought constantly. His birthmark intricately covered both his uniform's bare arm and the fingers on his clothed one. Pulling at the single sleeve, he eased his bulk into a remaining chair and stared at the bare, white wall before him.

As if visioning, he began, "You know why I am here."

"So," Kendro sighed. "You know."

"Which part? The fact that Mika is pregnant? Or that you intend to hide the Royal Heir away, so no one else will know?"

Kendro's face dropped. With all the power he held, he still could not keep his secrets from Wez.

Wez almost laughed. He knew his King all too well. "I was your father's advisor. I've been yours since you took the throne."

Kendro looked away to the open window, thinking, not wanting to acknowledge, at least for the time being, that his life would be so short.

"What else are you planning?" Wez enquired.

To talk about it made it too real. Kendro needed someone to discuss it with. But, staring at Wez's bare shoulder, he refused to answer.

"I don't see everything—" Wez prompted.

"I hope to get us to a new home with minimal casualties." Kendro knew this wasn't possible though. "What more can I say?" The unspoken lay between them in the near empty room—their survival depended on trying.

"Some individuals believe we should stay and fight." Wez's stare came straight at him, evaluating all that wasn't being said. "The other three Houses are struggling with the evacuation. Your handling of the next few days will be crucial."

3

Gritting his teeth, Kendro stood. He shoved a shaky finger at the window and countered, "They don't understand." Wez followed his gesture to their sun. "We have no idea what's in store if we go, yet we must."

"I know what you're doing." Wez joined Kendro. "Your shield might not be obvious to most, but some know it is there."

"I tried my best to hide it." Guilt flooded through Kendro as he blinked. "But…"

"Only the most powerful Aonise could shield so many."

Watching the teeming citizens below, bundled into their warmest for this arduous exercise as they loaded their shuttles, Kendro wondered if he was doing the right thing.

"Your Highness," Wez placed a hand on Kendro's arm guiding him from the window, "they don't understand because the truth would have terrified them all months ago." Wez's voice made no dent. "Please, do not distress yourself by their ways. Our dying sun is not something the houses want to admit. They would sooner blame you for the Zefron, as well as this upheaval."

Wez returned to his seat, shaking, and no longer the man he was when he advised Kendro's father these forty years past.

"You've seen something else, haven't you?" Kendro asked at last. "Is that why you're here now?"

Wez peeked back to the light from their glorious red sun. "I did see something."

"What?" Kendro's lips drew together, tighter.

"The Zefron. They…"

Kendro's body stiffened. "Can't leave us alone, can they?" His hands shook, his voice lowered to a near whisper. "We're leaving our solar system. They're still bent on our annihilation. Why?" Kendro's eyes flashed, his frustration peaking. These were answers he needed now. Spinning away from the window, Kendro searched the bare room for something else to destroy. It was no use. He fell into his chair, defeated.

Having seen many of Kendro's outbursts, Wez locked eyes with him. "You know none of us are sure." Withdrawing his hands from his sleeve, Wez spread them, as wide as the divide between the Aonise Houses over this harrowing move. "So much history was lost when we left our home world following the Great War."

"Yes," Kendro shouted, "and here we are again, forced to leave because of them!" Clenching his fists and biting his lip, he so wanted something to throw.

Scratching his nose, Wez's birthmark shimmered green.

Kendro's lips narrowed, sensing Wez about to shatter his world once more.

"The *Sol'Ishar* will be the only survivor. Unless you change your plans today."

The room spun. Change all our plans? Kendro's face dropped. "No." He leaned on his chair. It creaked beneath his weight. Taking a deep breath, he tried to stem the nausea sweeping through him.

Lowering his head, Wez sighed. Kendro read in the old man's mind. This was no time for indecisiveness. Bluntly, Wez laid things out for his King. "If, as you've planned, each ship carries a specific House, then only one will survive. Yours."

Over half of the Aonise 'working' society already lived on board the ships. He couldn't issue new orders now, with no time to implement them.

After a long moment, Wez probed. "Sire?"

Kendro remained silent. He knew there were choices. Dire ones. There must be an alternate one for him now.

A moment later, Kendro turned to a small computer, entering Ainoren Broki's personal comms number. "Call everyone together. We meet in an hour."

Captain Sheve Hadi stood, stretching his long legs the length of the bridge on the *Sol'Ishar*. He scratched his head. *I need another haircut.* Sitting again at first point, there was no time for that now.

Things were not going as well as the Captain had hoped.

At his command was a brand new ship, not even done with its first shakedown cruise, half-finished and full of glitches. It made everything extremely complicated.

Commander Vax monitored the transfers and incoming cargo beside him, tedious but necessary work, and she knew it. But together, they followed two three-dimensional view-screens, co-ordinating, and tracking the movements of the King and his labouring, dark suited soldiers. Sheve's fingers tapped his bare knee. This process was taking too long, and he itched to be back in space. His sharp jaw ground in frustration.

"Sir," said Vax. She pressed twice at her console, glancing his way. "The King is requesting to speak with you on comms. I'll put it through to your office."

Turning the shuttle images off, Sheve stood, "Thank you," and he made his way back through the bridge into his office. He ignored the sparse decoration of the mother ship. It felt nothing like his previous office on the *MarsDen*. When Kendro visited him six months ago, promoting him to lead command of all the evacuation ships, the excitement that rushed through his lean physique had left him humbled.

The task was at hand now, though laborious with not much time for

5

anything other than work, this sparseness would be his world for quite some time to come.

Sheve sat at his desk, placing a narrow hand on a clear panel to his right. His DNA accepted, the desk lit up. Kendro's face appeared. Over the last few months, Sheve had noticed his King had not only lost weight, but grey had appeared both in his hair and the beard he'd started to grow. Sheve felt a twinge of concern, but hoped it didn't show on his face. "Your Highness, everything all right?"

Kendro smiled. "Yes, Captain. Where are we in our evacuation preparations?"

"My weekly report will be filed with Ainoren Broki in the morning, as usual, Sir."

"I'm sure. Please run through it for me. Now."

Sheve touched his key-port bringing up the report he'd logged earlier. "We're almost fully loaded with today's tallies. Eight hundred seventeen thousand and forty-one citizens and crew are on board." He glanced quietly at some scrolling info, his birthmark colour flashing. Croex high, confidant. "Reports from the other ships are similar, Sir."

"I will be holding a press conference in the next hour. You must speed things up, as all citizens will be heading for the launch site tonight. Prepare your crew. Work through all watches, if you have to. Whatever it takes."

Sheve swallowed. Something had changed. He could see pain etched across the King's normally placid face. "Yes, Sir." He risked being disrespectful, and with a sharp intake of breath, he asked, "It's time, isn't it?"

The King nodded only once before severing their communication, leaving Sheve to initiate this new plan. Yet, the Captain sat there pondering his choices. Deciding, he hit his comms to patch himself through to the medical bays.

"Doctor," Katya Brie answered before looking, "Sheve, you're supposed to be on your way home!" his spouse pointed out.

"Oh, you noticed it was your mate, did you?" Sheve smiled at her. "I could say the same about you." Getting down to orders, he began. "Plans have changed. We're on twenty-four hour watch as of now. The King will be issuing a statement soon. Be ready. The Heiako elderly are next."

"I'm well aware of who's coming in next." She sighed, fingering a loose strand of her golden hair behind a shell-like ear, exposing her matching sunlit yellow birthmark in the process. "I'll let everyone know we're standing double watches."

"Thanks." Sheve could rely on her. Dealing with the lower class citizens came naturally to doctors. However, getting his top officers to do the same was going to be tougher. Like him, they'd pushed past double duty all week now, exhausted. Dealing with the Heiako lower classes tested everyone's patience.

Brie placed her palm up to him. He reciprocated before signing off.

Stepping towards the podium, Kendro fought for composure. The consequences of this decision would weigh heavy on his heart for the rest of his life. Aonise gathered below him, everyone from every House. Four large view screens connected him to camos on board their four escape ships. Kendro surveyed them all.

Standing with him to his right were the rest of his house and family; Ainoren Octav Broki, his wife, Frie, and Lieutenant Commander Lyrik Horr and his wife, Roma. Together, the six of them, not as broad as Kendro, but most the height of their King, formed the Royal House— House Niakrex.

Blue banners waved the royal colour, filling Kendro with more hope than he'd ever imagined possible under the circumstances. Smiles adorned his subjects' faces. A cheer rang out. Pointing their cameras and microphones towards him, with a nod, the news troop gave him the go-ahead.

Taking a deep breath, Kendro spoke loud and clear into the microphone. "I acknowledge every citizen, not just those assigned to a House. Our evacuation is steady. Each of you will be assigned a ship number. The evacuation procedure will be as follows." He peered from the sheet he carried back out to his people. Many more shoulders here were covered.

Only the Military and Government caste wore an arm or leg bare to show house birthmarks. "It does not correspond with any House, or any class. You will board the ship you are assigned. I implore you to stay calm." At that, the hum began. "These orders take effect immediately."

As Kendro completed his closing statement, Madrall, leader of House Flikait, caught his eye. Madrall bowed his very dark head once, his striking birthmark flickered his colour of yellow against his much darker Flikait skin, and, at this point, a deep gesture of loyalty. Kendro watched as several hands shot into the air. He appealed to them, "This is a testing time for all of us. We must survive, until we find a new home." *Deception kept at bay—they need not know we have not a plan.* A clamour rose for more information, assurances, hope.

Kendro had no time for questions, feeling overwhelmed by everyone's emotions, and his own. *I can do this. Given time to try, we can do this.*

Stepping away from the podium, he took Mika's small hand in his larger one. Holding his head high, they strode out through a corridor, and into their private gardens. Voices rising behind them, Kendro held tightly onto Mika's hand. Fighting the inner turmoil to rush back inside, insisting they be calm, and that they'd be all right, he carried on.

Mika tugged Kendro back, stopping the escape she felt within him. She leaned closer for an embrace, whispering in his ear, "Are you going to tell me?"

"I can't."

Mika began to protest, and then stopped. Her eyes growing wide, she pointed beyond the garden walls. "Oh!"

Kendro turned skyward. A tremendous solar flare licked their atmosphere. Gritting his teeth, Kendro watched the flaming tendrils strike his shield. He could do nothing to react. They curled along its protective layer, intent on decimating the surface of his world, while consuming everything in sight.

"Sire." Wez rushed on unsteady bowed legs towards them, shouting, "Get inside. Now!" Words couldn't describe the acrid burning that assaulted their nostrils.

Moving to protect Mika, Kendro found himself stuck, transfixed by their darkening world.

"What's happening?" Mika questioned Wez as he reached them.

"We're too late," Wez puffed. "It has begun. Inside. Now."

Tugging at Kendro, Mika tried to pull him back towards the palace, dread flooding through her veins as the tugging intensified.

"It can't be happening," Kendro said. Wez's ancient arms yanked him from the garden. "It's too early."

"You don't have time," Wez reprimanded. "Mobilize all your forces."

They raced back into the palace. Ainoren Broki threw open the doors, waving them on faster.

"Octav," Kendro mumbled, "I'm sorry." In the distance, the city lights blinked. All around them were screams, muffled voices, and the sounds of rushing footsteps.

Complete darkness.

"So quick. I didn't know." Kendro's birthmark flickered. With a flash of his croex, he lit up the room. Eerie shadows cast in every direction, heightening the rooms' emptiness.

"None of us did," Wez replied.

"What do you need?" Octav pushed him. "I'll retrieve it. You must head for the *Sol'Ishar*. Now."

"You can't get it alone," Mika said. "I've things hidden."

"Octav, Mika will accompany you. Thank you for your concern. Now, go. I must make one last statement before I leave for the ship."

8

Entering the main conference room, Kendro noticed one news crew remained, their equipment lighting the surrounding area. Approaching, Kendro demanded of them, "Are you still live?"

The shorter reporter nodded, patting an energy-pack on her hip. One of her assistants pointed at the camera. "Whenever you are, Your Highness."

Kendro stared into the dark lens, his jaw set with determination. "For those still watching, this is it. Take your family to the re-location centres. Put aside any differences, any prejudice. Be swift. More importantly, be safe. Leave everything. Go now."

Kendro indicated to the news troop. "Go. You have family to be with."

"Your Highness—" the reporter protested.

Waving them towards the far door, he repeated, "Go." Then he, too, hurried from the conference room.

Kendro needed to do something else before he made his way to the *Sol'Ishar*. He ran towards his private chamber, and out into the palace gardens.

In almost complete darkness, Kendro knew each step. He'd walked this path every week since he'd been anointed King.

In the gardens, he stopped by a wall taller than any other inside the palace grounds. It bore one symbol—the royal crest of the House Niakrex.

Reaching under his tunic, Kendro pulled out a pendant. It glowed against the darkness as it separated from its chain, echoing his dimming birthmark. Pressing it to the wall's crest, he waited a moment before the resounding click allowed him to pass straight through the now opened gap.

Once Kendro was inside the hidden space, the pendant blazed emitting enough light to guide him. Kendro followed the shape of the wall. The path ahead of him dipped, yet his steps didn't falter. He knew the terrain, every twist and turn committed to memory.

Further and further underground, he strode until he reached his destination—a hidden room. Kendro's birthmark flashed in the darkness. Several lanterns illuminated. With one quick glance around, he held out the pendant. At first, nothing happened, then once he felt the weight of it lift, he let go.

The pendant floated chest high to the King. In air, on its own now, it began spinning. A whirling rainbow of colours brightened the room, and then, stopped. A thin, bright, vertical line took form in the wall, widening until it formed a doorway.

"Why are you here?" came a voice. So long since Kendro had heard that voice.

9

Kendro spoke, "It is time."

"So soon? It doesn't seem that long ago you brought me down here." A withered arm protruded from the doorway.

Kendro sighed, completely overwhelmed. "It's happening quicker than we thought." Had they all made it to the ships by now?

The voice wavered with concern, saying, "It has started? Already?"

"Our people are evacuating as we speak."

The arm flexed, another pale limb appeared. "Are you sure no one will know what you've been doing?"

"No. If they do, then that is for me to work out."

"You will leave me, Kendro. Don't hesitate. We've done this for our people—remember that." The speaker faltered for a moment. "Remember my sacrifice."

Kendro's face creased. "Can we pull this off?"

"We will. We have to."

Kendro reached out, grasping the arm. Pulling on it, his older stepbrother, Nax, fell into the underground space.

The old man squinted. His tunic, although tattered, was clean. His mess of beard and hair met, almost covering his navel.

Nax stared into Kendro's blue eyes. "What aren't you telling me?"

"It hurts." Kendro gasped. The air around them sizzled. "A lot."

Red eyes glowed in the darkness before him. "Then, it is time for you to rest. Let me take the burden," Nax said.

"Are you sure?"

Nax smiled weakly. "Kendro, I'm dying anyway. Go. Save our people."

Kendro moved closer, croex exchanged, allowing Nax to take over the shield. A sigh escaped his lips, once Nax had control. The lightening of it almost drove Kendro to his knees, such a relief.

Nax's birthmark blazed red, lighting up the cave with an eerie glow of what was to come. "You were right. It does hurt. Now, go. Save our people."

Kendro hesitated at the last moment, Nax's eyes reflecting the pain he'd just received. "You'll never be forgotten." Leaning into his brother, they embraced.

"Now." Nax pushed him away. "Go."

THE SOL`ISHAR

OCTAV PALMED THE KEYPAD OUTSIDE the royal chambers, waiting for Mika to answer. She'd sent him to pick up one last item from the Royal Hold, before she would leave the palace. *Come on*, he thought, *we need to leave now.*

"Think she's still in there? Might she have gone on?" Special Officer Chace Monro pulled his uniformed cap down over his ears, hiding his growing dark hair.

"I know she is." Octav saw fright in the young officer's eyes. While they waited for the Queen to answer their call, his special ops-trained warrior shivered.

"We'll get off this planet, don't worry."

"I can't help but worry." Chace's hands shook as he locked eyes with Octav. "You know we don't have a destination."

"You're privy to that information." Octav shot him a glare. "Do not speak of it aloud."

Chace stepped backed. "I'm sorry, sir."

Octav stared at Chace's shimmering forearm where his birthmark betrayed his fear. Wearing their traditional uniforms had been Kendro's idea. He'd hoped to bring calm to everyone as their open birthmarks reflected their emotions. Winter wasn't the time of year to be showing bare skin though. The chill Octav felt inside was almost un-bearable, and not all of it from the weather.

Chace's emotions were there for everyone to see, from the flicker across his striking facial mark to the swirling pattern of his arm. He was terrified and more, his croex fairly shouted it.

"Listen to me." Against his better judgment, Octav reached for Chace. Pulling his own croex to the surface, Octav allowed it to trickle

11

through into Chace's skin. "Trust me. We might not know where we're going, but we will find a new home."

A spark ignited between them, the energy alive between the pair, this time Octav backed off. *What is this?*

Chace's birthmark slowed to a flickering, and then stopped. Chace lowered his head. "Thank you."

Octav turned back to the Queen's door muttering, "You're welcome." Pain resonated within him, and he couldn't explain why. With no answer, he again placed his palm to the panel about to use his security clearance. Patience wasn't his signature.

The door opened on Mika, a hand on the wall. Concern spread through Octav instantly at her casual stance. "My Queen! We must leave."

"Where's Kendro?" she said, allowing only Octav inside her quarters. Chace remained out.

Octav hesitated, he didn't want to worry Mika unnecessarily, but watching her flickering birthmark, he made the decision to speak the truth. "Word from the *Sol'Ishar* is the sun will continue to flare every five micros."

"Flare?" Mika's birthmark flashed, as her face paled. "I'm sure he'll meet us shortly. Kendro knows how little time we have."

Across their bond, Octav cast a glance around the almost empty room. The royal crest adorned each of the hand-carved pieces of furniture that would remain here forever. Their escape ships packed with only essential equipment, wildlife, and food stores. "It must be difficult," he said, feeling her sadness.

Mika ran a hand across the back of a chair. "Yes, it is."

"I'll find Kendro." There was no time for reminiscing. "We need to get you to the *Sol'Ishar* now. Please, do you know where he's gone?"

"Are we in immediate danger?" Mika stepped closer to him.

A small beeping alarm emitted inside Octav's only pocket. Pulling the small silver device, he barked, "Ainoren."

"You must locate the King. Explosions on the sun's surface have started a chain reaction." Even Chace could hear the Captain's static voice.

Mika snatched Octav's arm, her eyes wide. "The gardens!"

"You're coming with us, Your Grace," Octav said. "Anything more you need here?"

Mika glanced around, lowering her head. "No, everything else was sent weeks ahead."

"Then, we must leave." Octav gestured. "Pilot Munro will see you to the awaiting shuttle."

Kendro brushed the cobwebs and dirt off his uniform, hurrying back through the gardens, up the main steps to the Royal Palace. Octav came at a run, grabbing his King's arm. "We've been looking everywhere." Anger in each word, no longer holding back, he commanded, "Come on!"

"Don't panic." Kendro halted, ignoring this insubordination. "There's time."

"You're still my priority." Octav cocked his head to one side, in the way he usually did when something seriously annoyed at him. Kendro sighed. As the face of the Aonise military, his model good looks, and perfect wife, Octav had everything. Well, almost. He had yet to have children—but no time for this to bother Kendro.

A moment later, the two flew through the courtyard, and down a flight of steps. Octav ushered his King towards their awaiting shuttle, his thoughts invading Kendro's mind. *Thank Ari, I've found him in time.*

He would miss even the simplest things in life. Kendro ran a hand over the shuttle's shiny surface.

"Something wrong?"

"It's—" Kendro held a breath then climbed in, "—nothing."

"You're sure?" Octav probed, hopping into the seat beside his wife, Frie.

At Octav's nod, Chace typed in several commands at his console. The port closed with a snap as he manoeuvred the hovering shuttle several meters off the ground, and then away from the palace.

Kendro dared not look behind. His stomach churned the farther they rose from the garden.

Octav did watch as the palace dwindled in the distance. Frie squeezed his hand. "I wish there had been more time."

Kendro agreed. "We were lucky."

"Emmi refuses to change plans." Octav locked eyes with Kendro, reporting to his King on the state of the other houses. "So House Sonaya won't be joining us."

Emmi! Stupid, stupid woman! "That could cause major repercussions." Kendro opened a porthole, relieving his sudden nausea. "What about the others?"

"Both House Flikait and Magalite are on board the *Sol'Ishar.*"

"Good." Rubbing his forehead, Kendro stuck his face into the stream of rushing air. "And Mika?"

"You'll see her soon." Frie's words calmed him.

The shuttle slowed. Kendro noticed the thousands of citizens still lining the streets, the soldiers guiding them towards their respective ships. As their shuttle flew past, heads turned for a closer look, and then, chivvied by the soldiers, they were hurried aboard.

13

Looming above them, the *Sol'Ishar's* gigantic metallic hull darkened the sky.

Frie reached for her husband's hand again. "She's huge. Will we be safe?"

With a guilty look at Kendro, Octav assured her. "She's much like our smaller vessels."

Frie's gaze rose up at the ship. "Really?"

"Well, on a larger a scale," Kendro said.

Frie laughed, a tinkling sound. "To be sure, much larger," she said, as the loading dock hove into view. Underneath the ship, the shuttle eased into the loading bay. Sliding the door open, Kendro stepped onto the ship.

Before him, Mika tapped her long nails on a console. Shivering, she pulled at her cloak, a scowl settling on her face.

"We'll convene in an hour," Kendro commanded, glancing once at Octav.

"I'll gather the others."

"You look so pale." Mika's scowl softened. "Are you all right?"

"Much better now," he smiled through his pain, "seeing that you are safe."

Reaching, Mika took his hand, more than she normally would do in public. She led him in, and out of the cold. "Bar House Sonaya, things seem smooth at present."

"Yes." Kendro followed, never letting go of her hand, her affection much needed. "You've seen Emmi?" They made their way quickly up the steep ramp.

"They still smell so new," Mika said, as if she hadn't heard, and they traversed several shiny white corridors.

Kendro ran his other hand along the bulkhead, far from his focus on Mika. "We'll have to sort out House Sonaya. I've no time to argue with Emmi at present."

"Argue?" There was no way around this now. "She has to listen. She might be a House leader, but you're her King."

"She listens. Doesn't mean she'll obey. We need to meet properly."

Mika stopped before a lift. "Don't blame yourself for her insubordination. She's still very young."

"She needs more guidance than I have provided." Kendro's birthmark flickered with his frustration. "There's never enough time."

Resting a hand on her husband's shoulder, Mika's gentle words reminded him, "She has had your guidance."

"Destination?" the silvery voice of the ship's main computer asked.

"Royal Chambers."

The lift jerked, and sped towards their quarters. Turning his attention to Mika, Kendro reminded her, "Emmi makes everything difficult. It seems natural for her rivalry."

"Then, should you ask her?"

He thought for a moment, knowing it would come down to this. Kendro would have to assert his leadership with Emmi, and wasn't looking forward to it.

A creak echoed around the lift just as suddenly it lurched. Mika held her stomach.

Kendro steadied her. "What's wrong?"

"I don't think our son likes lifts." She wrapped her hand around his.

"You can feel him already?" Kendro placed a hand on her stomach. *I wish I could.*

"Yes. Can't you?" she stared at him with twinkling eyes, giving away her emotion.

Kendro knew her sadness. He tore away. "He's shielded." It hurt him to be separated from that wonderful new connection. "It stops me from feeling him."

"I'm sorry." Snuggling into his chest, Mika stroked his back, alighting desire inside, despite their topic of conversation. "I know how much it upsets you."

"Keeping Taliri safe is more important." Kendro returned her hug, wishing his son to be safe, always. "I'll have plenty of time to get to know him later."

The lift slowed, then stopped, yet they stood in each other's arms a moment longer. Leaning in towards him, Mika nuzzled into his neck.

Kendro paused, breathing in her fresh-washed scent, exhausted. "I must rest before this meeting." Pushing himself away, he moved through the door first, into a simple white hall, which led into their chambers.

"I'll prepare us some food." She moved deftly through the door, touching links until one turned on several dim lights.

"Prepare? You have people who do that for you," Kendro teased.

"You know I prefer cooking for us."

Kendro moved towards their sleeping space, but hesitated by the door. "Would you mind?"

"You want me to…" grinning, she nodded. "Of course."

Kicking off his shoes, Kendro fell onto the welcoming bedspace, feeling Mika climb in. She touched the side of his face, with long soft and delicate strokes, until he drifted to sleep.

Listening as Kendro's breathing slowed, Mika leaned over, and kissed the side of his face. Then, her eyes flashed red as she harnessed her croex, allowing her energy to seep into her tired mate.

"You've been doing far too much, for too long," she whispered. His

15

need to rest seemed out of place and albeit brief, Mika knew it was much needed for the strong presence in front of all his people, but not with her.

Looking to their porthole, she slid away, knowing he would feel her leave the bedspace.

She stood, walking towards their porthole to look out as far as she could. "The world we're leaving behind is beautiful, Taliri." Her hands instinctively rested on her stomach. "I would do anything, if we could stay."

Kendro grunted in his slumber, stirring. Mika stared lovingly at him, and back at the sky. She froze as the red shimmer blinked in and out like a warning beacon. With her stomach churning, Mika rushed to Kendro. "Something's wrong."

Fully awake in an instant, Kendro came shooting out of the bedspace, calling out on the run, "Comm the others now!" He rammed his feet into his shoes and flew out of the room.

Mika spoke into the communication panel. "Octav, the bridge quickly. Kendro's on his way."

Mika heard Kendro whispering as the panel whooshed shut behind him, "Hold out, brother. Please," knowing there would be no more restful interlude, no heads together on their pillows.

Their dying sun flickered through a port window, illuminating with an eerie red glow.

Storming onto the ship's bridge, Kendro returned Commander Vax's salute as she stood. "I need status reports on the citizens aboard the ships," he commanded. "Now."

Octav joined them a moment later. "Report?" The buzz of the night crewmembers growing with anticipation, they hurried about their business clumsily, making much more noise than Kendro would like.

"Is the Captain on his way?" said Kendro.

"He'll be here soon."

Frie, Lyrik, and Roma flew through the doorway from their quarters. "Here," they all reported in unison.

Kendro pointed Lyrik towards a console. "Status, now?"

Lyrik's huge frame almost pushed the ship's crewman from his station, frantically keying in several commands, until the screen lit up before him. "We're forty percent loaded. The *Sol'Tar* and *Sol'Rayn* are thirty percent. The *Sol'Delka* is at fifty."

Looking to Octav, knowing... futility. "Get them on any ship," Kendro demanded.

Moving towards Lyrik, Octav asked, "I need a live feed outside the ship. Can you get me that?"

"Give me a moment," said Lyrik.

"Bring up the outside view, too!"

Lyrik clicked a panel, and the windows before them flickered to life. Aonise citizens continued filing towards their ship, while Lyrik got the outside communications stations working alongside the internal ones. "You're live," he sat back, crossing his arms.

Taking a deep breath, Octav spoke clearly, "This is Ainoren Broki." Waiting a moment, he watched as they searched for him. How in Ari would they take this?

"Good. Lines one, two, and three. Board the *Sol'Tar*. Lines four, five, and six will join the *Sol'Rayn*. Lines seven and eight, board the *Sol'Ishar*. Do not run, please. Drop what you carry. Board your vessel, as fast as you can." Doing as he ordered, the guards backed away from the men and women below, who dithered, looking from their stations, mouths open, not quite sure.

"Now," Octav barked, his voice ringing with command above the citizens.

The main door burst open. Captain Hadi sped into the room while trying to straighten his uniform. "The lift. It malfunctioned." Holding onto his left side he panted. "Sorry. Six decks."

Appearing on the view screen before them were Captain Della, Captain Brayer, and Captain Gaal, their bleak faces staring at Kendro awaiting instruction.

"It is time. Start preparations for launch," said Kendro.

Captain Della and Brayer signed off with grave nods, leaving only Captain Gaal staring in contempt. "Now? Why?" He quizzed Kendro. "We're nowhere near capacity. Or ready!"

"Start procedures now. You must be ready when I give the launch codes." Cutting the comm, Kendro turned to Captain Hadi. "Comm anyone you have to, but get this ship ready to fly."

"Yes, Your Highness." Captain Hadi, hesitating before allowing himself to ask, "How long do we have?"

Kendro replied, "Not long enough," looking towards their darkening horizon.

With a loud hiss, the bridge door opened again, revealing the leader of House Flikait. His full military uniform gleamed against the flickering of his gold croex. "What can I do?" Madrall moving with speed towards Kendro, his second in command, Retray, only one-step behind him.

Polr from House Magalite stepped onto the deck a moment later, not in uniform. His mate and second-in-command, Jae, pulled her bed-tousled hair back into a tight band as Polr stood by his King's right side.

Kendro pointed at the office. "Join me." It was not a request.

Stepping towards the Captain's office, Kendro placed his hand on the side panel, waiting. The door's panel didn't budge.

Captain Hadi rushed towards them desperately to help, swiping his own hand across the panel. "The ship's full of—glitches. I'm sorry." No matter how hard he tried, it wouldn't budge.

No time. Kendro frowned. Pathetic! Turning back to Madrall and Polr, birthmark flashing its bluest, he risked non-house ears hearing this. He began, "I need to ask for your help. My brother—he's shielding everything while everyone's boarding."

Concern spread across Polr's face. He stared around the bridge, at the others. "You want us to help him, together?"

No House Leader had performed this type of task before anyone but their most trusted of family. "We'll have to use the bridge," Kendro said. This was not ideal.

Madrall regarded each crewmember waiting at their stations. He added, "I will trust them." Octav and the rest of House Niakrex smiled with relief.

Kendro nodded. "Good."

Stepping forward, Octav lowered his head with respect. Madrall listened with suspicion, knowing he was no match for Octav, obvious dread etched on his face at the words to follow.

"We're all sworn to the King," Octav said. "Anything that transpires here will not be spoken of."

"Thank you, Ainoren," Polr replied in the wake of his mate's stunned silence.

Kendro moved to the bridge's main doors, placing his palm onto the panel, a flashing blue light glowed above it sealing them in. His croex grew stronger, in the now quiet space. This was for the good of them all.

Madrall spluttered. "Nax." All faces looked to him. "That answers my next question."

"Nax took a year preparing for this." Taking a deep breath feeling his brother's pain, Kendro refused to let Madrall see this, though. "He can't hold on much longer."

"Why couldn't you trust us with this information before?" Octav stared at Kendro. No one else dared.

Madrall coughed lightly, and Octav turned to him. "I understand Kendro's decision. Information like this—think of the panic. Not only among each House, but more so, among the Heiako."

Kendro shuddered at the thought of the Heiako turning against him, or the Houses. They were the unwanted. The un-bonded Aonise citizens accounted for more crime and murder than any other faction. The King pushed such concerns away, much as he'd pushed them into the fortified bays while boarding. He concentrated on the task at hand.

Frie placed a hand on her husband's arm. Shrugging it away, Octav ignored the implications of another House's chastisement, and moved towards Lyrik. "Zoom in again on the people boarding."

Tapping in more commands, Lyrik brought the viewer back to life.

Although moving much faster now, the lines still stretched on and on. "Will we have time?" Octav asked Kendro.

"What are we? Zefrons? We're not the rushing kind. We'll have to make the time," Kendro replied, ushering the House leaders around him to begin the Scrie. "Come, form a circle. I need you to prepare—in case my brother…"

They choose an area beside the main consoles, no one asking him to finish that dire thought, struggling to establish a circle on the bridge.

"Nax—" Octav was about to say more.

"No." Kendro's face revealed what he was loath to say, his bright eyes dulled. "He will not survive the croex loss. His sacrifice, however, will never be forgotten."

Bang. Bang. "Let me in!" a shrill voice came. BANG.

Kendro sighed, turning to the pounding.

Mika wouldn't let up. "Let me in!"

Kendro placed his hand on the comms panel. "Mika, return to our room. We'll be launching sooner than planned. I need you safe!"

Mika banged. "You need me now. Let me in. Right now!"

"No."

On the small screen before him, Kendro noticed several other crewmembers joining her beyond the sealed door. He watched in dread as she turned, asking, "What can we do, he won't let us in?"

Soreea, Madrall's wife appeared behind Mika, shuffling sleepily towards the door.

Kendro reached out with his mind. "Soreea," he spoke in her mind, knowing she must do what he was about to ask.

Scanning quickly, unsure if Mika was aware of the familiar voice of her King, Soreea eyed the door.

Kendro spoke.

"Madrall?" she thought back at him.

"I will take care of your husband. I need Mika somewhere safe."

Nodding towards the security cameras, Soreea stepped towards her distraught Queen. Taking hold of Mika's arm, gently she murmured in her ear, "Come with me, Your Highness. All of you, come with me."

Kendro watched on as Mika pleaded low to Soreea, royal-to-royal, woman-to-woman, surely she'd understand with Madrall in there. "He needs me. I can't leave him."

"But you must." Soreea tugged at her sleeve. "Now come," lowering her voice, "it is his wish, Your Grace. Come. Show the others your strength, my Queen."

Kendro watched as Soreea and the Queen disappeared from sight.

"I am sorry, Your Highness," Captain Hadi said, bringing Kendro's attention to the room. "We're night staffed. I can't fly this ship alone. Could you let the rest of my crew in?" He pointed to the few people waiting, uniformed, and remaining outside the doors.

"Can you trust them?"

"With my life, Sir."

A moment later, Captain Hadi unlocked the door. "Do not disturb the King, or talk about tonight to anyone. Ever." Hadi closed the door replacing the security locks. "We must work fast."

His crew went about their duties preparing for launch, professional in every way. No eyes strayed.

Kendro took point at the centre of the Scrie. "This is not like the joining ceremony. It will be a hundred times more painful than anything you've experienced before." Hearing this, a crewmember pointedly stepped farther away, averting his glance. "Some of you might not be strong enough. Anything you give will help."

Turning towards the others outside the Scrie, Kendro warned, "We must start." His birthmark flashed blue as he called forth his croex. With his left hand, Kendro struck forth with an almighty crack, his croex focussing at the centre of the Scrie. With his right hand also glowing blue, he held his croex together. Then, reached inside of himself, he pulled out his core, his *Routui*.

Thousands of coloured life strands lit up the room in a rainbow of light. For the briefest moment, everyone in the room could see their own coloured strands reaching towards Kendro.

He didn't feel completely safe in bringing it forward here, out in the open, but all their lives depended on his actions. He had to trust them. Madrall and Polr were each connected to their house, and everyone beneath them, but they weren't connected to every Aonise as he was. Kendro could use the Routui to harness croex while Madrall and Polr could only give, not take.

Kendro regarded each of them. "I am passing you control. This once. I will expect it back. Soon, you will be able to draw from each Aonise citizen who you are connected to. Direct the combined croex towards the solar shield." Kendro smiled, as they seemed confused, wryly added, "Copy me."

Madrall and Polr raised their left hands in unison. Madrall's eyes flashed dandelion yellow as he hurled his croex towards the centre of the Scrie where it began to mingle with Kendro's blue energy. Polr's blood red soon joined it, crackling and sparking at the centre of the room. The complete life force of each person stood side-by-side, not some dull mingling of brown from the various life colours, but a rainbow of myriad strengths, bolstering each ones it touched.

Reaching into their chests for their own Routui, they each pulled. Polr gasped as it came away much easier than he thought.

"Be gentle, Polr." Kendro pointed at his Routui. "One wrong move, and it could be fatal for one of your house."

Kendro stepped towards Madrall, and without hesitation, he placed a hand on his shoulder. "This will hurt."

Turning his attention to his own swirling strand of colours, Kendro reached into it, and separated a single yellow strand out from all the thousands of others. As he plucked the strand from its pack, a silvery hue connecting it to Madrall glistened. "Although I am severing our connection now, I will require it back."

The single yellow strand floated in mid-air, waiting. Madrall gazed on as Kendro reached back into the pack pulling out Polr's strand of red, too. Kendro didn't hesitate as he severed their connection.

Madrall and Polr collapsed against each other, sweat dripped from Madrall's brow, while Polr struggled for breath. Their seconds, Retray and Jae, rushed at them, supporting them as best they could.

Kendro turned his attention to the centre of the Scrie, where the three brightest colours still mingled. A moment later, Madrall and Polar rose, wobbling. They stood by their King's side.

Madrall spoke softly. "It feels empty without you."

Kendro knew that pain. "I know. Concentrate. There is much to do." Facing the others, Kendro said, "Direct your croex at the centre of the room as I withdraw from the Scrie. You'll need to stabilize Madrall and Polr as they project everything they can to the planet's surface."

Kendro replaced his Routui. As the others cast their croex to the Scrie's centre, he withdrew. Polr wobbled again on his feet, but only for a moment. He stood firm, eyes on his Jae for support. "Good job. It will buy us a little more time. Keep going." Kendro praised them.

Captain Hadi pointed to the port view. "The sky's turned white."

Kendro regarded him. "Status report, please, Captain?"

Captain Hadi studied his console, relaying. "We're at eighty percent population. The *Sol'Tar* is at sixty percent, and the *Sol'Rayn* is at seventy."

"What is the hold up?" Kendro sighed, staring out at the sluggish lines of his people. He moved away from the Scrie towards the Captain's screen. "Zoom in there."

Captain Hadi obliged, the screen zoomed in, the line of Aonise citizens moving slowly before them. "Your Highness. They're still recording names of who's going aboard the ships,"

Imbeciles. "Get me those men on comms!" Kendro ordered.

Captain Hadi attempted to raise the men, turning only to apologize. "I can't reach them."

"Well, put me live on a comm." Kendro pointed to the sky. "We're out of time."

The soldiers and citizens looked up in shock as a massive explosion shook the very ground where they stood. Their attention turning to their dying sun, panic erupted. Even with their placid nature, they ran now towards the *Sol'Ishar*, scrambling everywhere.

Kendro's voice boomed across all the boarding parties below, "The soldiers taking names at gate seven. Stop. Get these people on board this ship. Now!"

Their red shield pulsed, weakened, almost blinking out.

TAKE OFF

FROM THE *SOL'DELKA*'S BRIDGE, CAPTAIN Gaal stared at the view-screen into his King's face. He waited until First Officer Chien approached, holding an envelope. How quaint! Snatching it, ripping it open, he scanned his launch instructions.

Five simple words— 'Do not start your engines' —followed by launch procedures he already knew. Captain Gaal's fingers clasped around the paper, scrunching it tight, furious. Did the King think he was stupid?

Turning to the communication screen, he locked eyes with Kendro. "If we can't start our engines, how are we supposed to get off this wretched planet?"

"Don't concern yourself." Kendro smiled with all but his eyes. "Make sure you're ready," his reply came.

Gaal opened his mouth to speak again, but the King severed their communication. Fuming, Gaal turned to his First Officer and the other members of his crew. "Ideas, anyone?"

They stared, afraid to answer. Eventually, a young female stepped forward requesting, "Sir?"

Captain Gaal glared at her.

Taking a breath, she continued. "Junior Officer Crey, Sir. Under Science Officer Jenile, Sir?"

Observing his Science Officer, the Captain nodded. "Speak."

"Sir, I've searched through the ship's inventory. We aren't built to carry enough fuel to launch, Sir."

Captain Gaal paced, looking for a quick exit, the need to flee overwhelming. His anger boiled inside him. "No one else paid attention to this. This. Very. Important. Detail!" He slammed his fist down on the nearest console, the screen shattering.

23

"Get the engineers on comms. I want to know why no one saw this oversight."

The bridge filled with murmurs. Annoyed, Captain Gaal commanded, "Quiet, all of you!"

The crew grew silent, buttons clicked, scanners read, as they carried on with launch preparations. Moving towards the science console, Captain Gaal inspected Officer Jenile's work. "I suppose you've looked over Crey's figures?"

"Only this morning, Sir."

"What did you think?"

"She is correct. Although, I saw several soldiers earlier today, as they loaded tanks on board. I assured her these held the fuel for take-off."

"And did they?"

Shaking her head, Jenile said. "No, Sir."

"What was in them?"

Jenile tapped, searching on the console bringing up images of the tanks, "*Atrei*, water, Sir."

On the bridge, hissing, the main door opened. Head Engineer Stylx stepped inside.

"Follow me," ordered Captain Gaal.

Following, Stylx stepped through into the Captain's private office at the back of the compartment. Once inside, Captain Gaal paced, clenching and unclenching his fists. "Can you explain why we have no fuel for lift off?"

"I can," Stylx said.

Turning square on, facing the engineer, Captain Gaal restrained himself from striking Stylx. Growling, he said, "Explain then."

"I knew something was wrong. I forwarded my concerns to the other engineers, and we met a month ago. I was approached by the King's second in command."

"Ainoren Broki?" Gaal asked.

Stylx clasped his hands behind his back, straightening his shoulders. "Yes. He told me the information was between us. I kept my word."

"But the other engineers—"

"—believed what I told them, Sir."

"You told them a lie."

"I told them the fuel was being loaded last, and that they needn't worry."

"So, Octav told you the real plan?"

"No, he asked me to trust our King."

"He did, did he?"

"Yes, Sir."

"You believe, even now with no fuel, that our great King can get us off this dying rock?"

"Yes, Sir."

He threw his hands up. "We're doomed."

Stylx stepped towards the Captain's desk, typing commands into the console. A 3D image appeared of their planet. "Have you seen the colour of the sky lately?"

"Why?"

Stylx enlarged the image, pulling up the view above them. The engineer pointed towards their horizon and the glittering rainbow of colours. "See that particular white glow?"

Captain Gaal said, "I see it."

"When a sun dies, it burns all its energy, generating massive solar flares."

"So? I've seen them."

Pursing his lips, Stylx queried, "Sir, you never read any of my memos at all, did you?"

Captain Gaal shook his head. "I don't have time for reading."

"For several weeks, I've reported our planet is being bombarded by radiation, Sir."

"Then why aren't we dead?"

Jabbing towards the image and the blue tinge, Stylx replied, "We're shielded, Sir."

"How?"

"Not how. Who."

Captain Gaal frowned. "But—"

"Exactly.

"All right. All right, so we have to trust him." The Captain relented, decision made. "You may leave."

"Yes, Sir." Saluting, the engineer removed himself from the Captain's quarters, leaving Gaal with his thoughts.

The Captain's hand hovered over the comms device, hesitant. Should he? Closing his eyes for a second, he opened them, pushing in a number. A low buzzing emanated around the room. "I need to see you right away," he directed.

"You do not demand of me," the voice countered.

"This is important, Dalamaar."

"Someone will meet you in the ship's social gardens. Twenty-five minutes."

The line went dead.

Staring at the console with no focus, Captain Gaal couldn't understand why Dalamaar would cast him off so quickly. To send an underling to meet him wasn't good either. Dalamaar had trusted him, once. Gathering his thoughts, he exited his private office.

"Location?" the lift spoke.

"Social gardens," Gaal said, and entered. With a jerk, the lift moved away.

When he arrived at the gardens, Gaal strode in, strutting his way past several on-looking scientists. The Captain moved towards his usual rendezvous point, admiring the lush green grass beneath his feet, breathing in air fresher than any pumped around the ship.

Weeks ago, because he met Dalamaar, his family now had safe passage to stay on board the ship, avoiding all the rush of those still waiting to board. He neither liked, nor disliked, him; he was using him to forward his career.

As Gaal approached the central lake and ecosystem, a man waited.

"Why couldn't Dalamaar meet?" Gaal asked.

"Busy. Other things. You may tell me what you know," said the man.

"I'm uncomfortable speaking to anyone else."

Turning on the Captain with brusqueness, the man introduced himself, "I am Trax. I am not just anyone else. You get me?" His eyes glowed, fierce, red. "If Dalamaar trusts me, then know I am capable of ripping you to pieces, with just a thought. Understood?"

Gaal swallowed hard. Noticing the extensive detail flickering inside Trax's birthmark, he shivered. Glancing towards the scientists to see if they watched, Gaal realised he was alone. "I'm sorry, Trax," he added, standing tall. "I need words with him about Kendro."

Trax's glowing birthmark dimmed. "You call him that like you're part of his family. I wouldn't let anyone else hear you."

"No. Of course not," Captain Gaal replied, proceeding to inform Trax of his conversation with the ship's head engineer.

"Thank you, Captain. You may return to your duties," said Trax.

Hesitating, Captain Gaal turned, walking past the scientists, who now acknowledged he was there. Typical.

Trax moved about freely within the ships confines. The *Sol'Delka* had been first to be loaded, and settled quickly, leaving corridors and gangways free of any Heiako.

Several Aonise stood waiting for one of the main lifts, so he instead used a maintenance one, stepping inside to the familiar greeting, "Deck?"

"Cargo bay six," Trax replied. Waiting, he tapped his fingers against the metallic wall. The lift moved off.

When it stopped, he alighted, walking through the corridor towards the main cargo bay. Trax placed his hand on the panel. When it lit green, he entered.

Stepping onto a gangway, overlooking a hundred fighters and men, Trax continued. When he reached the gangway's end, he followed a small flight of stairs down to a glass office. Inside the office, there stood two other Aonise men. They nodded towards him, opening the door.

Moving through the control station towards a back office, Trax knocked on the door before him.

"Enter," Dalamaar spoke from within.

Trax closed the door behind him, lowering his head, as he moved to stand before Dalamaar, without making eye contact.

"Were you correct, Trax?"

"Yes, Sire." Once addressed, Trax looked up. "No fuel for lift off. It seems Kendro thinks he has enough croex to power all four ships."

Chuckling, Dalamaar pushed his chair back.

Trax cocked his head to see his master's amusement. "Why are you laughing?" he asked.

Dalamaar's eyes flashed. Pushing his long dark hair away from his elaborate birthmark, he tucked the stray hairs neatly behind his ear. "Getting these ships into space will not be easy on our King, especially after he's been shielding the planet for so long. Our plans for an assassination might not be needed after all."

"You think lift off may kill him?"

Dalamaar laughed once more. "We're about to find out, Trax. Then, maybe, I can take my rightful place as King."

Captain Hadi spoke, bringing Kendro's focus back to the main bridge. "Your Highness, ships two and four are at ninety percent. We are full."

"Seal us tight, Captain. Get me Gaal on the comms. No video."

Captain Hadi turned, swiping his left hand over a console. The comms flickered to life. A moment later, Captain Gaal's shrill voice sounded, "We are awaiting final instructions, Your Highness."

"Inform your Science Officer." Kendro looked towards Science Officer Lynj, and added, "Open all type two conduits from the engines." He signalled for Captain Hadi to close the comms.

Watching as Officer Lynj typed in several commands, Captain Hadi waited, the intense knotting of his stomach growing tighter with every passing minute. "All conduits are open," Lynj reported.

Turning his attention to Captain Hadi, Kendro ordered, "Relay the message to the other captains as soon as their ships are loaded and sealed. When they are, alert me. You must give the launch command when the ships are at full power. We are last, even if our engines are at full capacity. Launch before the others, and it might be over for them."

"Yes, Your Highness," Captain Hadi replied, questioning none of the directions.

Kendro moved away from him to the centre of the room with the other family. Captain Hadi watched, mesmerised by them all. Kendro paused as Madrall's bright dandelion yellow faded to a dull eggshell.

Captain Hadi moved towards Officer Lynj's console, peering over her shoulder he reported. "The *Sol'Rayn* is at full capacity, Sir."

Kendro observed the room, noticing the female crewmembers for the first time, feeling an unexpected amount of vulnerability. "I must undress. It helps with the croex transfer." Captain Hadi smiled, as Officer Lynj blushed, looking away from the King.

Captain Hadi watched as his female officers turned away from Kendro, yet the male crew stared. Partial nakedness accepted as normal, yes, but none other than the King's family had ever seen his full birthmark. A nervous twitch from his stomach reminded Captain Hadi that Brie was the only woman to see him naked. Curiosity got the better of all his crew in the end.

Hadi drank in the King's glorious birthmark. It stretched from the nape of his neck around both shoulders and torso, then down his left leg and ankle. Hadi watched as Kendro flexed his muscles. His birthmark glowed, shimmered, changing shape. A smile spread across Captain Hadi's lips. Kendro's power left him awestruck.

Kendro's croex pulsed, flowing across his birthmark. A wonderful display of light that could keep everyone entertained for hours. Captain Hadi watched him wobble on his feet. Kendro reached out to steady himself.

"I can do this," Kendro whispered.

Nausea hit Captain Hadi. *He thinks he can't! Oh, Ari help us.*

Hadi pulled up a different screen where he could view the citizens below. Almost all were now aboard.

The static electric croex building on the bridge raised the tiny hairs on the back of the Captain's neck, his own croex boiling to the surface.

Hadi knew Kendro had never attempted anything on this scale before, shielding the people from the dying sun's effects seemed trivial to lifting four ships from the planet's surface.

Kendro's breathing continued steadily. In. Out.

As the final ship loaded, Captain Hadi edged towards Kendro, tapping his shoulder as requested. Hadi then stepped back, as Kendro let the full force of this gathered croex loose.

As he focused on Kendro, a blinding blue light exploded, then pulsed. In the end, Captain Hadi had no choice but to look away. It hurt.

He could see the rainbowed croex pouring out of Kendro as it reached the walls of the *Sol'Ishar*, then out to all of the other ships.

"Engine, status?" Captain Hadi asked, smiling at Officer Lynj, who stared, completely transfixed at their King.

Lynj shied away, her face flushing pink. "Sorry, Captain." She pulled up the required information. "Our engines are at thirty percent, Sir."

Captain Hadi touched his console, bringing an image of their engines. Tiny squares filled and stayed filled, indicating the rise in power.

"Forty percent," Lynj said, staring at the King. "He's amazing," she said to Captain Hadi.

"Get me all the other ships," said Hadi, turning to his communications man, Officer Reel.

Nodding, Officer Reel switched all comms over.

"This is Captain Hadi. Your ships are powering up. When you reach full capacity, initiate launch sequence."

Captain Gaal's voice came through. "Where is this energy coming from?"

Hadi sighed, "None of your concern. Watch your gages. Prepare for launch, Captain."

Captain Hadi turned back to Lynj, raising an eyebrow.

"We're at eighty percent, Captain," she beamed.

"Fast. How are the others?"

"Also coming on at eighty percent, Sir."

Drawn back to the King, Captain Hadi experienced calmness as never before, transfixed by the swirling rainbow of colours before him.

Lynj smiled at him this time. "I've never seen anything as beautiful."

"Neither have I, Officer Lynj. Especially in another man."

Lynj smiled. "No, I guess not." The screen in front of her flashed green. "Captain, we are at one hundred percent."

"Hold for the others to launch first, Lynj."

Captain Hadi watched on. A blue croex surrounding all three evaporated, as the engines fired up. Huge bellowing dust clouds blew from beneath them as the trio of ships lifted.

With three ships airborne, Hadi's heart soared with them as they moved further off into the planet's depleted atmosphere.

"Take us up," he commanded Lynj.

The surface beneath his feet quivered as their own ship eased off the planet's surface. Captain Hadi took his chair.

A siren blurted blurted as the ship shook with tremendous force. Hadi stood again, "Report!" He ordered.

"We're losing power, Sir."

"Why?" Hadi shot at Lynj. "Explain."

Science Officer Lynj regarded Kendro. "The other ships are using more power than he thought. We'll hold until they're in space."

Rivers of sweat ran down Kendro's back. Captain Hadi checked the monitors watching as the three other Aonise ships ascended into space. "What's our capacity?"

"We're at forty percent power, Sir."

"Nowhere near enough!" Hadi approached Madrall and Polr. "They have to drop the shield. He needs their help." Captain Hadi reached out, touching them each on the shoulder.

Madrall snapped from his trance, and then collapsed in a heap on the deck. Hadi supported him, as he struggled getting to his feet. The others stirred, moving around them, confused.

"Captain, the solar shield has failed. We're experiencing a rise in outside temperature."

"The King needs you. Help him. We don't have enough power for lift off."

Madrall stammered. "Exhausted, but I'll give it my all."

Polr focused his croex towards Kendro, with Madrall following a moment later.

Turning to his crew, Captain Hadi ordered, "Help him. Forget your duties. I'll get us into space."

Joining with Madrall, Polr, and their house heads, the crewmembers poured their power towards Kendro. The room sparkled with pure croex.

Rushing to the engineering console, Captain Hadi brought up the information he needed.

Sixty percent. The squares on the console before him filled.

Seventy percent. Waiting, Captain Hadi's heart thumped.

Eighty percent. Thump.

Ninety percent. Thump.

"Come on, you can do this," Captain Hadi shouted. "I believe in you."

One hundred percent.

With a flicking of his wrist, Captain Hadi keyed in the launch codes. The room vibrated once again, the ship lifting free.

Dripping down his face, Captain Hadi wiped his single sleeve across his forehead absorbing his sweat. "Come on."

The power fluxed, dropping. The ship shuddered violently beneath Captain Hadi's feet while fear engulfed him. Whirling into the room was a bright red burst of croex. A man's image formed before Hadi. He stared into the eyes of Kendro's half-brother, Nax.

Moving away from Captain Hadi, Nax turned his attention to Kendro. "I give you my life, brother. Save our people."

Reaching, Nax touched Kendro's back. His red croex met blue in a swirling cloud of deep purple. Their commingled energies exploded.

And Nax vanished.

The ship's croex peaked at one hundred percent, with one last push. Captain Hadi propelled the ship off from the planet's pull.

Everyone on the bridge, bar Captain Hadi, then collapsed.

Typing in for the ship's medical bay, Captain Hadi ordered, "Medics to the bridge. Multiple casualties. Code red." Leaping to his feet, he ran to Kendro's side, covering him with his own clothes. He struggled to find a pulse, fearing the worst. Kendro's skin clammy, finally a faint pulse beat beneath his fingers. Thank Ari!

"I've never done anything like this before. I am not very strong." Swallowing hard, as his eyes flashed his colour green, Captain Hadi focussed his croex into his hand. He placed them to Kendro's forehead. "Take what you need to survive. We need you."

As Hadi's mind touched Kendro's, the Captain wailed, the whole world collapsing around him.

SPACE

CAPTAIN HADI FELT INTENSE, STABBING pain. His skin itched as Kendro absorbed his life force. Nothing mattered more than saving his King. Hadi's croex levels dwindled, the bridge darkening around him as Kendro took life from his touch.

Kendro sucked in a deep breath. "Enough," he spat shoving Captain Hadi away. Hadi fell backwards with tremendous force breaking their connection, his King having taken at least ten years from his life.

Hadi sprawled across the deck, slamming into his chair. Breath escaped from his lungs as he struggled for more air, clutching at his chest. "Sire?" Hadi sighed warm relief spreading through him. Hadi straightened himself, a muscle in his neck cramping. Massaging it, he winced.

"C—cold!" Kendro stuttered. Still only capable of single words, he collapsed again.

As Hadi glanced to the rest of his unconscious crew, worry lines stretched across his face. Hadi assured, "Medics are on the way, hang in there."

Loud banging ensued. "Captain, it's the Doctor. Let us in." A woman's voice came across the comms.

Captain Hadi eased up into his chair, feeling such weakness. He pressed his hand to a panel. Medics filed onto the bridge carrying bags and other equipment. His wife, the lead physician Doctor Katya Brie, stood mouth agape for one brief moment before she assessed the situation. She rushed towards Captain Hadi, touching his hand quickly. "What happened?"

Hadi clasped her hand, their fingers interlocking, feeling instant comfort, reassuring, safe. "I'm fine. Just help the King." He pushed her warm hand from him.

"What did you *give?*"

Hadi noticed her glance to his hand, his flickering croex giving it all away. "Enough."

Nodding, Brie bent towards Kendro placing her fingers to his carotid artery. "He's quite weak." She turned, "Lalia, help me get him to the medical bay."

Lalia pushed a floating medical bed, reswae, towards their King. They had Kendro up in a moment, ready to transport him to the infirmary.

Mika stormed onto the bridge, stopping the trio in their tracks. "You are taking him to our quarters," she ordered.

"But," Doctor Brie prickled, "he needs expert medical attention."

"Doctor, I know what he needs. You can't provide it for him. Now, take him to our quarters."

Mika stood firm, "But—" Brie started. Two soldiers by Mika's side. "You mus—"

About to protest again, Brie had no choice but to watch the King's reswae whisked from her. Their King floated from the bridge, his spouse following.

Focussing her attention on the next patient, Madrall, Doctor Brie sighed, feeling his clammy forehead.

Madrall roused. "How did we do? Are we in space?"

"Well, you don't look so good," she glanced towards Hadi, "but, yes, we're all off the planet," she told everyone.

Madrall, smiling through his mustachio, murmured, "I can rest now," and promptly fell asleep.

When the nurses had several members of Hadi's crew up, ready for moving, they turned to the doctor for her orders. "Infirmary." She pointed.

Hadi grabbed at her arm, once more nearly falling to the deck. "Will my crew be all right?"

"They'll all be fine, but they're exhausted."

Raising an eyebrow, he warned, "I can't fly the ship on my own. I need them back to full health as soon as possible."

"I never thought of that." Doctor Brie looked around the now emptying bridge. She scowled at his directive. "Are there no secondary crewmembers?"

It was a joke. "Of course. These are just my most trusted. I'll be fine."

Stepping towards her husband, Doctor Brie felt his forehead. "You look like you've been through hell. You should rest, also."

"I can't."

She placed a hand on his shoulder, offering him her other. "Doctor's

33

orders."

Hadi wobbled on his feet, reaching for her hand. "I need to brief the skeleton crew when they arrive. I promise I'll see to those doctor's orders, as soon as others are on deck."

Doctor Brie reassessed him with her every eye movement. "I'll be back in a little while to make sure you are resting, Captain."

Kendro winced, stirring as Mika tucked him into their bedspace. The pain inside his mind so severe, nausea climbed, and the room started to spin.

Sliding in beside him, Mika said, "Darling, Taliri would also like to help. Please let him." She took hold of Kendro's hand so it rested on her stomach.

"I couldn't shield him anymore." Kendro moaned softly, "They'll know. I'm sorry."

Mika leaned over him, kissing the side of Kendro's forehead. "Don't worry. We can face the consequences later." A glowing white light emerged from the centre of Mika's stomach. "Let him help you, my love."

White light reached out, wrapping itself around both of their hands, then it snaked into Kendro's aching body. Mika's red birthmark sparked and danced in response.

With the sudden boost from his son, Kendro focussed more. Looking to Mika, he pulled his hand away from her stomach, feeling awful relying on Captain Hadi earlier, and now, their unborn son. "Enough," the King said, once more.

Kendro glanced at the porthole above his bedspace. Fear swelled in him as the reassuring blackness stared back.

Captain Hadi straightened as Doctor Brie returned through the sliding doors. She coughed, annoyance showing. He'd been on the bridge too long, despite her orders. "Maintain this position," Captain Hadi instructed the last of the crew to arrive on the bridge. "It's to be in effect until their situation can be assessed properly by the King."

"Sorry," Hadi attempted to rise from his chair. Feeling weak, his feet struggled to hold him, and he slumped back. "I got carried away."

"You should have listened." Brie moved to help him. "There was no need for you to stay so long."

"I just—"

"—I know."

"This is the first time any of them have served on a ship this size."

Accepting the doctor's help, Hadi stood, stumbling, attempting to walk. "Puswer," he cursed himself.

"It's the first time for any of us. The infirmary isn't even finished yet. The whole ship is full of—"

"—glitches." He pulled her closer. "Yes, I know."

Brie stepped in time with him for support as they moved to the main doors. "Will the House leaders be all right?"

Leaving the bridge, Doctor Brie slid one arm around his waist and her hand into his. "Yes. Now, let me get you to bed."

Hadi smiled. "Only if you join me?"

Brie laughed. "No time for that. I'll have to get back to the infirmary," she paused, "What happened on the bridge?"

"I can't discuss it, you know that." Hadi held his eyes with hers. "But it was exhausting."

"Well, I'll run a few tests. Madrall seems to be the worst off, like the life was sucked right out of him."

Hadi shivered pulling his tunic tightly to him, knowing exactly what they all felt like. "Everything will be all right. Don't worry. Just give us all a few days."

They came upon a technician working on the lift Hadi wanted to use. The tech stood when they approached. "Captain, sorry. Please use another. This one's just malfunctioned."

Brie laughed, turning her patient around. "I don't think any of us are getting much rest."

Stretching his arms above his head, Kendro pushed his covers off, his vision blurred, head banging. Every muscle ached.

With a creak, the door opened. "Good. You're awake," Mika whispered. "Everyone's been so worried."

"Madrall and Polr?"

"They've been camped outside our quarters, along with Octav and Lyrik."

Kendro stood and reached for his tunic. "I need— Get—" Sickness spread through him. He wobbled, sank on the bedspace, off his feet. Frustrated, he slammed his hand down, defeated.

Mika adjusted the lighting. "You still need to rest."

Kendro looked around. "There's no time for resting." That sick feeling knotted his stomach with realization. "The ship's not moving."

"No. We've been immobile for a sixer."

"A sixer!" Staring at Mika in shock, he attempted to push himself up once more. "I've been unconscious for a whole six days?" Feeling nothing but weakness, Kendro held out his hand for aid.

"Do not worry yourself." Mika moved to his side, clasping his hand, her fingers squeezing. "Our people are quite capable of looking after themselves for a while."

Kendro made another attempt at standing. "We must leave. Now!" But in his head, the pounding grew worse. He rubbed his temple trying to stem the pain. "I—"

Mika reached for a glass of atrei. "You're dehydrated. The doctor tried to get you to drink, and so have I, but it's been near impossible." Doctor Brie had complained that nothing worked. "In the end, the only way was to put a special tube she designed down your nose. Without that, you might not be here."

Running a hand over the skin of his arm, Kendro laughed. "Impenetrable when it wants." Fire at the back of his throat made him realise how dry he felt. The atrei tasted wonderful, but hardly quenched his thirst.

"I had a tube down my nose?" His hand rose, a finger gently touched his tender nostril. "Strange." He drank more.

"Slowly," Mika moved the glass from his mouth. "You don't want to be sick, do you?"

Kendro sipped the atrei, savouring it as it eased his throat's throbbing, settling his stomach.

"Better?" Mika smiled.

Kendro nodded. "I need to—"

"It's late." Mika pushed him back gently. "You should stay in bed."

Kendro wasn't taking 'no' from her. He attempted to rise once again, looking into Mika's eyes, pleading.

"All right." She offered a hand to help. "I'll make us a snack while you organize a meeting."

"A shower would be nice first." But not wanting to offend, Kendro agreed. "Could you call Octav for me?"

"Careful." Leading him into the bathroom, Mika turned on their sonic, testing it before she let go so Kendro could step inside.

Kendro let out a deep sigh, the pain in his head almost gone. But something else gnawed at his insides. The sonic beat gently from all sides. No connection with Madrall and Polr, Kendro knew this must take priority. He would not survive for much longer without them, or their houses, the connection with all Aonise a vital part of his strength.

A few minutes later, Kendro, dressed, and slipped on a pair of sandals. The drifting aroma of fresh cooked garbael tantalized his senses. He headed for their utility station.

"I messaged Octav." Mika set a plate in front of Kendro. She joined him at their small table. "He said he'd organize a meeting in an hour."

Kendro devoured everything she'd placed in front of him, chomping away all the lingering soreness. "Thanks."

"Hungry?" Mika chuckled.

Kendro coughed, setting his fork down. "I guess I am." Pouring himself another glass of atrei, he drank gingerly. "Sorry." Watching as Mika stabbed at her food. "Everything all right?"

"I'm queasy on board." Mika pushed her plate away. "I don't think Taliri likes the ship."

"But, everything is all right?"

She forced a smile. "Everything seems fine." Her hand instinctively rubbed her stomach.

Kendro puzzled for a moment, 'seems' wasn't good enough. "I'll ask Doctor Brie to come take a look at you later."

"But—"

"No buts. Your pregnancy is probably already circulating around the houses."

"No one has said anything."

"They won't, yet."

Finishing off his meal, Kendro pointed to Mika's plate.

Mika gave it a shove in his direction.

"I'll find out if they know anything. You see the doctor."

"All right." Mika sighed. "The doctor can't tell anyone though, can she?"

Kendro raised an eyebrow. "It would be on her life, if she ever spoke about seeing you. I'll ask her to stop by after the meeting to look at me. No one needs to know she's seeing you at the same time." Kendro sat back, patting his full stomach with a sigh. "That feels much better."

"Go. Get out of here." Rolling her eyes, Mika added, "Just take it easy, please?"

This time, Kendro stood with no wobble, some strength returned. He moved to Mika's side, kissing her before he left.

Kendro stepped inside the council room, pulling up the ships statistics before him. Finding out exactly how ready they were. He studied them for some time before Octav arrived.

Greeting the Ainoren with a handshake and an embrace, Kendro's birthmark flickered with emotion, ecstatic to see him, and glad they were all alive.

Octav smiled, letting Kendro go. "I'm glad you're back on your feet. We've been worried sick. Lyrik has done nothing but pace the corridors."

"I'm fine, I've had some rest." Kendro leaned onto the chair with a sigh. "Though I'm not getting any younger. It was harder than I'd ever imagined."

"You did it, though. You lifted four ships off the planet!"

Seeing the amazement on Octav's face, he replied, "Yes." Kendro chuckled. "Some feat, huh?"

"Everyone's speculating, but even knowing, and being on the deck, hasn't given me any insight."

Feeling his legs grow weak, Kendro reached to steady himself on the table. He missed it.

Octav caught hold of him. "What aren't you telling me?" the Ainoren probed as he gently lowered Kendro into his seat.

"Polr. Madrall." Kendro panted, "Are they——"

"Why?" Octav eyed him.

"I need you to wait outside." He looked to the door for Polr, or Madrall. "Keep the others out until I give the all clear."

"This is to do with what happened on the bridge, isn't it?"

"Yes." Kendro's breathing steadied. Octav's concern stretched across his face reaching his eyes. Kendro didn't want to worry him unnecessarily, so he added, "I lent them something that needs to be returned. Go. Hurry them to me."

With no thought for decorum, Octav raced out the council room, leaving Kendro to lay his head on the table's coolness.

Too much time passed. No one returned. Kendro's pain grew worse as the room spun violently around him. Bile burnt the back of his throat. With a hard push, he swallowed.

Kendro's mind drifted away, and he passed out.

Bursting through the door, Madrall and Polr roused him. Kendro sat straight. Octav waited a moment before stepping out, closing the door as he'd been asked.

Madrall regarded Kendro with certainty. "You need it back."

"Of course." Polr's birthmark lit up. "We should have known."

"But we didn't. Let's just get on with it." Sitting opposite Kendro, Madrall tested. "How do we?"

"It can't be taken by force."

While the King stared at Polr, concern spread through Madrall. Polr stared right back. "You have to give it back to me," Kendro stated. "You have to want to give it back."

"I do!" Polr spat, his face flushing red. "I do want to!"

Ripping through his mind, the severe pain made Kendro gasp. "You say that." His eyes flashed blue, illuminating the room. "Yet, I can see that you don't."

Polr lowered his head. "I do. I've—just grown used to the power, and feeling this good."

"I agree. It feels amazing. However, there is one thing missing." Looking towards Kendro, Madrall also lowered his head. "Our King."

Polr repeated, reassuring the pair, "I do want to give it back."

"Then call your croex forth," Kendro commanded.

Kendro watched Polr's birthmark flash red around the room. Reaching inside, Polr pulled out his Routui. The shimmering strands of all the Aonise linked to House Magalite shone brilliantly, directed towards a single spot.

Madrall followed suit, his croex directed toward the same spot. The pulling sensation was painful, but bearable this time. The room sparked and crackled with their combined croex.

Swallowing hard, Kendro opened himself last. Yet, his depleted Routui just wouldn't shine as it once had.

Madrall offered Kendro back his connecting strand. His birthmark dimmed as Kendro accepted, the power loss immense, but glad for it to feel normal.

Stepping forward, Polr held his strand towards Kendro.

"You must be sure," cautioned Kendro, locking eyes as he braced for the push from Polr.

"Yes, Your Highness," replied Polr, submission in his tone.

As he reconnected the strands to his Routui, the power's sudden surge overwhelmed Kendro. With a flash of light, the croex in the room vanished.

Kendro rose from his chair, feeling almost normal. He moved closer to Polr. "If it hadn't been given freely, then I would have died. Thank you."

At this, Polr dropped to his knees. "Forgive me!"

"Rise." Offering Polr his hand, Kendro paused for him to accept it. "The survival of our species needed me to make that decision." Kendro tugged Polr to his feet. "Our people owe you both a debt of gratitude."

"We owe you the debt, Sire. Our people would not be alive without your sacrifices."

Kendro studied the console. "Well, now, that is over. Shall we get down to these other pressing matters?" Walking towards the door, Kendro released its lock, seeing Octav, as he paced at the far end. "You may call on the Captain, rejoin us," the King ordered, returning to his seat, and leaving the door ajar.

Madrall growled, "Why is Captain Hadi joining us?"

"There is no one better to advise us. We will discuss his crew, the workings of this ship, and what's happening now. House matters will be taken care of later."

Bidding Captain Hadi inside, Kendro pointed him towards a seat.

"Glad to see you in health, Your Highness," said Captain Hadi.

"Should we not comm Emmi?" Octav asked.

"Eventually. There are things I must say to you first."

Octav frowned, something Kendro didn't like to see, but he carried on. "I trust the four of you. I hope you trust me." Looking to each of them, Kendro continued. "The Zefron will follow us—"

"The Zefron, still!" Madrall's outburst reverberated through the others.

"Yes and my last recon came back with nothing," Octav said. "We still know nothing else about them. They're bent on our annihilation, with no valid reasoning."

The Ainoren waited for their acknowledgment. "Staying away from the Zefron won't be an option. I believe we will have to fight."

With a hand slammed on the table, Kendro brought up a holosnap. "Octav smuggled this off the Zefron home world." A holographic image rotated over the centre of their table. "Like us, at first, we thought they were fleeing the solar system." Pointing to several areas as the ship rotated, Kendro added, "Initial scans from Octav's team were conclusive. It's a battleship. I can presume they will be coming for us."

"Puswer," cursed Captain Hadi. "We escape a dying planet to be chased across the galaxy."

Octav shot the Captain an angry glare. He had reminded him about using general outbursts at a meeting. "Where are we on tactical weapons?"

Swallowing, Captain Hadi sank back in his seat, overwhelmed and out of his depth. "Yes, Sir. We're—"

"This will be a long night." Kendro's thirst pulled him to the other side of the room towards several drinks. Damn it all, forget custom. He gathered and passed bottles to his men.

Taking a much smaller swig than his King had, Captain Hadi started reporting for Polr and Madrall's benefit. "We were informed a month ago that we needed to arm the ship."

Touching his control console, the Zefron ship vanished, and was replaced with an image of the *Sol'Ishar* now. "At the time, we had no defences." Hadi leaned across, touched several areas of the hologram, which grew larger, proud at the intelligence his crew had gathered.

"Our ships were fleeing vessels. However, with some quick thinking, we were able to bring in these."

An elongated cannon came into view, slick, deadly. Captain Hadi tapped the last image until it was large enough for clear viewing. "I am sure you are familiar with these."

"Designed to disrupt engines," Octav smiled at Hadi, "with a few modifications, we've given them a lot more fire power."

"Excuse me," Madrall asked, staring at Kendro's birthmark, hopeful in his query, "is there nothing you could do?"

"What you witnessed no one else ever will." Kendro sighed at the thought of raising those several million tonnes of spacecraft. "There is no easy option. The Zefron are an imminent threat. They must be defeated by other means."

"I had to ask…" Madrall's hopeful look gone, he remembered, and added, "Your Highness."

"Are our cannons ready? For testing?" Polr held Captain Hadi's stare.

"Of course," Hadi smiled, hiding nerves, yet knowing Polr would see through that, he pulled up another holosnap. "We're training several gunners now," with a glance, the Captain tossed the lead to Octav.

"Good," Kendro broke in, just managing to stifle any groan as a sharp pain hit. 'Taliri,' his mind screamed, hand to his midriff. Within the sharpness, his eyes closed. He drifted away from his council members, searching for Mika and the boy's presence.

"Your Highness, are you—" Captain Hadi rose, as did the others.

"Forgive me." The King snapped back into the room. "If there is nothing else—" Octav and the others clamoured to his aid, Kendro held his hand out. "No."

Polr, about to speak again, halted at Octav's swift gesture. "It can wait. Captain Hadi, escort the King to his quarters, please."

Captain Hadi placed an arm out, steadying the King. "Thank you," Kendro grumbled. "I can walk myself." At the door, Kendro turned to Octav, "Ask Wez to stop by in the morning."

"I'm sorry, Sire." At this, Octav lowered his head. "He's not on board this ship, Sir."

"Find him," Kendro demanded, dread adding to the earlier sickness. Outside, Kendro paused as Captain Hadi ushered him from the room. Leaning on a wall, he breathed in deep.

"Should I send for Doctor Brie?"

"No." Kendro forced himself upright, wobbling down the hallway. "Thank you." He would make it back to his quarters unassisted. Stepping into the lift, he paused, Hadi happy to see him relent, "Ask her to come, after I've rested."

Captain Hadi nodded. "Of course," then he risked an impropriety, "It's really not okay, is it?"

"That information must never leave your lips." Kendro flashed on their energy bond. *Did Hadi know now?*

41

FIND WEZ

WHAT IF I CAN'T? A shiver ripped through Octav, stopping him as he left the council chambers heading for Security. 'Find him,' Kendro had said. Octav's stomach churned. Wez—his abilities were important to Kendro as well as all the Aonise. Octav punched in a number. He waited. They'd have to be woken. No choice.

"Hello," Lyrik's gruff voice echoed through the comms.

"Meet me in Security."

"Yes, Sir."

Octav flinched at Lyrik's dry response, not meaning to sound so official, not with his friend. He'd apologize later.

Head of Security Officer Chen showed Octav inside the Sietev, the ship's main computer. Chen's face showed confusion, but the Ainoren didn't explain himself. He dismissed Chen, and then ran a hand over the armrest of the fuse chair, goosebumps exploded. He never liked merging with the larger ships.

Image upon image, every conversation, and each report filed would flood his mind. The extreme effort it took controlling this deluge was always painful. Sinking into the chair, Octav took in a sharp breath, and then, slid his left hand inside the operating glove—their croex merged—the rush forcing the breath from Octav's lungs.

The Sietev's silvery voice thrummed in Octav's mind, "Heart rate above normal," as if he didn't know, "May I assist you, Ainoren?"

Gasping, gripping the second armrest, face contorting with the overload of data, Octav mustered a few terse words, "Reroute all new information—Central Two." Hoping the information overload and pain would stop.

"All new information rerouted, Ainoren."

Thank Ari. Octav sank back into the chair.

"I need all footage from the palace filos from the hour we left Letháo."

Several auxiliary screens materialized in front of him, each one a different angle. Using all his croex, digesting the lot, Octav watched everything simultaneously, barely hearing the sliding of the chamber's door.

Lyrik staggered in, open-mouthed, hair dishevelled, and rubbing his tired, red eyes. He towered above Octav, his bulk almost blocking out the light. This disturbed Octav's concentration. Grateful, he withdrew his hand from the glove. He knew this giant, his family, cared more for others than he did himself.

"Kendro?" Lyrik's detailed birthmark flickered his colour—purple.

"He's weak. But he'll be fine." Octav pointed at the chair opposite. "We've got work to do."

Lyrik exhaled, slipping into it, and facing his own display screen. He evaluated Octav's state, allowing his croex to reach out for a merge, but finding only empty space "Are you all right?"

"I—" Octav felt the guilt rise up from his demanding tone earlier. Yet, he fought off the urge to open himself to Lyrik.

"It's good." Lyrik nodded at the computer's rising readout. "We're good."

"It's Wez." Octav leaned over to a console, typing in several commands. "He left after the conference. However, he hasn't shown up on any camos."

Lyrik squinted to see, he viewed an image of Wez's curb shuttle, pulled up at a docking port, not more than three hours earlier. "That is our ship." How could Octav not see the obvious? They watched on, studying a hooded figure exiting the shuttle, slipping inside their ship a moment later. "I don't understand?"

"Wait." Octav touched at the panel, pushing in closer. The view inside the ship popped into focus. Zooming in, the figure exited the shuttle.

"Who—" Lyrik leaned in even closer, dread in his voice when he realized. "That isn't Wez."

"His name's Yuko. A Heiako. Living under Emmi's protection."

Lyrik's birthmark flickered at Emmi's name, changing its shape in the artificial lighting, unable to match control as Octav could. Showing pure white teeth, Lyrik's grin spread wide, excited now. "You thinking what I'm thinking—"

"Time to visit Captain Gaal."

Separating from Lyrik, Octav next dragooned his pilot. If they were to search Gaal's ship, he'd need all the help he could gather. Waiting for Chace to answer his comms, Octav ran other names through his mind.

Chace's half-naked torso appeared. "Ainoren?"

Octav coughed. "Suit up, Monroe," looking away, cheeks flushing, "Grab Veco. Meet us on the flight deck—"

"The mission?" Chace mumbled, cutting the video.

Octav smiled. "Recovery." He heard Chace dropping equipment on the deck. Best pilot in the fleet, but the clumsiest... "Pack light."

"Yes, Sir," said Chace, disconnecting.

With minimal night staff on the flight deck, Octav searched, but found no one at hand, until he heard clanging ahead of him, and followed it.

An engineer poked his head out from under a fighter being repaired, and reading Octav's green flickered birthmark, immediately rubbed his hands down his uniform. "Ainoren. How can I assist you?" Jumping up, smoothing out the crumples, he saluted.

"Prep Lyrik's ship," Octav ordered, "and mine."

Saluting sharply, the engineer ran off, alerting other unseen staff. Octav observed while they started prepping the fighters. A few moments later, Lyrik joined him, closely followed by Chace and Veco. Smiles and laughter all around, they were more like old friends than a mission group.

"Bit of an impromptu visit, isn't it?" asked Veco, whipcord thin, and older than all but Octav.

"I briefed them both on the way down." Lyrik squinted around at the group. "They know the stakes."

Octav gave a curt nod at that report.

Chace stifled a yawn. "I'd be guessing it might be more than a surprise. There is no love for us from Emmi."

"Understatement," added Octav.

One of the engineers paused, not wanting to break in. "Your ships are ready, Ainoren."

"Shall we?" Octav said, the urgency of finding Wez, safe, forcing him on.

They separated for their ships. Reaching out, Chace placed a hand on Octav's shoulder. Octav flinched, fighting to hide his weakness.

"You've had no rest at all, have you?" Risking severe reprimand, Chace ventured, "I'm taking control of the Vichi."

"Insol—" Octav's legs buckled. He fought stronger for control.

The grip on Octav's arm became stronger as Chace edged closer. "I'll look after you. At any cost." Chace flicked his head towards the watching night staff. "I'm not one of your house. Court martial me if you must, but listen, please."

Swallowing, Octav regained his composure, attempting to use his croex. But unsuccessful at reading Chace's thoughts, he acquiesced. "Just board the damned ship!"

"Is this really a good idea?" Chace slid in behind Octav, picking up his helmet, tapping Octav's chair. "Surprising Emmi... I mean?"

Given a breath, Octav replied, "The ship doesn't belong to Emmi." He held his helmet for a second. "She will let us do our job, and not interfere."

"I doubt it." Chace slipped his own helmet over his curls, brown eyes flashing his colour blue. "Awkward woman!"

"Take it easy." Octav sensed his aggression. "She isn't the enemy."

"Yet," Chace mumbled, punching in launch procedures, his console lighting up, and the engine roaring to life.

Octav ran through all the checks before the engineer's voice echoed in his helmet. "You are free to launch, Ainoren."

"Let's get outta here!" Had Chace even heard a word he'd said?

Sliding his right hand inside the fighter's main control glove, Octav's eyes flickered with his croex, as he felt the computer systems jolt and hum.

The fighter roared to life, filling Octav's veins, the rush kicking him in the guts as he handed control to Chace.

Chace hollered his familiar, "Wooo hooo!" as they accelerated into space.

He set coordinates for the *Sol'Delka*, and darkness enveloped the fighter. "Should I raise the Captain?" Chace asked a moment later.

"No. He'll know we're there soon enough."

Chace touched a section of his console. On cue, Veco and Lyrik's fighter shimmered with light, almost vanishing. Octav closed his eyes as sleep's pull was finally allowing him to put full trust in Chace.

Octav felt a tap on the shoulder as Chace shook him awake. The fighters were closer to the Sol'Delka than he'd liked, but Octav slid his hand back into the control glove, opening up communications with Lyrik. "Use docking bay four. They know we're here. I'll send Gaal a message when we're on deck."

"Affirmative," the response came.

Octav guided the fighter down towards the *Sol'Delka's* lower belly approaching the docking bay.

Several officers, guns at the ready, bound toward the fighter. Upon sighting the disembarking pair, Security Officer Tao shouted, "Weapon's away!" All hands dropped. "Ainoren Broki." Tao saluted. "To what—"

Interrupting him after returning the salute, Octav ushered Tao beyond hearing distance from his men. Chace and Veco secured their fighters. Lyrik stood at ease waiting.

"You may inform Emmi and Captain Gaal of our arrival, but for now, I'd like to ask you some questions. We're looking for a member of the King's personal staff."

"Of course." Tao nodded.

"We're looking for Wez Chant."

Tao regarded the rest of his men, now at port arms. "The Seer?" His soldiers remained, watching Octav's conversation.

"Something wrong?" Octav raised an eyebrow at his own men. Knowing, but—

"I..."

Hating to do it, Octav, knowing the gesture would be seen as a threat, clasped his arm around Tao, pulling him closer. "Do we need to go somewhere private?"

"No. Sir, I—" swallowing hard, Tao came clean, "I've seen him. Seer Chant."

Excitement pulsing through Octav's veins, his eyes flashed blue. Really, so easy? But this bit of luck felt wrong. Looking towards Lyrik, Octav commanded, "Clear the decks."

"Yes, Ainoren." Lyrik approached the pair as the soldiers double-timed off the landing deck behind him. "What's he got?"

"Seer Chant," Octav repeated.

Officer Tao's birthmark, beetle-sized, glimmered then faded, "A few days ago. In one of the Heiako bays."

"How did he look?" Lyrik asked.

"Was he with anyone?" Octav overrode the first question.

Wiping sweat from his brow, Officer Tao hesitated between them, not knowing whom to answer first. Behind Tao came Chace, a single finger raised for Octav's benefit. "Ainoren, may I?"

Chace ushered Tao backward into the waist-high wheel of one of the fighters, leaving Octav's blood boiling at the interruption.

"I guess we can be overwhelming," said Lyrik, friend to friend, knowing the Ainoren would not normally stand for such, skirting Octav's glowering look and clenched fists.

Stemming his anger, and through gritted teeth, the Ainoren relented the slightest bit. "With something this important? Yes. But I will have words with him."

Lyrik reached out, seeing Octav's mounting anger. "Maybe." He smiled. "But remember, he's not just a subordinate. Chace is your friend, and saved your life on many occasions."

Octav's birthmark flushed green, guilty for wanting to lash out. Unclenching his fists, he wiped his hands across his forehead. "I'm not with it. Am I?"

Lyrik turned away, but the flash of his birthmark agreed.

Unable to stop, Octav stared in the pair's direction. "When we're back, I'll buy the first round."

"That's more like it!"

Watching Chace with Tao, Octav made a move as anger tweaked his innards. Lyrik pulled him back. "Let him work his magic. One-on-one, like he does."

Octav stood still. Torn. The more he witnessed, the more his stomach knotted. Bile burnt at his throat's back. Patience wasn't something he could do.

Chace eventually walked to them. "Tao's promotion came through a few days ago," he began, "nervous, so the other men think he's not up to the job."

"Did you get the information?" asked Octav, taking a deep breath.

"Yes, Sir." Chace read the glower in the Ainoren's look. He straightened, and reported, "He saw Wez in one of the bars after shift, looking uncomfortable, and he had two other men with him."

"Would he recognise those other men?" Lyrik asked, on task.

Running his hand through his hair, eyes up through cheeky lashes, Chace's eyes flittered side-to-side. "Said he'd never seen them before."

Octav shifted his attention when Officer Tao drew nearer, head lowered. "Ainoren, I was out of line."

Chace's firm stare eased Octav's instinct to reprimand Tao. Octav questioned, "You'd never seen those others with Wez before?"

"No, Sir. One was called Trax. My informer didn't give a second name though. Sorry, Sir."

Lyrik and Octav traded glances.

"What is it?" Chace asked.

"Dalamaar's right-hand man." Octav's tension at the mention of Dalamaar shone clear on his cheek. "We need to locate Wez."

"I can take you to the bar," Tao offered, "if it will help?"

Octav decided. "Yes, but I must visit with Emmi first."

"You're sure?" Lyrik asked his face awash with concern. Lyrik waved Veco over, deciding without a response, "Come with me."

Once they left the deck, Octav moved onto Chace's instructions as the man stood patiently. "Lyrik knows how important this is. My mission is different."

"Kendro asked you to find Wez? I don't get it."

Grinning, Octav said, "Time to wake the head of House Sonaya."

"Yes, Sir."

At Emmi's private chambers, Octav pushed the comms. No answer. He banged loudly on the door.

A very tired woman popped onto a viewing screen. "What's the problem?" Sleep-filled eyes saw Octav. Clasping her mouth shut, she stifled her surprise. Opening the door, ushering them in, she said, "I'll wake Emmi." Then she shuffled away.

Stepping towards a drinks unit, Octav poured two glasses of atrei, offering one to Chace.

A seductively dishevelled Emmi whirled into the room, her elaborate birthmark shimmering through her thin nightdress. Blonde ringlets cascaded down her back, swaying with her, until she stopped before Octav. Until now, he had never noticed her beauty. The standard uniform did nothing for her figure, but this nightdress accentuated every curve.

"Ainoren." Emmi pulled her gown tighter around her. The uneasiness in her voice sharp, concerned.

Octav regarded her for a few moments, drinking his atrei. He commanded, "Wait outside, Chace."

Chace placed his drink down, slipping from the room, glancing back to check the Ainoren.

"You know why I'm here." Octav turned his attention back to Emmi. "So, don't ask."

Emmi's eyes flashed a familiar purple. "You may talk to Kendro how you please," her birthmark flickered, angry, "but you will respect who I am."

She looked no older than his wife's sister—eighteen summers young. Octav caught himself before laughing. "Of course, Ma'am." His agenda to gather the Houses all on Kendro's ship might fail, because of this girl.

"I cannot—" Emmi poured herself a drink, "—help you."

"Cannot, or will not?" he challenged.

"I cannot leave the ship. I've unfinished business."

"Unfinished business." Octav slammed his glass, atrei spilling over the unit. "The King's safety is our top priority!"

"Do you not think I know that?" Taking a step back, Emmi touched above her heart. "I've felt his pain!"

"Then why disobey him?" Octav couldn't understand. Her need to protect Kendro must be as strong as his. Surely. Yet she seemed to turn her back.

He struggled to keep his composure, his breathing quickening. "Grow up!" he all but yelled.

"Grow up? Why, yes, my Ainoren. Of course." Stepping closer, Emmi caressed his uniform's insignia, her eyes sparkling with her croex.

Octav swallowed hard. Though she was the youngest head of any House, her croex seemed phenomenal. He fought the urge.

"Don't worry, Ainoren." Emmi withdrew with a sly smile on her face. "I have the utmost respect for your marriage."

Pulse settling to normal, Octav quizzed, "Then what are you doing?"

"With your permission," she held his gaze, holding up a hand that sparkled, the intricate birthmark curled around her every finger. "I must show you the truth."

Can I trust her? A shared bond with another House wasn't common, yet it would give him the opportunity to see the truth. For his King's sake, Octav held his hand towards Emmi. He needed to see deep inside to who she was. "You have my permission."

Emmi tucked a curl behind her ears. "I have a lot still to learn. This won't be gentle."

Octav held firm, studying her wavering hand. Their palms touched. "I'm used to rough."

Letting out a laugh, Emmi's smile was intoxicating. Octav drew his croex forth, the strands entwined where their hands met in connection.

Octav felt an instant pain. His birthmark flickered, and then, stayed illuminated. She wasn't lying! Stifling a gasp, he squeezed his eyes together, and then, opening them. He locked with hers, the bond complete.

Through a fully connected Scrie, their energies mixed. Emmi bit her lip, holding his stare. For the first time, Octav glimpsed the terrified young leader before him, the very sight causing his own barriers to shift. "Here, take my right hand." He extended it to her, waiting.

"It's not custom." Emmi's hand wobbled, unsure.

"Forget custom." Octav winked at her, despite his pain.

Emmi placed her right palm to his left, trembling with the strength of his croex. Octav steadied their exchange. "Better?"

"Thank you." Her pain subsiding, she sighed. "How do you do that?"

"Experience." Octav's breathing slowed. "Although, it is hard with a partially nak—"

"You jest." Emmi almost broke contact, the croex flow revealing his truth. "May I take the lead?" she asked.

"Please."

"Close your eyes, Ainoren."

Octav obeyed. Within a purple vision, Emmi whisked him back.

The plum-tinged strands glistened at the edge of Octav's sight of Letháo. Emmi had full control of this vision. Octav's persona stood before Wez, observing all. She'd taken them to her private chambers. He now witnessed Wez and Emmi, as they talked on their home planet.

"You must stay on the *Sol'Delka*," Wez commanded her.

Emmi's face contorted with obvious confusion. "Kendro's ordered me to move."

"Emmi, listen." Wez took hold of her hand. "I've been a King's advisor for longer than you, or our King, has been living. Kendro needs to do this without you."

Emmi's cheeks, flushed. "Why?"

"You know why," Wez chided.

"I can't be—" She tried to stem her nerves as her body shook.

"There, there." Stroking her cheek, Wez leaned in, kissing her forehead. "Everything will work out, my child."

Straightening, Emmi composed herself, sucking in a breath. Octav heard her inner thoughts. *I'm before the King's man.* "I will stay," she said aloud. "I will not be the downfall of our species."

Wez regarded her with a sly smile, leaving her alone to her thoughts.

"Why are you showing me this?" Octav asked from within the vision.

"Wait. You'll see."

Octav consented, moving with Emmi's vision as she called forth a view from several camos, observing as Wez walked from her chambers. An alert came through from the *Sol'Rayn*, 'Cargo is secured.'

I'd forgotten. Puswer! Emmi's inner curse shocked Octav.

A hooded figure joined Wez outside her corridor, along with a second—Trax. They left her deck, huddled together.

Octav's mouth dropped open. "Dalamaar!"

"That is why."

Octav's lips tightened. Breaking the vision, he thought only of smashing the first thing he came upon. The table before him crumbled to bits as his angry fist struck.

Emmi stood firm. "I stay not because of Wez. Dalamaar is a bigger threat than you know."

Deep creases sat across Octav's forehead. "I'll call someone—"

Emmi kicked a splinter of wood to one side. "It's no bother."

An insistent knock came through the door, "Everything all right?" shouted Chace.

"We're good!" Octav yelled. To Emmi, his frown said something else. "Why is Wez with him? I don't understand?"

"Wez kept that side of his family a guarded secret. Very guarded."

Octav sat now, head in his hands, not wanting to think about these last words. "Impossible."

Kendro won't believe this. Many things started to make sense now. *I can't believe it.*

Joining Octav on the divano, Emmi nodded. "I know. You have to trust me."

"Your ruse with Kendro? All the arguing—"

"Yes. I'm playing two roles, Ainoren." She touched his arm. Smoothing her nightdress, she whispered, "But I am on your side."

Octav sighed. "What about Wez?"

"I can't answer that one. But I will find out, if need be."

Octav faced Emmi, the croex flow from her was pure. No malice. He had to trust this. "I saw the whole truth," pausing, Octav added, "I should keep this from Kendro, yes?"

"Yes." Emmi frowned. "Neither side suspects me. It must stay that way."

Noticing a purple shimmer flickering around her, "You're shielded." Octav smiled. "You have talent beyond your years, Emmi."

Emmi winked, smiling back. "That comes with practice, too."

"All right." Pushing up, Octav stretched his legs. "I'll pull Lyrik and Veco back. What will you tell Captain Gaal?"

"That you attempted to persuade me to join Kendro on the *Sol'Ishar*. I declined. You left. Simple."

"This is a private channel." He moved from the young girl, keying in a number. "No one will hack it. Comm if you need anything. Anything at all."

Emmi rose, walking him to the door. Once outside, she leaned in close to Octav. "Cute. I see why you like him."

She closed the door, leaving Octav fighting sudden nausea. What did she mean? Looking to Chace—had he heard?

Chace's puzzled look left Octav feeling even more unsure. "What was that?" he asked.

Octav steadied himself against the bulkhead. "Call the others, we're leaving."

The docking bay buzzed. Several engineers worked on Octav's fighter as he strode in. "Are they ready?"

Nodding, an engineer ran off in a different direction. A few moments later Lyrik, Veco, and Officer Tao joined them.

"We're leaving? So soon?" Lyrik asked. "I don't—"

"I'll fill you in on board," Octav snapped. "We're leaving. Before Gaal arrives."

Echoes of Emmi's words taunted Octav. His stomach churned waiting for the all-clear to board. Yet he couldn't stop himself from watching as Chace walked around their ship.

In space, Chace punched in the coordinates for the *Sol'Ishar*. "Everything all right?"

Octav had grabbed for a bag, bile rising at all that Emmi had shown him. The burning deep within exploded, easing the sickness he felt. Now, he could look at Chace.

A red dot flashed, bleeping on Octav's console. Flicking a switch over on comms, he choked out five syllables to Lyrik. "We. Have. Company."

"See it," the reply came. "Past the *Sol'Delka*. What's it doing?"

Wiping his mouth, he had no more time for sickness. These were the enemy. "Full attack," Octav commanded.

A DRONE

"YES, AINOREN," SAID LYRIK THROUGH comms. "Full attack."

Stars zipped by as Octav's fighters chased after the Zefron ships. If they escaped, it could be the end—death to all Aonise.

Pushing at a different control panel, Chace turned off the automatic guidance system. Handing control back to Octav, he watched as Lyrik's ship shimmered, vanishing.

Octav scanned the vastness before him, his birthmark flashed green. "Where are you?" he snapped searching for any signs of a ship ahead. Within seconds, merging with the fighter's controls, he was then able to see much more.

The Zefron ship hove into his spherical vision. "Got you!" Octav shouted.

"You see it?" Lyrik hollered through the comms.

"Class two, recon bird," Chace informed them both. "No more than a drone."

Two shielded Zefron fighters dropped in behind their foe arming their weapons to fire.

"Evasive manoeuvres," Octav ordered. Too late. The Zefron fighters shot off two rounds. At the impact, sparks scattered from Lyrik's ship. On the second shot's strike, dead centre, his shield splintered. They could feel its reverberation though their hull.

Octav retaliated instantly, his enhanced abilities firing missiles at three Zefron ships without a thought. Bursting into flames, the class two banked sharp, colliding with its fighter, both destroyed instantly. The remaining ship spun, dipping its tail at the sharpness for the manoeuvre, and fled.

Instincts wanted the enemy completely destroyed. But Octav's House responsibilities allowed it to get away. A thought turned Octav's ship, then moments later, it flanked with Lyrik's damaged fighter.

"You should have gone after it," Lyrik stated.

"No. You need assistance. They have our coordinates. Damage is done. "

Lyrik sighed through the comms.

Feeling some pain across their bond, Octav asked, "You're injured?"

"No. Veco caught the blast. Get the Doc to meet us."

Octav cut their comms, changing channel for Captain Hadi. Worry lines etched his brow. They'd been found.

A knock at the door roused Kendro. *Thank Ari.* Leaning over, he pushed a panel, and a video image of Doctor Brie appeared. "Come in."

Stepping inside, she asked, "You called for me?".

"Please—" Kendro said, waving her from the doorway.

The Doctor moved, assessing the King's condition. "How are you?"

"Better." Kendro could see her confusion. "Thank you." He glanced towards the bedroom. "It isn't me I've asked you here for."

Her face dropped, panicked. "What's wrong with the Queen?"

"I'll wake her. Then, we can both explain." Kendro's anxiety allowed Brie through the door first, and then, he followed.

Mika slept. Sitting on the bed, Kendro leaned in, kissing her cheek. "Sweetheart, Doctor Brie is here."

Stirring, Mika beckoned the Doctor closer. She smiled, "It is all right, come."

"What can I do for you?" Instead of the panic she first felt, her Doctor's instinct kicked in. Settling her medical kit on the bedspace, she edged closer.

At Brie's hesitation, Kendro announced with pride. "Mika is pregnant."

"Pregnant?" Brie's mouth fell. "I had no idea."

Continuing, Kendro enumerated, "Difficulty eating. And keeping fluid down. Feet swelling. Is there anything you can do?"

Taking a cuff device from her kit, Brie held it out. "May I?" she asked the King. "It will take preliminary readings. Hopefully, the full scan will let me know what's going on."

Remembering the Doctor's atrei tube, he stepped aside, "Should I leave?" asked Kendro.

"No need, Sire." The doctor lifted Mika's hand. "This won't take long. We can then discuss what's happening." Attaching the device around Mika's wrist, Doctor Brie touched an interior button. The device lit up. A humming noise commenced as the scan proceeded. "How far along are you?" she directed at Mika.

"Kendro has him shielded," Mika shrugged, "but no more than a couple of months."

"Has 'him' shielded? You already know."

Grinning, Mika winked at Kendro, whose joy sparkled back blue at her. "I knew the moment we created him."

Doctor Brie choked, embarrassment flushing her cheeks red.

Noticing, Mika grinned. "I apologize. My manners escape me—"

Kendro's colour rose also, "—our relationship—" Mika's cuff beeped, disconcerting the King even more. "Much like you and Sheve."

"Don't apologize," Brie said, removing the device. Plugging it into her handheld reader, she scanned the information. "I'd blame the hormones." She studied the results.

Kendro hoped nothing was wrong, but Brie considered something. Kendro wanted to read her thoughts, restraint so tough with his croex.

"He's a hundred and eight days old. Growing very well. Croex output is weak, though." Brie touched Mika's abdomen. "How long have you been unable to keep food down?"

"Before the evacuation," Mika replied, lowering her head.

Kendro's upset instant. "Mika!" Anger surfacing, he clenched his fists. "You didn't say."

Mika concentrated on the doctor, avoiding that look. "What can we do?"

"I should take you to the infirmary." Doctor Brie packed away some of her equipment. "You need fluids. I can hook you to a croex infuser. Your baby needs a lot more than you at the moment."

"Mika's not going anywhere." Kendro stood before Brie. "This can't get out."

Doctor Brie stopped packing. "Yes, Sire, but your wife and son are in grave danger. Your Highness," staring at the King's expression, open-mouthed, Brie stuttered, "with— without proper treatment, both risk death."

Kendro's heart skipped, yet he held fast. "Collect what you need. Have it all come here. She's not moving."

"I must do my job."

"You can't move her." He couldn't let Doctor Brie take her. It was too dangerous.

"Doctor, my husband does not joke." Mika reached for Brie's arm, she had to understand. "There are death threats circulating." At this, Mika touched her birthmark. "If it's known I am carrying, my life is forfeit, too."

Pausing for a moment, Brie stared from one to the other. "I will need help getting the equipment."

"Octav will help," Kendro said.

"No, it must be someone I'm seen with on a regular basis," she replied, "or suspicions will be raised."

Kendro declined. No one else could know about the situation.

"Sire, if I may." Brie reached out, palm up. "Take my hand."

Kendro didn't move. Staring at Brie's outstretched palm, he sought Mika's eye for approval.

Only when Mika nodded, did Kendro hold his palm out, unintentionally hearing Brie's thoughts, *The King has ultimate decision, surely?* "Trust me," she said aloud, with a pearl white smile.

Kendro's blue mark shimmered, allowing his croex to trickle down his arm. Tickling him as it surged, it settled in his palm, the static between his and Brie's own palm intense. Allowing her croex to flow into him, Kendro stepped back with shock.

"Do you see—" the Doctor held his stare as he realised, nervousness creeping within him, "—now?"

"Yes," looking towards Mika, Kendro announced, "she's pregnant."

"I didn't realize—" Mika said. "I thought you'd know," looking to Kendro.

The doctor temporalized. "My daughter's only a few days old." Lowering her hand from Kendro's, Brie's connection vanished. She tried again. "With your weakened state… yes?" She waited for a reply.

Kendro fought with that answer. Someone had to know the truth, even at the risk of seeming vulnerable. "She's right," he admitted. "I can't feel anything. It might take months for those connections to return."

Brie laid a hand on Mika's. "Let me ask Sheve. He can help with the equipment."

Kendro stared at Doctor Brie, and then, relented, "We hadn't planned to tell anyone else. However, I do give permission for you to tell Captain Hadi."

Mika smiled at Brie's intent. "Will this work?"

"No one will suspect. I don't mind sharing I'm pregnant with anyone who asks." Brie gathered her bag, adding, "We'll wait until the shift changes, then fetch the equipment."

Doctor Brie's thoughts raced, her palms leaving prints on the bulkhead. It had been a lucky guess that Kendro wasn't in tune with everyone. Brie knew their King should be tuned in with every single Aonise. He, alone, knew beforehand. That was the King's horrible gift—that connection to each. From the moment that they're conceived, until the moment they depart.

Now, she faced a problem bigger than even what the King had. *I want children, but does Sheve?* None of this had been planned. She didn't know how he'd react. With the responsibility they'd just been given, it came at the worst time.

She also didn't know everything that had happened on Sheve's bridge that previous week, and it worried her. Constantly. Especially, now that they had a baby to think about.

Now, or never. Brie entered their quarters.

She came upon Sheve with his usual mountain of paperwork. This wasn't going to be easy. She edged in, waiting for him to notice her.

"Hey there." He smiled with a wink that made her knees tremble. This broke her. Instead of responding, tears burst free.

In a second, Sheve was up, and by her side. "Katya, what is it?" Cradling her, rocking back and forth until the sobs subsided, he soothed her with gentle cooing while stroking the hair that covered her yellow mark allowing his croex to seep through to her soul.

Hugging him tighter than ever, Brie didn't want to let go. But as the emotion subsided, she had to push him back. "Sorry."

"Stressful week," kissing her, Sheve added, "Want to talk about it?"

Lowering her hand to his stomach, gently rubbing it, she began. "Sheve," she whispered, "I—"

His eyes widened. "I don't understand." For a moment, Sheve stared, as what she'd been saying sank in. His thoughts reverberated in her mind. *No.*

"I—I'm just overwhelmed," she said.

"A baby." Guiding her towards a seat, Sheve sat them down. "Whatever you need will be fine. I'll work around it."

"I'm not the only one pregnant."

He looked puzzled. "You're the only one that matters to me."

Brie's heart melted. He could be so sweet, one of the reasons why she loved him.

"The Queen is sick, and needs our help."

"Both of you! Katya, that's wonderful." He started rambling as usual, over excited. "Our King will have an heir."

She grabbed his hand. "No, no one must know." Her words were fast and low. "All right? They can only know about me."

"I guess." Running a finger over her skin, Sheve's face beamed. "I'm thrilled. Do you kn—"

"A girl!" she said, the earlier nervousness gone.

Sheve's eyebrows rose. "A daughter." The words etched lines over his face. "What about inertia? And the Gs when we have to accelerate? Not good for babies, any of that!"

Brie let out a laugh. "We're a long way off yet, and we do have plenty of doctors on board." She stared at the paperwork. "Do you have much more?"

"As always." Sheve turned, looking at the mountain. Brie heard. Heck. That could wait. "Do you need some food? An early night?"

"Can we take the nasci equipment to the Queen first?"

"That's brilliant." Smacking her hand, Sheve laughed at Brie's deviousness. "Pretending the equipment is for you."

"Five minutes and shift changes."

"Better I'm in uniform." His grin tautened. "Instant authority." Sheve shot from the room, calling as he went, "Will she be all right, Katya?"

Inside the infirmary, Doctor Brie's mood switched. She smelled it right away—the dark undertone everyone knew. Death. Scanning around, she found the covered body, and sighed, walking over with Sheve in tow.

Doctor Vawn approached. "Sorry, Doctor. I couldn't raise you," he said. "We lost this one, thirty minutes ago."

"We can't save everyone, Dex."

Vawn acknowledged the Captain's presence. Brie watched as he noticed Sheve's bags under his usual bright eyes. "Are you here for a check up, Sir?" They all needed more rest. She knew that.

Brie directed him away from her mate. "I'm pregnant. We've come to borrow one of the nasci generators. I need the extra croex."

"I'm thrilled." Doctor Vawn's mouth tightened, though his words sounded benign. "Do you need a hand?" He regarded Captain Hadi. "This is the best news."

"We'll be fine." Brie glanced back once more to the covered body, sadness filling her. She hated losing anyone, even if it was from old age.

The couple moved together to the equipment, Brie pointing at what she needed. "Take this," she directed, "and this."

Sheve hefted objects from the shelf, feeling their weight once their gravlocks clicked off. "Anything else?"

"Yes, one more thing." Brie continued towards a wall, sliding her hand on the console as a cupboard opened. Inside, stacks of vials lined up. Routing through them, she found ones she needed, pulling a few out to take with them. "I think that's it. If we need anything else, we'll come back."

With a heave, Captain Hadi lifted the cumbersome equipment, lugging it towards the corridor.

A buzz alerted Kendro that visitors waited. Half asleep, and not dressed to receive, still he moved to greet Doctor Brie and Captain Hadi.

"Your Highness." Giving his attire a surreptitious glance, the doctor apologised. "We're disturbing you."

Kendro rubbed sleep away. "We were just resting." He bid them inside. "Please, come."

Hauling the equipment, Hadi said, "This is heavy, Sire. I can manage it for you." He settled it on the floor.

"Was it difficult to procure?"

"No, Sire." Lifting the fusion equipment, Brie pointed her husband towards the King's bedspace area. "Will you take it through for me?" Turning to the King, she continued, "I'll get Mika settled first, before I sort out the fluids."

Captain Hadi placed the equipment down, and quietly left the room. Brie attached several nodes to Mika's arm, sternum, and abdomen with quick precision. Turning on its gentle rhythm beat, in tune with Mika's heart, she handed her a glass—medicine, which the Queen sipped at reluctantly.

"It is on the highest setting for now," she instructed Kendro. "It will need turning down a notch in the morning."

"Thank you, Doctor."

Hesitant to ask outright, yet needing to know, Brie said, "May I ask a personal question?"

Stiffening, Kendro replied, "Yes?"

"Your son. He gave you some—of his life force. Didn't he?"

Kendro floundered. Wanting to answer, but struggling for words, Mika reached out, taking hold of his arm, answering for him. "Our son did. It was his choice to do so."

Brie frowned. "I thought so. He's taking in a lot of your croex, even as it made him weaker." Checking the machine once more, she added, "We'll monitor him for a few days. You're on bed rest for now."

"Bedrest. But—"

"Total bedrest." Moving to tap in a number on a console, she spoke firmly, "This is my personal comms. Any problems at all, reach me here. All right?"

Tossing and turning throughout the night, Brie snuck out of their bedspace, more than just the ache of her stomach plaguing her. She sat in their dark living room with a warm glass of atrei, hoping not to disturb Sheve. A sharp pain ran through her abdomen. Doubling over, she clung to the divano barely stifling a scream.

Rising to rid the pain. "Please. No. This can't be happening." Her eyes drifted to where she'd been sitting. Blood. Her comms buzzed. What now?

Brie reached for a light. *I can't lose you. Not now.*

Her private comms pierced the night. Mika? Hitting the panel, she answered, "Sire?"

"Come. Now."

The line went dead.

Brie grabbed an infusion guin, duty to her King ruled over her own health, injecting directly into her thigh. With the relief, she flung on some clothes, snatched her bag, about to head out the door.

"Need me to come too, Katya?" a sleepy Sheve asked at the door.

"No." She kissed him briefly. "I'll be back." She headed for the royal chambers.

The lift wouldn't come. Brie slammed the panel, cursing. "Come on!" When it opened, she stepped in as the door closed, pushing at a second panel. Nothing.

Brie's blood began to boil. "Puswer!" Looking for the nearest emergency hatch, she slung her bag over her shoulder, opened a panel, and squeezed herself through the tight spot as it started to ascend.

She'd climbed several decks, pain ripping through her, her hands slick on the rungs she climbed, finally emerging on the King's private level.

Pausing at the King's door, injecting another dose, she banged on it. No answer. She swiped her emergency pass across the panel, entering.

Mika screamed. Brie ran for the bedroom, fearing the worst.

"So, bad," Mika spat as several spasms wracked her body.

"Please," Kendro paced, lost. "Do something."

Brie checked—the equipment was working. Mika thrashed, banging her head on the bedframe with a sickening thud. Her skin split open, blood spurting over the sweat-laden bedclothes.

Brie reacted quickly, grabbing a cloth to stem the bleed. "Something for the pain." Brie took her infusion guin, placing it, and she pulled the trigger. "You're losing him." Kendro's eyes widened at this pronouncement.

"I'll give it back," he cried, "I'll give it back."

"Taliri wouldn't accept it." Brie knew that was his son's sacrifice to give. His choice. "You were too weak. He saved you with his last gift."

Brie flinched. "I really am sorry," she murmured, shivering at the sudden chill.

Picking up a table, Kendro hurled it, smashing it to pieces.

"Shh. My love. It's all right." Crying, Mika held her arms out to Kendro. "It isn't our fault."

Gathering up her med bag, Brie resigned to the lounge. Already knowing the worst, she attached a wrist device to herself, refusing to bite her nails as the pulsating light initiated a full body scan. Brie eased back. Please Ari. Help us both.

The scan over, she read the results. Brie swallowed hard, her worst scenario confirmed. If only she could leave this minute. Reaching for the nearest comms panel through tears, Brie keyed Sheve. "You'd better come."

Brie waited for someone—anyone to join her. Kendro exited his bedroom, looking towards her the once. She noticed his red face and teary eyes. Slamming open a cabinet, he pulled out a bottle of bright orange liquid. Pouring a drink, he downed it, coughing once as it burned his throat before filling the glass again.

"You look like you need one," he said, sitting across from her, offering her a tumblerful. Brie stroked her stomach as the cramps continued and declined the glass. Kendro twirled the drink around and around. "Our future depends on Taliri's survival." His shaking hands starting to calm, "Without him, we've lost." His next swallow slower, savouring the strength.

Brie had no comforting words, inner turmoil pulling her in every direction.

The door buzzed. Weary, the King still stood to answer it letting Hadi in. Brie at once ran to him, clutching and sobbing in a way no doctor would.

Brie never noticed Kendro slip from the room.

"What's wrong?" asked Hadi. Brie looked around worrying at the King's swift departure, her words about to shatter their joyous day.

Reaching for Sheve, Brie knotted his fingers in hers. "Our daughter's dying."

"I—I don't understand—what?"

Brie fought back sobs. She was still the doctor, her patients a room away. Yet she wanted to let so much out. Trusting her medical calm, she began, "I may carry her for a month. Maybe longer. But—"

Sheve's skin paled. "I— Is there nothing we can do?"

Lowering her head, Brie whispered. "Nothing. I'm sorry."

"I thought—the problem—the Queen's baby."

Glancing towards Mika's bedroom door, "The heir is—is—"

"You're joking?" Sheve sunk back. "Please say you're joking."

Brie's eyes filled again. "I want to carry our daughter." The tears kept coming, stinging, and burning his words into her. "I want to give her a chance," she grasped at anything.

"But?"

"But—" she sobbed. "She'll still die." Brie stood, pacing the room,

61

pulling what little strength she had left from within. She faced Sheve. "There is one thing," she hoped he'd remain calm. Fearful for the consequences if Sheve didn't understand. "Our daughter could save the King's son. She has the one thing he doesn't. Life force."

"You want to sacrifice your baby?" His face boiled red, "for theirs!" He stalked to the door. "Let's go to the med bay, to Doctor Vawn."

Shaking, Brie lifted her shirt. Perhaps this would stop his rant. Sheve recoiled at the patch of blood that stained through. "Ari, no."

"There's no time for false hope," Brie almost shouted.

"Nothing at all?"

"No." Brie pulled him close. "Nothing." Knowing there was no way to save this baby, she offered what little comfort she knew she could. "Kendro can help us speak to her—once at least."

"Please, then—if he's the one who can help."

MEETING ALEXA

KENDRO COUGHED FROM HIS BEDSPACE, grasping Mika's hand. "What's going on?"

"Apologies for this personal intrusion." Sheve lowered his head, touching his birthmark. Brie knew this habit. She listened as he spoke calmly. "Your Highness, we need your help."

"You only need to ask." Kendro walked to Brie's side. Reaching her, he lifted her chin. "Why the tears?"

At his kindness, Brie's soul ached. Breathing slowly to stop the sobs, she admitted, "Our daughter is dying." Saying the very words hurt her so deeply. "I'd like to speak to her i—if it's possible, Sire?"

Kendro took in a breath. "I—I don't—" *Oh my Ari, help me, your servant.* "—kn—know if I can."

Brie insisted. "I must ask her something. Important."

"I will try." Kendro regarded Sheve. What was the Captain thinking of this? "Only if you are both sure?"

Brie sought Sheve's hand, cold in hers now.

They both stared at each other for a long moment. Kendro knew their thoughts, although he didn't want to.

Finally, Sheve added, "We're sure," clenching his wife's hand.

"Make some space." Kendro indicated the divano, preparing himself to open up to their connection. As the feeling of sharp pricking needles stabbed through him, he fought the urge to moan, knowing it wouldn't help.

"I won't lie. This might not work." Kendro knelt.

"You're willing," Brie said, as she lay down. "That's enough."

Kendro witnessed Sheve flinch. "I won't ask for croex, Doctor." Kendro held out his hand to Brie. "Sheve and I will bring forth your daughter."

63

Brie prayed her thoughts clear, *Please work.*

"Face me," Kendro ordered Hadi.

Brie closed her eyes, Kendro knew her pain was unbearable, yet the darkness comforted.

"Focus in," Kendro spoke softly. "Focus deep within on your daughter."

Flashing blue illuminated the room. With his left hand, Kendro brought his croex to the centre. Allowing it to gather into a swirling mist, a shape formed. The outline of a young soul emerged, bright red fiery hair, wild around her small pale face. She waited as if they could reach out to embrace her, smiling at them in turns.

"Here," Kendro moved himself aside, allowing the trio what privacy he could by shutting down that portion of his contribution to the connection.

Sheve stared into his daughter's crimson irises, squeezing Brie's hand, he whispered. "Look at her!"

Brie hesitated, unsure if she was ready.

"Please, Brie, open your eyes," Sheve begged.

Sitting up, she breathed slow, taking in her beautiful daughter, fully formed before her, smiling in anticipation. In Brie's mind, the name arose—Alexa.

Alexa spoke. "Do not be sad. I'm not hurting."

"I am sorry, Alexa," cried Brie unable to contain her tears.

"You gave me life," Alexa looked to Sheve, "and I am happy."

"I have som—" Brie choked, "—ask of you."

The little girl shifted closer with outstretched hands, almost touching Brie's face.

Sheve leaned in. "The decision is yours, daughter of mine."

Alexa allowed him closer. "I know." With a glance to Kendro, she smiled. "The answer is yes. The answer would always be yes."

Sheve gasped, letting go of Brie's hand.

"Father," Alexa pulled his attention back, "it is not yet my time. But it will be soon. I will see you again. I promise."

Brie inhaled as the image began fading. "I love you, baby girl." She sobbed. "We love you. Never forget that."

Their daughter had gone.

Brie collapsed into Sheve's arms.

"She'd be just like you, full of love." Sheve kissed her. "We should tell him."

Kendro was back with them now. "Tell me?"

"Our daughter. She's willing to save Taliri."

As his emotion bubbled, his birthmark flickered, changing shape. "What? Why?"

Brie took hold of Kendro's shoulders, then realising who she'd touched, let go. "Alexa wants to help Taliri."

"But..." Kendro's tears formed much easier than his words. "Are you sure?"

Their sacrifice was great. Their love for him, and the royal family, was strong. All three of them were crying, yet smiling.

"Come," Brie stood, tugging Kendro to his feet.

"T-th-is will work..." he stuttered as Brie led him to Mika. Sheve, crestfallen, shuffled behind.

Perching at the edge of their bedspace, stroking the side of Mika's face, Kendro whispered, "We have a gift. A gift of life."

Behind him, the young parents shifted, and Kendro turned, asking one final time, "Are you sure?"

"No." Sheve wouldn't meet his King's eyes, pain evident as his emotion flickered through his birthmark. "I am not all right. This is Alexa's life force. Her choice." Sheve lifted his face to his King. "If your son, our heir and future King survives because of Alexa, then I am deprived, but a happy man."

"Thank you for your honesty." He touched Sheve's arm, knowing it could have gone differently.

Brie returned in some of Mika's clean clothes, too long for her, the pants dragging along the floor. "I'm glad she's still asleep," said Brie, laying herself down next to Mika.

Sheve lowered himself next to his wife, "What can I do?"

"This is up to them."

Closing her eyes, Brie grasped Mika's limp hand. Silence prevailed. Brie's mind raced with all that could have been. With a shiver, she forced herself to stop, and blanked the thoughts off, concentrating her breathing.

Kendro watched. White glowing croex from Brie travelled up her chest and into her arm. He traced it down to her hand, willing it to pass across into his wife. Please work.

Brie let out a sob and opened her eyes. "She's gone!" She flung herself into Sheve's arms.

Sheve, holding tight for fear she'd break, could only whisper his love in her ear. He turned to Kendro, "I'll take her home."

Kendro, wanting to say so much more, grasped Sheve's arm. Reaching out, their eyes locked. *Give us time*, he heard Sheve's internal plea. Kendro allowed them to leave.

Sheve found his wife some medication to help her sleep. She lay next to him, her breathing slow, steady. He should have taken some himself.

Instead, he stared at the ceiling, thinking about how short their time with Alexa had been. Feeling guilty for not wanting to help the heir to the throne, but more importantly, for not sleeping.

He slid out of their bedspace, found his slippers in the dark, and wandered into the lounge. The never-ending pile of paperwork stared at him from his desk. Not a chance. Pulling on his uniform, hoping to find something that would numb his feelings, he headed out.

Corridor after corridor, he wandered. Not noticing where he was until he stood eyeing the gardens lifts. Palm pressed to the panel, he waited. When it came, Ainoren Octav Broki greeted him from within, out of uniform, the same tired bags under his eyes.

Octav moved aside, making room. "Can't sleep?"

Captain Hadi didn't respond.

"Me neither," Octav said, performing a hamstring lunge. "I'm going for a run. If you'd like to join me, you're more than welcome."

The gardens, designed to make the ship self-sustaining, stretched on and on. Hadi stepped inside and breathed in the clean, moist air. It was so much fresher than that circulating through the pipework on the above decks.

"Beautiful, aren't they?" Octav asked, stretching out the full of his back muscles. "Do you get any exercise?"

"Not as much as I'd like," Captain Hadi replied.

"I have a good pace." Octav grinned. "You don't have to keep up." He started to run, Sheve followed. The steady slapping of feet on the grass invigorated him. Sweat dripped down the Captain's back. Although his breathing wasn't laboured, he found the pace draining.

Octav banked left, bringing them into a vast grassy area where he stopped. Sheve's thrumming heart pounded in his head.

"Do you get to let loose your croex much, Captain?"

"Not really, why?"

"That's a shame." Octav's birthmark lit up his colour of green. "It's part of exercise for me."

"I had always wanted to command a big ship," Hadi said, feeling his croex tingling inside, bursting for release. This was something he'd not done in years. He wondered for a split second, even if he could. "I never really learned how to master it. Even in training."

"Do you want to?"

"I—" Hadi shrugged, feelings urging, begging him to at least try.

Octav's brow creased, letting his croex form into a swirling orb. He threw it into the centre of the field where it floated.

"Go on. Hit it."

Sheve glared at the green orb, hearing Katya's cry in his mind again.

Reaching within himself, he found his croex. Knowing it could be used as a weapon, yet not quite remembering how.

"Think of something that upsets you." Octav waved his hand before the Captain's face. "This is how I gather croex. Through emotion."

Hadi's mind, primed with pain so deep, so intense, blasted Octav's green orb into nothing.

"Great," Octav said. "How about a moving target this time?"

"Sure," Hadi grinned dismally. Finally, something that made him feel better; his spirit lifted at the scent of ozone from the blasted orb.

Octav released target after target, while Sheve blasted each one with alarming precision. He tired quickly, sinking to the floor, a physical and emotional wreck. He had nothing left to give.

The emotional outburst caught Octav by surprise. Placing a hand on Sheve's shoulder, he allowed the Captain to cry. Not saying a word.

"Excuse my behaviour, Ainoren." Hadi straightened his back, and risked standing. Lowering his head out of respect, he rubbed the last tear from his reddened cheek. "I should—go."

"Anytime you can't sleep," Octav smiled, "you know where to find me."

Kendro felt Mika's pain as she shifted in their bedspace. He reached for her instinctively.

"Some atrei," she murmured.

When he returned, she was sitting up.

"How are you feeling?" Kendro held the glass as she sipped.

"A little better."

Taking her hand in his, feeling how cold she was, Kendro reached down the bed for an extra blanket, pulling it to cover her more. "We almost lost our son."

"Yes." Mika's face dropped, her hand covered her mouth. "The doctor? Did she lose—"

Kendro couldn't meet her gaze. He should have stopped it, allowed nature to take its course with both these lives, but he hadn't. *Am I selfish to want my son to live?* He pushed the thought aside, knowing his choices affected everyone's future, not just his own. It was for everyone, not just himself.

Mika reached for him, touching his cheek, turning him to her. "Don't do that to yourself. Please?"

She knew him all too well. He said, "It was their choice to give Taliri the croex he needed so he could survive."

Mika's eyes filled with tears. "But—her daughter—"

"I know." Kendro leaned forward, kissing her. "Will you be all right? I have to go."

She pointed to the glass. "Another drink. I'll read until you get back."

Octav met Kendro on the way to the bridge. "Long night?" He stared directly at him. "You look tired," the Ainoren started at this.

"Yeah, I can't settle." Octav sighed. "Everything here is different. You know."

Kendro motioned for them to continue walking. "You've never been home so much. Frie must be happy about that?"

Wrinkles crossed Octav's forehead, "She is, bu—"

"You're not?"

"I feel lost sometimes. In what to say…"

"Women are complicated creatures—that's for sure. Mika's one of the strongest women I know, until you put a furry animal before her. Then, she melts."

Octav laughed. "Frie is the same, animals and babies."

Kendro raised an eyebrow at this. "Babies, is she broody?"

Taking a step back, Octav almost fell. "I hope not, least not yet."

As they neared the bridge, a figure appeared, head low, shuffling along. Almost without trying, Octav took in all details—hidden from view, a detonation device.

Without forethought, Octav forced Kendro back. *Not on my watch.* He grimaced, seeing the man launching the device toward them, throwing up a shield. A lightning energy blast struck, blasting the bulkhead in two. The percussion tossed both Kendro and Octav against the deck. Pain shot through Octav's shoulder as his shield vanished. He lunged for their attacker, grappling him backwards. The Aonise man tried to defend, but was no match for the Ainoren's strength. Octav retaliated, smashing his King's assailant into the partly destroyed bulkhead. Octav had the male pinned now, the traitor squealing like a girl.

Octav pounded his palm on a comm panel. "Security to Deck Six."

Seconds later, three security officers appeared, running towards them. "Take him to a holding cell."

Octav turned to Kendro. "I'll deal with him." He offered a hand, which hardly shook at all.

Octav stood firm, watching Kendro walk away. Only when his King stepped through onto the bridge safe, did he make his way to the Security holding cells. He would rip that traitor to pieces if he had to, but he would get the information he needed.

Octav entered and, Chen stood, saluting. "Ainoren." He saw him glance to the awkward prisoner, who shifted in his seat.

"At ease, Officer."

Chen relaxed a little, shoulder dropping. "The prisoner is secure." Indicating his reader, he said, "Running DNA checks now, Sir."

"Has he spoken?"

"No, Sir."

Approaching the cell, Octav placed his palm against it, feeling the electrical energy it possessed. "Turn off the barrier."

"Sir. He is dangerous."

"Turn off the barrier."

Officer Chen placed his palm to his console, and with a flash, the protective barrier vanished. The prisoner didn't move. He stared, eyes unwavering. Chen shouldn't be allowed to see this. With a flick of a wrist, Octav dismissed him.

The Ainoren hoped for some answers, but knew he wouldn't get any soon.

"Who sent you to harm our King?" Octav asked.

No answer.

He asked again, louder this time. "Who sent you to harm our King?"

"Why try? I won't tell you."

"Oh. You'll talk. You all do. Eventually."

The traitor struggled against his restraints. Licking his lips, he shut his mouth.

Grinning, Octav had another go at his prisoner. "You say you won't, but you're already losing faith." He observed the shaking legs, and the prisoner's facial twitches.

Octav had removed his shirt. His birthmark, grasping his torso like a widespread hand, shimmered in the light. "The superior who sent you. Name him."

Still nothing. *As stubborn as Chace, I see.*

Flexing his muscles, Octav allowed his croex to trickle out into his skin, changing the mark's shape that cloaked him. He stepped closer. "The man you're protecting. Did he teach you anything about torture?" The room flashed green. "I've been doing this for years."

At last, the man responded. "And your King sanctions this?" The prisoner spat. "Pahh."

Good. Octav snickered. He wanted to crush this man before him. Traitor. "Sanction it or not is irrelevant." Bringing forward his croex, focussing it into a thin pulsating creature, Octav teased before he struck. The man watched—before he screamed. Red-hot energy sliced a neat hole in his chest. "Can you take pain? Much? "

Officer Chen's knock disturbed Octav's rhythm. A voice came though the bulkhead. "We have an I.D. on him, Sir. His name is Yuko. He's on Lower Deck Four with a group of Heiako."

Octav nodded. He hadn't thought for a moment Yuko belonged to a house. A Heiako made it much easier for him to deal with, near-slaves in some Aonise eyes.

"Unwanted, huh." Octav laughed at Yuko. "You're not grateful enough that your King saved you from a painful death on our home planet? You make an attempt on his life?"

"I'd sooner die," Yuko spat, "than serve under a false King."

Octav's anger surged as he reached, grabbing Yuko by the throat. "You're one of them. Aren't you?" Octav shook him until spittle ran from his mouth. "Finally, we're getting somewhere. It was Dalamaar who ordered the attack?"

"No." In fear, Yuko shook his head. "No, Dalamaar would do nothing like that."

Octav dropped him. "For that, you will suffer." He released the portal door. Turning to Officer Chen, Octav spat, "Tag him as a deserter. He'll be trialled as soon as we finish the courtroom."

Officer Chen, not knowing where to look, stared only at Octav's shoes asking, "Will we continue with capital punishment?" And Octav heard the unspoken. *There are so few of us now.*

"That will be up to the Houses to decide," Octav replied, grabbing his shirt as he left.

Commander Vax stood as Kendro stepped onto the bridge, which bustled with various activities. "Your Highness." She saluted.

"Is Captain Hadi available?"

"Yes, Sir." Vax escorted Kendro through the bridge to Captain Hadi's private chambers and knocked.

"Come," Hadi called.

Kendro stepped inside. "I wasn't expecting you here this morning."

"I have a job, Your Highness." Hadi neatly placed files on top of each other. "I still intend to fly this ship, to the best of my ability."

Understanding the Captain's need to work, it had taken Kendro's mind off his problems many a time. Kendro took a seat across from him, making eye contact. Seeing the pain etched on his Captain's face was hard, though. "How are preparations for the tests going?"

Hadi checked his reader. "Ready tomorrow. Barring contingency."

"Good. Well done."

"Our men have been working double shifts, Sire. We're sure it will work, without glitches. The *Sol'Ishar* still operates at a hit and miss calibre."

Kendro's lips tightened. "I had noticed." Having to climb ladders instead of using lifts was frustrating. "Smaller glitches are fine.

Defending against an attack, that's a must."

Octav made his way to the bridge, thinking hard about Yuko, about the information he'd gathered, and what choice he must recommend to his King. On their home planet, deserters were punishable under the strictest law. Death. Would it be different now? He didn't think so. Any attempt on the King's life had to be taken seriously. Would one death for effect cause Dalamaar's minions to retreat, their plans foiled at the last minute?

Rubbing the lines from his face, Octav wished he'd had more sleep. Frie's company, however, grated on his every nerve. They argued at the slighted things. Every time he walked through their door, her conversations were childish in nature, driving him to wander the decks at all hours.

Alive with activity, the bridge crew had settled into perfect sync. Everyone functioned as one entity. Octav's salute to Commander Vax accompanied a shout from one of the crewmen, "Ainoren on deck." Vax returned the salute.

"At ease, Commander."

"Ainoren. Everything is as requested for today's testing," she reported.

"Excellent. Is Captain Hadi in his office?"

Pointing, "Yes, Sir," Vax stated and stepped aside.

Octav moved to knock, but there was no need. Captain Hadi shouted, "Come."

Smiling at Kendro, who was still seated before Hadi, Octav stood before them ready to report. "The prisoner?" Kendro asked.

"Secure." Octav's birthmark twinkled. Not wanting to be the bearer of bad news, he glowered before going on. "Dalamaar's faction is alive, though."

"Who is Dalamaar?" Captain Hadi asked, staring at Kendro.

Octav saw Hadi's confusion as the King replied, "He's not in a House. Something completely different. He did captain one of our ships." With a nod to Octav, he asked, "Ainoren, bring him up to speed?"

Octav limped to the Captain's desk. Pressing his palm over the security panel, he typed in several slow commands. A holographic image appeared. "This is Dalamaar," Octav informed Hadi. "He takes on many different guises to evade us." Several other images appeared. Octav pointed to each one of them. "And he's leader of this faction." He ran through names. "Trax, Imamu, and Rade."

"I don't understand why you haven't eliminated them," Hadi wondered aloud.

"It isn't that easy." Octav frowned. "The moment we get close, they relocate. It has cost more men looking than it has allowing them to carry on."

"What are their plans?" Hadi asked.

"His main plan—"

"—is planning something bigger," Kendro filled in. "Small attempts on my life are nothing but distractions. His plan is the throne."

Hadi asked, "He has rights to the throne, if you're dead?"

"He has no rights!" Kendro slammed down his hand. The floating rebel images vanished. "Whether I'm dead or alive."

"No right, if you have an heir," Octav was reluctant to add.

Octav saw Hadi beginning to speak, but the Captain stopped himself, casually moving his hand over his mouth at Kendro's glare.

Silence prevailed for a while until Hadi came back with, "Should be easier to capture Dalamaar surely, now that our people are on four ships?"

Octav agreed with a nod. He brought up schematics from one of their ships. "They hold near a million citizens. We've asked everyone to register. However, with folks like Dalamaar, there are at least ten thousand per ship who haven't registered. When the evacuation was quickened, several hundred thousand were distributed to the wrong ships."

Hadi studied the schematics, all thoughts of heirs forgotten. "What are we doing about it?"

"We're going through the ships. Room by room. There are some who aren't cooperating."

"They're scared of being moved," Kendro reminded them. "It wasn't long after we boarded that Dalamaar let everyone know his supposed future vision, and that only the *Sol'Ishar* survives. Trax must be a Seer. There's no other way Dalamaar could get that information."

"He's effectively one step ahead," Captain Hadi said. "I can see why it's a problem."

Octav took a seat, rubbing his temples, trying to ease his painfully clotted brain. "A continuing problem."

"Tired?" Captain Hadi asked.

"Migraine."

A knock came at the door, and Captain Hadi's screen announced the person waiting. "Madrall." He checked the time. "This gathering is big enough. We'll meet to discuss these issues after the defence testing."

Kendro stood with more grace than he felt. "I agree, Ainoren. Let us prepare for the test."

With a decline, Captain Hadi swiped 'No' to the door buzz. Watching as Madrall, frustrated, turned leaving the bridge.

"He doesn't like us discussing things without him," Octav stated.

"He's unsure of everyone's loyalty."

"Don't forget, Octav—" Kendro interrupted. "Madrall has Retray."

"Retray is also a Seer." Noticing the Captain's puzzled face, Octav explained once more, "Third generation. He's not as powerful as some are. Can't see everything. Hence, Madrall gets nervous."

"Who can see everything?" Hadi asked. "If Retray is third generation, who is second—or first?"

"There are only two first generation seers still alive," Kendro replied. "One is my advisor, Wez. The other hides well, known to no one. Even me."

"For good reason," Octav said. "She, or he, is very powerful. In the wrong hands, a first generation seer can do more harm than good."

"They're on board this ship though, right?"

"Perhaps." Kendro smiled. "Let's get to the testing site before any more secrets are revealed." He looked to Octav. "Agreed?"

SIMULATION

KENDRO LED HIS ENTOURAGE FOUR decks below the bridge into one of the ship's wing sections. Underneath the wing spanned a vast shuttle bay, hundreds of fighters flanked side-by-side, their sleek metallic edges as sharp as their weapons. Once in unison with their pilots, these single engined fighting machines were super fast, and they easily manoeuvred around a larger target, perfect for fighting the Zefron.

Kendro watched as his officers waited. Dressed in full battle uniform, they saluted towards him in unison; a full squadron of the best available soldiers. Kendro took in the dock's view below, happy for the effort he witnessed.

Lieutenant Euro stepped forward addressing Octav specifically. "Ainoren. We are awaiting final instructions, Sir."

"Ready." Octav waited for Kendro to turn around.

"Are you pleased, Your Highness?" Euro asked.

"Yes, Lieutenant. Perfect job from all stations."

"Thank you, Sir. My men will be glad to hear so." Euro faced the others officers. "Shall we?" He waved to the ladder, pilots, up and down in both directions. "The men are eager for testing."

Lieutenant Euro walked up the central line and turned about. On the hanger deck stood soldiers, primed and ready for battle simulation. With a salute to the Ainoren, he shouted, "Battle stations!"

The men scrambled at Euro's command, scurrying to their ships, prepped and ready for launch within seconds. Kendro, impressed, let himself believe for a moment that perhaps they could fight the Zefron after all.

"I think we should take a step backwards," Octav whispered to the King. Kendro obliged.

Within minutes, the deck was a hive of movement. Engines fired. The ground humming, the fighters began launch sequences.

"We should return to the bridge, Your Highness," Madrall said. "A better view from there."

"Prepare a shuttle," Kendro ordered. "Our best view will be from space."

"Agreed." Octav motioned. "The shuttles are below. Won't take a moment to prep, Your Highness"

"May I assist, Ainoren?" Lieutenant Euro turned briskly to his second. He directed commands to each officer, then stepping lightly aside to join the King's men.

On the deck waited twenty shuttles, much larger than the fighters, designed for exploration and science missions, rather than war. Kendro stood as Octav placed a hand on a panel, opening the gangway. The others followed a few moments later, until all were aboard, and Euro had checked they were all strapped in securely.

Once sitting, Lieutenant Euro took to the controls, double engines purring to life.

Gripping the arms of his chair as the shuttle's confines closed in on him, Kendro's birthmark paled as he shivered.

The shuttle dipped, lunging forwards into the void.

Ahead, in a brilliant twinkling of the stars, blackness stretched before them. Kendro's stomach churned. *Should have eaten breakfast.*

Lieutenant Euro promised his King, "You're in safe hands." He slid the controls down a notch, rechecking the King's seat was secure before saying, "Much better view from up here!"

The Ainoren expertly manoeuvred the shuttle above the *Sol'Ishar*, leaving Kendro to admire their ship's sheer size and power. *She dominates everything in their sights.*

"She's magnificent." Kendro offered that praise to the crew around him. "Planet side, you couldn't comprehend her size."

"Isn't she?" Octav boasted with a quick wink. "A sheer feat of ingenuity."

The hundred fighters sprung for the test flight spread, swarming the *Sol'Ishar*, poised for their attack. She seemed helpless, but Kendro knew differently. Formidable.

"They're ready," Lieutenant Euro reported. "Awaiting orders, Sir."

With Kendro's approval Octav tapped his comms. "*Sol'Ishar*, this is a drill. To battle stations. Say again. Battle stations."

Octav pulled up the command deck's internal image. Captain Hadi stood proud, leading his *Sol'Ishar* head-on into the simulation.

"Red alert, Commander Vax," Captain Hadi ordered, hearing the call to battle stations. The alarms sounded, and red-flashing lights pulsed around the room. Adrenaline flooded his veins. He knew every officer on deck felt as edgy. Simulation or not, how they performed on this day would be recorded for all to see.

"One hundred fighters swarming the ship, Sir."

"Shields?"

Commander Vax read the screen before her. "Full capax, Sir."

"Fighters moving in," Science Officer Lynj spoke loudly.

"On my mark." Hadi anticipated. "Fire."

The fighters made their pass towards the *Sol'Ishar*. Her cannons roared into life. Sparks flew from behind. More sparks exploded around them as they powered up about to fire on their target.

Kendro's eyes widened, seeing the splutter, all cannons faltering.

"Aren't supposed to do that," Euro whispered.

"Cannons are responding abnormally," Lyrik reported through comms.

"No." Octav, watched as their cannons swivelled tracking the incoming fighters, their sparks lighting up the side of the *Sol'Ishar*.

"Dammit!" Octav slammed his hand on the console. "Abort drill. Repeat. Abort the drill."

"What's going on?" Kendro asked.

"Not sure, Sire." Octav checked as cannon stats came through from Lyrik and their mother ship. "All energy should be diverted through the forward sections. There's a fault."

"Take us back." Kendro sighed. "Please, Ainoren," he added. At this, Euro busied himself programming their return.

"Let it be an easy fix," Lieutenant Euro said while he plotted the course. Octav spun his chair from the console wishing to talk over the cannon's readings, but not in this full company of listeners.

"Sir." Euro brought them in safely. "If you need my help investigating, I'm more than willing to do whatever is necessary."

Octav agreed, yet gut instinct told him Euro knew more than he was letting on. It didn't feel right, so he added, "I'll keep you in mind."

"I don't understand. I checked everything." Octav stared at Kendro. "This morning, there was nothing amiss."

"You think someone has done this on purpose," Madrall broke in, "don't you?"

76

"I do." Octav straightened, hating to be uttering the word. "Sabotage."

"No," Kendro said to the five he'd gathered behind closed doors. "It doesn't make any sense at all. Death to us would be death to them all. Saboteurs as well."

Octav surveyed the small grouping. "Why then? Everyone on our 'watch list' is on board this vessel. Why would they sabotage their own ship?" He would gut anyone who was trying to hamper the battle plans. "You have other agendas for discussion now. I will find out who did this."

"We will re-convene after your investigation." Kendro waved them to the door.

Octav separated from the House Leaders and his King, heading straight for the Energy cannons. Several minutes passed for a lift to reach the weapons deck. *Dodgy mechanics. We're dead in the event of the Zefron attack.* Burnt metal stung his nostrils. Tapping the console, he'd left scorch marks.

A beeping alerted him to a private comms.

"Octav," he barked.

"Ainoren, where are you?" Captain Hadi's voice came clear across the comms. *At least we have that.*

"In Section Five's lift, headed for the Energy cannon relay."

"I'll meet you there."

Still, the lift could not have been slower. *Thank Ari that at least I'm moving.* With a jerk, the lift stopped, opening two decks away from where Octav needed to be.

Curious, he stepped into one of the lower decks, glancing around looking for a second lift that might be in better repair.

This wasn't right.

Door after door stretched the full length of the companionway. Heiako men stood ahead, one staring right at him. Octav pushed the panel on the second lift, trying to force the doors open. They wouldn't. Stuck. Straightening himself, he stepped from the lift, heading down the companionway toward another way above.

As he drew closer to the waiting, staring men, a door opened beside him. A little Heiako girl scarpered after a quick moving sable wielse. Octav was swift, grabbing the creature by its long, spindly tail, holding it at arm's length so it wouldn't bite.

"I'm sorry," she said, holding her hand out for her pet. "He just won't settle."

Octav held on tightly. The wielse stopped trying to bite, cooing at him until he stroked its puffed fur. Frowning at the girl, he chastised, "You weren't authorized to bring any pets onboard."

The young girl stared up at Octav, noticed his uniform, and started to cry. Her mother appeared, cuddling her daughter first, then seeing Octav with the squirming wielse.

"Ainoren." She stood saluting even though she wasn't in uniform.

"At ease—"

"Petty Officer Cryz, Sir."

The wielse cooed louder as Octav rubbed its ears. Casually observing the men still at the bottom end of the corridor, he knew they were watching.

"Petty Officer Cryz, you are aware of this direct violation. No animals are sanctioned on this vessel."

She lowered her head. "I'll dispose of it." Her daughter's cries rose in the echoing companionway.

Octav regarded the little girl. It saddened him. He never liked anyone crying. "There's no need for that." He held out the wielse as the girl took possession gingerly. "There is a condition, if I let you keep it."

The little girl glanced quickly to her mother, checking first. "Y-yes?"

"A report every week. You'll write it now. I want to keep an eye on its progress."

"Run inside." Petty Officer Cryz patted her daughter on the head. "Please, Daya."

Two of the men edged closer. "Are you proficient in self defence?" he asked Cryz, indicating down the space towards the men.

"Sir?" Cryz followed his gaze. "Oh. Of course." She stepped out from her door, closing it.

"Easy—" Octav whispered. "Don't want to start a war down here."

The men drew closer still, their eyes glinted a dull orange in the darkness, croex already harnessed.

Cryz and Octav stood fast, flanking each other—a strong defensive stance.

Doors opened behind Octav. He knew then they were surrounded. "What do you want?" he called.

One man stepped forward. "Ainoren." Hands in sight. "A quiet word. If you don't mind."

"Russif—" whispered Cryz. "Local gang leader."

At that, Octav waved Cryz away, his anger threatening to ignite his birthmark. "Just to talk to me?" He noticed the man's birthmark wasn't anywhere near as detailed as his own was. He was appalled that this someone demanded to speak alone, and directly. Octav's croex pulsed strong though his annoyance at the obvious deception. "You hijacked my lift!"

"We mean you no harm," Russif said. "Octav. Please, stand down."

"Sir, you aren't going to trus—" from behind, Octav saw the glimmer of Cryz's croex flicker, "are you?"

"No," he addressed Cryz. "Not in a crowded corridor." Turning back to Russif, Octav demanded, "You know who I am." It felt strange to be using such language with a Heiako of low standing. So be it, if it got him the information.

"I'm Russif." The damned man risked standing firm, not bowing or saluting before Octav, watching him close. Without breaking eye contact, he gestured back. "These are my men."

Octav noted each of them. His men? "They're not bound." He sensed their loyalty to Russif. How unusual for the Houseless.

"No. I choose not to do such."

"Even though you're strong enough?"

Russif smiled. "Yes."

The other men seemed shocked at Octav's statement. There were murmurs around him: '…slaves,' 'never,' and 'why.'

"Even though I am strong enough." Turning around, Russif pointed towards an open door. "Please. Come with me."

Octav took a step, followed by Cryz.

"Alone."

"Go back to your daughter." Octav smiled. "I will expect her reports as she promised."

"Please," Cryz said, "let me know you are all right?"

With a nod, Octav stepped away with Russif.

Octav sat. A young woman brought them a pair drinks. The room contained only a bedspace, a few chairs, and a control console. She ogled the birthmark and Octav's uniform with shaky hands, holding out warm alcoholic drinks for the men.

"Thank you." Octav took one, addressing Russif. "Yenjo," Octav smelled the aromatics wafting from the steaming cup. "Very nice."

"Yes, it is." Russif drank. "Not much is on board, I believe."

"Lots of trouble for you to bring me here. So, please enlighten me."

Russif shooed the girl away, then pulled out a crystal disk. "I came into some information." He tapped his offering. "Valuable information."

"You want me to buy it?" Octav gestured the room. "Can you not see where we are?"

"Not to buy, but I do want something in return."

"What is this favour you want?" Octav drank more deeply, feeling the glorious intoxication settle his stomach. "I don't have time to be messed around."

Russif placed his cup down. "I don't know yet."

"You don't?" Octav's birthmark glimmered, a warning.

"This information is, as I say, very valuable." Russif, between thick fingers, played with the rhombus disk, a small wave. "I am trusting giving it to you that you will hold to your promise."

Disks were rare. Russif held the enticement out, piquing Octav's attention. He had to ask, "May I?"

"Of course." Russif passed the disc across. He swivelled his control console around for Octav to use.

He placed the disk into its reader, and within seconds, the information loaded. Octav read the plain text and turned it off. Thank Ari. He pocketed the disk, his stomach knotting. "Who has seen this?"

"The man who brought it me. Only him."

"Not the girl? Not your men? Can you guarantee this will go no further?"

"Yes, on both our lives."

"If I can corroborate the information herein, then I owe you a debt to be repaid at your request."

"Thank you, Ainoren," Russif said.

"There is one condition."

"Is that fair?" Russif's palm-sized birthmark flickered. "I give information, you make conditions?"

Octav stared him down. "I will not harm without reason. And I will stand by our King."

"Oh, of course." Russif croex flicker diminished. "I'd not expect anything else."

"Do we have a deal?"

"Yes," said Russif holding his hand out for Octav, shaking it firmly.

Octav looked to Russif's door. "Are all your men registered down here?"

"Ainoren." Russif stood. "May I show you some of 'down here' if you have time?"

Octav checked his reader as Russif stood at the door waiting to lead him outside before joining the Heiako who walked ahead. Octav warned, "I'm short on time." He should have met Captain Hadi ages ago. And the board meeting with Kendro was in less than an hour.

With a touch to his woman's shoulder, Russif motioned towards the corridor. "Please."

Taking Octav further into the belly of the ship, Russif turned, asking, "There was supposed to be room enough for all of us, right?"

Octav knew it was a mess. Was that why the saboteur struck above decks? "Indeed, there should be a room for every family." But, they had run out of time.

He just hadn't seen it first hand.

Russif opened the first set of double doors leading them to a platform above one of the hanger bays. "It is what it is, Ainoren. Is that what you'd tell me? Perhaps with your own eyes you can understand how your King's people are suffering."

The bay sprawled below them. Packed tight. Over a thousand citizens huddled, waiting. Octav took a deep breath. The smell knocked his stride. Reaching for the barrier, he steadied himself. "I know it isn't ideal—" Octav swallowed. "We had no choice but to stop building individual rooms. We did our best to fortify the space." He stopped speaking, adding only, "I can feel this pain—we had no choice."

As they witnessed the bay below, whimpers of children rose and fell. Some men noticed their arrival, immediately heading over to the ladders.

"Ainoren," Russif indicated the whole space with a wave of his arm, "please do not misunderstand me." Pure exasperation resonated in his eyes now. "Our people know you've done everything possible. We know where the Heiako stand. Now, we're in this space, settling into routines. They want to do things."

"What do you mean—" Octav watched as men below drew closer up the ladder, suddenly aware all eyes were on him, "—do things?"

Russif pointed to a group of youngsters. "The children are bored. The adults are frustrated. Without privacy, tempers flare. Accidents happen. We are not inanimate machines to be rolled in and out of some bay at need. This is a huge, ungoverned space for so many."

"I see." The Ainoren watched the queue for the shower facilities, stretching half way across the bay, moving ever so slow. "How can I help?"

By now, the climbing men were almost upon them. Octav didn't feel threatened. These men weren't the Zefron. One of them approached along the platform's rail, smiling broadly, holding out a hand. "Ainoren. Good to see you here."

"We've heard reports." The man shook Octav's hand. "An attempt on the King's life earlier?" His birthmark shimmered noticeable at his hairline, under locks of dangling hair around his face.

So quickly!

Confidentiality, a strict onboard requirement had been forsaken. Humm. Anger bubbled, and concern for the King's safety was still foremost in his mind. Octav forced himself to stare each man down. *A report? More a leak.* "We're doing everything. We'll find the men behind your report."

"Ainoren, we're not soldiers." Another man stepped forward, bright-

81

eyed, eager. "We're workers, designers. Teachers and chefs. We're willing to help above deck, or below."

Taking in the bay before him once more, Octav could only agree—they should be using the Heiako, not hiding them. This meeting above the bay drew more attention. Many gathering below, mumbles and cries drifted upwards to them.

"I can see." Octav turned to Russif. "Let's join them." He moved to the platform's ladder, quickly descending.

A young man snuck in between the adults who'd gathered around Octav, tugging at the Ainoren's arm, birthmark glimmering with nervous excitement as he looked up at him.

"Yes, young man?" Octav asked.

"My father, he's sick," the youngster lowered his head. "He needs some medicine."

"Has no one seen him?" Octav turned, asking Russif.

"No, no medical staff has been below decks."

The teen shrugged, lowering his chin, staring at the floor. "My name is Sylkx."

"Take me to him, Sylkx," Octav commanded, a little too sternly. But smiling, Sylkx grabbed Octav's hand.

Sparks flew as their touch connected. *Unbelievable.* Octav recoiled at the tremendous power contained within such a youngster.

Reading something in this touch, Sylkx withdrew his hand taking hold of Octav's uniform instead, pulling him away from the gathering group. Russif and the others followed behind, as Sylkx led them deep into the midst of the thousand restless souls.

Reaching a section of handmade sleeping quarters, Sylkx pointed towards a single bedspace where his father lay.

"Lace." The group approached the man who stirred, trying his best to sit on seeing the Ainoren.

Kneeling down before the boy's father, Octav asked, "What is it you need?"

Lace shook his head. "Not—" he coughed violently.

With a nod to Octav, Russif eased the worried youth toward the group who had followed. "Your father's thirsty, boy. Take some with you, and go gather atrei. Bring what you can for him."

Sylkx eyes glinted, full of hope. Poor boy. Octav knew his world would soon shatter.

Octav turned back to the father, kneeling once again. "You're dying?" he asked.

"Yes." He coughed harder. "Medicine—the sun—"

"There is nothing else?"

"I don't know." The coughing grew worse. "Not for a Heiako. My son?"

"Be assured he will not go without," Octav replied.

Octav spoke to Russif, "I'll collect the medicine myself, and send medics down." Pausing, Octav watched those around him. "Form a task force, Russif. Your men will help get these people registered. Once they're registered, they can be assigned jobs."

"A good idea."

"It seems my men are lacking the discipline to obey orders. They'll be dealt with accordingly."

Russif laughed at this. "Your men are scared."

"I can see why." Octav scanned Lace's small bedspace again. "Orders are orders. They will need to answer for not doing their duty, regardless. Make sure—"

A siren echoed throughout the bay followed by a flashing orange light.

Octav shook and banged on his reader, which lay silent in his hand.

Panicked, Russif confessed, "I'm sorry," he said, "we jammed your personal comms."

"We're under attack?" Octav ran for the nearest hatchway, slamming his palm on the wall comm. "Lock down, now!" he shouted.

THE ZEFRON

"CITIZENS!" KENDRO'S VOICE BOOMED, URGING Octav to run faster, as he sped towards the bridge. "This is not a drill."

Reaching the bridge, so out of breath he struggled to keep upright, Octav smashed his hand on the control panel. The door slid open.

He joined utter chaos.

"Thank Ari! Where have you been?" Captain Hadi demanded. "We sent a search party."

"Explanations later. Report!" Octav's observed the whole room assessing the needs on deck around them Kendro's voice repeated 'Battle Stations!'

"Two Zefron war-birds. Sitting just on scanners range, Sir."

"What are they doing?"

"Nothing, Sir. Just waiting." Hadi looked to Kendro now.

Octav met the King's calm stare. "Waiting for what? More ships?"

"I don't know."

"I've been—below—can't we engage the energy cannons?"

"Sabotage." Captain Hadi broke in, turned his console around for Octav. "Someone's pulled out several relays. We're tracking down when. But the camos have been doctored."

"Impossible." Octav scanned the room. Trusted crew, or not? "They're guarded. How could anyone get past?"

"Drugs," Captain Hadi sighed.

Octav stared through their viewport into the blackness of space. "Have you managed any repairs?"

"I have men on it, Ainoren."

"Puswer!" Octav cursed under his breath.

"The Zefrons have broken positions." Science Officer Lynj shouted,

84

"Heading for us, Captain."

"The other ships?" asked Octav.

"Their war-birds, plus—" a crewman answered.

"—large weapons!" Lynj spoke aloud what they all witnessed.

Kendro's birthmark flashed around the room. "They aren't standard Zefron weapons."

"How close are the engineers to finishing repairs?" Octav ordered towards Reel. "Get me the engineers."

"Yes, Ainoren."

"All cannons. Fully operational," Chief Engineer Zyler wheezed through the comms, "Sir."

"Fire on my command," Octav barked. *They won't know what hit them.*

Officer Lynj checked her scans. *Was this right?* A glance to her King, she knew he heard her thoughts, not her commanding officer, before reporting. "Your Highness? They're heading away."

Everyone watched in silence, hands on controls. The war-birds manoeuvred into a wide sweep past the outskirts of the *Sol'Delka's* range, all but skittering away. The crafts diminished, finally on the view screen nothing more than points of light.

"Stand down, Captain," Octav said.

"Yes, Ainoren."

With a nod to Kendro, he said, "We should talk." Then, to Captain Hadi, "We'll be in your office."

Octav ushered Kendro inside, palming closed the door, locking it, and then, checking once more. No one else must hear this, only the two who had stepped inside.

"Quite an operation, this sabotage. Wouldn't you say?" Kendro stated, sitting in the Captain's chair, rubbing his forehead.

"What happened?" Kendro raised his face to his Ainoren. "Not just now," with a wave to their Captain on the other side of the door. "Hadi was losing his mind comming you! Were your comms off?"

In one breath, Octav explained all. Finishing with, "I'd been taken off-grid by Russif's order."

"Off-grid?" asked Kendro.

Octav knew the sudden lurch of his stomach would give away what information he had. "It is said you have an heir," Octav stated, raising an eyebrow. "To some, an heir who must be eliminated. For us, one who must be protected."

"Some? You mean this Russif?" Kendro met Octav's puzzled gaze.

"I'm sorry, old friend. I couldn't tell you."

"How far pregnant is Mika?" Octav wanted to congratulate him, to hold him tight. Their House, family, was very important to him.

"Enough to be safe." Kendro beamed, but that faded. "There were complications. Doctor Brie's attention these last few days meant a great loss. For both her and the Captain."

"Ah." Poor man. Now, he understood. "Hadi needed to vent last night."

Kendro lowered his head. "Yes."

"Awful." The Ainoren paused, wishing Hadi had told him something, but understanding his choice. "Mika's pregnancy won't stay secret for long."

Kendro diverted the conversation. "Tell me more about Russif."

"He's decent."

Octav wondered where to start. The *Sol'Ishar's* failing structural problems? Conditions below? Russif's followers? "He's thinking of the Heiako," he said eventually. "The conditions down there, we hadn't— it's cramped, Sire. No prospects. If anyone can, Russif can help bring order."

"We need to minimise all threats," Kendro commanded. "Mika must be in no danger at all. Treat this man with respect, but see that he stays quiet." Walking around the desk stretching his legs, he added, "I'll address everyone. After today's scare, they need to know we're ready for an attack. From without, at least," he added grimly.

"The Zefron. As soon as they know the cannons work, they'll not bother."

"Oh, they will. It is just a matter of time."

Octav watched Kendro, noticing how his King looked away—a tell that didn't want pushing further. Yet… "How much time?" He needed to know to prepare the fighters for battle.

"Soon."

Octav understood. Saddened, he probed, "How many?"

"Getting the names of the citizens from each ship is essential. Some must board with us. I will not allow them to die." At that, Kendro unlocked the Captain's door. "Be ready for anything."

Within the quarter hour, hoping to obtain supplies for Mika and the Heiako, Kendro and Octav entered the medical bay. Several nurses stopped at seeing their Royal visitors.

A redheaded young man lowered his reader to intercept them. "Your Highness." He clenched his hands as he stood nervously. "What can we do for you?"

"I'm requesting supplies for one of the Heiako bays." Kendro observed the busy staff under a sheen of palpable sadness and worry. So many sick? How could they beat the Zefron in these conditions?

"Of course," the young man regarded Octav as his King held out a reader. "Yes, Your Highness. Right away, Your Majesty." Scanning the list, the redhead strutted away.

"I'm very thankful—" Kendro placed a hand on Octav's shoulder, "you are my second."

"As am I," Octav paused, Kendro's expression had glazed over, silver swirls consuming his irises, "thankful—" Octav added, worried at the unusual public display, "Are you all right?"

Octav knew what was coming. Taking Kendro's arm, he guided him towards an empty bay. Once there, he eased the King down to a chair, closing a veil around them.

Kendro's face shimmered once before returning to normal. This vision hadn't lasted long, or his control had grown much stronger. Was he getting better?

"I'm fine." Kendro massaged his forehead, blue sparks from his fingertips matched the pulsation within his birthmark. "It was nothing new."

"May I ask," Octav probed, wondering indeed if he should. "Have you seen a boy named Sylkx in any of your visions?"

"Not that I recall." Puzzled, Kendro thought on that. "Why?"

"He's the son of the sick man these meds are for. In the bays. When he touched me, well, I've never felt anything like it in a Heiako."

"We're connected in many ways." Kendro smoothed over the crease in his uniform trrobhas, standing. "I'm sure there's a reason for what you felt."

When he slid the veil aside, the buzz of the infirmary became louder. Kendro scowled. *I want to do so much.* The sick lay in their beds, coughing, being seen to by many a nurse. An older woman waved for someone, but there were only so many hands to offer help. *This is no way to treat our elderly.* Kendro turned to Octav. "I'm sorry. You heard that, didn't you?"

"There are times when I do hear stray thoughts."

The woman struggled to sit. Kendro and Octav moved to her side. Placing his hand on her frail arm, Kendro gently restrained her. "Don't—" Both he and Octav could feel her agony. "You're in pain, Chion?" Kendro scanned the reader hovering above her bed.

Chion wheezed. "Tired. They—" She winced grasping her King's hand, trying to point toward the nurses, "mean well." Octav nodded. Such grace under all the pain.

"Do you mind if I—" Kendro glanced to her hand.

Chion tried smiling at them. "No," her face formed a grimace.

Gently, Kendro took her hand. In that brief moment, sparks flittered around the bedspace. In the exchange of croex, they held each other's gaze, transfixed.

Letting go, Kendro looked once more to the busy nurses. They took no notice as he closed a veil around Chion, shrouding this trio from sight.

"If you want to leave—" Kendro's birthmark flickered quickly, all his focus on Chion. "It's all right, I understand."

"I'll stay," Octav replied, curious. What was he about to witness?

Kendro's birthmark pulsed stronger while flashes of blue crossed his brow. "Chion, are you ready, love?" Octav barely heard this last syllable.

Chion's face lit up hearing her name. "With my King—" Her deep wrinkles lifted with her smile. "You do me a great honour."

"The honour is mine. This won't hurt." Kendro whispered, leaning closer, "Rest now."

"Choose honour, Ainoren." Chion met Octav's eyes. "Through life. In death."

A prescience filled Octav's chest. Kendro took Chion's hand in his again, placing his other on her forehead.

A red light from Chion's heart glowed so low. Kendro's blue joined the red, guiding it aloft, away from her body. Entwined, these spirits lingered for a moment dancing, an exotic display.

Octav, mesmerised, watched as the red light dissipated, then vanished. It was then tears flooded his eyes. He wiped them away.

For a moment, Kendro paused before lifting the bedspace sheet over Chion's now peaceful, pale face.

The curtain pulled back, Doctor Vawn stuck his head in. Taking one look at the stilled body, King or no, he demanded, "What have you done?"

"What Chion wanted me to—I've given her a serene death."

Doctor Vawn stared.

By his mark! He was challenging his King. Octav made ready to jump in, but Vawn's expression changed, "Your Highness," along with his demeanour.

Kendro stepped towards Vawn, who backed away. The nurses' chattering stopped as the King's flashing blue birthmark illuminated the entirety of the room.

Kendro clenched his fists. "No matter how busy we are—" speaking calm and loud enough for all, "make time for our elderly. Have I made myself clear?"

"I'm sorry." The doctor flinched. "It will not happen again."

"Make sure that it doesn't."

As they waited for a lift, Octav handed Kendro the Rakia that the redhead had given him, meant for Mika.

"I'm sorry."

"Sorry?" Octav questioned. "Why are you sorry?"

"I should keep tighter control of my anger."

"The pressure you've been under, I think a little anger is normal."

Kendro paused. "Still, I must remain calm for them, at all times."

Octav could understand this. There were many occasions he wanted to lash out, but as Ainoren, couldn't. "I didn't kn—" deep sadness filled the Ainoren's heart after witnessing Chion pass over, "—who showed you that gift, that you could do that?"

"To take a life needs careful thought." Kendro pressed his hand to his chest, avoiding the actual query, lowering his head. "It leaves a mark, you know. It isn't something I would normally share."

Stepping into the lift, Kendro wished for nothing more than his quarters and Mika now. "Doctors keep people alive because that's what they're trained for." He held the lift's door. *Octav must understand this.* "When it is against their patient's wishes, I will step in." He waved for Octav to join him.

But Octav demurred, looking the other way.

Blunt, thought Kendro, who only smiled at the refusal. "I'm heading back to the Heiako bays," his Ainoren explained.

"Just for a moment, a deck or two." Kendro held out his hand. "Please."

Octav stepped into the lift, wary only for a split second as to why. As the door slid closed, Kendro stopped it, entering in several codes. Octav witnessed the camo as it blinked out.

Kendro, his birthmark flickering, faced him. With a single hand wave, he conjured a sparkling image of Octav's Routui before them. He began, "This is what your Routui looks like, as you know." Kendro pointed to the lit strands that wove in and around each other. "Each House is linked to all the other House members. You can feel everything that Frie, Roma, and Mika do, can you not?"

"Yes," Octav said. "Pain, anger, everything."

Kendro looked about the lift, and finally placed Mika's meds at their feet, to illustrate more fully, pointing at each of the strands connected to Octav's Routui, his hands doing a dance around this conjured revelation. "Yet, you are connected only to the four of us." As they twirled around each other, Kendro let the image fade, watching Octav's face light up as he pulled forth his own Routui next, a sacred connection exposed. One solid white strand connected with millions of others.

The Power of it all, thought Octav, suppressing a reaction, but touching his birthmark unconsciously admitting that emotion.

"This is what you saw on the bridge. I see, hear, and feel, everything they go through."

"That would be horrendous." Concern stretched across Octav's face.

"When my father passed me the throne, there was unimaginable pain."

"Life and death." Octav's hands trembled, struggling to imagine what it could feel like. "What would've happened if we'd lost you the other night?"

"I don't know—" Kendro steadied Octav's hand, before letting the image go. "Taliri might not have survived the transfer invitro."

At these words, the royal Routui vanished.

Octav wandered the lower decks, mulling over the events of the hospital and lift. Thoughts of Kendro, Chion, and Sylkx's croex spike whirled with confusion. *Why's this boy special?* Reaching Officer Cryz's corridor, he noticed Russif ahead, chatting to some of his men.

"Ainoren." Russif met him half way, extending a hand in friendship. "You came back." Russif waved over one of his men.

"I've medical supplies," Octav reported. "Distribute them properly." He held the bag out to one of the gathered men, only then, taking the offered hand in his emptied one. "This is specifically for Lace."

Russif lowered his voice to Octav, as the man hurried away, "We had no idea the Zefron were so close." Shame came over in his demeanour, "The comms jam—forgive me."

"Forgiven—we have important things to do." Octav paused, glancing towards the open bay. "We must make these bays safer for the Zefron's return."

"Will they?"

Octav walked forwards, knowing they would, but confirming so to Russif with only his silence.

"Then, we must work quickly." As Russif palmed the panel, it wobbled and groaned into the open space. Russif said the obvious. "These sections aren't strong enough at all."

"Agreed." Octav looked the panels up and down. *Deplorable.*

"I've deployed men, as you asked." Russif frowned, the revelation of possible annihilation sinking deep. He shivered. "Double them?"

"Get as many engineers as you can find." Octav paused. He'd fight Kendro, if he had to, over this. "Bring them out of retirement, if you need to."

"Lace was one of the best. If he's well enough with your Rakia, I'll have him to put a crew together."

"Think about it a moment, just to be sure." He pulled the new ally's arm. "Report back in two hours."

"You're really bothered by this, aren't you?" Russif dared to touch the Ainoren's arm, even though he might be punished for it.

Octav did not shake him off. "Without everyone pulling their weight..." he took in the view before him, still fighting the urge to gag at the intense uric smell emitting from the bay, he answered honestly, "...I fear for all of us."

In echoing silence, they watched the citizens going about their dreary businesses.

A loud beeping sounded, Captain Hadi's voice following, "*Sol'Ishar. Two Zefron war-birds passed today.*"

Every citizen stared towards the comms, freezing at the announcement. Until seeing Octav among them, and with pointing fingers and shouts, they rushed to the pair. Octav made his way down to the bay, Russif following down the ladder to the deck. *First thing, we need better access to these levels.*

"Before the Zefron return, we must work together." Hadi's announcement continued.

"What about my children!" Many of the women called out with fear in their voices.

Several of the younger men yelled, "Sign me up!" and "We'll fight!" as they pushed and shoved to get to the Ainoren's side. For the most part, the reactions were slim.

Only a few voices rose, calling out. "We're not fighters anymore." An elderly couple groaned, edging to the back of the crowd trying their best to melt away.

The Captain's words bounced over the head of the Heiako.

"I have medical skills," a young man shouted, also. That was good to hear.

This announcement over their head, urged each citizen—"...name and skill sets to the office stations."

A child cried, holding onto his father, "Don't go."

Yet, the cowered citizens still stared towards Octav. It was then he realized the Captain's words meant less to these below. At a lull, Octav spoke clear and loudly to them all.

"I appointed Russif today as part of a special task force. I ask you to cooperate with him." But too many of them only moaned, heads lowered, deflated. Octav knew he did not have their support. *What chance do I have here?*

"How long have we got before they come in for the kill?" one shouted. The men around the speaker agreed with irritable and petulant complaints. "Aren't we just wasting our time? These ships aren't fighters!"

"Listen," ordered Octav, "we will protect all of you. And," he paused to gauge their reactions, "we're not done for yet. We will fight the Zefron to our final breath." He'd made the bold decision to give them the truth. "We left no one when we evacuated our planet, but we're still guided by her laws. I ask that you work with us."

They're not stupid. "You know there wasn't enough time to finish these ships." He pounded on a bulkhead making it rumble like nearby thunder. "These bays need fortifying, if we are to stand a chance against a Zefron attack. I ask anyone with skills in engineering or construction to step forward."

The crowd's face did not reflect compliance. They moved menacingly, causing Octav to flinch, but no—they were merely opening a path.

Sylkx, smiling proudly, led his hobbling father to the crowd's front. With a nod to Octav, Lace faced the gathering, speaking loudly from the base of the ladder.

"You know me! I'm Lace Grec, Chief Engineer for thirty years at the LU corp. I designed the first Curb shuttle." He coughed, gripping his son's arm. Octav could see his pain, but Lace continued, "I can design the supports, but I'll need help. H—he," Lace touched Octav's shoulder, "gave me the Rakia to get me standing. He is a good man. Form a queue to my left. My son will take your details." Pointing opposite him, he made a request, "Everyone else, please give your names to Russif's men. Everyone has a skill. Let us use them to better our lives here!"

As several moved towards Sylkx, Octav watched him enter names to a reader. "Thank you," he said to Lace. Holding out his hand, Lace shook it. "You just saved my hide."

Lace coughed harshly, yet stood straight, and proud. "Honoured to be of service, Ainoren."

Lace and Octav stood further into the Heiako bay. Lace pointed to several sections of bulkhead.

"Compartmentalisation was already started." Lace grimaced once, coughing harder. "There wasn't time to continue."

Octav looked back at the sheer size of the bay, more of the Heiako stepping forward to add their names to Sylkx's list. Some fete indeed. "How's the pain?" he asked.

"Bearable." Lace shook it off. "I'll be good for a while."

"Then carrying on from those designs—we can further alter the structure as originally intended."

Lace nodded with a stricture of pain on his brow. "We'll build shields around the perimeter bulkheads, inner protection for these." He made a rumble, hitting a panel.

"Sorry." Octav rubbed his forehead, his birthmark flickering, pain or confusion. "I'm no engineer, Lace. I must trust you implicitly."

"Our biggest threat is from space." Lace began moving towards one of the far bulkheads. "If the Zefron were to puncture through the shielding, and this—" he tapped the cool silver wall, "then we would lose this whole section."

"I understand." Octav saw they were at a risk even Kendro might not realize. *Unacceptable. Why did we not get to shielding each space at this level?* He spoke what they both already knew— "This just has one band."

"Exactly." Lace waved his arms, and then, banged on his chest, coughing, amid the still streaming line of volunteers. "If something comes through that wall, everyone will be sucked out. One shield won't—it'd be over."

"This needs to be ship wide." Octav stared back at the main ports. A huge undertaking. *It will be done.*

Lace puffed out a sharp, "Yes."

Octav rubbed his forehead, pain turning into a heavy throb. He wanted to leave the bays, lay his head down for a while. It wasn't possible yet.

"Sir?" Lace probed.

"I'm fine," Octav lied, leaning against the bulkhead. He watched the citizens still queuing before Sylkx, the young man's shoulders almost as tall as each man that approached him. For his age, he was a big child. Octav was sure he was the cause of his pain. *Why?* He'd need to ask the boy questions, but there was no time.

"We can do this," Octav stated. "Trust me."

Making his way towards them smiling, Russif acknowledged Lace with a curt nod. "Glad to see the meds working."

"If it weren't for the meds, I might not be offering my help." He then added, "I have a list of engineers. If I give you their names, can you find them in this crowd?"

"I'll have them report. To you, or the boy?" Russif asked.

Octav straightening himself, prepared to leave. "Do you know if they're here with us?"

Octav viewed the cavernous space. "How many bays are there like this?"

Lace had to look away with his reply. "Over a hundred."

At that, Russif interjected, "Then the quicker we find them, the better." He pointed, adding, "If the Zefron knew where each bay was on their first strike, they'd wipe out this ship."

As if two mismatched cogs clicked, Octav understood now. "That is exactly what the war-birds were doing. They weren't about to attack. Puswer! They were recon!"

"Wouldn't you detect those reader-waves?" Russif asked.

Octav pushed away from the bulkhead. "Lots of the ships systems are down. I'd guess that system wasn't functional." He knew exactly what he needed to do now. "Get me those names. Talk to the people willing. Bring them to the boardroom. We need plans in motion. Fast."

TOO LATE

OCTAV APPROACHED THE BOARDROOM WITH his King by his side. Ahead, loud voices echoed while thoughts of the next Zefron attack fuelling his speed. "Seems they're waiting on us." Octav quickened his step, needing to work through Lace's ideas.

Palming open the door, Kendro stepped inside first. The room stilled. Several men stood before him, unsure whom they should address first. At last, Lace bowed. "Your Highness." A holographic image of the *Sol'Ishar* spun at the room's centre.

Indicating the older Heiako man by his side, Lace began introductions. "Sire, we've gathered the best engineers from below decks." The elder man hobbled a step forward, his silver hair framed around a pale birthmark. "Maurdo."

"I'm afraid I cannot bow, Sire." Maurdo lowered his head. "Malinga through the spine."

"No need." Octav felt the sudden longing from Kendro to reach out and touch this man, but in his weakened state, the King couldn't heal everyone. "Your respect is noted."

Lace waved past the image of the *Sol'Ishar* to the next in line. Two men moved beside him. "Hax and Crey," said Lace, and then introduced the last. "Jefl and Kiin." Each bowed to their King as Lace continued, "We can't locate our senior specialist, Demak. It seems he's on one of the other ships."

"We'll do our best to find him," Octav assured Kendro. There had been so little time for a thorough briefing.

Moving further into the room, Kendro finally took his stance before the spinning image. "Ideas?"

Lace leaned on the table, tapping in commands. The view of the ship vanished, and a three-dimensional design of one of the bays appeared.

"These structural alterations should sufficiently thwart any attack."

While Octav studied the design, Kendro sat at a different console with Octav's assurance that these handpicked engineers were the top of their field. All that was needed was to let the Ainoren lead completely. To Octav, the energy in the room seemed positive. *Chance is a fickle thing.*

Thoughts drifting towards him from Kendro, *Who are they, really?*

Octav noticed Kendro quickly brought up each man's personnel file, studying while the others debated and pointed at the technical schematics.

"We'll need a team for each bay." Lace nodded towards Hax. "You will be our foreman." Kendro stared at him, so Lace turned, explaining, "And he'll deal with all the team heads, Sire."

"We have enough men," Hax reassured Octav. "I understand the size of this project. Trust in us. I—we can handle this."

Octav grabbed a glass of atrei to stymie his sudden nerves, which flooded through him. He drank slowly while holding Hax's gaze. All eyes turned to Octav when he coughed.

Hax went on to speak with such confidence, the room relaxed, shoulders dropped, hands unclenched.

Impressive. Octav still held his gaze noting his youthfulness and striking birthmark. *Another Chace,* he thought. "I will trust you."

"Without Demak," Hax continued, "we can't get the shielding joined with the ships." He spoke specifically for Octav's benefit. "Unless you can spare one of your programmers?"

"You can have our top man while we track down Demak. I'll request him personally." Testing to see if Hax turned away first, the confidence he oozed, Octav continued their gaze. "If we don't find him before you're ready to merge the systems…"

"Wonderful." Hax's birthmark sparked his colour—yellowing suzsrai. His gaze lingered on Octav just that bit longer, but then he turned away.

Octav grinned. *I always win.*

"Then, we have lots to do." Lace addressed Kendro, "If you agree of course, Your Highness"

"Yes." Kendro flicked his screen around displaying the files. "You all have exemplary bona fides." He continued the praise, a tactic Octav had seen many times. "Glad you are willing, talented people." Kendro raised an eyebrow though at Hax, whose cheeks flushed. He understood the younger man's game, even if Octav hadn't caught on.

"Hax is the best." Lace's pride showed as his paled birthmark shimmered. "He's been in the field only a few years, yet his designs are amongst the highest sought after."

"Wonderful." Kendro tapped his reader. "We should get this operation moving. The day has flittered away."

Octav beamed. *Not on our side.*

Kendro went to his quarters. In the corridor, he paced, exasperated. *Need sleep.* Placing a palm to the console, the door slid open.

He stepped into their room catching another glimpse of his ripe wife. Kendro nearly fell rushing to her. "Are you all right?"

"I think," Mika rubbed her stomach, "something else is going on."

Kendro stroked the obvious bulge. Proud and worried. "You're double the size you were this morning!" He felt a strong kick from his unborn son.

She waddled over to their divano, "I knew everyone was busy, I—" and eased herself down, out of breath.

"Everyone's busy." Kendro sighed. She would never comm him, even in the direst situation. Women. "You are a priority though, Mika. I'm calling Doctor Brie."

"Kendro," she pleaded, "can we leave it until later, and let poor Brie sleep. Please?"

"All right." Kendro fumbled with his shirt. "You have to let me know if anything happens. Anything."

"It just feels weird, that's all." She rubbed her stomach.

Kendro held his hand out, then pulled her up, and wrapped her in his arms. Squeezing gently, he nuzzled into her neck, breathing in her scent.

"I promise you," she kissed the side of his neck, "you'll be the first to know if I feel different."

"Good. Then, Brie, right?" Kendro pushed her forward gently. "Bed."

Work commenced on the bays as fast as materials could be gathered. Octav dropped into bed with his sleeping wife each night, exhausted. But still, real rest never came. *Please, Ari, no dreams!* Nightmares plagued him as he dozed. Horrendous Zefron attacks. All their ships totally annihilated. Pushing his covers back, he slipped from Frie's embrace, trying not to disturb her.

"Morning?" Frie grumbled. "Already?"

"Go to sleep," Octav whispered. "It's still early."

With a deep sigh, she pushed off her covers. "You can't carry on like this," she said, "and neither can I!"

"You're complaining?" Octav slipped on some trrobhas, watching her eyes flare in the darkness. He knew what was coming.

"You know what I'm saying," she said.

She really is going to argue. Right now. Exasperated, he tried diffusing things. "I don't want a fight."

"I'm not fighting," she spat. As bright as daylight, her yellow birthmark illuminated their room. "You spend more time with them than you do me."

Please let it go. "I can't sleep, Frie. That's all." Octav moved from the bed with Frie in her nightdress almost slipping off, a step behind. *Since when did she become so small?*

"You can't sleep," Frie stared at him, "because you're with me."

"Can we talk about this some other time?"

"Fine!" Frie threw her hands in the air as Octav laced his boots with angry yanks. "Ignore me as usual." Yellow sparks flew from her fingers in the dimness of their quarters. Octav ducked as the fixture above exploded, shards of glass everywhere, a sharp acrid burning flooding his nose. Any other fight and he might have cleaned up such wreckage, but not tonight.

Octav left their quarters.

Walking through the dim corridors, he strode until the hum of the lights above settled him. Something internal pulled him down to the lifts. He entered from a new doorway into the first Heiako bay. Chaos looks organized.

Making his way into the thick of that chaos, he spotted Russif and Lace over by a bulkhead. He greeted each citizen working this mid-watch, smiling as they offered him a nod or a wink. Hope, a wonderful gift. "Things are looking good," Octav shouted over hammering machinery.

Russif waited, offering a hand to the Ainoren as he neared. "How are people sleeping?" Octav asked, indicating the bedspaces with tucked up bodies.

"Sorry." Lace laughed. With both hands, he pulled two tiny devices from his ears. "They're silencers. Can't hear a thing."

"No wonder they're snoring." Down here was relief. At least some people could rest. "How's it coming?"

"We have enough men to keep a team going through the watch." Lace motioned the humming machinery. "It's tough, but we're on schedule."

"Brilliant." Octav noted the structural supports. Their sheer size split the bay into sections. "It looks much better. Did Hax devise these?"

A shrill sound echoed followed by flashing Amber lights, bright enough to wake any sleeper.

Octav's reader buzzed. Dread sank in. Fishing for it, he read the message. He slammed his hand on the nearest comms panel. "Report!"

"We're not ready." Lace's face reflected sheer panic.

"Wake everyone." Octav slapped his shoulder.

Captain Hadi stood over Lynj's shoulder. Together, they watched her screen as a single war-bird powered their way, flitting from one position to another with no regularity at all.

"A lone fighter, distressed?" she asked. "Or is it lost?" Somehow, Hadi didn't think so. Spells trouble.

He waited, not wanting to issue a higher alert just yet. His stomach knotted, gut instinct knowing what was coming. The ship's orders already issued, his men would stand by them. The war-bird dodged toward the outer edge of their range. Another recon? But it headed in.

"Six off the starboard, Captain!" Lynj pointed, blips appearing from the blackness. Puswer!

"Set amber," he commanded. Officer Lynj reacted, tapping the command. Amber lights flashed. Hadi motioned for Officer Reel. "Ainoren Broki on comms. Now."

A locator soon found the Ainoren. "Deck Seventeen. Heiako bay one." Reel keyed further commands, but comms didn't respond. "Comms are scatty, Sir."

"Everything on this ship is scatty." Hadi already knew it would be so.

In response, Gaal's voice boomed from Lynj's comms, "*Sol'Delka* Reporting! Do you have them in sight?"

Captain Hadi thumped his fist against the console, a finger pointing at Reel. "Get our Ainoren on deck before those ships open fire!"

"Captain," Reel's face in the amber lights glowed pink, infuriated, "I can't reach him." Frantically, he continued typing to no avail.

"I will not accept can't," Hadi spat at Reel as the comms finally beeped. "Get a body down there to drag him back!"

A second ship's voice cackled over Lynj's comms, "*Sol'Tar*, here, we count war-birds. Ten at least! They keep scattering. No firm count!"

At that, Ainoren Broki's voice came though on the bridge comms. "Status," Octav ordered. But the viewports filled with war-birds told all they needed to report.

Closer, the Zefron ships sped towards them, defying their known laws of physics. Their weapons glowed, online, yet they didn't fire.

"What the hell are they waiting for?" Hadi spoke aloud, fed up with their strange dance.

"I said 'Status!'" the Ainoren roared, not there to see the spectacle. Hadi was at a loss.

"This…" Officer Lynj flicked her hand, tapping the console, an image, a new ship, appeared, "it's within scanners range, Sir."

"What is that?" Hadi's face froze, turning white. At the centre of the room, the new ship's image spun.

Octav's panting over the comms drowned out the Sol'Rayn's harried, "We're surrounded, Ainoren."

On both sides of this new monster, war-birds flanked. Single engines lit the blackness of space on fire. Like thousands of fleas on a beast, they swarmed around and around, choosing their moment to strike, altering their trajectory for the *Sol'Ishar*.

"Red alert!" Hadi shouted with a deafening siren following.

Finally, Octav stepped onto the bridge. "What is that?" He echoed Captain Hadi's exact words as he studied the image confronting them of the Zefron's new ship.

Are we done for? Hadi thought.

Officer Lynj stepped towards the image pointing at the large ship. Octav glared at her. "These," she touched several sections of the enemy ship, the cylindrical shafts sticking out from their forward section and starting to glow, "—are weapons."

Hadi and Octav shared a look. Hadi licked his dry lips, swallowing.

Seeing indifference in the Ainoren's eyes, Lynj ran for her controls. "Shields are at full capax."

"Who's manning the cannons?" Octav asked.

"Hanger Bay Two's engineers."

Not good enough! Hadi stepped back, fearing what came next. Shocked at the thought crossing into his mind from Octav's, "I'll take forward base," Octav shouted. "Scramble all fighters." To Reel he barked, "Tell them I'm heading down!" He turned, with a jerky nod to Hadi, "You've got the bridge, and the command, Captain."

"We need you here, Ainoren." Hadi had to control the situation. Trust in Octav's abilities, yet he struggled almost grabbing for him, restraining himself, as he tried his best to keep the Ainoren on the bridge.

Octav's brow creased, glancing to Kendro. "You need me firing that cannon. You have the fleet, Captain."

"Zefron ship fired! First projectile away. Tremendous speed." The Sol'Tar confirmed what they'd just witnessed.

From behind the cylindrical shafts emerged one massive squared opening. It flickered once, silver twinkles, then out shot a second weapon. Much different in design, half the size of the first. Hadi's attention turned to commanding all their ships.

"Impact two minutes," Lynj reported.

Ari, help us. Captain Hadi pushed for ship-wide comms. "*Sol'Ishar*. Brace for impact. Others, you see the new target—fire at it!"

Lace held tight onto Sylkx. "Away from the walls!" They crammed together as Russif pushed everyone under the panelling where wires stretched the full length of the bay, hanging, but not connected to the shields. "Close as you can."

If only there had been more time.

Sylkx clung to his father, eyes wide, fighting back tears. "It'll be all right, Son." Lace hugged tighter, hoping the show of affection would calm them both.

"I—I'm scared."

I will not fear. "When you were a baby out on the streets, and really scared, do you remember what I used to sing to you?" Lace lifted Sylkx's chin, staring into tearful eyes. His son's birthmark shimmered.

"Yes, Father." Lace caught the fear in everyone's demeanour. Heads low, single cries echoed around them as they waited. "Could you sing it now? For everyone?" his son asked.

So thoughtful. Lace followed Sylkx's gaze around the space. His colleagues, friends, people he knew well, all huddled close with their whimpering children. Lace answered. Wanting to please his son, yet worried his voice would waver, "I guess."

Before so many? Such a small thing to offer them.

"Try," Sylkx pushed. "They're scared, too."

Lace eased Sylkx away, limping towards the centre of the bay, pain wracking his body as he coughed. With Sylkx's help, he climbed aboard a Tripax, its three supporting legs perfect for the platform he stood on, tapping into its comms system. "My colleagues, friends," he raised his voice and implored, "Please listen."

The whimpering slowed, and then stopped.

Sylkx's face beamed. "Go on."

Lace cleared his throat. "The parents, the old, among us will know this one," he said. In a deep, silvery voice, he began, "Don't be afraid of the dark, little one. I am here. Don't be afraid of the wind, my dear—"

A chorus of 'I am here' resounded through the bay.

Faster, Lyrik ran. According to his reader, Octav was just ahead. Adrenalin flooded his system, igniting his birthmark. "Octav!"

The Zefron's first strike hit, knocking them both off their feet.

Lyrik flew into the air, slamming into the overhead. Octav, an arm's length away, tossed and pounded against the deck. When gravity took, Lyrik hit the deck with a sickening crunch.

Vision blurry, Lyrik felt his left side. Intense stabbing pain with each breath. He'd had this before. Broken ribs? As he lay, it seemed an age passed. Faintly, the sound of an urgent order reached Lyrik. "Get up."

The loud pitch of the sirens brought him around. When he pushed himself up, pain shot through his back. He gasped aloud.

"Are you all right?" Octav crawled to his side.

Through stabbing agony, Lyrik allowed Octav to help him to his feet.

He would not let them down. Not now, not ever. "Where do you want me?"

"Lower cannons." Octav eyed him as his friend clenched with pain, concerned. "I'll take the forward sections."

Lyrik hung back not wanting his Ainoren to witness this distress. Octav took off in a different direction, but to reach the lower decks, Lyrik would have to negotiate several floors. With each step, the throbbing worsened. Turning a corner, the ship shook, throwing him once more against the bulkhead. He barely caught himself, having to rest now and then the whole way down the corridor.

Come on! Lyrik drew on all his strength, his birthmark flared purple. With a deep breath, pain ripped through his lungs.

Lyrik wheezed by the lower cannon bay, barely upright. Taking a moment, he watched as Chief Engineer Zyler manned the cannon from a remote console, already unleashing their defences. Lyrik forced the horrific pain away, and straightened. Striding under the cannon's bay, he commed the chief. "I'll take over."

The chief refused this direction. "You need a medic… Sir."

"Stand down, Chief."

"Yes, Sir," said Zyler, reluctant, yet he stepped away.

Lyrik waited for access into the cannon needing to vent his immense pain out into space at the Zefron. Struggling into the chair, consciousness slipping, he fought onwards.

"You all right?" Zyler asked in his ear. "Vitals are off the chart."

"Start the cannons, Chief."

Whirring sounds echoed through the cockpit that Lyrik had squeezed into, as the vibrations exaggerated his pain.

Gritting his teeth, he slid a hand into the operating glove. *I can do this.* The cannons systems merged, overriding the pulsing pains. *I can do this!*

"All fighters launched, Captain," Lynj reported.

"Evasive manoeuvres," Hadi ordered.

Kendro knew their ship wouldn't avoid the next projectile. Their shield flickered, power dimmed as the hit struck like a fist.

"Shields at forty capax, Sir."

Please, no. Immediately, Kendro braced himself against the back of the Captain's chair, preparing himself for the onslaught he knew would reverberate through every subject, and so, through himself.

With the same ferocious intensity as the first, the second Zefron projectile slammed into their shield, changing their ship. In a rainbow of colours, their shield shimmered, blinked once, and then, failed.

"Captain," Lynj said. Her voice wavered, "We've los—shield down,

Sir."

Tell me something I don't know. Captain Hadi's fingers ran over the main controls, typing futilely at comms. "Repairs, Zyler! Now!"

"That second weapon!" Lynj's hands trembled as she spoke. "I'm reading fluctuations throughout all systems. There is no croex left."

This can't be happening. Kendro heard Hadi's thoughts loud and clear. He touched Hadi's shoulder, and Hadi pushed for another comm link to open. "Deep breath, Captain."

"Ainoren, where are you?"

"Forward cannons, all firing," Octav's voice came across the comms. "Not making a dent, Captain."

Hadi viewed all from his position. The *Sol'Tar*, *Sol'Delka*, and *Sol'Rayn*, fought equally as hard against the swarming enemy.

As a section of war-birds broke away from the Zefron main ship, Hadi knew their trajectory. "Several war-birds heading your way, Ainoren."

"Consider them dealt with," Octav spat. "Lyrik, you ready for these monsters?"

Lyrik's voice wheezed over the comms, "Ready, Sir."

Hadi met Kendro's glare of concern. "He sounds bad."

Kendro rubbed his left side. "His pain, I feel it."

"Fit enough to fight?" Hadi asked.

"Oh, he'll fight." As the intensity of Lyrik's pain increased, Kendro leaned against the console. To the Communications Officer, he barked, "Have a medic stand by."

Reel raised Doctor Brie on the comms ordering her to the cannon bay. The bridge clambered on, a hive of motion, as the Zefron closed in.

"They know... they know we're weak, Captain," Lynj spluttered.

"Ari, help us all," Captain Hadi prayed.

"Ari isn't here to help," Kendro retorted.

Taking stock of where his pilots fought, Hadi ordered, "All fighters to the Heiako bays."

The crew watched on as their thousand one-man crafts intercepted the Zefron's war-birds, clashing in huge waves, almost pushing them back. Diving in and out for distraction, as the larger ship advanced.

"Get me ship-wide comms," Kendro demanded of Reel. "I must speak with our citizens."

"Ship wide," Reel confirmed, keying the last of the codes. "You are live, Sire."

Kendro scrutinised the screen before him as the Zefron war-birds advanced to firing distance. Their firepower was small, but with no shields. It wasn't their weapons he worried over, though. He spoke clear and strong. "Aonise citizens. Do not panic. It will only set in. I ask that you fill your hearts with love. Do not let a single bad thought into your mind."

Kendro's birthmark flashed blue, and then started to change. As dark as it was, white swirling lines grew from within until it was all white. *I have no choice.*

Stepping towards the viewer, gazing into the blackness of space, Kendro's hands glowed white hot with this croex. He placed one hand, then the other, onto the viewport. The white croex spreading from his hands— "Do not be afraid. We will defeat these Zefron."

The Zefron war-birds approached Octav's firing position. Luckily, manning the other cannons around the ship were Chace, Hanya, and Lyrik. Coordinated, they had hope.

The bleeping of the war-birds grated on Octav's nerves. Flexing his fingers inside the control glove, he held fast—cannons, hungry for action, itching to let loose pent-up croex.

The war-birds turned, dipping underneath him. "Dirty Egma," Octav cursed at the screen. They sped inwards for the ships underbelly where metal thinned. They knew.

As they approached range, Octav rolled his chair around aiming at several ships. With the extra cognitive abilities from the merge, he controlled the cannons several hundred feet above him fully. His precision exploded with its first pulsating energy blast.

War-bird number one split asunder, jagged metal ripping into opposite trajectories. Octav spun the cannon aft, adrenaline rushing his system with the first successful hit. Firing upon a second, striking its left wing. It burst into flames, headed on a collision course with the *Sol'Ishar*.

"Starboard, bay one!" Octav shouted, reaching instinctively within his mind towards Kendro. Hoping somehow his King still had the strength to protect them.

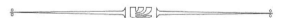

Huddled together, focussed on the love that their King had asked of them, Lace and Sylkx squeezed each other tight. Love and hope.

Lace risked opening his eyes. "Wha—" Pulsating white energy enveloped the far weakened bulkhead. Kendro?

Metal screeched against metal. Imploding inwards, it deafened them all. Russif's wife screamed, but Sylkx held tighter to Lace. The bay creaked with the impact, buckling. Then, it bent back outward with the blow from a monster these Heiako could only imagine. Impossible. The love had overwritten any scenario of dread in their minds. They remained surrounded in white croex. Undamaged.

Lyrik aimed for the third war-bird. It swung around, launching several primitive missiles his way. Puswer!

"Ignore the missiles for now," Kendro's voice echoed around his cockpit. "Their ships do more damage."

A sharp pain ripped through Lyrik's side. He coughed at the rusty metallic taste as he wiped his mouth. *Not good.*

"Hang in there," Kendro's voice whispered.

I'm sorry, my King. I've let you down.

Staccato beeping brought Lyrik back. Two Zefron ships had locked sights on him, preparing for an assault. He grimaced, but through the pain, he simultaneously launched his own threat. The cannon blast, like a fist, smashed on through the war-birds missile, splintering its hull.

It smashed into its companion, destroying them both.

Captain Hadi's heart sat in his throat as their cannon operators battled the Zefron war-birds. He could do nothing but bark for details, listening greedily as various solitary reports came through the static.

"How many left?" Lyrik's voice drowned out the others.

"One heading your way." Captain Hadi scrutinized the ship's defence screen. One tiny blip, their fighters had seen to the rest of the war-birds.

Come on!

Lyrik's cannon glowed as it prepared to fire.

Don't let it get away.

Sparks lit the screen before them. The cannon's energy struck the war-bird's engine.

Kendro shouted, "Get him out of there. Now!" Every pain of Lyrik's glowed hotly in Kendro's brain—the King crumpled to the deck.

"Extraction!" ordered Reel to the medics.

"Done!" Brie's echoed back. Confident.

Hadi rushed to Kendro's side. This will finish him.

"I'm fine." Kendro struggled to rise. "Causalities?"

"We lost many fighters," Hadi reported, indicating his hand once more.

Finally, Kendro took the proffered hand. Hadi helped him to his captain's chair where he leaned. Shaking. *Too many.*

A ROYAL INJURY

"YOUR HIGHNESS!" COMMANDER VAX CORRALLED him towards a chair. "Please."

The pain emanating from Lyrik burnt Kendro's lungs with such intensity he doubled over, his pale birthmark flickering wildly. The medics sprung to action. "Where's Doctor Brie?"

Vax waved a nurse over. "Where is Doctor Brie?"

The King's pacing slowed, he stopped to grasp his side, reaching out for something to steady himself.

"In theatre, operating on Lyrik." Tentatively, the nurse approached the pair. "Is there anything I can get for you, Your Highness?"

"No." Kendro rubbed his side. "Thank you." The pain eased a little. "When the doctor is free, I wish to see her immediately."

"Of course. I'll send her to you." With this, the nurse touched her own small birthmark and withdrew, leaving Vax to consider Kendro, resting his head in his hands.

Kendro sat where he'd all but collapsed moments before.

Will he be able to weather this loss? Kendro ignored Vax's thoughts projecting towards him. He had reason for hiding his face. This vision hit him with full force. With no warning, the world around him vanished.

Sunlight shone above him. He shielded his eyes, readjusting to the intensity of it. This plane, something he'd never witnessed before. The air crisp, clean. An undertone of metallic dust here and there.

Looking to the skyline, Kendro saw it. Heading in. Its large structure and wings spanned a huge distance, though nothing compared to their own ships. Closer and closer. Kendro felt its engines rumbling.

It dipped a wing, coming in to land. He covered his ears. It careened overhead, its wheels hitting the terraformed ground beneath him with a

106

screech. Fumes choked him.

Where am I?

Then, it was gone.

On hearing a door slide open, Kendro shook away the vision. Doctor Brie emerged. Blurry, wobbling to his feet, Kendro almost ran to her seeking answers. Pain in his side, dull yet unrelenting, knifed through him with each step. He forced himself upright despite it. *I must not show fear.* He walked to her, head held high.

At the door, Kendro saw his wounded friend. Lyrik lay suspended within a light animation chamber. He turned to Brie. Seeing her demeanour, yes, he knew. Inevitable.

Kendro let out a low gasp. "How bad? The truth now."

"Blunt trauma."

Kendo's shoulders slumped. Lyrik's left side, his exposed birthmark battered and bruised. It pulsated slowly in time with his heart.

"His ribs are shattered, he's bleeding internally."

Please, Ari, save him. For me? Kendro stepped forward placing his hand on Lyrik's. "Stay with us, brother of my heart." At these words, their birthmarks fluttered briefly in unison.

"He's lost a lot of blood, Your Highness." Brie touched Kendro's shoulder, then realised whom she had hold of. About to pull away, her surprise evident when he reached for her hand, holding it gently in place.

Kendro's shoulders slumped, weariness setting in.

Brie pointed to a chair. "Rest yourself, please." She then carried on with her report, trying for an uplifting word of hope where possible. "He's strong, though, and the operation went as expected."

"Are there other injuries throughout the ship?"

"Minor bumps. Bruises. Many burns, but all are being seen to."

I can't lose him. Kendro frowned worry deepening as he felt Lyrik's life force slipping away. "I'm going to stay." Kendro sat this time, taking Lyrik's hand in his, stroking his fingers.

Captain Hadi sat away from the bridge for a moment's peace, studying reports as they came flooding in from all decks. They'd sustained heavy structural damage. The more he read, the more he doubted they'd make it in another fight.

Commander Vax returned from the infirmary, taking her seat beside him. "Are you all right?"

"The Zefron scanned us, dammit. Take the bridge, Vax."

Heading to the lower decks, Hadi paused only to use a comms panel. "Zyler."

"Meet me in Heiako Bay One," came the command.

Chief Zyler paced about waiting for Hadi outside Bay One. "Captain, why am I down here?" he asked.

"You're the only available engineer to help secure these bays." Hadi noticed his Chief's stance. Arms crossed. On defence. Fire in his eyes.

"You want me to help the Heiako?" Zyler spat. "I can't."

"What you can't is irrelevant." The Captain took a step, his words curt. "It's an order."

Zyler backed away, eyes narrowed.

"Yes, Captain." With his feet tramping along the deck, and his scowl almost burning a hole in Hadi's head, he followed the Captain into the bay.

Hadi worked his way through the Heiako crowds to one of the cranes, noticing Russif. Changing course, he walked towards him. "How is it looking?"

"The war-bird did its job. We took a full throttle hit." Russif picked up some debris. "A real battering. We're lucky."

"Chief Zyler's here to rig your system into the shields." A nod in Zyler's direction gave Hadi the shivers. Zyler's birthmark paled before him, almost vanishing. *Why the hostility?* He couldn't fathom it. "Head over to the wall," Russif directed the chief. "Lace is coordinating our efforts there."

As the unexpected vision hit Hadi, the intensity increased. Silver lines swirled around, overtaking the view before him. Images flashed of a beautiful, petite woman, silk dress flowing around her intricate birthmark, accentuating each curve. Swaying before him, seemingly unaware of any admirers, she mesmerized him.

Rapt, Hadi could not look away. Only to then hear the shouts. Four men came at her, dragging her away.

Hadi didn't want to witness more, but the flashing images of her attack continued.

Russif's face loomed into view before Hadi's puzzled face. *What's this?* Hadi leaned to one side, vomiting over the deck.

Reaching out a hand, Russif asked, "Captain?"

Forcing himself straight, Hadi pushed at it, brushing Russif's hand away. "Ignore that."

Hadi didn't know how, but now, he knew everything. Had Zyler shown him this? He wanted to rescind his orders, and take Zyler away from the Heiako who caused him such pain. *I can't.*

Indicating the far wall, staring at Zyler, the fire within him burned deep. "You're the best man for the job," Hadi stated, no way out. "Save our ship."

Storming to the far wall, Zyler turned to Lace who wielded and shifted debris with several others. Hadi hoped 'save our ship' would be enough to get Zyler past his grievance with the Heiako.

Russif signalled to a woman, who rushed over with a pail and mop. Hadi smiled, but got no eye contact. As soon as she finished, she hurried away.

"We still haven't located Demak," Hadi informed Russif.

"I gathered. I hope Zyler is of the same standards."

"He is, trust me."

"Do you think we can get it stabilized soon?" Hadi asked, turning to the damaged wall. No time for 'assery.' "I don't fancy our chances with it weakened when the Zefron return." At this, Zyler's huff came loud and clear. "Keep me up to date. I'll organize whatever I can."

"Some of us will work right through." Russif kicked the shattered debris at his feet. "We need teams on the outside, too. If they hit us in the same spot, we're done for."

Kendro's loss was not the only one bringing someone low to the point of anguish. Octav's need to numb the pain he felt from Lyrik, spurred him to a secluded bar in the lower decks. The Heiako had not wanted him in there. He knew, still dressed in full uniform, that he stuck out. He didn't care. His aim was to get as drunk as possible, as quickly as he could.

Placing enough gems on the counter to alert the barman, Kale, to his needs, Octav swiped the full bottle from the man's hand before he could pour.

Kale leaned across the bar, indicating the corner of the room. "Ainoren, I'm sure you're going through hell, but you should leave."

Octav glanced to the Heiako sitting there, eyeing him. "I'll not be chased out of a bar." He poured himself a large measure, downing the burning shot quickly.

Kale moved away to stack glasses, and then, picked up a reader, sending a message. Octav knew Chace would soon be there. *Knew I should have gone to another bar.*

The bottle stood almost empty.

Chace strode through the doors, assessing the situation, carefully glancing around the bar. He saw Octav, back to him. He did insist on putting himself in harm's way.

Kale called out, smiling, "Chace."

Chace noted him behind the bar, working hard as usual. He headed over, sitting on a stool. "Thanks for the message."

"He's in a state. I thought it was only right." Kale poured Chace a drink, sliding it across to him. Chace reached for the glass, their hands touching. Kale's birthmark flickered yellow as he tried to interlock Chace's fingers.

"Not now, please." Chace downed the short drink. "I need to see to Octav."

Kale's smile faded. "You always need to see to him, when's my turn?"

Chace shook his head, turned away. "Not now!"

Taking the bottle from Octav, Chace poured himself his own measure. "You don't like the crappy stuff," he asked, "do you?"

Octav's birthmark flickered differently as he glanced over Chace's trrobhas and shirt.

Chace glanced to his attire, sleek against his physique. *I should have dressed properly.*

Octav shook his head, looking back to the bar. "Kale comm you?"

Chace sat, lifting his glass. "You know he did. He looks out for all his customers, especially my friends."

"I know." Octav glanced to Kale.

Chace caught Kale's stare. *This night is not going to be easy.*

Knowing Octav needed the space, Chace just sat in silence. *I hate seeing him like this.* He wanted to reach out, help in any way he could, but not here. "Shouldn't we get you home?"

Octav poured himself another. His eyes held Chace's gaze, cold. "I'm not leaving."

Chace settled, and reached across Octav's glass for his reader that was sticking out of his pocket. Not a normal to do thing, but needs must. "The Captain has been asking for you." Before Octav could protest, he tapped in Hadi's personal comms, sent a message, and then, handed back the reader. "At least now he knows you're safe."

Chace signalled for Kale. "Any chance we can get something to eat?"

"Chef is still here, I think." Kale indicated behind him. "I'll ask him to whip up something."

"I'll have roast garbael," Octav slurred.

"Two garbael, then?" shouted Kale.

"No, I'll have the Roots, please." Chace rolled his eyes. *He knows I hate the garbael here.*

Chace offered Kale a smattering of gems, which were declined. "He's paid with more than enough."

Chace picked up their glasses and the bottle. "Let's sit somewhere more private," he said, moving away. Octav stood, wobbling slightly, but followed Chace into a corner opposite.

They sat in silence. Octav turned his cup round and around in his hand. Chace remembered the day they left Letháo, when Octav had broken protocol and reached to comfort him. Chace glanced left then to

110

the right. No one watched them.

Slowly calling forth what croex he could, he reached for Octav. Not quite touching, but allowing him to see his intentions.

Octav's glazed eyes stared at the offered hand. Before his eyes, Chace witnessed the battle raging on. Knowing Octav's worries—to accept this from someone not in his house… The others would frown upon it, especially, his wife, Frie. Chace pushed the thought of her away, focussing on only helping his friend.

Octav turned his palm outward, and Chace's croex connected with his.

Wanton emotions shook Chace through to the core. He stifled a gasp as Lyrik's pain hit him hard. Octav's abandon didn't shield a thing—it hurt more than anything else in Chace's life.

Both fought back the tears wishing to erupt. Concentrating on allowing his strangely rising thoughts through into Octav's mind, Chace thought, 'So complicated.' He'd never witnessed this from the Ainoren before, or felt as he did. Chace wasn't sure on how to accept this full connection. But he wanted to—he wanted to feel more.

"Hmpppp, sorry," Kale's voice, sharp.

Chace broke their connection, turning to Kale who shifted awkwardly while holding two plates.

"Thanks," Chace said, motioning for him to sit the plates down. Sure, his embarrassment was obvious as warmth spread to his cheeks.

"Is there anything else you need?" Kale eyed the empty bottle.

"Just atrei, please."

Kale took up the empty bottle, backing away. Not moving his eyes from Chace, disgusted. *I'll have to deal with him later.* Chace let out a sigh.

Turning back to Octav, Chace was about to ask what had just happened between them, but he saw Octav pushing his food away.

"Eww, I can't." Octav looked to the differing plates of food.

"You need something." Chace picked up his fork, about to dig in.

"Yours looks better than mine. They overcook their garbael."

Staring at the dish, Chace agreed, and gave his roots a shove towards Octav. "Take mine, then."

"All right." Octav pulled the plate closer, inspecting the roots, fruits, and vegetables.

Chace tucked into the garbael, hungry. Indeed, it had been overcooked, and a lingering aftertaste of burnt spices assaulted his senses. "It's food. We should be thankful there's plenty to go around."

"For now."

Chace knew he was right. Things were already showing as desperate, but he tried his best to keep positive thoughts foremost in his mind.

Captain Hadi had to stay strong. *I can do this.* He bit his tongue, a stress habit he'd picked up years ago, as thoughts flittered through his mind. This past week everyone pulled together, making things easier. *Kendro has put such trust in me. And I must go check on Lyrik's progress, comfort Roma, if I can.*

In the infirmary, Hadi couldn't ignore the injured. The nurses ran about under pressure, exhausted to the end. Damned Zefron. A young redhead scurried up. "She's in her office."

"Thanks." Heading to the far side of the bay, he palmed the control panel for entry.

"Come in." The door slid open.

Brie jumped from her chair, running to his arms. Hadi whispered into her ear, "It's good to see you, my jeno."

"And you." She squeezed him. "You need sleep."

"We all need sleep." He gathered her close, kissing her. "Unless we can get on top of things…" He paused, holding tight, nuzzling into her neck. Safety. "This new Zefron destroyer—fired twice. It came in with the war-birds, fired, then retreated. I think they were testing us."

"Testing?"

"Long range scans show they have two others—four days away."

Her eyes widened.

Hadi put a finger to her lips, but he wasn't able to quench her panic. She sputtered, "They plan to attack? Three ships? It doesn't make sense!"

Hadi rubbed his eyes. "Nothing the Zefron do makes sense." Desperately needing sleep, he could only add, "If they return sooner—"

"I don't want to know." Brie turned away.

An alarm sounded from the infirmary. "What is it?" he shouted as Brie ran.

"Lyrik," she called back.

Kendro's white face greeted them. "He—"

"His lungs are filling." Brie screamed, "Get him to theatre," as Vawn whirled into the room. "We have to go back in."

"What can I do?"

Hadi stood beside Kendro, mouth open as they rushed Lyrik away.

"I can't lose him." Kendro stared, shaking. "I just can't."

"He's in the best hands." Hadi swallowed hard. He knew his wife's skill, but still hoping his words rang true.

Kendro sat on the bedspace as Roma whirled into the room, her short-cropped hair sticking to tear stained cheeks. Taking one look around, she demanded, "Where is he?"

"Back into theatre," Kendro informed her.

"Oh, no." She broke. "Please, no."

With Kendro and Roma, Hadi waited, watching the clock on his reader. *Why did it go so slow?*

Silence remained.

Hadi watched as Roma's hand touched above her heart. "No," she shrieked, collapsing in a slither to the deck.

Hadi dropped his reader. He watched helpless as Kendro scooped Roma into his arms. *Oh, please, Ari, no.*

Lyrik's fate was confirmed, long before Brie showed up.

Attempting to cover her bloodied clothes with a borrowed smock, Brie knelt before Roma where Kendro rocked her back and forth.

"We did everything we could." Roma's sobs grew louder. "We couldn't save him."

LYRIK'S FUNERAL

OCTAV FOUGHT HIS BUILDING EMOTIONS, croex burning underneath his skin's surface, power itching to let loose. Grief, pain like no other was tugging him apart. His House stood on deck, in full military dress.

Frie had put Lyrik Horr's funeral together with the utmost respect to their House. The bare flight space they stood in was arrayed in beautiful banners, as their old tradition for ascendere called for. The *Sol'Ishar* mourned Lyrik as a hero. House Niakrex mourned him as family.

Three young men, Lyrik's sons, pushed the floating casket down the centre aisle, where the families were gathered. The women around Octav dabbed their eyes dry out of respect, no crying, as was their family's way.

Octav fought within himself. He couldn't let the loss of a dear friend show, not in such a public place.

Even that morning, Frie had sat before him, patiently covering his puffed, red eyes with the last of her dim-alieve. "It will help." She knew him all too well.

The itch to rub them, removing the touch up, was deadly. He focused out into the crowd, and to his King, whose head was lowered, grief all too much for him. *It should be you speaking.* But the weariness he felt oozing from Kendro indicated why now he had to take charge.

Octav lowered his head as the casket drew level with the aft porthole where Lyrik would be committed to space.

The words he'd speak were going ship-wide, everyone taking a few moments of silence, blessing Lyrik's departure.

A far portal beckoned Octav, his instinct to bolt strong. He wanted to drink until he passed out, yet he had to stay, mourning his friend in public. Clenching his fists, he took a deep breath. Kendro motioned for him to take point.

Octav, to the front of the hall, began, "Lyrik was the bravest Niakrex I've served with." Resting a hand on the casket, he continued, "I've lost my best friend, my brother. Today, we will mourn him." His eyes scanned the group. "Tomorrow, we celebrate, for his life was filled with love, joy, and laughter." Then, with a nod to Lyrik's eldest, together they intoned, "We commit Lyrik's body to space. We commit him into our memories. Those who have loved him, may they continue to do so forever."

Octav turned over and over in his bedspace. *It should have been me.* Leaning up on one arm, he checked the time, knowing already that it was far too early.

Frie stirred. "Can't sleep?" She ran a hand down Octav's back, his birthmark flickering green light around the room. "You should get something from the Doc."

Her concern touched him, but did nothing to comfort. "Nothing," Octav threw the covers aside, "will help me sleep."

Frie tried pulling him back to her, but he shook her off. "Don't—" he spat. "I can't!"

"I'm sorry." Octav knew he'd hurt her, and felt the cringe with her apology.

Dressing quickly, he fled their quarters, needing something more. Would Chace be awake? Pausing by a comms panel briefly, he shook away that thought. *No, why wake a third person? I'll cope.* He headed for the one place he would get comfort, alone: the gardens.

In darkness, the natural hum of the ship gave him peace as he wandered alone with his thoughts.

Why, Ari, why take my kin? Anger built within. He lifted a hand, green sparks flickering from each finger. Octav knew what was coming, so he shoved his hand into his only pocket. *I can't, it's too small here.*

By the lake, Octav sat starring out at the lapping waves. *Why not me?* His twists of mind matched his knotting stomach.

Darkness grew lighter as the lonely hours dwindled. A thigh brushed against his extra weight as the bench creaked.

"Hello." Captain Hadi's simple greeting brought Octav back with a sigh.

It took so much to return it though.

Silence didn't worry Octav. With Sheve there, his croex had something to reach for. It slithered across the bench's gap querying Hadi's aura momentarily.

Octav felt his Captain's pain. Expecting him to pull away, he was surprised when Sheve didn't. Instead, their internal chaos reciprocated the exchange, easing grief for a briefest of moments.

"I'm sorry." Octav yanked at the connection, cutting it. "I shouldn't have."

"Customs seem to be changing. I'm honoured you felt comfortable to share."

"Your daughter—" The fractional second of Octav's vision had shared Hadi's deepest wound.

"I—" Hadi clenched his fists against the bench. "How do we move on?" he begged. "I don't—how—talk to Brie anymore."

Such heartache. Octav did not need to see tears brimming in his Captain's eyes. He felt the same pain too, for Lyrik, but the urge to remain Ainoren overcame emotion. "We have to believe this isn't the end, if you understand me?" His words kept him calm, in spite of it all.

"Kind of."

"We're protecting our future, Sheve. So our future children can grow, play, love, and lose as we have."

Hadi sighed, rubbing his hands up and down his trrobhas. "We will survive, won't we?"

Octav refused to look to the lake. Its gentle, glass-like surface, usually soothing, irritated him instead. "Damn lake."

"Fancy letting off some steam?" Hadi finally suggested, feeling tension rising, even though both sat mostly silent.

Octav's birthmark lit up. "I thought you'd never ask." Pushing himself up off the bench, he flexed his muscles, and turned away from the lake.

The practice field they used stretched on without a soul.

Octav smiled. Nights were the best time to be here. *Why doesn't anyone else use them?* He felt his croex bubbling to the surface—this time he'd harness it properly.

"I'll be the prey first," Hadi goaded, as a small red globe lit up in front of Octav. It darted left to right playfully. "Rank has its privileges."

"I'll detonate you, Captain." Octav's croex begged to be let loose. The green globe shot off. The Ainoren's eyes flashed brilliantly. With a swipe, he missed Hadi's globe.

"Hah!"

Off the globe shot in another direction, Hadi taunting Octav with his target.

Commander Vax sat on the mid-watch bridge, looking into the space, contemplating life, and Lyrik. She hadn't known sorrow like this on Letháo, even though she had only known him by association. Their total losses from the battle were harsh, but losing a member of the Royal

House devastated everyone. Her attention drew to the Captain's office. Kendro had appeared at the start of her long night, locking himself away.

"Commander?" Science Officer Lynj approached, biting her nails. Vax knew the habit of hers. A nervous officer, unacceptable to her, yet Lynj's resume had been exemplary. "We have energy fluctuations. In the gardens. Unusual."

"What sort of fluctuations?" Vax turned to this new concern.

"Aonise based, Commander. House Colours."

"Someone's fighting on this ship? My ship?" Vax stood, stepping to the science console. "Get me the images from that area now."

Lynj clicked on console portions, birthmark flickering at the commotion below. "You'll need to input authorisation," she apologised.

Vax slammed her palm to the console, the view from the gardens popping up before her, feeling panic rise at recognising the combatants. Captain Hadi and Ainoren Broki.

"Security, get someone down there right away!" she barked.

Hadi's office opened, and Kendro appeared. "Stand down." He directed his remark to the SO.

"They're not fighting, Commander." Kendro marched to her. "They're practicing."

"Practicing?" Lynj nearly squeaked.

"Maybe practicing isn't quite the right word." Kendro closed down the viewer. "Venting is more accurate."

Commander Vax opened her mouth, but nothing came out.

"It's their private time, Commander." Kendro clicked once and the links died. "Respect House grief."

Sweat dripped down Hadi's back, soaking him through. Directing his globe to avoid Octav's energy strikes seemed simple at first. Octav missed more than he hit, his focus way off. "Octo to penhex," Hadi taunted, feeling a sense of achievement in besting the Ainoren.

The longer their practice continued, the more Hadi realized that Octav's struggle focused with his inner turmoil, instead of his target. Octav fumbled, once again, striking a nearby tree instead of the orb he aimed for, shattering it into slivers. *The science team won't like that.*

"Come on," Hadi goaded, "Penhex. Can't hit a little target?" He hoped this taunting wasn't doing more damage than good. "What's wrong?"

Something snapped. Octav's birthmark flashed green, his aura changing with it, darkening to a colour Hadi had never witnessed before. As he took a step back, a figure appearing at the edge of the tree line drew his attention away. The energy signature from them both made them easy to locate. *Who else would be out at this time?*

Octav saw Hadi lose concentration. *I'll get you this time.* But the Ainoren's croex level had other ideas. Reaching to harness the green pulse, it fought back, upping the turmoil; Octav against himself, snapping his mind in two. *That target will be decimated.*

Screaming, he let his power unleash. Octav's force whipped away from him with such intensity, he dropped to his knees, the release overwhelming.

His strike heading for the target shook the ground beneath the garden. Hadi didn't move. Octav saw genuine fear etched in his face. *I'm sorry.* There was nothing he could do.

Octav's croex blast destroyed the target in a split second. But it didn't stop, the strength behind it intensified, and headed directly for Sheve.

"Move," Octav shouted before collapsing, exhaustion finally beating him.

Kendro felt Octav's intense spikes of sorrow growing within his own mind. His steps quickened. *I must contain him.* Hadi knew nothing, he wasn't versed in House grief. And as strong as the Captain might be, he wasn't capable of keeping Octav under control. The latest spike struck into the King's heart.

He felt the heartache too, but his people needed him. His own grief would have to wait. He pushed his basic needs to the back of his mind, his quick walk turning into a run.

Octav had loosed his croex in its purest form. Bursting from the tree line, Kendro harnessed his croex, letting a protecting shield race after Octav's blast.

The blast rocked the ship, but a blue surrounded the green, dissipating it evenly. His mourning would cause no permanent damage to his, or any other, House.

Kendro and Hadi ran towards Octav, reaching him simultaneously. "Help me. We must sit him up."

They pulled Octav into a sitting position. Kendro took out a small vial of fluid that he dripped into Octav's mouth.

"What happened?" Hadi demanded. "The power of it!" Hadi was at a loss for more words. "The strength."

"Grief," Kendro replied. "Let's get him back to Frie."

"I'll call for a—" Hadi moved toward the closest comms.

"There's a reswae," Kendro called after him, "far doors."

Kendro ran a hand through Octav's damp hair. "You'll be all right, I promise." Both their birthmarks responded to the touch.

Hadi returned quickly, only to face Kendro. "Sire, you knew of this danger, and what might happen… you knew." They eased Octav on the stationary. "Why didn't you stop him?"

"You have to let it out, no matter how hard it is. For someone of your power, it has no major consequence. For us—well, he might have, at a minimum, destroyed the gardens. No disrespect."

"None taken," Hadi replied. "I shouldn't have teased him, should I?"

"It's part of our healing process. It would have made no difference." Kendro placed a hand on Hadi's. "You've done more for him than you'll ever know, just by being here, Captain."

Frie paced the corridor, hair dishevelled, gown tangled tight around her. *He'll be all right. He's strong.* The lift at the far end of her corridor opened. The King and Captain pushed Octav out on a stationary towards her. She ran to them. "I was afraid this would happen." She looked down at her husband laid out, pale, lifeless, her birthmark flickering. *We all feel the pain.* "He'll be all right, won't he?"

Kendro touched her shoulder. Between family, this was an unusual display of affection. The slight brush of his fingertips meant so much to Frie. "He'll feel better in a couple of days. He needs lots of rest."

Frie glanced to the Captain, dipping her head slightly, "I want to thank you."

"Why, what have I done?"

Frie smiled, a weary hand gesturing to his sweaty attire. "He's taken to you over these last few weeks. Your nightly exercises have been good for him. Lyrik was—" Her voice trailed, catching a sob as she touched Octav's hand. His birthmark responded, colour returning to his skin. "Having you to help see him through our loss will be important."

Hadi looked confused. "Friends like him are hard to find." He touched Octav's hand himself, a small energy exchange between the three of them wavered momentarily.

Frie saw tears in the Captain's eyes, emotions so strained. Leaning forward, she kissed the side of his face, whispering, "You will always be welcome in my home. And my heart."

119

GRIEF

WITH THE RETURN OF THE day watch, Captain Hadi took the bridge. "Dismissed, Commander," he said smartly to Vax, sitting in his chair as she gathered herself to leave for her well-earned rest. *Just give us a break, Ari, please?*

"Captain?" Officer Lynj approached them, stemming a yawn. Hadi pretended not to notice, seeing as she'd been on duty for over sixteen hours. But Vax's raised eyebrows and frown reflected disapproval.

Noticing this silent exchange only brought the weary thought. *Give us all a break.*

Lynj broached, "Captain, for your eyes, before I'm relieved?" She held out a reader, Hadi took it, scanning the device while Lynj's jaws flexed, suppressing a second yawn.

"What is it?" Vax spat.

Lynj ignored that, addressing the Captain, "Data collected from after the attack, Sir. We're being shadowed."

"Zefron?" Hadi stared at her, anger building within.

"This mass here—the readings aren't accurate," Lynj pointed, and her flickering birthmark paled, "would indicate several ships are at starboard. Hiding."

"Zefron. They're waiting for something?" He sighed handing her back the reader. "Why wait? Surely they must know we're rebuilding."

"I don't think they are waiting." Lynj held the reader at the newer angle, pointing at another mass several light years ahead. "They're flanking us. An ambush."

Hadi cast a glance to Vax, her anger at Lynj's contempt evident in her flushing cheeks. "Not good, Vax," Hadi said, too tired to bother dismissing Lynj.

"I know, Sir. If Lynj sees what might be a trap—" Vax added, "we must retreat."

"Wouldn't work. We'd still have to turn back. There're huge systems these ships can't navigate through. How long have we got?"

Vax considered this. "If we slowed our speed, a couple of weeks. They'd know if we slowed too much though."

"They think we're stupid." Hadi tapped his console, sending a message for all House heads to meet within the hour. "So, let's play stupid."

"I have some ideas," Officer Lynj offered. "If I may, Sir."

He noted the black circles and pale birthmark. "Yes, of course. Dismissed, Lynj," he said, wishing the command was for himself. "We'll work out plans after you get some down time."

Sheve found Katya in her office. *Working again!* He watched as she agonised over a chart, then as the tears came, he moved to pull her away from it. "It's all right," he whispered. "It's all right."

As she clung to him crying, Sheve glanced over what she'd been studying. "I should have done more!" she wailed.

"What else could you do?"

"There was plenty. I'm the doctor. It's all my fault," Brie's cries grew. "I missed it."

"Missed what?" He could see nothing on the screen.

"There was a tear we didn't close. I missed it."

"You did your best for Lyrik." Lifting her chin, Sheve wiped her eyes. "You know that."

Katya took a deep breath. "I'm sorry." She kissed his hand.

Watching the emotion play on her face, Sheve probed deeper. "What aren't you telling me?"

"I'm just so scared," she admitted, "of—"

"I thought the injections were working?" Sheve perched properly at the end of her desk, keeping hold of one hand. "Are they?"

"No." Tears bubbled again. "I'm useless."

"You are not useless," Sheve said. "Without you and our daughter, we wouldn't have an heir to House Niakrex."

"I know."

"Come." He lifted her chin. "Let's go get something to eat."

"I'm not really hungry." She sighed, reaching to switch her systems off. "Can we go home? You can make us a nice snack."

Mika screamed.

Kendro woke immediately, pain ripping through his stomach. "What is it?"

"Get the Doctor." She wheezed. "Taliri's coming."

"Now?" Kendro fumbled in the dark for his clothes. "He can't be."

"Ohhh." In dimness, Mika screwed her face. "He's coming all right!"

Kendro banged onto his console, keying the Doctor's private code. Mika shouted, "The baby!" before he had a chance to speak.

In Kendro's ear came, "On my way."

"What can I do?" Kendro touched Mika's shoulder. She'd managed to raise the lights. A contraction once again ripped through them both. Horrific.

Kendro knew this was too soon, as Mika made a grab for his hand. "Anything!" she spat.

"All right. Take a deep breath." *I'm not ready for this.* "Calm now. Doctor Brie's on her way."

Mika's one hand gripped too high on his leg, squeezing so hard Kendro bit his lip, tasting blood. *The pain!* He'd no idea.

Doctor Brie rushed in. "What the?" *What did we do? Mika's protruding stomach—this couldn't—* "Can this be possible?"

"I know." Kendro slid down the bedspace, giving them room. "Last night. She wouldn't comm you."

"Contractions?" Brie attached a wrist monitor. No wasted motions.

Mika's mind screamed towards him. *More help, less questions.*

"He's full term? Am I wrong?"

Taking stock of the monitor's results, Brie overrode Kendro's next query. "I don't know."

"How's that even possible?" Mika gasped.

"Well, we're delivering this baby." Brie smiled, trying to alleviate tension. "It's all right," she soothed. "I've done lots, you know."

"I'm not ready, I—" Kendro rubbed his own abdomen, low, as Mika cried out in sync to his touch.

"Sheve's outside." Brie pulled equipment from her bag, offering an escape. "This may take a while."

"No," the King said.

Again, Mika wailed. Kendro's birthmark paled, feeling her pain. He kissed Mika, and she whispered in his ear, "Go. You must. This is too soon after Lyrik."

As another pain ripped through them both, Kendro looked to Brie. "She'll be okay," she promised. "Please. Go. Shield yourself."

He frowned and gritted his teeth. "I'll be back soon."

Kendro's hands were cold, numb. In the living room, he greeted Sheve. The younger man must have felt it in his grasp, too.

Sheve flinched, asking, "Everything all right?"

Kendro sat opposite him, rubbing hands over his thighs.

"Nervous?"

"I'm having a baby!"

"Well," the Captain laughed, "Mika's having the baby."

"Is this all right? Being here?" *At least I've company, but this must be so hard for them.*

"I'm happy for you." He nodded. "Really."

Mika howled. Kendro jumped, and restrained himself from rushing in—his only option was to start pacing.

"It'll be all right." Hadi reached out, clasping his arm.

Kendro froze, but didn't chastise. Their customs were changing. As a species, all were becoming closer. Instead, he merely shrugged off Hadi's touch, continuing across the quarters.

"A drink?" Hadi brightened. "Could be a long night."

Kendro sank back down. The drink provided him something to do with his hands. "A royal shouldn't be so—so—rattled."

Hadi reached out again, placing his hand direct in contact with Kendro's. This time, Kendro did not shrug him off, feeling a brief connection.

A ping at the door roused Frie from her slumber on the divano. She checked her reader for the time, brushing herself down, going to at least see who was there.

From the security camera, she saw a young man, hesitating, about to ring the comm once more. *I'm sure I know him.* She watched him bite his lip, his birthmark flickering turquoise. *It's much too late.* She turned away, but stopped herself.

Curiosity getting the better of her, Frie opened the door. "Can I help you?"

"I came—how the Ainoren—was?" His birthmark aquiver, adding, "The other specials, we are all worried."

"He's asleep." Frie watched the young man take a step back. She smiled. "I'll tell him you stopped by." As the man teetered back and forth, it pained her. "I'm sure he'd be grateful. It's Chace, isn't it?" she asked. "Would you like to come in? He might wake soon."

"No, Ma'am." Worry lines formed, stretching beads of sweat across his forehead. "I'm sorry. I didn't mean to disturb you."

Was he sick? She was about to try once more, but he'd turned, running. He stopped at the end of the corridor, wobbled, but looked back once. Frie closed the door, holding his gaze until it was gone.

She glanced around. Although filled with belongings from home, their onboard space felt wrong. She stepped through to their bedroom.

Frie crept to the side of the bedspace. Watching Octav dream fitfully, she leaned over him, stroking a finger along the side of his face. His birthmark responded to her touch, their connection still strong. "What happened to us?" she whispered. "We used to be friends."

On the *Sol'Delka*, Emmi flicked through her reader, the day's reports leeching into her night. *Well, this warrants a meeting.* She leaned, keying in for Anrel. "Come to my quarters," the House leader commanded.

Anrel entered her room, waiting for the acknowledging nod to speak. *If we were mated*, he thought, *there would be none of this ignorance. She would see me.*

Emmi ignored his inner thoughts, instead studying the last report. Only then did she regard him, indicating a seat before her. "Have you read this?"

"Our men are doing their best."

Emmi tapped comms, this time external. *Sol'Delka*-to-*Sol'Tar*, she was reluctant to go though the comms officer. "Captain Della," she snapped.

"In a meeting, My Lady," a voice came back. Mas, if she wasn't mistaken. "Shall I disturb her? Or ask to comm as soon as she can?"

Emmi replied, "No need to break in. Thank you, Mas." Her eyes locked with Anrel, unsure. *Did she need him?* Ending the comm, she told Anrel the truth. "We're struggling, but her reports are much worse."

"You're worried for them?" *I wish she would just relax for once.* He moved to behind her chair, her shoulders hard beneath his fingers as he massaged. "Understandable."

"Could you see to it? That an extra team is sent to her?"

With a flick, Anrel spun her chair around. "Is that a good idea? We're already stretching ourselves."

"Gaal would never agree to it." Anrel's face softened at her realisation. She didn't need to, but added, "Please, for me?"

"I will do as you ask."

Emmi would not push him off tonight. Her need greater than his, she placed her arms around him, and his grin spread. She knew the best ways to manipulate. Pushing herself against Anrel, his breath quickened. "You have my gratitude."

"My lady."

Emmi allowed his lips to trail the side of her face, and then, she kissed him deeply. "We have more work to do." She pushed him away.

"All right." He moved away, his birthmark flickering as he settled himself. "Let's work." He raised an eyebrow at her. "We play later."

Checking Mika's results, Brie saw the truth. Not so good.

She lied, "You're both doing fine."

"Why does it hurt this much?" Mika gasped, gripping the bedspace. Her birthmark lit the room in red bursts.

Brie reread the vial she'd picked out. *This really should be helping.* She checked the contents before administering more. "Any better?" Hoping the answer would be in the affirmative.

With a sigh, Mika's fingers relaxed, her birthmark paled. "He's really strong."

"That's better." Brie considered Taliri's stats. Stronger than ever.

"How. Much. Longer?" Mika panted as the room spun, seeing not just one, but two Doctors. "I feel awful." Leaning left, Mika vomited.

Brie felt Mika's forehead, pulling her long hair aside in case more was on its way up. "Reaction to the drugs." Both mother and child's heart rates spiked. "It will pass."

Brie looked to the door. *Could do with some help.*

Mika gripped the covers, screaming. But no, Kendro remained stoic, even with his child in jeopardy. *Does he trust me that much to keep them both alive?*

"Fully dilated." *Thank Ari.* "Won't be long now." Brie assured.

Emmi noted Anrel's unrest as he squirmed in his chair. *He'd really do anything for me.* His fingers tapping on the metal surface started to annoy her. With a nod, she pointed to the door. "Go fetch us something sweet to share."

"Wonderful way to coerce me, My Lady." Stretching his legs, he left the room.

Emmi's comms buzzed.

Captain Della's young, round face, her cerise birthmark flustered, filled the screen. "These meetings—" Della raised an eyebrow, placing her palm to Emmi.

Emmi reciprocated.

"I'm sorry I missed your comm."

"I understand. You have a ship to run." Emmi removed her palm, resting it on her knee. "Our cargo, is it safe?"

"Everything is as it should be—secured, safe."

"Good." Emmi looked away. She should have kept the Powex with her. "I just don't like it too far away."

"Trust me. No one knows it's with us. Better here, than with your other guests."

Still. This—Emmi's gut ached. Primal instinct had been drilled into her by her mother to guard their most prized possession. "I know. Thank you for aiding me."

"How are you really, Triaon?"

Emmi's birthmark flickered at her cousin's use of her pet name. "Really?" Emmi let out a sigh.

"Yes, Cousin. Really—"

She paused, avoiding the question. "Anrel is a wonderful man. Gaal—a strong, but devious, Captain."

"And you?" Della prompted, her stare never wavering.

"Stuck in the middle," Emmi admitted. "Wish I wasn't, but I must make the best of it."

"Anrel sent notice about the crew, thank you. We're so far behind." Della's face lowered, breaking eye contact. "I'm scared of the next attack."

"I'll message Ainoren Broki," Emmi reassured. *He'd help her, wouldn't he?* "He'll have protocol ready and waiting for that. Keep your men, and the Heiako, working."

"Perhaps we got the raw end of the Heiako. Very helpful, yes, but slow."

"Do we need to send more?" she asked, panic for her dear friend. "I could try again?"

"No," Della beamed, placing her palm to the screen. "You're sweet, Triaon. Must concentrate on your own ship." Her birthmark flickered, unspoken gratitude.

Chace staggered, and wended his way back to his quarters. *What now?* He'd hoped when he'd knocked that Octav would have been up. Talking to his wife, Frie, was always awkward.

Entering his living space while unbuttoning his shirt, Chace threw the crumpled uniform to the divano, his skin itching. Moving to a cabinet, he reached in, extracting some cream. After that night in the bar, when he and Octav had shared their croex, things hadn't been the same. He felt different, more alive than ever, but also, something felt off.

A buzz at the door, and a second later, it slid open. Kale stood there shaking a bottle of booze.

"It's a bit late." Chace sighed, not wanting to see his partner right now.

"Come on, I need to see you." Kale made his way inside, moving to collect two glasses on the way to the divano. Pouring them a drink, he sat down, waiting for Chace to join him.

Chace sat opposite, tucking his legs underneath, he reached over taking a glass. "Thanks."

"I've not seen you since you were in the bar a few nights ago." Kale moved closer, running a hand up Chace's thigh.

Chace flinched, "I've been busy," and brushed him off. "We've all had to cover Ainoren Broki's detail."

Kale shook his head, downing his glass, and pouring some more. "All I ever hear is Ainoren Broki this, Ainoren Broki that."

Chace put his glass down, knowing. "This is about what you saw in the bar, isn't it?"

"What I saw," Kale fumed, "was improper conduct between two officers. One being a much more senior officer."

Chace put his glass down. He stood, pacing the room. "I was helping out a friend."

Kale slammed down his fist, splintering the table.

Chace glared at the broken shards, fear curling down his spine.

"A friend?" Kale demanded, "If you two had been in a private room, what would have happened?"

Chace faltered, remembering all those feelings whirling around inside Octav's head. Yes, there had been lots of pain from Lyrik, but there was also much more. Chace managed to spit out in response, "Nothing."

Grabbing hold, Kale pulled Chace into a kiss.

In this drunken state, he didn't want this. Chace tried pushing Kale off, but the older man had the upper hand, shoving Chace back, his weight pinning him against the wall.

"Kale, please." Chace struggled. "You need to go."

Running his hand down Chace's bare chest, Kale waited for a response from his birthmark. Nothing.

Frustration and anger seared his lips tight.

Chace managed to push him off. "Leave, now!" Chace moved quickly to the door, about to palm it open, but Kale was too quick. He grabbed hold of him from behind, forcing him down to the floor.

Oh, Ari! No.

Chace struggled, but couldn't get Kale off him.

"You will love me," were the last words he heard as Kale's fist connected with the back of his head.

BIRTH

A SQUALLING CRY ECHOED THROUGH into the living room. "That's him!" Kendro jumped up, and then, stopped. "That's Taliri."

"Go to them," Captain Hadi urged. "Don't be shy, Your Highness."

Kendro rushed for his bedroom. There lay his exhausted wife, and a perfect baby boy. *I mustn't fear.*

"Everything is good," Brie assured, tidying around her patient, replacing her tools in her bag. Finally, she pushed a hand to the small of her back, stretching sore muscles. "All vitals on mum and baby are stable. You can relax."

"He's so small." Kendro moved towards where Mika reclined, touching his son's back. "But perfect."

"Yes, yes, he is," Doctor Brie agreed. "I'll give you some time."

Brie stepped from the room. Once beyond, she sought Sheve for a supportive hug.

"They're not ready for him." Hadi gestured towards the bedroom. "Any idea what's going on?"

"None. He's fully formed." Staring at her husband, she hoped he felt what she was going through, having to deliver a baby so soon after... "Perfect in every way. I'll get some scans later." Seeing his birthmark shimmer in response to 'perfect,' she knew he felt the same.

"How—?" Sheve asked her. "She was nowhere near due, days ago."

"I know. He's here, and very much alive, though." Feeling her emotions bursting for freedom, her eyes filled with tears. "Sheve, can we try again. Soon?"

"Of course." Sheve stared into his wife's befallen face. "We'll have the most beautiful family. A family the Prince can play along with."

She tucked into his chest as he kissed her forehead. A tear ran down his cheek, falling in her long hair.

Chace felt someone gently shaking him. Double vision. At least he was in his own room.

As Hanya's face came into view, he remembered his last moments.

"Are you all right?" she yanked a blanket from his divano.

Chace attempted to sit up, aware of his nakedness. "No."

Hanya knelt before him, her face saying everything. "I should comm Octav." She reached for his comms panel.

Chace placed his hand on her's, stopping her. "No."

"But you've been assaulted?"

"Just keep him away from me, forever." Chace grasped her hand tight.

"Chace, he needs locking up, he'd no right to—to—" Hanya couldn't even say the words.

"Here, hold him, he's heavy." Mika held Taliri for Kendro. *Already, she needs a break.* "While I clean up."

Gently taking the boy, Kendro cuddled him to his chest, staring at the tiny bundle—his son. Taliri's bright face stared back. *I'm a father.*

At Kendro's elbow, Mika's breathing deepened into calm. Taliri rested as Kendro held him. Carefully, he watched as Taliri opened his eyes, a glorious blue gazed at him. "You are smart," Kendro whispered to him.

"Do you need any help?" he asked Mika. *My son.* "I'll shout Katya."

"I'd just like some rest."

Kendro turned his attention to Taliri and held tighter. "Yes, little guy." The baby's extensive birthmark ran from his forehead over the front of his torso and left arm.

His father ran a finger along this. It crawled over his bottom, down his left leg and over his ankle. *My son.* It was the largest Kendro'd ever seen, covering more than eighty percent of the baby. *He'll be powerful.*

Tickling Taliri's belly made the boy arch and twist. Kendro amazed by him. *I'd do anything for you.*

"You must be chilled, though." Kendro walked to a dresser. Opening it, he pulled out a blanket, dutifully wrapping it around his son. "Must turn up the heating."

Mika opened her eyes. All that pain was worth it, smiling at the bundled Taliri. "The perfect father."

"I hope so." Taliri cooed in his hands. "Can we take him to see Sheve?"

"I'll rest." Mika yawned. "You take him."

Stepping toward his King and the baby Prince, Sheve ran a finger over Taliri's birthmark as it glowed intricately in the pale light. With Taliri holding his gaze, Sheve could see the new Prince loved being the centre of attention. Taliri reached, and Sheve let him take a finger. Their brief connection shared pure love. Sheve pulled back. *I so want a son.* "Sire, I— I've never—"

"Kendro," Brie almost forgot her place, "he's gorgeous." Not sure if the baby's touch would mean anything yet, but her internal worries concerned the King. "I need to run a few tests."

No. I'd forbid it! Kendro's grip tightened on the tiny bundled, and then the King understood it would be for his best. "It won't hurt him?"

Brie felt awful at lying.

"No." She knew the tests were not on a normal newborn—this newborn for certain. "He won't feel anything. I promise."

Kendro clutched his son to him, pacing the room, not wanting to let go. She'd no idea he could see right through her assurances, and so did his son. *What must be done, will be.*

Brie moved to take up her tiny patient. Taliri's birthmark flashed a brightest blue. Kendro watched his son's croex pulse to the surface, still holding on tight. "You really want to come near him, like that?"

"I don't mean you any harm." She held a finger out towards him, which Taliri took. Kendro listened, amazed, as she spoke to Taliri—not a doctor, instead oozing motherly coos and cajoling comforting words for his son. "I must see what's going on inside your body. New baby such as you. Tell your mummy all the news. All right?"

Kendro frowned. "Should he be so aware?" Awed as Taliri's croex dissipated. "Of everything already?"

"No."

Uncovering the child, Brie attached a device to Taliri's forehead. "I've never seen any child develop so fast. I must rule out anything genetic."

Kendro's worry spread in deep lines across his face.

"Brie knows what she's doing." Sheve placed a tentative touch on Kendro's shoulder.

Watching Taliri closely for discomfort, Kendro squirmed as the device clicked and recorded, obtaining the data it needed.

Removing it a moment later, Brie looked over the results, curling her lip. "I've never seen anything like it. His cells are growing at such an exceptional rate."

"Does that mean a genetic disorder?" Sheve asked.

"I'll need to analyse more." Brie pulled out a guin, clipping a vial to it quickly. "Blood sample."

Not a chance. Kendro stroked Taliri's head. "You don't know too much about Royal blood, do you?"

"Sorry, Your Highness," confused, she lowered the guin, "No."

"You won't get a blood sample. Although if you want to try—be my guest."

"I—" Brie looked to the guin, which shook gently. "I have to try—" Approaching Taliri, she placed it to the bottom of his foot. *Please work. I hate to look foolish.*

Taliri made a soft whistling noise, trying to wriggle away.

Brie pushed the device against him. The needle snapped. "I don't —
"

Taliri let out a cry, more frustration at his heel being held still than pain. "I didn't think so." Kendro gathered him to his chest. "Although not impenetrable, by any means. We only give it up willingly."

"You're saying he doesn't want to?" Brie stared. *Why? I'm only trying to help.*

Taliri yawned as a clumsy hand covering his small face.

"He's adorable," Brie leaned closer, "the way his eyes sparkle."

In the main meeting room, Captain Hadi mulled over several reports. A message popped up from Frie, 'Apologies, Octav still sleeps. He will not be at your briefing.' Hadi flicked it from the screen. *Time to wake my friend. We need our Ainoren.*

He'd not slept much the previous night, lying awake, and thinking about Taliri's birth. He wanted to announce it over the ship's main comms, proud of Kendro, and Mika. An heir preordained their survival. It meant so much to him, and would for the rest of Kendro's people.

The King arrived first, greeting Hadi with a firm handshake, although large dark circles graced his happy expression. "Glad you're here. I wasn't quite sure if I'd make it, after last night. I expected him to cry. At least that." Kendro's exhaustion slumped his shoulders, glancing only once to the closed reader. "Babies need so much."

"Is it Taliri? Aware that silence is needed, perhaps?"

"I never thought—" Kendro glanced from the reports. "Mika's the doting mother."

"He has no need to cry then." Hadi closed over the reports, his King's happy mood catching. There would be time for news in a moment.

"Something to tell me?" Kendro, knowing the motives behind Hadi's gesture, was willing to wait for Octav and the others.

"We're doing everything we can," Hadi reported. *How can you hide anything from someone who sees all?* "But it's not fast enough."

"Inevitable. The Zefron are coming for us."

Hadi saw it. The death toll to come, his King's fear. "You're more than worried," so he pushed, "Sire, if I may?" Kendro's eyes met his. He didn't falter. "You don't talk to Mika, do you?"

"For many years, I've relied on my foresight." Kendro lowered his head, breathing out a sigh, reluctant, yet willing to trust Hadi as he did Octav. "There are Seers more powerful than I. When a Seer tells you something will happen, it will."

Hadi hadn't meant for Kendro to really open up to him—or had he? His King's birthmark shimmered. With a flash, the room's door locked. Hadi swallowed. *Oh, my Ari. What?*

One fine line of Kendro's croex reached across the table, slithering towards Hadi. The Captain almost backed off.

"You're wondering about us?" asked Kendro. "Our connection?"

He was. Tightness gripped Hadi's insides. *Trust your King.* Their energies arrived at a connection—a myriad of colours twirled, dancing between the two immobile figures.

Hadi, allowing his own croex forward, reached for Kendro's strength, and understood. "You're connected to everyone! But—it's only one way. That day I helped you—"

"It woke your side of the bond."

Hadi allowed feelings to flood his system. *Is it supposed to be like this?* It confused him. "I'm not—I'm with Katya."

"No, and I know, my love knows no societal bounds."

At Hadi's protest, Kendro hesitated, unsure. "There is a lot you don't know. I—I…"

The door buzzed. Their meeting's participants were late.

Kendro disconnected.

Before the door was freed from the King's control, he whispered, "I hope you will get to know."

Chace busied himself with the Ainoren's orders. His task to make sure everything was perfect for the test. His pain, deep-seated. *How could he?*

Hanya had asked him every day to report Kale for what he'd done, but Chace wanted—no, needed, to forget. That relationship one of his worst mistakes, ever.

Greeting Chief Officer Zyler in the forward bay, Chace went through to the cannon. Distracting himself was his only option. That, and he needed healing time. There was only so much *female* dim-alieve he could muster to hide the dark contusions on his face, if it managed fooling anyone at all.

Chace ran his hand over the chair before taking position. This merge would allow him control of not just one, but several cannons above. Information and camo views from each one might overwhelm him at first, but it needed a test. And he would do it. For Octav. Seated, sliding his hand into the glove, Chace allowed the sensations from outside the ship to take over his mind. Finally, free from Kale.

"Zyler's been a great help," Lace started. "We also located Demak," indicating the Aonise sitting to his right. "Together, they've got the shields fully functioning in all Heiako quarters, on all ships."

Both Hadi and Kendro sighed. The King probed, "We're ready for their next attack, then?"

"I don't know about ready." Demak smoothed his trrobhas. "We're better prepared."

Kendro regarded Madrall. "Our other plans, they working out?"

"We've managed to move some on your list—" Hesitating, he reached for atrei. "They're asking questions."

"We need them on board—"

"Yes, Your Highness."

Hadi listened in, regarding everyone's composure. Why would the King be unsure?

"The training for the Cannons?"

"We've picked the best, so our pilots can man the fighters." Madrall lowered his head, in speaking the name. "No one could ever replace Lyrik's abilities, though."

"Thank you for the respect." The stabbing to Kendro's heart struck hard. "He is greatly missed, even more so in battle."

"We still can't locate several men. Doing our utmost to find them, though, aboard the other ships, Sire."

Octav woke with a start. "But—"

"It's all right," Frie soothed. "You're home."

"But—" came again, in his confusion.

"No." She stroked the side of his face, calming him. "No, buts. Take a moment. Breathe."

"I didn't—" Octav took a breath. He gazed into her eyes, noticing the redness. "I'm sorry."

"Don't be." She touched the side of his face again, but now aware, he shied away. "Just talk to someone, promise me?"

"N-No—" he stammered. "What's happening?"

"It's not good." Frie glanced out their porthole window into space.

"We're heading into an ambush."

"I must get up." Ambush? Octav struggled. How long? Weakness throughout his muscles. "I need to see Kendro."

"They'll be asleep. It can wait. You've been on a drip for a few days. You'll need something decent in your stomach before—"

Octav pushed himself up, feeling a little of his strength return. "How many days have I been unconscious?"

"Four."

"I must get up." He tried once again to get out of bed, but Frie held a hand against his chest.

You can be so stubborn. Her thoughts were loud and clear. "You're lucky Kendro's attuned to you. He managed to contain the blast, knowing you'd discharge."

"I put people's lives at risk." Octav threw the covers off. Seeing his nakedness, he grabbed for his trrobhas, feeling conscious before her. "I shouldn't have done that. I should have more control."

Frie laid one cool hand on his now-covered thigh. He pushed her away.

"I'll get some food." She sighed.

Returning later with a cold dish when he was fully dressed, she kept her eyes down. *Was she giving up that round?* Octav wasn't so sure.

"Thank you. I've never felt so hungry." Octav tucked heartily into the offering. "Anything would taste good."

"I'm glad," she murmured, watching him crunch through what she'd set before him. "You're making me nervous." He laughed, setting down his plate.

"We need to talk," Frie's words came to his ear, blunt, "about us."

Octav could not do this. Not yet.

On his reaction, she changed direction, rolling a lock of hair through her fingers. "But we do have some additional news." Her hair, that's a thing she only does when very upset. "Although none of us are supposed to know, I guess."

Octav lowered his fork. "What is it?"

"I felt a presence a couple of days ago." She grinned. "A new bond. Could only be—"

"You know."

"I'm bound to Mika, the whole House. I know. Our King has an heir."

It's too soon. Octav searched within himself to see if his wife was right. There it was—a new bond. Sudden excitement flooded him. "It's not possible—"

He couldn't believe it, but there, inside his awareness, it stood proud.

Frie paused, adding, "Please, tell me it's true."

"She's pregnant," he admitted stuffing one more bite into his mouth. "Shouldn't have given birth yet."

Frie's face fell. "You knew." Her birthmark flickered, upset— "If she shouldn't yet, then something's wrong. I—I should go see her."

"We'll go—"

With Frie's help, Octav wobbled on his feet, leaning, steadying himself against the corridor wall that led towards the Royal chamber's lift. *I will see them*, Octav thought.

"Breathe," Frie reminded him as the lift finally opened.

"I'm just nervous." Octav gasped, exhaustion racking his body stem to stern.

"I know. I feel it, too." Frie offered her arm. He leaned on her, careful not to weigh her down.

Octav knocked, instead of using the comm.

At the open door, Kendro's face dropped. "Octav!" Then a grin spread. "You're up." The King, embracing him in the corridor, added, "I'm so pleased."

A shadow moved from inside the royal chambers. *I'm not ready for this.*

"We want to come in." Frie raised an eyebrow to her King. He was family, after all. "We know—"

He couldn't hide it any longer, not with Frie's tongue. Kendro stepped to the side, and allowed them in.

Mika came from their bedroom, holding the baby close. "I should have known I couldn't keep Taliri from you," she held out a hand for Frie. "You're kin."

"My Ari," Frie exclaimed, rushing forward. Taliri stared, holding his hand out to her. "I don't understand—he's so big. Like a full cycle, why?"

"His growth is a stress response..." Kendro informed them both, while he helped Octav into the most comfortable of seats.

"We thought something was wrong," Mika added holding her son all the tighter. "But Brie insists he'll be all right."

"With a price on his head," Octav explained to Frie. "We had to protect everyone."

Taliri reached for Frie straight away. "Of course," said Frie, opening her arms, hoping Mika'd let the now burbling child into her arms.

"He already knows what he wants," Mika grinned. "I can't stop him."

"A little learning machine," Kendro said from the divano.

"Will this growth hurt him?" Octav asked the King, feeling the worry oozing from both mother and father.

"Not that we know of," Mika replied quickly, unsure.

"He's amazing," said Kendro.

"I love him already," Frie cuddled into Taliri, busily playing with her hair.

No. Octav stared at her, knowing Frie's thoughts. "Don't be getting any ideas!"

"Why shouldn't I?" Frie faced him, Taliri chuckling away. "We have a population to increase, do we not, My King?"

Two broody women faced him. Octav didn't know where to look. He had thought about children, it just hadn't happened. For the most part, he was away. "I—"

Frie tried to laugh it off as she watched him. A million thoughts ran through his mind. "Relax, husband," she said. "You'd be lucky. I'm not ready for children."

Kendro helped himself to a seat, patting the space for Mika. "Our species needs to see where it's going, where it wants to be, and why. Your children will come into this, even if you've not yet decided."

Octav turned white. "I—"

"Lyrik and Roma never thought of kids," Mika broached the subject from another angle, "until it happened."

Octav continued to watch Frie with Taliri. *Should they?* "Soon," he almost whispered, "we'll get there."

Frie tickled Taliri. "I'd do anything to protect him." She was trying her best to turn attention away from her mate's floundering.

"He is our priority. He must live," Octav spoke loud, what they were all thinking.

Taliri gurgled, pushing Frie's hand away. Mika took her son. "He needs feeding. Let's leave them for a while." Taking Frie's hand, she said, "Come."

"How are you coping?" Frie asked, taking in Mika's pale skin and sunken eyes. "Is your body still supporting his?"

"I'm binging on garbael, eating it all day long. I can't stop." Mika motioned for their bedroom. Taliri fidgeted, his hunger growing by the sounds of his fussing. "I've never eaten so much in my life."

The women's voices faded as Octav decided it was time to get down to business. He eyed the drinks Kendro poured, both large ones. "From what Frie tells me, we're heading into an ambush?"

Handing Octav a glass, Kendro sat toying with his own. "We've upped defences." He stopped short, downing it in a swallow. "Chace has drawn up a full training schedule."

It was not like the King to drink so openly. "I'll fit in as soon as I can."

Kendro held his hand up. "You will rest. A coordinated jump, even a tricu, is risky."

Octav knew when to push, and when to back down. His King

wouldn't take a 'no' lightly.

"It was a difficult decision. But the jump is small. I believe Captain Hadi has thought about all coincidentals for the Tricu."

Chace was Hadi's idea? Octav's birthmark flickered, pride. "I will look over the plans."

"I expect nothing less. I couldn't ask for a better second."

Octav forced a smile at that. He knew everything had changed. His responsibilities as second, doubted? Did he really understand all the consequences?

A baby's giggle echoed from the bedroom. "You're more a target for Dalamaar now than ever, Sire."

But Kendro knew this. Hearing it aloud struck his King hard. "I'll always be a target for that snake. He believes he has claim to the throne. He'll try his best to take it—"

"Dalamaar isn't just criminal," Octav stated. "He's devious, and more. He's organized."

"I know, I'm waiting—" Kendro clenched his fists, wanting only to take Taliri, and flee off the ship. "I'll destroy him first."

Watching Kendro's reactions, it was inescapable to Octav's weary eyes. The King's need to save his people, as much as his son, was tearing him in two.

AMBUSH

OCTAV FOUND HIMSELF STILL WANDERING the corridors at night. His route now passed the Heiako bays, and then, under the Royal chambers, around them to the gardens. There, he ran until sweat dripped from every pore. Protecting his King and Prince was his utmost priority. Thoughts of Yuko, the assassin, even in memory, plagued him. *What if they try to assassinate the heir?* Only when he was exhausted beyond reason did Octav retire to quarters, hoping for sleep.

Collapsing on his divano, he pondered the days ahead—wanting to fight the Zefron now, knowing their ships were in tip-top shape. He believed, as Kendro did, the Aonise stood a chance.

The next morning, he woke to a stiff neck. Stretching out, he massaged some pain away, and then showered, dressing in full uniform. Entering the lounge, Frie surprised him.

"I love a man in uniform." She whistled flattening his shoulder creases.

"To do battle without wearing it today would be dishonourable."

"You should eat first."

Octav sat, crunching his way through the dry meal she'd prepared, while she poked at her own. *Would she settle, if they tried for a family?* "I'm sorry things have been so strained."

Watching her shifting her food about, not eating, and hearing no response, Octav wished he'd said nothing.

"Let's not do this today." She finally spooned something into her mouth.

"I need a clear head." Even though this meant pain, they needed to talk. "It's not working, is it?"

Frie's birthmark flickered, her eyes filling with tears. "You really want to do this today?"

Octav wanted to get it sorted though, but the fear he'd never see or hear her again, was real. "I—I don't know what to do." He placed his spoon down. "I can't read you anymore."

Frie stared at him, her mark flashed once pink. She really was upset.

"Frie, talk to me."

"No." She sighed. "This isn't working. I'm not used to you being around so much."

Octav pushed his breakfast away, nausea flooding his veins. "You're saying you don't want me around?"

"I never said that. You need to focus on the battle, not me."

"We need to work this out, now. We are in space. Puswer."

"Yes, I know, but, not now." Frie pointed. "Not when our lives depend on you."

"Frie, I might not get another chance."

Tears welled in his wife's eyes. "No, you will survive. We will survive. But we'll talk later. I promise."

Octav stood, silent. Without a glance back, he walked to the door, catching her whisper, "I do love you."

Was that ever going to be enough?

Simultaneously, Captain Hadi, Kendro, Madrall, and Polr convened at the boardroom entrance. Officer Reel proceeded to comm the other ships' Captains. Their faces appeared in the room, with the others' shadows surrounding their images, just out of view.

Hadi stood, ignoring his seat, pulling up images of the Zefron ships awaiting them.

Octav stepped forward, pointing to the area they intended to come out of the tricu. "We managed to get the full view of what we face as we arrive. Seven destroyers wait, two flank us." Nine points on the image at the predicted ambush site faced them all. "We must strike first. If they disable any of our shields, the other ships must defend."

The time is right, Kendro sent silently to all.

Captain Hadi concurred. "No hesitation. Our fighters will launch as soon as we complete the tricu. They will take on the war-birds, distracting them from our ships."

Captain Gaal piped up. "We are at your disposal, Ainoren."

"This will not be an easy fight, Captain." Octav frowned at Gaal's sarcasm, choosing to ignore it. "Expect heavy losses." Pointing, he took in what they faced. Heavy losses would be an understatement. "This is a test of everything—our ships, our personnel." Everyone in the room agreed, as did the other three Captains on screen.

Coordinated, Octav hoped to hit the Zefron, and walk away with minimal losses, despite Captain Gaal's attitude. "We launch in an hour. Let's make history—and may the Zefron hate us more."

"May we have a word, Ainoren?" Madrall whispered.

Octav nodded tersely. Polr and Madrall waited while the others departed, and the room emptied.

"We're asking permission to join the battle." At his side, Polr nodded in terse agreement. Octav wasn't quite so sure. "You, The King, are wasting us. We're capable fighters, and you know that, Ainoren," Madrall stated.

"You are both too valuable, beyond comprehension," their expected reply, "as heads of your Houses." Octav admired them both, but he couldn't put them in the midst of the battlefield, could he?

He glanced to Kendro waiting at the War Room's door. These two stood firm. Madrall held his gaze. Octav smiled at Kendro's simple gestured 'yes,' the King's nod. Turning to the young men, Madrall and Polr were fighting men, not leaders. "The only way you're going out there is with me at your side." Octav took Madrall's hand.

Giving a resounding sigh, both men said as one, "Thank you, I'm honoured."

Octav raised a brow at Polr, also waiting to shake hands. At great times of need, they'd rise to the challenge, as would any Aonise. "We have several targets to strike, if the tricu isn't as much of a surprise as we hoped. I'll need the best. Are you up for that?"

"That we are, Ainoren," Polr assured, with a sheen of sweat at his birthmark now.

"Good, I have three of my best men on standby. We must be ready as soon as the tricu's complete." *We will beat them.* "Do anything you need to first. Meet me on Deck One."

Hope filled their minds and souls. He felt it. "We'll be there." They saluted.

"You think they're doing the right thing with Madrall and Polr? Going out there?" Captain Hadi pondered, approaching the bridge.

Kendro stopped, placing a hand on Hadi's arm. "Don't worry," he assured, "they'll be fine. We must concentrate on the whole plan, not individuals."

Hadi tried a protest, "But, as House Leaders—"

"— and Octav. Well, you've grown close to him. Trust this—he's a venerable warrior."

"We've never taken on any foe in this capacity. Without a planet, we've a do-or-die plan here."

"I know, Captain. This is new for our civilisation. In every aspect."

"I—"

Kendro's eyes flashed blue. Birthmark flickering, he knew he needed to settle Hadi's feelings properly. The King reached, croex seeping through his palms. "Do not doubt yourself, Sheve. Draw strength from me."

Hadi calmed, hearing his name from the King's lips. "I'm sorry, I just…" And the rest was unspoken between minds.

Kendro released him. "Don't be. We all have our moments." *Mine was back on the planet, facing my brother.* "We have a plan, a place for us. Believe me."

Captain Hadi straightened. "Thank you, Your Highness." Renewed, he strode onto the bridge with confidence.

Commander Vax saluted, standing down from her post. "We're ready, Captain. Every team, every person on board has reported in."

"Good, then let them wait no more." With a nod to Officer Reel, Hadi commanded, "Shipwide comms, now."

In seconds, Reel gestured to his Captain. "All Comms, Sir."

"*Sol'Ishar*, this is your Captain. Your tasks have been assigned. We will engage. Perform to the best of your abilities. This is your thirty-minute warning. We'll take the Zefron down today."

With his final words, Hadi's birthmark flickered green. "Battle stations."

Octav, Madrall and Polr arrived at Deck One in good time. Three other pilots waited there, along with several engineers.

Standing before them, smiling proudly, Octav introduced the flyers. "Madrall, Polr, three of my finest, Chace, Veco, and Hanya."

Madrall shook each flyer's hands, and to Hanya's surprise, he held on gently, lightly kissing her hand.

Polr also shook their hands. "Pleased to meet you. You're not military trained?"

"Originally, yes," Octav answered for them. "Special ops now, answering only to me."

"Well, then," Madrall grinned, "let's go kill some Zefron."

Chief Engineer Zyler stepped up before them, saluting. "All ships ready for launch, Ainoren."

"To battle stations," Octav ordered, "and may Ari allow our safe return to our loved ones."

On the deck, everyone raised a hand in salute, shouting, "To Ari!"

Captain Hadi observed Officer Lynj monitoring her screen. "Approaching the tricu coordinates, Captain."

A fluttering of his stomach only evident to himself, Hadi swallowed, taking a deep breath. "On my mark—" He counted silently.

Three.

Two.

One.

"Mark." With Lynj's word came a low grumble, the ship powered.

Then, leapt.

Nausea hit them all, Hadi felt himself swaying. He swallowed through it, straightening his back, head high.

"Four minutes until deceleration," Vax stated, adding, "Captain," belatedly.

The novelty of stars zipping past their viewer, lost on Captain Hadi, whose only focus was the four minutes dragging by.

Observing the holo-clock tick before him, forced him to breathe slower, thoughts of the battle ahead and their future raced through his mind.

Hadi felt sure the whole of his ship watched, as much on the edge as he seemed.

"Captain. Thirty seconds out."

"Stand by to engage."

The Aonise fleet dropped out of their tricu, right in the midst of the Zefron destroyers.

Captain Hadi leaned, pointing, as if he could do it himself. "Fire!"

Every Aonise flyer launched the moment their ships dropped out of tricu, a swarm of fighters descending on Zefron war-birds. Octav, Madrall, and Polr realized instantly—the destroyers were unprepared. Much smaller, their fighters were able to shield themselves all the quicker.

"Keep them from the *Sol'Ishar*," Octav broadcast. "Under no circumstances are they hitting her."

Firing up weapons had been accomplished in the interminable four minutes of tricu. Now, the only one to have been retrofitted—a smaller version energy cannon, sprung alive to Octav's senses.

"Ainoren," Madrall laughed, "seems an unfair advantage, no?" as Octav's first salvo launched into a war-bird's heart.

Octav laughed along. "It is a fair advantage—when I'm on your side." Sobering with the opened bay doors on war-birds two and three, he added, "Radio disciple, men. Fighters launched. Clear shots. All of you."

Watching on, Zefron fighters were targeted, and picked off by the

Aonise ships, Octav had to smile. He noticed a flicker out the corner of his eye then. Hailing the *Sol'Ishar*, he spat, "Captain. Destroyer Four. Powering weapons."

Captain Hadi's fleet struck at the Zefron destroyers, blasting four into oblivion before they'd even had a chance at manoeuvring.

The destroyers' debris spread out, knocking Zefron war-birds about.

The remaining three Zefron ships powered up shields, jockeying, and returned the surprise fire.

Before he could ask, Commander Vax spoke, "Shields at maximum, Captain."

"Who's the target?" Hadi shouted.

"Trajectory's the *Sol'Tar*."

Hadi flicked his comms. "They're firing on the *Sol'Tar*, Ainoren."

"In pursuit!" Throughout the deck Hadi's crew heard the slam of Octav's hand on his console.

"Get us in the path of those weapons," Hadi ordered.

The first destroyer let loose its weapons. Nothing stood in its way. It struck the *Sol'Tar* with tremendous force. The second blast split its shields in two.

"Captain—" Commander Vax began.

"—what's their damage?" Kendro demanded.

"Shields are zero. They won't sustain another hit."

The second destroyer had weapons locked. It powered up to fire.

"Get this ship in front of that destroyer!" Captain Hadi screamed.

Octav spun his fighter around, pure croex flooded his veins, but he couldn't fight alone. "Head for Destroyer Four," he ordered.

As he neared the *Sol'Tar*, the view of their flickering shields gave him his answer. They had no protection. The next projectile to hit would rip their ship apart.

"Ainoren. We can't stop it!"

Octav slammed his fist on the screen.

The destroyer let loose its missile. Watching on as it struck, Octav could do nothing.

Fire ripped through the *Sol'Tar*, dead centre in a massive explosion. In several places, her croex stations and hull splintered, breaking large chunks from her central core.

Metal disintegrated into space, leaving a trail of debris. Octav could make out cargo and tiny bodies floating in the distance. Bile rose in Octav's throat.

In a dizzying move, he pulled his ship away, focusing on the destroyer. Revenge would mean everything.

"You will not fire again!" he yelled. Then, into the comms, he shouted, "Launch everything we've got. Now!"

Captain Hadi recoiled as the *Sol'Tar* took the full blast. "Damage report?"

"Internal structure compromised." Commander Vax pulled up an image of their fallen vessel. "Forward sections destroyed, Captain. She's breaking apart."

With a tap of his finger, Hadi spoke to all fighters, "Defend the *Sol'Tar*. She still has people alive on her."

The other two ships acknowledged, slowly moving into position.

The *Sol'Ishar*'s crew watched hundreds of fighters hit the destroyer with a barrage of missile fire. The destroyer's shields failed, sparks shooting. There was no time for this enemy to discharge anything else. She crumpled, exploding.

Kendro shouted, "YES!"

"The others are ready to fire. The Ainoren is right in their path."

"Ainoren, get out. Now." Hadi leaned over his console—if he could manoeuvre Octav out of there himself, he'd do it in a second.

The tiny fighters jetted out of range. Nothing could stop the last two destroyers. They powered up.

"Brace for incoming," Hadi announced as the third destroyer turned to fire at them.

The projectile hit. Rebounding. At full force, explosions from its charge resounded in space.

"Shields are holding," stated Commander Vax, a newer edge now to her report.

"Second projectile launched. Counter measures," Hadi commanded.

As hard as it was to bank their ship left, it manoeuvred just enough so the second projectile hit only their aft shields.

The ship shuddered at the impact. Hadi asked Lynj, "Report?"

"Fifty percent, Captain."

Captain Hadi decided in a wink, "We can take another hit. Keep us in the path of those destroyers. They'll not hit the *Sol'Tar* again."

Its aim straight for the *Sol'Ishar*, the fourth destroyer let loose its projectile. Several of Hadi's fighters picked at it, crippling its left side. It retaliated with smaller weapons fire, but couldn't chase the careening harriers off.

Moments later, the projectile struck, the shudder almost throwing Hadi from his seat.

"Captain. Shields at zero."

Finally, the fourth destroyer succumbed to the fighter's onslaught. Sections folded, exploding into molten chunks under weapons fire as the comms filled with shouts and whoops.

Vax was heard over the celebration in everyone's ears. "One destroyer remaining."

All three Aonise ships concentrated upon it. Its shields held.

"It doesn't stand a chance," Kendro said. "Why aren't they retreating?"

The destroyer let loose one last projectile before a final volley shook it to bits.

"Captain?" Commander Vax shouted.

Without a pause, Hadi ordered, "Evasive manoeuvres!"

Commander Vax glared, "You can't!"

Their helmsman cranked the steering.

Octav turned to watch as the last salvo headed straight for the *Sol'Ishar*. The King! He could do nothing more. The destroyers were gone, and the war-birds calling a retreat.

"For Ari's sake, turn it," he begged, "Turn it."

The *Sol'Ishar* turned. Too slow?

The missile flew past their belly, just missing. Relief flooded through his veins. Finally safe!

It sought another target—the *Sol'Tar*.

Octav's heart sank. The *Sol'Tar* turned white, blowing outwards. Within a moment, they lost her in an array of fiery pieces, littering the darkness of space.

"Ainoren to the bridge," Octav radioed the *Sol'Ishar*. "We're heading home. Recall all fighters. The Zefron are in retreat."

Octav turned his fighter, her wings as heavy as his soul.

"There was no other choice," Madrall spoke across the comms.

Almost two hundred thousand souls were gone in a second. Octav stared where the *Sol'Tar* should have stood, a fireball in its place.

He'd thought the pain of losing Lyrik felt—immense. Kendro won't weather this. Would he survive?

Kendro had heard those words. "Evasive manoeuvres." Gripping tightly to the back of Hadi's seat, he'd watched as their ship tried desperately to shift its massive bulk bending from where the enemy projectile had come.

No.

His belief had held. The Captain had done his utmost to defend every Aonise on board all their ships.

But that last order!

The *Sol'Tar*. Every soul on board ripped away in an instant. Kendro let out a blood-curdling scream, collapsing. Captain Hadi rushed to him.

The agony, nothing The King had felt before. The white flash of his birthmark lit the room as rage engulfed him.

Captain Hadi loomed before him. He dared not touch him now. "We are stronger together," Hadi said, speaking softly. "Sire, our people need you now."

Kendro's anguish subsided, remembering his citizens. A moment later, his colour returned. Swallowing, he bit down on his tongue, tasting more than his own blood.

He stared at Hadi, whose tears streamed down his own face, calmer now. "They did not die in vain. Each will be remembered every day, as our lives go on."

"Officer Reel, are comms ship-wide?"

"Yes, Sire."

Kendro took a breath. He stood.

"Citizens, the Zefron are in retreat. This battle came with heavy losses. One hundred and seventy thousand, two hundred and four perished on board the *Sol'Tar*. We survived because of them. Do not feel defeated. Though we mourn them, carry on your duties with love." With that, he signalled for Reel to cut the comm.

Commander Vax spat, "With love. You say it. Yet that move abandoned our brethren."

Kendro whirled to face her. "It was the right call, Commander. If he had not, the Zefron would have eliminated both our ships."

"Liar," she shouted. "You're both murderers! My family was on that ship!"

"Commander, you're relieved from the Bridge." Captain Hadi motioned to Security Officer Chen with a nod.

"You did the right thing." With Vax in tow as Chen left the bridge, Kendro's mind wandered. Wearily, the King repeated, "You did the right thing."

146

THE VISION

LYNJ SAW CAPTAIN HADI'S BLANK expression. The pain of his decision. She knew it would weigh on him his entire life.

"Yes," he murmured at Kendro's words, "but—how many lost." Hadi turned away. "I need all reports," ordering Lynj, "as soon as our fighters are aboard."

Kendro wobbled on his feet. Lynj saw the Captain notice, but he walked away. One final order over his slumped shoulders, "See to our King. He needs to rest."

Lynj choked, looking to Kendro for guidance. But he had nothing to give her, an empty feeling inside ached.

"Sir, who has the bridge?"

Ainoren Broki manoeuvred over a squadron of fighters, setting down on a narrow platform where Chief Engineer Zyler awaited. As soon as the locking mechanism clicked into place, Octav popped his canopy and disembarked.

"Well done, Ainoren," Zyler said. Octav ignored him, racing from the deck.

Kendro. But would that help? He headed for the bridge instead, to see Hadi. As it climbed, the lift struggled. He straightened his uniform as he tried to wipe sweat from his face.

Stepping onto the bridge, Octav found no one at the helm. "Where is he?"

Officer Lynj paused, uncertain, and then pointed. Octav approached Hadi's door.

"Come."

Octav entered. "I've sent rescue shuttles to scout the remains. Some

147

pods were launched. We'll pick them up."

"Survivors?"

"We're looking."

Octav slumped into a chair at the news. Captain Hadi placed a drink before him, which he didn't hesitate to down, lifting the bottle at the side of Hadi's desk to pour them both another.

"Are the Zefron really gone?"

Octav downed the next glassful. "For now, they are. Two destroyers are still following us. They'll regroup, meet with others, and then, make another pass. We might not be able to surprise them next time."

"Well, at least we learned more during this attack. I have teams analysing the information. We'll get full reports shortly."

"The shields held. Lace's crew did an excellent job with the modifications."

"Indeed, but—"

"The *Sol'Tar*'s loss is great. Focus on the living."

"It's been the hardest few weeks of my life," Hadi admitted.

"And mine. For all of us. We're not alone. That matters. A lot."

"Everyone will judge me on that decision. T—to move."

"Yes. It was a decision you made. For every life on this ship. Your ship. The ship that carries our King. Don't dwell on it."

Captain Hadi swallowed. "Thank you."

"Don't question yourself," Octav said, remembering some of his earlier decisions in the field, those that cost many lives. "More important—don't let others question you. You're our Captain because of your training, the choices you've made. People know you're a strong man."

Captain Hadi laughed. "I don't feel strong."

"We don't think we're—" Octav knew questioning those decisions could break a man, so he spoke a truth not many had heard. "You were there the other night. We are strong for others. We put on that face. We let no one see what we're going through—" he tapped his chest, "—on the inside."

"I should be on the bridge," Hadi said, pushing his glass aside.

"Yes." Octav waved to the bottle. "No more, get me those reports. And get yourself some food."

Octav returned to his quarters, needing to see his wife, marriage over, or not. Out there in the midst of battle, his only thoughts were family.

"Frie," he called. No answer. There on his desk, a scrawled note, 'I'm with Roma. I need time to think. I'm sorry. ~ Frie'

Octav ran a finger over her signature.

148

Changing out of his uniform and into trrobhas, he pondered over the drinks cabinet, wanting something strong. Instead, he poured atrei, savouring the cool taste.

Kendro.

Moments later, Octav knocked on his King's door.

"Is he here?" asked Octav, as Mika greeted him, Taliri's soft gurgle beyond her shoulder.

"I don't know where he is." Mika's nails tapped the smooth surface of the bulkhead. "I can't raise him on comms."

"May I?"

Mika moved to the side, allowing Octav in. Taliri played in the corner. Octav stared for a brief moment, still not believing how quickly the baby had grown, almost as big as three cycles now. Placing his hand to Mika's comms panel, he accessed security systems. An image of their ship appeared.

His heart skipped, sure the blood drained from his face. *No.*

Mika grabbed his arm.

"He's not on the ship!" Octav said.

Covering her mouth didn't help, Mika gasped. "How can he not be on the ship?"

Octav raised Captain Hadi. "The King's missing. Get me all security footage. From the moment he left the bridge."

"He left with security. They escorted him to quarters."

"Meet me in five." Octav reached for Mika's arm, hoping his touch would help her. "I'll find him."

"He's never vanished befo—"

"Trust me." Octav knew otherwise. "He's vanished, just not in a confined space. He won't have gone far."

She'd want to search the ship herself. But he couldn't let her do that. "Look after the heir. Please." Taliri had stopped gurgling. *He knows.* The toddler's birthmark flickered many shades of blue. "Please, both of you, don't worry."

Kendro's Routui needed fixing, fast. Only a full discharge would help. He still needed to vent his anger over the *Sol'Tar's* demise. His frustration, and his loss. His—

He couldn't discharge on the ship. He'd have to leave. Getting Captain Hadi to agree to this—would not so easy. He'd pointed out that Hadi had witnessed Octav's discharge. It wasn't a stretch to see that his King's would be infinitely more intense.

The Captain gave him permission.

No one could help him as he had helped Octav earlier. His pain must be let out, and somewhere safely, away from others.

The bays were still overflowing with men and women, maintenancing their fighters. So Kendro found a departure bay lower down the ship, where there weren't as many that his grief might accidently damage. Two other ships, Hadi had demanded, must accompany him. Kendro allowed this reluctantly, ordering them to keep as far back as possible.

He needed to be on his own.

With no idea how he'd manage a discharge on a shuttle, solo, he at least recognised that being alone calmed him; the peaceful hum of the mechanics, the dimmed lights just bright enough so they didn't hurt his eyes.

The King sat back in the pilot seat, resting, focussing on breathing. In. Out.

A blurred silver twinkle appeared to the side of his vision. "Please, not now," he begged.

He couldn't stop. Silvery lines of reality faded. The cockpit replaced with a towering building.

Squinting, Kendro focussed on one spot until the blurred vision dissipated. Taking a deep breath, he turned away.

He found himself standing on land, no longer on board, no longer in space. This was a planet. A planet with life, humanoid life, like himself.

As he stared at the face of a passing woman, humanoid, yes. But he noticed one difference. No birthmark. Watching as more of them passed, both men and women—he saw none. A race without a mark.

These folk continued walking past the King, oblivious to his presence. He joined the throng, following one man inside a building, through several busy corridors, until they stopped in a room filled with other of their kind in beds.

"Morning, Doctor Challand."

"How are the patients today?" asked this doctor.

Kendro could see all the markless ones in the beds—young children, boys and girls, each covered in heat rash. Tossing and turning, sweat dripped from their bodies, staining their sheets.

"They're doing well, and responding to the medicine, Doctor."

Kendro wasn't sure how sick they might be. He stepped towards one. The young girl looked right through him. Sweat dripping from her forehead, soaking in her lank hair.

He watched the doctor insert a needle into the girl's arm, withdrawing vials of blood. Kendro walked away from her to a window. The planet glowed with life. Real life. The grey buildings scattered beneath him intersected with amazing greenery.

What is this place? Kendro could see nothing from the window, except the planet below. *Where am I?* Then something popped and spluttered in the corner of the room. He turned to see what might be a view screen, it blared to life with a woman's face.

Kendro's birthmark shone blue around his visions edges. Primitive, but effective. *I think we can track the signal from that.* He watched the screen as the woman pointed behind her. Kendro's smile faded. This alien species appeared to be at war.

He sighed, one monster for another?

He turned back. The nurse helped the little girl take a drink, fussing over her as only a mother would. This act alone gave Kendro hope. They could love.

Soon, along with the hospital, the silver twinkle around Kendro's outer sight began fading. It was then the little girl looked right at him, choking. "There! A strange man!"

The nurse turned, seeing nothing, Kendro leaned in quickly, not wanting to lose this opportunity. "What's your planet's name?" he begged the child.

The little girl giggled, reaching for his birthmark. "Earth, silly. What's yours?"

He tried to smile. "Shh, Earth girl, it doesn't exist anymore." With a nod, he added, "We'll see you soon."

Kendro came out of the vision, feeling the grief in his chest had worsened still.

He pushed up from the controls, stepping towards the back of the shuttle. Yes, there was somewhere for them.

But—

One chance, a few seconds, that's all it would take.

Harnessing the pain, Kendro's croex swirled—darker and darker. The cockpit flashed blue around him.

He strapped himself in, placing his palm against the control's panel, opening the shuttle doors. Oxygen whooshed from the cockpit. He didn't need to breathe to let his croex loose.

The security footage told the tale. Captain Hadi watched Kendro board a shuttle, leaving the ship. "I shouldn't have let him go. Should I?" Hadi asked Octav, the newest level of guilt tugging at the old knot in his stomach.

"Scan our surrounding area. He can't be hard to find."

"I'm not sure we will." Hadi frowned out at the surrounding area filled with debris.

A bright flash drew their attention—a shock wave that followed rocked the whole ship. Captain Hadi fell to the deck, banging his arm.

Octav sighed. "He'll be fine. Just get him back aboard."

"I have his location." Lynj scanned, nodded, and adjusted controls. "The King's shuttle has decompressed though, Captain."

Octav clenched his fists, feeling croex rushing to the surface. "Can you seal the doors? Pressurize it from here?"

"I'll try, Ainoren."

Octav stared her down. "Don't try. Do."

Lynj gulped, her hands flying across her console.

Hadi moved to the comms console where Reel sat. "Get me comms access?"

"Yes, Captain." He swiped over the console. "We are connected, Captain."

Octav said, "Kendro, can you hear me?"

No response.

"Kendro."

Lynj interrupted. "The cabin is sealed and re-pressurized, Ainoren."

Octav tried again. "Kendro, please answer me."

Static.

Then, a voice came back clearly. "I can hear you, Octav."

Captain Hadi jabbed a fist skyward to his crew's cheer. "We're bringing you back, Your Highness."

"Captain, I'm sending over some possible coordinates, Cepheid variables, I'm hoping," Kendro's command came over the comms. "Ask Lynj to see what she can do."

Octav and Hadi shared a glance. "Cepheid?"

"Yes, we have a new destination. We're heading for a planet, a planet called Earth."

Kendro landed safely on the deck. The escort fighters weren't happy with him. *Please, don't get us in trouble like that again,* one thought, looking at the floor.

"I'm sorry," Kendro said, placing a hand on the officer's shoulder, "—forgive me?"

The officer, humbled by Kendro's gesture, nodded, bowing low before his King turned to leave.

Octav intercepted Kendro as he cleared the deck. His glare spoke loudly. He had no need to voice any other thoughts.

"I'm a little thirsty," Kendro said. Octav, at the ready, held a bottle towards him. Kendro took it. "Thanks."

"Hadi's waiting. We had to silence the crew. Too excited over what you said on unsecured comms."

"I hadn't realized." He felt chastised, but the news, so worth it. He drank the cool atrei deeply. "I'll make a public announcement when we reach the bridge."

"You're sure about this? We're heading for this one planet. In all the millions out there, it is this one?"

"Yes, I've never had a vision so real. A child there saw me."

Octav stopped in his tracks. "You spoke to her in a vision?"

"Yes." Kendro laughed. "She didn't see me at first. She was ill. Had doctors treating her. She only noticed as the vision faded."

"What were they like?"

"A lot like us." Kendro started back to the bridge. "They don't have our birthmarks."

Octav raised his eyebrows. "No marks. They were plain?"

"Yes, quite plain. Their planet had such life. I think it has plenty of room for us."

"Will they accept us?"

"Good question. The girl wasn't frightened—" Kendro smiled, feeling intoxicated still by the vision. "—doesn't mean the adults won't be. We'll have to take things slow."

"Is it close?"

"I only figured a general location, did Lynj not say?"

"Too excited." Octav grinned.

"Your Highness," Captain Hadi greeted when they stepped onto the bridge. "You had us worried. Good to have you back on board."

"Don't worry about me. I can take care of myself." He tapped his Captain's shoulder. Hadi choked, patting his chest.

Kendro knew he was holding back comments, but couldn't hear those thoughts. *How strange. Am I being blocked?* Kendro shivered. *Impossible.*

"We're ready to hear your announcement, Your Highness."

Kendro cleared his throat, and stepped to the comms Reel offered. "Aonise citizens, thank you for your calm, and for your mature patience through this difficult day. Even with the great loss we've suffered, I give you hope. A few moments ago, I was whisked away within the silver realms of Ari. He showed me a beautiful planet. Green with life, filled with wonder and love. I believe Ari showed me our destination. Somewhere we can call home. A planet called Earth."

Kendro paused for a moment. Then, he carried on. "I don't know how long it will take us to get to the planet Earth. Keep faith everyone, and pull together. This journey will not seem so long."

He looked to Reel who cut the comms broadcast. Kendro turned. "Hadi, full status reports from the other ships yet?"

Captain Hadi pointed to his office. "Yes, you must be parched. I've asked for some refreshments to be brought through. Please—"

Kendro moved from the bridge with Captain Hadi, Octav in tow. Straight for the atrei he went.

Kendro drank one bottle then, another, until only one of the five remained. So thirsty!

"Are you feeling all right?"

"A little hot. I'm all right." But in all honesty, he knew he wasn't. "What's the status of each ship?"

"The *Sol'Rayn* took severe damage to its portside, some injuries on board." Captain Hadi brought up images of the three remaining ships. "They lost sixty-four fighters."

Kendro sat watching as Hadi turned to the third ship. "The *Sol'Delka* lost the most fighters, two hundred and seventeen. But, because of it, they suffered no damage."

"And how are we?" asked Kendro.

"No damage, a few injuries. We lost a hundred fighters."

Kendro swallowed, taking another drink. "We didn't lose the thousands we were supposed to. I am glad the battle turned in our favour."

"We sent shuttles into the debris right away." Captain Hadi frowned. "Over two thousand pods detached." He noted to Octav, "We didn't lose as many as you thought. Our doctors and medical staff are with them at the moment." To his King, he added, "We must relocate them. Some may billet here, others will board the other ships."

How? Kendro stared. "Two thousand pods escaped?"

Hadi smiled. "Yes. With four or five to a pod. Although, how they managed to squeeze in, I have no idea. Eight-thousand, three-hundred, and ninety-four survivors."

"According to one of the occupants," Octav added. "It was Captain Della who saved them. She ordered all to the pods when the ship took its first hit."

"And Captain Della?"

Octav lowered his eyes for a moment.

Kendro sighed. "At least she went down fighting. Please pass my condolences to Emmi." Fanning his shirt, Kendro took another drink, and then focussed on the good. "But survivors. That is the best news. Thank you."

"Our doctors are struggling with injuries," Captain Hadi reminded. "I've asked the other Captains to shuttle over what relief they can."

Octav reached for a slice of meat sitting before them on the Captain's table. "You should be proud of our people."

"I am. Proud and honoured."

"Captain Della will be remembered with the highest of honours, as was Lyrik," said Hadi.

Kendro, pale, glanced away. Thoughts of Lyrik and his young sons flickered through his mind. The pain was still so very raw. "Yes, of course. But later…"

Octav studied him. "You look off-colour."

From beneath his shirt, Kendro pulled the item he'd been touching. "I need to do something first."

Octav watched the royal pendant glint. Captain Hadi averted his eyes. "Yes," Kendro spat his tone, rude, "of course."

The two others shared a glance.

Kendro slurred, "Not now."

Reaching across, to take hold of Kendro's arm, Octav barked, "Call Doctor Brie to the bridge!" Octav managed to hold his King upright as Kendro collapsed.

"The King." Captain Hadi tapped into comms. "Brie! You'll have to suit up. We don't know what this is!" Hadi then turned to Octav. "I want everyone who's had contact with him isolated."

"I don't understand."

"Kendro said the girl in his vision was sick. What if she touched him, too? I'm not taking any chances. A virus we've never come across could wipe this ship out."

Kendro stuttered. "W—w–wa is this?"

"You're right. Isolate everyone." Octav held Kendro's arm. "Lock this room now. Are you sure Brie will be all right coming in here? Even with a suit?"

"She's the only one I trust. Yes."

Hadi issued orders to his bridge crew, and then, to the flight deck. The corridors they'd walked through were shut down, and decontamination protocols were issued.

A knock came at the door. Captain Hadi saw Brie waiting. He allowed her in.

"What happened?"

"We think it's something he was exposed to on the planet called Earth," Hadi said, watching her face crumple with confusion. "All theory right now. Can you run tests?"

"Maybe, but—" She looked to Octav asking, "Will he let me take blood?"

Octav's fists clenched. "I don't know." Kendro moaned. "We need to try something. He isn't himself at all."

Kendro turned to the Doctor. "I need to see Mika."

"Your Highness, we need to run a few tests. If you'll allow me," Brie reached for the bag she carried, "I can send for her. You're not feeling great, are you?"

"No," Kendro looked at the concerned faces staring down at him. "I'm hot. Can we turn the coolers on, please?"

Doctor Brie motioned for Hadi.

Hadi shrugged. "They're already on."

"Higher then, whatever it takes." Brie held a bracelet device for the King to see. "Will you let me pop this over your wrist?"

Kendro held out his arm.

Attaching her device, Brie ran its pulses through a portable console. "I might not need to take blood, if nothing is present."

The three waited, silence echoing, until the device bleeped. Brie read, looking to her husband. "You're correct. An airborne pathogen. Unknown. If it's already in our environmental systems, we can't stop it spreading."

"The ship's on full lockdown. No one in, or out."

Kendro sighed. "At least we've contained it here."

"We'll need the other ship's doctors. I'll set up a lab, analyse these results. But I will need samples from all who've come into contact with the King."

"Is it worth isolating us still?"

"Yes, we're stuck for now. Let Vax know what supplies you need. Until tests get started, I'm not going to know the hows and whys."

"I—I—can he—hear you, Doc—tor." Kendro tried standing, but couldn't. "No need to sh—out. I fe—f—eel hot. Sticky."

"Perhaps we can alter the systems?" Hadi suggested.

"Yes, cool it down some more."

"Sounds real nice." He shivered. "Thank's, D—doc."

Brie selected a guin from her bag, administering a sedative. As Kendro started to relax, they helped him lie down.

"We've a special connection, Sheve, I really like you." Kendro drawled, glancing left to right.

"I've something to ask you and Katya, but not yet."

Octav confused, shrugged his shoulders. "He's not in a fit state."

Brie picked up the guin again, and gave him a different shot. "This should keep him calmer."

THE VIRUS

OCTAV COULD DO NOTHING BUT keep Kendro sedated. This quarantine was driving them crazy. *Please, Ari, you know you can help him.*

His thoughts slipped to his wife, Frie. Then to Chace. Making a quick comm, Octav reassured himself Frie was fine. He commed for Chace.

There was no answer.

Doctor Brie's face displayed before the three men on a large view screen, telling Octav all he needed to know. She struggled, even though monitoring everything from the med bay.

"Is there nothing else I can do?" Octav's shoulders slumped.

Brie motioned to the table behind, equipment whirled, working to analyse blood. "We have to wait."

Her husband sat unpacking supplies she'd sent on. At least they were a little more comfortable. Pockets of isolated patients might, or might not, be the answer. Brie was taking no chances.

"Reports are coming in from all decks—" Hadi flicked through the updates on his reader, speaking calmly, despite the silence in the room, "from the officer's stations to the brig. Yuko might never make trial, he's very sick, could be dying."

Hadi glanced to Octav, whose thoughts still hoped Chace would comm back. Hanya had mentioned the young officer's fight with his current friend, the barman Kale. But Octav thought there had been something more. Perhaps he'd been wrong. His stomach churned nonetheless as he waited.

"Damn. The lower bay," Hadi said, reading the dispatch. "They've started with fevers and sweats, the elder Heiako are suffering the worst."

"It's spreading fast." Brie sighed.

Glancing at Kendro, Octav could nearly see through his pale skin.

"Your machines, how is he doing?"

Brie rubbed her forehead. "It is getting worse." Octav noted the internal struggle facing her. *Is there nothing?* "Little I try is working," she admitted.

Thinking, trying to force a solution from his tired mind, Octav's brow furrowed. *We can't lose him. Not now.* "If only we c—" he rubbed the side of his temple, his birthmark shimmered his colour, green lighting the room around him.

Brie eyed him as he processed his thoughts.

"Could we induce another vision, and somehow get him back?"

"To that sick child," concern spreading across Brie's face. "To what end?"

"Just tell me. Is that possible?" Hadi asked.

Brie gazed at them, thinking. Her normal bright yellow eyes had faded. Tired or sick?

Brie frowned, turning to the sureness of the equipment, gauging her machines as they hummed. "That might be something." Stepping away, Brie vanished from their view. They listened to her voice, calling, sending feet running. Then, she returned. "This might work. But give me a few minutes."

She held it for them to see. A vial in hand, it contained a pink liquid. "It's an old medicine. We used to use it as an anaesthetic, but it caused hallucinations."

"It won't hurt him in anyway?"

"No. I'll be right down."

Mika paced up and down in her quarters, ignoring the wailing cries from within the safe room. Sweat poured down her back, staining her dress. She drank from an atrei jar, not bothering to pour it to a glass.

"Please, Ari, stop his crying." The jar slipped from her fingers crashing to the floor. Atrei everywhere. Mika grabbed a towel, mopping up the mess.

Until Taliri's soft cough broke though her worry. Turning, she found him standing in the silver doorway.

"Oh, baby," she held her arms out to him. "Three cycles old maybe. You're too young still." Taliri toddled over, wobbling on his tiny feet.

Mika scooped him into her arms, cradling him, cooing into his ear. Taliri's birthmark responded, lighting the room with a cool blue shimmer.

A knock at the door, Mika pushed herself up, cradling Taliri close. Quarantine meant complete isolation. Even with that, Taliri had gotten a fever, which spiked earlier. Mika palmed the comm panel. "Yes?"

"It's Frie and Roma. Please let us in. We know Taliri's sick. You need help."

Mika's stomach knotted, looking to her child, his once bright blue eyes and birthmark, pale, sick. "Oh, Ari, help us all."

From inside his mind, Kendro smelled something different. He opened his eyes, finding himself back on the strange planet called Earth that he'd visited earlier. Looking up, he scanned, peering into darkness. A light at the end of the corridor provided just enough for him to see the many sleeping children, tossing and turning in their beds.

Feeling woozy, Kendro pushed himself up. Something wasn't right here. But why? He forced himself higher, managing to stand, with a draining of effort, but stand he did.

From under her covers, a girl peeked at the stranger in her ward. "You're back." She turned on a nightlight, illuminating her area.

"Yes." Kendro recognised her, the one who saw him. "What is this place?"

She hugged a small blue animal to her chest. "A kid's hospital." She stroked its head as if to comfort it. "Are you sick, too?"

"I am," Kendro admitted. Regarding his surroundings, the walls near her decorated in bright colours. In the corner, more fluffed animals of some kind. *Had they caught them? Were they preserved?* He rubbed his arms, chasing away a shiver. "What is this illness?"

"Wetwither. It's bad, though."

Poor child, he should have known she wouldn't be able to tell him much. "You don't look too sick," Kendro said.

"I'm getting better." Kendro moved to sit at her bedside. "Some of the other kids aren't."

"They die?"

"Some do." The little girl broke eye contact. "Anna died."

"I'm sorry…"

"My name's Jane. Jane Feltz. What's yours?"

"It's Kendro." He shivered again.

"She was my best friend." Jane reached out, touching his face. "Your tattoo is funny." His birthmark shimmered, lighting the room, and her eyes widened. "You don't scare me," she blurted.

"Scare you?" His hands rose over his head, shaking them about, he smiled again. "I'm not scary." Jane let out a giggle, attracting the attention of a nurse, who looked up from her reading, seeing nothing.

When the nurse looked away, Kendro continued, "The doctors give you medicine. What is it?"

Jane rubbed her watering eyes. "You need some?"

"Yes." He knew he did, he felt sicker with each passing moment. The knots in his stomach tightened. "I really do."

"They keep records at the end of the bed. You can take a look at the pages."

To Kendro, it seemed so far away. Dragging himself, he reached here she'd pointed.

"You can get it," she whispered. "A little more."

Kendro made a grab, picking up a board. Was this real? Could he physically be here? The notion had his head spinning.

Glancing to the nurse's station, Kendro made sure his actions had gone unseen. He then stared at the board, its hand written passages. How barbaric. Flicking through these pages, he wondered aloud. "I don't understand it."

"I'll shout the nurse." Jane called, "Miriam!"

Miriam came over, her stiff uniform crinkling in the night. She took Jane's wrist, counting not quite silently to ten, as she checked Jane's pulse. "Time for your medicine," she handed over a pot containing small tablets.

Jane, looked to Kendro, grinning. "If I were a Doctor, what would I call these?" She took them in her mouth, swallowed and waited for Mariam's reply.

"A Doctor, is it? You must be feeling better. These are Crixolin." Miriam nodded. Taking the pot, she tucked in the edge of Jane's covers, patted the small animal, and turned back to her book.

Behind Miriam's back, Jane then spat out the tablets, again in a whisper, "Here, you heard. I'm getting better. You need them."

Kendro took her pills. He, too, risked patting the small animal. Popping them into his mouth was a totally different risk.

Kendro's vision faded quicker than he hoped. It wasn't soft, or reassuring. The hospital vanished. And in a blink, he was back on the *Sol'Ishar*. Not quite coherent.

It took all he had to put a finger down his own throat, as Octav and Brie watched.

Brie stood at the ready, caching the golden vomitus.

"She didn't know its name. If you—" said Kendro, turning on his side. Octav only just got a second bowl to his lips as he heaved once more. Another tiny pill rested amongst his lunch.

Brie grabbed the bowl, sticking her head in close, sniffing. "I'll get these to the lab right away"

Kendro wiped vomit from his mouth. "Mika. Taliri?"

Octav handed him a towel. "Don't worry."

Kendro studied Octav, sweat dripping down the Ainoren's brow. *If it*

160

Brie entered her lab, two tables, a bedspace, and several pieces of med equipment. Doctor Vawn was surrounded by nurses as they worked within its confinements. Brie coughed, holding out the bowl of vomit.

"Get this analysed now. It will give us the answers we need."

"How long do you think it will take?" a nurse asked.

"Soon." Sweat dripped down her back, her vision blurring. *I hope.*

Doctor Vawn cast a glance at the bedspace where their sickest patient lay. "I'm hoping soon, he doesn't have much time."

Brie strode to the bedspace, picking up the reader, examining the old man's results. "More. More are falling past the point of help." She admitted, "I don't feel well either,"

The nurses traded glances, and Iryn spoke up, "Neither do we, even with taking pain meds to stem it off."

Brie smiled at their ingenuity. "Does it help?"

When they nodded, Brie went straight for a guin, injecting herself. Relief flooded her system, her eyes focussing once more. "Go get some rest, you two. Vawn and I will work through the night."

The two med students didn't argue, and they left the room.

Vawn held out a reader. "Check through these numbers while the main computer analyses the vomit."

Taking the reader, Brie sat, hoping the pain meds would last. Her focus was dropping already. Vawn yawned, tried covering her mouth, and only yawned even wider. "Sorry."

Brie couldn't help it, her mouth opening, she yawned, too. "Go, I'll wait for the results."

Vawn left her with the computer analysis. Brie studied the numbers herself. Some of the compounds of the pill remnants were similar to what she could pull from the frozen archives. Waiting was all there was to do for the finished scan before going near the bowels of the ship to fetch the ingredients. Resting her head on her arms her breathing slowed, and within a minute, she slept.

A tiny alarm sounded, Brie forcing herself upright, rubbed her eyes, focusing on the readers screen. She had her list of ingredients. It took her some time getting below decks to the main storage facility. There in almost complete darkness, Brie followed aisle after aisle, picking out the frozen canisters she would need. She handed them off to the lone tech who'd miraculously managed to still be steady enough on his feet to accompany her.

Once back in the lab, she'd run a synthesizer, mass-producing the serum she was intent on making.

"Thank you, Ari," she heard the young man whisper.

Brie returned to the lab, clicking, tapping commands for the computer to calculate correct amounts of the drugs she needed. It seemed to take days, but finally, she had it.

Then she contacted the Ainoren. "We have something. I've worked to recalibrate its delivery. It might take a few more hours. I think we can disperse it via air now. The circulatory system."

"I kn–new you—" Octav's voice faltered. "C–c–could d–do it."

"Octav?"

"No, hurry, Doc."

Brie knocked off the comms, and set to working with renewed energy. *This must work.*

Like a whirlwind, she bounced from a Dregnot to the computer to a Rastrom. Within an hour, she'd synthesized all she could. Time to start administering.

One of the nurses, Kritchi, came back, moving towards the bedspace at the centre of the room. "Oh, no."

Brie followed her gaze. The old man. I never heard the alarms. She went to Kritchi, placing a hand on the young woman as tears spilled over her cheeks. "I'm sorry."

"Do we have a cure?"

"Yes," Brie held up a guin, "I think we have it. If it works, it'll be delivered via air. I'll need at least twelve empty canisters."

"Several deaths have been reported." Kritchi coughed. Wiping her mouth, she found blood. "I hope this works."

Brie's face fell, handing her a cloth. "Someone should have come to get me!"

"That's why I'm here. Do you think it will work?"

"I'll need someone to test it on." Doctor Brie pointed to a seat, knowing Kritchi's answer.

"Yes, I'll take it," Kritchi said. "You'll monitor me?"

"Deal." Brie reached, inserted the vial in the guin, with one quick jab, and administered it before Kritchi could protest or change her mind.

She clipped on a wrist monitor, watching as data recorded.

Kritchi waited, neither making a sound.

Doctor Brie took hold of her other hand, feeling its clammy composition, checking. "Vitals improving. We did it, dear. Look."

"I'll be fine in a few hours?" Kritchi asked.

You're lucky. Everyone else will get this airborne. Not as quick a remedy that way."

"Wow, that stuff is incredible!"

"Not so sure. Might be amazing—it targets the sickness, you're proof of that. It's all I'm interested in knowing."

"No, Doc, I mean, this stuff feels amazing. Literally. It is like I've just taken in a hit of croex."

Brie turned back, studying her statistic's readouts. "Ahh, I see, yes. It is indeed raising your trexon levels. Like pure croex."

Kritchi's grin spread. "You'll have to be careful when you do this. Or the whole ship will be run by 'spaced out' soldiers."

Brie paused, thinking for a moment. "I'll order everyone to 'Drink up. Then go to bed.'"

"Great. Although, I thought it wouldn't feel as amazing as this!" Kritchi laughed. "This is just fab, Doc, you have to keep this stuff. You could sell it."

"Not a chance. I'm going to knock you out now. You do know that?"

Kritchi frowned. "Aww, Doc, please don't."

Brie turned to a drawer, taking up another vial. "Come on, go lay down. When you wake, this'll all seem like a dream."

With a sigh, Kritchi nodded, stepping into one of the few remaining spaces of floor. She lay, trying to make herself as comfortable as possible. With Brie's injection and a blanket, Kritchi fell asleep.

It took another twenty-five minutes to vaporize enough to be dispersed through the ship.

Brie's next thought. Contact Octav.

She got no reply. *No!*

Programming the computer took seconds, and then, stepping into her suit, locking on her helmet, she rushed out to the next task. She'd need to monitor the computer systems when the chemicals dropped into their air ducts.

Eventually finding the hold, watching the systems connect, the pale yellow cure flooding into the tanks gave hope. Swirling as the air generators mixed it, an extra addition putting them all to sleep, and the job was complete. Happy that the two potions seemed diffused enough, she left.

Several beds stood littering the corridors as she passed on the way to the bridge. In one, a nurse curled on her side, although she should have been on duty. Brie paused, checking for a pulse. *Yes, alive.* So, she continued.

Taking the Captain's seat, Brie placing her palm against the main console, she heard, "Doctor Brie." A computer voice. "What is the command?"

The three functioning crewmembers remaining waited to hear as well. "Initiate program delta seven," she stated. "Authorisation, Katya Brie, one, four, two, seven."

The ship automatically sounded the siren.

Reel and Lynj exchanged glances, both looking none too well. The computer system spoke. "Initializing, sequence one." At this, Brie removed her helmet.

Watching the readout for air vents to the bridge, Brie just made out a faint yellowing colour drifting from above as the room filled with a hint of crulang, instilling calm within her mind. Around her, the crew dozed fitfully at their stations.

As the drugs settled into her system, Brie's lids closed as well, breathing slower, and muscles relaxing. Within seconds, she too was sound asleep.

She heard no more.

Kendro stirred, focusing on the conference room, and seeing Octav asleep on the floor. Reaching down, tapping his Ainoren's shoulder, but he didn't wake.

With sagging arms, he palmed the console nearest him. Nothing. Puswer! Kendro managed a push to stand upright. Leaving the room, he made for the nearest console.

"Kendro to the bridge. Report, please."

For a few moments, no answer, then a foggy voice replied, "Your Highness. Doctor Brie here." The voice stopped, worrying him, and then, continued, "I've control of the bridge. How are you feeling?"

"Tired, weak. Like I haven't had a good meal in a week. What happened?"

"You don't remember?"

Bringing the memories forward, Kendro's birthmark flashed around the room. "Ah. We quarantined the ship."

Brie reported. "We found a cure. It's administered through the air system. You'll notice a side effect. It's the meds. I've had to put everyone to sleep. It may take most several hours to come around.

"I need food." Kendro's stomach growled. Rubbing it, looking to the slumbering men strewn around him, he said, "We're still in a lot of trouble."

Doctor Brie laughed. "Try getting Sheve up. I'll head down to meet you with some food."

"Sounds good. I'll do my best."

"It's fine now, Sire. Brie out."

Moving toward Octav, shaking him once again, Kendro, ordered, "Wake up, Ainoren."

Octav mumbled, "Chace?"

"No. Kendro." The King thought of Chace in his bunk recovering, also.

Focusing, Octav's glazed eyes fell on Kendro as he struggled upright. Trying but failing to rise before his King, "I feel like I've been out for a month."

"Same here. No fever though?"

"The Doctor?"

"All her doing." He then added, "She's gone for food."

Octav rubbed at his eyes. "Good, I'm starving."

A few minutes later, Hadi stretched, wiping drool from his mouth. Kendro informed them everything would be clear soon enough.

Into the corridor, Brie stepped around several makeshift beds, and headed towards Kendro and Octav. Delivering a bag full of fresh rations, she handed Octav the broth-tubes, and passed Kendro the atrei.

"There was nothing else?" Octav stared at the meagre liquid nourishment.

"It's the best fuel for your body at this time. You try feeding an entire ship all in one go. Drink it, you'll feel much better."

"Yes, Doc." He drank, swallowing the meal as quickly as possible.

"The ship is waking slowly. Captain Gaal's monitoring us. The illness hasn't spread to any other ship."

"Good news," Kendro swallowed. "Do we know where it came from?"

"You don't remember anything, do you?" asked the Captain.

"Nothing." His normally blue mark flashed a sickly, darker tone. "Care filling me in?"

"It was a planet. You told us it is called Earth. In a vision. Different. A young girl saw you, but she was sick. Somehow, you contracted what ever that was."

"Impossible." Kendro's realisation struck. *My vision?*

"That is what we thought, but it had to come from somewhere."

Kendro drank his atrei, taking a second of Brie's broth-tubes from her outstretched hand.

"I'll get us some more drinks. We should drink plenty to rehydrate. That fever was quite something."

Kendro, plonking his tired yet wired body down, mused, "This is just sooo good, yet so wrong." He took a sip, swallowing. "So, tell me, if it was a visioning, how do you think I could contract an illness when I wasn't actually on that planet?"

"This is all theory. I'm not yet sure how a sickness can be passed from one realm to another, but I do believe it possible." Doctor Brie perched on the edge of the table. "The child you spoke of saw you. As you tell it, she'd been given medicine, fluids. Others in the room were dying, but your little friend, she was getting better. She was the one who gave you her meds."

"A little difficult to believe." Kendro remembered the handwritten notes. "I couldn't even read their language. How did I speak to a child there?"

"Hadn't thought of that," said Hadi.

"The whole experience was beyond strange."

"I agree," Brie downed some atrei herself. "My scientific mind is saying, even though the illness was airborne, it couldn't possibly have been passed like that. I am hitting at malcracs here, but Sheve, I believe Ari did this for a reason."

Her husband quizzed, "You think—we needed to contract this virus?"

"Yes. For whatever reason."

Hadi took a tube for himself. "I guess we may find out one day."

"So, we should infect the other ships?" Octav stated.

"I still have lots of tests to run. I'm making sure the illness is gone completely." Brie sighed. "I don't know if we should infect anyone else yet—Sire?"

Kendro looked through the porthole. "I think it is a must. We treat this as we would when vaccinating our youngsters."

Moving behind the desk, Brie swiftly tapped in commands. "I'll organise it so we can control the spread. And the cure."

Octav frowned, "Any reports on how many died?"

"Deaths?" Stroking his forehead, a sharp pain struck Kendro's mind. "So much death lately."

Captain Hadi lowered his head. "We lost forty."

"No," Kendro cried, the pain settling deep within his mind.

He continued. "The virus took the elderly, mostly Heiako's. With changing body temperatures, they just weren't able to cope with it."

"I don't want any more dying," Kendro stated. He rubbed his tired eyes. "I can't take any more of this at the moment."

"We have to accept some will be lost along the way." Octav placed his hand on Kendro's shoulder. "We're doing our utmost keeping most everyone alive."

"I won't accept any of it." Kendro's croex surfaced, the sting of it pushing Octav away.

"Kendro, you aren't alone with your grief for those who have died." The Doctor's eyes met Octav's, tearful. "This has been very stressful for us all these last few weeks," she paused. "You may feel it personally. We all feel it in a different way."

"You are correct." Kendro's eyes teared as well at Brie's words.

166

"There's nothing harder than trying to move on."

For one bold moment, Hadi spoke up, "It's easy getting stuck in the past."

"We won't give up looking forward," Octav added. "None of us will."

Sheve moved towards Katya pulling her close for a much-needed kiss, "Pheeewww, you smell." He laughed, forgetting for a moment his unusual show of affection before royalty.

Brie slapped him across the head. "After all we've just been through?"

Octav laughed, loosening the direness of the group's thoughts, "I think the whole ship stinks. We should issue some extra relaxing time, let the ship run a little longer on auto-pilot."

"Agreed." Kendro yawned. "We all need food. More sleep." His commands were truncated. They all saw it.

"Sleep, again, no. But I would love a shower." Brie smiled.

"Let's not have the whole ship taking a shower at the same time. We might lose power."

"Now that might be funny," Brie said. "Imagine all of us in the showers when the lights go out."

Kendro's lids drooped. *I can't be tired still.* Then with an image of them all towelling off, he laughed loudly. "That would be a sight to see indeed."

Octav stood at his King's chuckle, directing Hadi. "I'll contact Captain Gaal. Inform him of our plans for resting one more night. We'll pick up everything in the morning."

SECOND ATTACK

THE OCCUPANT'S OF THE *SOL'ISHAR* slept peacefully with Captain Gaal monitoring from a safe distance.

Gaal noted everything ran smoothly while flicking through the ships reports, studying in more detail Doctor Brie's account of its most recent events.

This planet's sickness, Earth, would be coming here next, he was sure of it. Under controlled conditions, no doubt. Gaal wasn't looking forward to it. The Heiako numbers on his ship were twenty percent higher than the King's numbers.

A tiny blip in the background, Gaal glanced across to Jenile.

"The Zefron!" Jenile let out a gasp. "They're firing—"

No second to spare, Gaal ran for Jenile's console. "Evasive manoeuvres!"

Jenile banked their ship, but the explosion rocked through her layers like jelly.

"Raise Kendro! On Comms," Gaal shouted. "Now!"

Seconds before, Kendro felt the vibrations of the *Sol'Delka* through his bond. He sat up, throwing covers aside, grabbing for his clothes.

Taliri's cries echoed through the room.

"What is it?" Mika's first reaction was reaching for him, but he slid away, dressing quickly.

"The Zefron." Kendro gasped, leaning over her, planting a kiss on her forehead. His fingers fumbled for his shoes. "Get dressed, into the safe room. Now!" As Mika got out of their bedspace, he pulled her to him, hugging tight. "I love you."

Then, Kendro ran, sliding into his shirt as he did, punching for Octav and Captain Hadi.

"Sire?" Octav mumbled, half asleep.

"The bridge. Now!" Kendro ordered.

Moments later, Octav, whirled onto the bridge, spitting out orders, just as the comms call from Captain Gaal came through.

"Red Alert!" Gaal screamed. "You have incoming!"

The view-screen flickered, all eyes watching the Zefron weapon strike Gaal's ship.

Single handily, Octav took control of weapons, almost shoving the Duty Officer out the way. *We're not ready for this.* As their siren's echoed, goose bumps rose along his flashing birthmark as he shivered.

"All personnel. Battle stations! This is not a drill. I repeat. All personnel. Battle stations."

Still half dressed for bed, Hadi entered, moving to tactical command as Kendro joined them. Octav spun the *Sol'Ishar*, helping defend their two other ships, shouting at Lynj. "Target the Zefron defences."

"How many?" Hadi pulled up reports from their scans. "No one is manning the cannons."

If only Lyrik were still here to command. Octav touched Hadi's arm. "I'm heading below. Buy me some time."

Hadi could do nothing but nod, as Octav whirled from the bridge.

Time almost paused as the Zefron drew closer. "Several war-birds," Lynj reported. "Four destroyers."

Hadi pressed his nose so close to the view screen that the incoming destroyer seemed to fly into it.

The Destroyer fired again on the *Sol'Delka*. Her shields took this blast, but wouldn't take another. They all knew it.

"Manning the forward cannon." Octav's voice came over the comms from his station on the fighter deck.

"Target and fire," growled Hadi.

The *Sol'Ishar* swung around hard. At Octav's barrage, the Zefron destroyer splintered in two, bursting into flames.

Right behind it, the second destroyer sped closer, opening fire, two of their projectiles exploding against the Sol'Ishar's shields.

They watched in horror, the destroyer turning to starboard. It didn't want the *Sol'Ishar*, instead aiming to hit the *Sol'Delka* again.

169

Kendro pointed to an empty spot on the radar screen. "We must get between them."

"Yes." To their helmsman, Hadi barked, "Match their trajectory, and get on their starboard side! Manoeuvre, damn you!"

"Shields. Seventy percent," Lynj reported.

Chief Engineer Zyler's voice echoed over the comms. "Fighters are ready for launch, Captain."

"Launch!"

Kendro's heart skipped a beat as the command echoed out to all stations. The *Sol'Delka* met with two projectile's lots, their shields failing.

Captain Gaal opened fire on the destroyer still aiming its weapons at his ship. The Aonise couldn't get past its shielding. "Taking heavy damage, Captain Hadi!" Gaal's shaky voice came through comms. "We can't stop it!"

Kendro recoiled, feeling what everyone would see in seconds. The destroyer powered up once again, firing, this time aiming for the *Sol'Rayn*. The projectile hit the ship's forward deck with devastating consequences. As the ship broke apart, the souls aboard screaming, pain and fire, hit him squarely in the face. Kendro struggled. *Focus!*

The war-birds' fighters still zipped in and out like flies. Battling with the outnumbered Aonise, losing either way.

Madrall led the fighters in Octav's specially kitted-out ship. The Aonise fleet opened up on the destroyers, while Madrall and his fleet aimed for the second destroyer.

"Keep firing, Octav," Kendro screamed.

The second destroyer was kept at bay, and manoeuvred around, but was continuously thwarted. The *Sol'Ishar* firing constantly, the destroyer finally began buckling.

Octav had the destroyer in his sights. With one more hit, it collapsed in on itself, a popping noise heard through comms as it exploded.

The destroyer fired its last before the Aonise fighters could reach it.

Kendro's heart sank hearing Gaal's internal pleas, *Ari, save us.* Both projectiles had separate targets. The first struck Captain Gaal's ship breaking through their left side. Flames erupted, spreading quickly.

Kendro's legs gave way. He tried blocking the screams he heard from inside. But he couldn't. Leaning against the console for support, he let out a sickening wail. None of members of the crew could bear looking his way.

As he singled out the last destroyer with his cannon, and just as Madrall fired, Octav hit the destroyer square on. It was history.

The last Zefron projectile had locked onto its target, and nothing could stop it. It struck the *Sol'Rayn* with complete precision, breaking the ship into burning sections.

Inside Kendro's mind, Captain Brayer's last orders echoed, 'All hands abandon ship.' Kendro sank to the deck. Then, there was nothing to reach for but pain.

As their fighters focussed on the remaining war-birds, Captain Hadi watched a glorious showdown of power. They had annihilated them all. *Hopefully*, he thought, *none survived*.

Captain Gaal commed in. "We're badly damaged. Requesting immediate repairs. Life support is failing." He coughed. "On several decks."

Kendro winced. Could he bear this? Yes. He must. "You'll have everything you need. Captain Hadi will organize it."

Pushing himself to his feet, Kendro knew there must be some survivors. He tuned in the standard frequency—projecting this with his mind might kill him off. "Survivors of *Sol'Rayn*. Hold on. We will find you."

"All fighters can search. We might have one problem though, Your Highness—"

Frowning, Kendro knew what Hadi was about to protest.

"Landing the fighters? Enemy survivors?"

"We'll do our best. Salvage what we can. If we have to leave fighter ships behind, so be it. Get as many aboard as you can. As for any surviving Zefron—" Hadi lowered his head, pleading. "We're already stretched to capacity."

"They decided their own fate." Kendro's face screwed, wrinkle lines deep in his forehead. "Leave them."

As casualties continued flooding the infirmary in the hundreds, Doctor Brie determined quickly who should stay; a simple matter of their forehead colour. The walking wounded were sent on. Empty fighter bays waited where nurses saw to lesser injuries. It had been a perfect idea. It meant that the cramped Heiako bays were not overloaded, giving the seriously wounded access to top medical staff.

Captain Hadi entered the infirmary, waving his hand high, trying for his wife's attention. She noticed, but a wounded man leaned, coughing up blood. She grabbed a bowl for him, holding it under his mouth. "Nurse!"

A redheaded nurse ran to her, taking the bowl while Brie loaded a guin, injecting meds. Brie placed a green dot on his forehead then made her way over to her husband.

"How's everything?" Hadi saw the slump in her shoulders, bags under her eyes. "You look exhausted."

"They're still bringing in the wounded," she said, through a yawn.

"Can you take a break?"

Brie's eyes were glazed, a weary nod as more Aonise wandered in, some carrying others on reswaes, Doctor Vawn assessing them, sending some on their way. "No."

"I can't trust him to make all the right calls."

Captain Hadi wrapped his arm around her waist, watching her reactions closely. "You are taking a break. Come, you need food, Katya. And, by the looks of it, fluids," He pulled her closer, holding on tight, "and a hug or two."

She stared at him, tears dripping down her cheeks. "I'll need more than a few hugs."

"I know." He stroked the side of her face. "We need a new home." *What else should I say?* "Soon as we're up and running on full capacity, we'll be heading straight there."

"How long will it take us? Really?" She wiped the tears with the back of her hand and sniffled.

"I don't know, neither does Kendro."

"I just want a rest." She indicated the whole room, "We all need a break. This—" her sight full of injured people brought a sigh, "—is relentless, Sheve."

Hadi walked her away from the injured Aonise. Pulling her closer, refusing to let go as a nurse waved her hand, a frantic motion for Brie. Another doctor meeting the Captain's stern glare rushed over to help instead.

Sitting her down on her desk, he ran a hand over her thighs, trying to stem the cold.

Brie asked, "How many?"

"Kendro won't speak of it. No one can get him to talk. He's shutting down."

"We thought losing one ship was bad," Brie choked up, "t–this is—"

"I know." He rubbed her bare skin, hoping, warming her. "I can't contemplate what he's going through. Just empathise."

"He's strong, he'll fight for us," she said.

"Is he?" He wiped an eye as he watched the nurses busily dressing the wounded outside the office door. "After this, I'm not so sure."

"I am sure of it," she replied.

Hadi sat on the desk with her, placing his hand in hers, their fingers interlocking.

"How's Captain Gaal's ship?"

"Badly damaged. I've sent over two hundred crews to help with repairs to the hull and other essential structures. It's not looking good."

"Will it ever be flight-worthy again?"

"I hope so. There is no way we can get anymore people on this ship."

"If we had to, I'm sure we could."

"Oh, Katya." He moved in to nuzzle Brie just as the door burst open.

"Doctor, please, we need you!" a young nurse called.

Sheve held onto her hand, locking fingers with hers. "Love you lots," he promised. Then, he let her go.

Hadi looked around the corridor, thinking for a moment. He tapped a comms panel asking for Lace.

"Lace here."

"Ask around any of your Heiako mothers. I'd like some volunteers for the infirmary. No med experience needed, just compassion. A willingness to help."

"I'll see what we can do. How's it looking, Captain?"

Hadi took one last look around. "It looks bad, but we'll be fine. And at your end?"

Lace laughed. "It looks bad here, but we'll be fine, too."

Captain Hadi headed back up bridge side, meeting Octav on the way.

"Ainoren," he said. "Anything I can do for you?"

"I don't know. I hope so."

Captain Hadi motioned and continued walking. "I've just asked Lace to send some of the Heiako women to the infirmary. The staff there could do with the extra help."

"Good idea. I've come to request leave from the ship."

"Leave the ship?" *Ari, what now?* Hadi's birthmark flickered, his brows furrowing. "Why?"

"Something is hiding in the debris from the *Sol'Rayn*, it looks odd. I'd like to get there before the search and rescue shuttles."

"What is it?"

"That's what I aim to find out. It's giving off strange readings." Octav held a small statistics reader. Captain Hadi took a quick look.

"Bizarre. I've never seen anything like it."

"Nor have I. I don't think we should leave it in space for anyone else to salvage either."

"Yes, then. Permission granted." Hadi handed back the reader. "Do you need anything else?"

"I'd like Zyler and Chace accompanying."

Hadi rubbed his forehead, his finger catching his birthmark in a glimmer of red. "You'll have to get Zyler back from Gaal's ship though."

"Puswer!" Octav tucked his reader away. "I don't think we have time for that. Is there anyone else you'd recommend?"

Captain Hadi's face lit up. "Me."

"I can't ask you to leave the ship?"

"You're not asking me. I'm going."

Octav grinned. "Can Vax cope?" He looked to the bridge.

"She'll be fine." Hadi continued towards the doorway. "Meet you in ten."

Octav took time gathering all the equipment he wanted for the task, and joined Captain Hadi and Chace on the shuttle deck.

Chace's birthmark flickered as they all shook hands. His hand lingered that bit longer with Octav. "Good to see you, Ainoren."

"Never enough time in the day, is there?" Octav felt the severe heat from Chace's handshake. "We'll catch up soon, I promise." He gave a light squeeze to Chace's shoulder.

They took one of the larger shuttles in the hopes it would be sturdy enough for getting the object aboard. Like Zyler, Chace could fly all ships.

Octav gave him guidance, navigating the debris field.

Hadi mentioned, "Search and Rescue will be here soon enough. Hopefully, they'll find other survivor pods."

Chace carried on, weaving his way through the debris with skill. But as Octav watched his adept manoeuvring, he couldn't help notice beads of sweat on his top lip. *Something's wrong. Is he still sick?*

"Easy." Chace grinned at him, wiping the sweat with a flick of his hand. "It's just ahead." Hadi focused on the scanner at his elbow. Chace moved the ship closer until the object drew into physical view.

It loomed in front of them—long, silver. Captain Hadi pointed, hands spread, gauging the size and shape of it. "Bulky. No small trinket here, men. Will we get it on board?"

Octav gazed, too. "I don't know."

"If we can't, we'll tow it in," Chace assured.

"We can use a helix beam to bring it closer." Octav agreed. "We'd need to guide it in the rest of the way by hand."

"Suit up then." Hadi moved towards several suits anchored along the bulkhead.

Chace steadied the ship, hovering as close as possible. Beautifully entwined writing marked down each side of it. "Have you seen anything like this before?"

Captain Hadi, before setting his helmet and toggling it down, said, "I haven't."

"Let's get it on board," Octav slipped into his own suit, "as fast as possible, then."

174

Above their deck, Chace programmed the Nelliss beam bringing the object as close as possible to the bay where the other two waited. Opening the hatch doors, he called though comms, "All yours."

Octav and Captain Hadi waited with magnetic handholds to grab and adjust.

The object pulled closer. "Can you hear that?" Octav strained his ears—*was it real?*

"Hear what?" Hadi shook his head.

"My mark is humming."

"I can't hear it. Mine's not."

Octav noticed Hadi's face pale white. *Him, too?* "Are you all right?"

"Just not keen on actual space, if you get me."

Octav laughed. "Captain of the Fleet, scared of space? Never!"

"Don't laugh." Hadi focused on a single spot. "It's not fear. I just don't like it much."

Octav turned his attention to the glyph-decorated object. "I'll step out to try to lever it inside."

"Check your tether," Hadi yelled, but Octav had jumped.

Captain Hadi had often wondered what it would be like to drop off a ship, floating. Looking downward sent his head spinning—all he wanted was that object inside. Fast.

Octav approached, herding the bullet-shaped prize. With a gentle tug, Hadi grabbed hold of the side he could reach. He pulled it towards himself.

"Won't fit!" Hadi shouted. "Try the other side first!"

Octav squeezed round its bulk, back inside the shuttle, moving the object's nose to the left. Manoeuvring, nudge by nudge, settling it down within another minute. It finally rested inside their shuttle. "Got it. Chace? All clear. We're in."

Hatches closed, Chace, repressurized the cabin, switching off the Nelliss.

Captain Hadi removed his helmet with a sigh of relief.

And the two stripped off their suits.

Chace entered wanting to see it for himself now that it was on board. "I wasn't sure. But you did it."

Sliding towards the side of the object, Octav wondered at his mark, still at a hum, though a softer key now. "It looks like someone's final resting place, don't you think?" He ran his hand over the metal. Cool to his touch. "What were, they giants?"

Hadi said, "Big coffin."

THE PRISON

"NOW IT'S ON BOARD." CHACE, touching a few console keys, pulled up scans of the internal structure. "I'll let you know the results in a moment." He read the stats, spinning his chair around to watch them with the object. "Hadi was right. It certainly is a coffin."

"Two occupants." Chace reported. "Unfortunately, not a giant. One didn't make it."

"It looks ancient."

Hadi didn't like the feel of this. "We should get it back before something happens."

"What do you mean?"

"I just have a feeling this should be locked up. It was on board the *Sol'Tar*, no log for it. There's no record of anything this size. This isn't something we should be touching."

"Kendro will know what it is." Chace spun his chair around to face his console again.

Hadi's birthmark flickered, "I don't think he will."

"Agreed, this is ancient." His fingers traced the glyphs. "A few thousand years old—could be before Letháo."

"No way." Chace laughed, nervously.

"We don't know everything, Chace." Captain Hadi pointed to the scan. "I sense danger. Lots of it."

"I think it's beautiful." Octav stared at the image, mesmerised by the fine lines and ancient lettering. "If it were my coffin, I'd be happy."

176

"You're missing my point." Hadi sat back in his chair next to Chace. "It's not a coffin. It's a prison."

"Let's see what Kendro thinks of it," Octav buckled himself in. "Return us."

"To the *Sol'Ishar*," Chace replied.

Chace brought the shuttle, hovering over the *Sol'Ishar*'s dock, easing in, pushing thrusters forward slightly until the engineers clamped it onto the deck.

Octav issued orders clearing the deck, relieving all officers on duty, before he went for a set of three reswaes. *The thing was that large.*

He'd spoken to Kendro on their way back. This was the best plan, considering the humming and Hadi's worries. Checking that all of the corridors they planned traversing were empty, Octav and the others transported the salvage from their shuttle into a secured room.

"I'll see if Kendro will come now," Octav said.

"Is he well enough?" Hadi asked in a lowered voice.

"It will need guarding at all times. Chace, can you see to that?"

"Yes, Ainoren."

They left Chace, and headed for the royal chambers.

"You trust him with it?" asked Hadi.

"Why?"

"I don't know him that well."

"Don't be paranoid. He's solid, we go way back."

"It makes me nervous." Hadi frowned, eyes darting back up the corridor. "Doesn't feel right."

Octav stopped, glaring at Hadi. "I said I trust him with my life. I mean that."

"Did he look all right to you? Some residual effect from the planet Earth's illness maybe?"

Octav looked back now, thinking. "Yeah, I thought he might have been feeling sick still. Seemed he didn't feel it necessary worrying the Doc though."

"Shall I ask if Katya will check on him?"

"Good plan, I'll meet you in a few hours."

Chace watched the wide silver coffin, wondering who or what was inside. At first, he guarded the door, but curiosity got him. He stepped closer, a vibrating hum drifted towards him, inviting.

He stopped, listening, and wondering, *is it getting hotter in here?*

Chace moved to a comms panel, pulling up the stats on the room.

Optimal conditions. Loosening his shirt, the sweat dripped down his back. *Then what was this?* He itched. Scratching his stomach, his fingers touching raised, bumpy skin.

With a quick tug, pulling his shirt clean out of his trrobhas, Chace peered at the itchy patch. His birthmark was the source of the raised bumps. He touched at it lightly, running a finger over the redness, expecting the usual response. But the mark didn't light up. It seemed darkened. *Wrong.*

Chace shook his head, the hum from the object louder. Reaching towards it, he felt its cool metal. "Whoever you are." He spoke aloud. "I'm sure you've one heck of a story you'll tell us."

Octav commed through at the Royal door, waiting. Mika opened it, rubbing darkening eyes. "I'm sorry to disturb you, Your Grace."

"He's resting, but you can go through, if you like."

Octav rapped on Kendro's bedspace door, and entered.

Kendro smiled, pushing himself up, curling the blankets around his chest. "Good to see you." He patted the end of the bed. No need asking if everything was all right.

"How are you doing?" Octav moved closer. He looked nearly well. Coming around, he saw that Kendro's eyes seemed brighter, yet weariness resonated through his birthmark. It was flickering pale blue.

Kendro's mark shimmered once, and stopped. "I'd be telling you a lie if I said I was recovered fully."

Octav's birthmark flashed green, tinting the bare walls. "I hate seeing you like this." He held out his hand for Kendro.

"I—" Kendro hesitated, not ready to share his exact feeling.

"Just take it," Octav moved closer, "please."

Finally, Kendro took hold of his hand, his eyes flashing blue as they touched. For a brief moment, they shared.

"Thank you." Pulling away, Kendro smiled. "Even a brief moment of peace helps. You know me too well, Octav."

"As I should," Octav let his hand rest, croex dissipating around the bedspace, "we're family. Even within protocol, I'm allowed to share."

"I should get dressed." Kendro threw off the blankets. "You obviously want me for something, yes?"

Octav stood. "Yes." *Should he, though?* "We've found something that needs your attention. I said we'd meet Captain Hadi back down in the unoccupied bays."

"The locked ones? Give me a few minutes. I'll come out."

Octav withdrew. He met with Mika, waiting with a hot cup of Reingo. He smiled and sipped, glancing around. "Where is Taliri?"

"Here, I'll show you." Mika moved towards a silver wall. "We've relocated him—" Mika stepped forward, the wall was still, then it shimmered and shook. Vanishing through it, she then returned a moment later through the still shimmering space. "Genetically engineered for Kendro, the doctor, and myself at the moment."

"Brilliant."

"Yes. He's getting so big. We couldn't have kept him quiet while we had visitors."

"How quick he's growing." The pair smiled at Taliri's progress—doting mother and gracious uncle.

"Doctor Brie thinks he will be the equivalent of a three year old in less than a few weeks."

"What does Kendro think?"

Stretching to her left, Mika lowering herself beside him, began, "Well, we've talked about it a lot—"

Dressed, Kendro appeared in the doorway, having heard it all. "It's a stress reaction."

"Because he's a baby?" Octav stared towards the secret room.

Mika, temporized, "He can't react. Not about things going on around him. But his mark is so active."

"Always shimmering," Kendro added.

"Exactly, he's already mumbling words, talking. And, boy, does he!" Mika laughed, her birthmark twinkling. A good sight to see.

"When will it stop?" Octav saw Mika's twinkle fade, her eyes flittered to Kendro, then back.

"We're not sure, but soon, I hope. We'd like him to have some childhood."

"Come." Kendro motioned. "Let's go."

Octav stood. "I'll come back soon to see Taliri." He smiled at Mika. "And you, of course."

Mika reached for him, the silk dress she wore slipping from her neckline. She kissed Octav's cheek. "Please do."

As they entered the small lock-up, Kendro and Octav acknowledged Chace. Chace made sure the door closed behind them, allowing Captain Hadi in moments later.

Kendro walked around the object, carefully studying it, not saying a word.

"What do you think?" Captain Hadi broached.

Kendro's birthmark warmed his skin as he harnessed his croex before approaching it properly. "I don't know. Stand back." He reached out.

Octav jumped as the object reacted to Kendro's touch. From the centre of the device a circular wheel turned, protruded. It grew in size until it extended several inches above the smooth surface.

Chace gasped aloud. "Is this safe?"

Octav stepped towards it, leaning in for a closer look. "Something fits inside this."

"Yes. This—" Kendro reached into his clothes, pulling out an object that glinted in the light above their heads.

"The Royal Pendant," Chace said, instinctively dropping to his knees.

"Please. Stand," Kendro said, holding his pendant out for both Captain Hadi and Chace. "I forget how powerful its presence is. Not many people get to see it up close."

Chace gasped. "Amazing. Will it fit?"

Kendro removed the circular part from the main clasp. He held it towards the object.

"Let's find out," said Octav.

The energy inside the room sparked. *No!* Octav stepped in Kendro's path, glancing to the others. "Kendro! Don't!"

Kendro remained still. Octav's warning held no sway over his judgment as he kept the pendant towards the device. "The only way we'll know anything is by trying."

Chace stared at Octav. *Did our scan malfunction?* "Someone's alive in there. We've got to get them out!"

Hadi spoke the unspeakable. "Why don't we just leave them?"

"Them?" Kendro ran his hand over its full length.

"Initial scans show two bodies." Chace held a reader for Kendro, an image of where the bodies lay within the vessel. "One's alive, suspended. The other—"

"We should comm Brie." Kendro motioned Hadi towards the comms panel.

"I don't think we should risk anyone else." Hadi's low statement challenged Kendro. "Any number of toxins could be in there."

But, if needs must. I will. Kendro knew Hadi just didn't want them comming his wife. "I understand." He ignored Octav's insubordination, knowing better of his Ainoren. Gently, he pushed past him. "Let us see what's really inside."

As the pendent connected, the room sparked with all their primary colours. With a click, the lid of the prison slid open.

The four of them peered over. The occupants of the prison came into view as the lid revealed a woman inside, moving, coming around, with a fluttering of eyes.

"She's Aonise, that's for sure." Kendro secreted the pendant back under his tunic. "See? Her birthmarks." An intricately layered pattern snaked around petite ears, over the bridge of her nose, down the right side of her face. "Pretty powerful, too."

Her eyes popped open, staring right at Kendro. "Calmarix Shruz?" she commanded, bolting upright.

Octav motioned Chace. "An ancient dialect?" Octav then immediately programmed a reader.

She spoke again. "Calmarix Shruz?"

A moment later, the reader's voice spoke. "Identify yourself."

Kendro ran a finger over his pendant, such power within. It vibrated with his touch, taking it back from the device. "I am Kendro Makshaw. May I ask who are you?" He trusted the reader, assured it would speak for him.

"Lady Verona Katesh." The reader spoke.

Kendro's heartbeat skipped. *Katesh, I know that name.* But, he wasn't quite sure.

Her eyes flitted from one face to another, fearful. "What is the meaning of this?" Her eyes flickered blue. "Where are we?" Then, she gasped. Lady Katesh let out a sob, scrabbling to climb over the centre section of the space. The other man's lifeless corpse lay still in her arms.

Octav stepped in, restraining her. "I'm sorry." Octav's birthmark flickered, feeling her pain. "He's been passed a while."

"Why?" she cried, staring at Kendro, knowing instinctively who he was. "Why?"

"I, too, am sorry." Kendro lowered his eyes. "Malfunction, maybe. I don't know the reasons."

Lady Katesh pushed back from Octav, pulling herself out of her prison to stand before the quartet of strangers. Straightening her back, her head high. "Malfunction—" she spit out, wanting answers, placing a hand on a control panel, which emerged, illuminated.

With a light touch, several commands were entered as the others watched. She traced over the console with a finger, answering, "We've been in stasis for a thousand years longer than we should have." She shot at Kendro, her face, red. "Why were we not awakened properly?"

She pointed, remaining calm, not a flicker from her mark, Kendro noticed.

The Lady demanded, "It wasn't a malfunction—see? Someone tried raising us three hundred years ago! Without that—that—" She pointed at Kendro's chest where he'd secreted his pendant. "Why?"

The King had no response for this. "I don't know anything about you. Or who may have tried raising you—"

"You don't know who I am?" Her nostrils flared, she spoke with eyes widened.

"No," the reader replied, speaking for them all.

181

She seemed bewildered, repeating, "Who are you?" Then, passed out. Octav caught her before she fell to the deck.

Captain Hadi punched at the comms now. "Infirmary!"

Emmi paced her office, grief overwhelming her at their losses. Reports were coming in from all over their ship. Irreparable damage. Death. Tears ran freely down her cheeks. *Why, Ari. Why?*

Anrel burst into the room, without asking her permission. "This can't be happening!" She broke down, sinking to the floor. With one stride, he was kneeling with her, holding her against his chest. "I'm here now, I'm here."

"We lost—everything." She cried, gripping onto his skin, nails digging.

"Not everything," he soothed. "We have each other, my love."

Emmi looked into his eyes. Tears evident, but also his need to fight them back.

"The Powex?"

"I can't find it. I'm sorry."

The truth hurt, Emmi had lost family. But also, the most sacred item she owned too was gone. "Other survivors?"

Anrel's lip curled into a smile. "There are many. We've not lost anywhere near what Kendro first predicted."

Emmi tried to take comfort in that. Their species would thrive. The Zefron, gone.

When the reswae arrived in the infirmary, Brie was waiting. Around them, the infirmary swarmed, packed with injured people. Hadi felt a twinge of guilt pulling her from them. Kendro scrutinized doctors and nurses as they sifted through patients as quickly as they could. He hoped everyone was given the attention each deserved; Officer and Heiako alike.

Brie broke away from the confusion around her, passing her husband. She lowered her head to Kendro. "The Lady Katesh? We have one private space left." The medical staff all running and attending the neverending cycle of patients would deal on their own for a moment. "Let's take her in here."

Octav pushed the reswae after Doctor Brie as Chace slipped the reader into his pocket. When they were safe from intrusions inside, they transferred The Lady onto a sturdy bedspace.

Brie attached a monitoring device on The Lady's wrist, accidentally touching one of her birthmarks. She pulled back, startled and stating, "This is fake!"

Kendro suspicions confirmed, *Yes!* Not a flicker from The Lady's mark. "How?"

"Here," Brie said, taking his hand. "Feel this." She ran his fingers over the birthmark. Rough to the touch, it tickled.

"It really is fake." Confused, Kendro scratched the side of his face.

Octav could not believe his eyes. He'd held her, kept her from hitting the deck, had seen her tears of discovery. "Why? She's gone to a lot of trouble making it look real."

"She purposely hurt herself." Hadi also leaned forward, touching the false mark. "Who would do that?"

Octav surmised for them all. "Someone who is frightened."

"For protection?"

Brie checked the cuff's readings. "She's in good health, considering she's been in suspension for two thousand years."

"Poor woman," said Octav. "Two thousand years!"

"Her DNA is clean. In fact, I know of only two with DNA markings like this." Brie pointed on screen to irregular shapes. "The other traits I've not seen, ever."

"Whose?" Hadi wondered aloud.

Octav followed Brie's gaze to Kendro.

"I just can't work out why?" Brie's birthmark flickered as she checked her reader again.

"There's only one explanation." Kendro paused. "She's a direct descendant of Ari. We're related."

Hadi coughed. "She's Royal?"

"Somehow, yes." Kendro grasped Lady Katesh's limp hand, holding it gently. "We're family."

"She's in deep shock." Brie reminded them all. "She'll need lots of rest. In the meantime, I can run more tests."

"I'll stay with her for now." Kendro smiled. "Octav, will you inform Mika?"

"Of course." Octav backed away.

Captain Hadi asked, "Anything I can do?"

"We need her guarded. Securely. Two thousand years or no, whoever locked her away did it for a reason. I fear The Lady may be in danger."

"I'll see Chace stays. Octav trusts him."

Kendro looked to the door. "Just don't tell anyone anything yet."

In the corridor beyond the infirmary, Captain Hadi turned to Kendro, again asking what no one had. "If she is family, then who was the other she was imprisoned with?"

"I don't think it was a prison," Kendro replied. "She was hiding."

"That would make sense. Still. Two of them in hiding?"

"We'll take things slow. Even though we have lots of questions."

Kendro stayed with Lady Katesh. Brie returned often, attaching a drip, checking stats on both her patient and her King throughout the night, concern for both evident, as she fussed over them.

The next morning, Kendro waited as Lady Katesh went on sleeping. Eventually, she stirred, her wide eyes focussing towards him. *Where am I? Puswer?* Kendro felt her thoughts, understanding them even in her ancient dialect.

Lady Katesh glared straight at Kendro. "Where are we now?" she demanded.

How was this all possible? Inside, Kendro felt no connection.

So many questions. He knew he couldn't overwhelm her though. "How are you feeling?"

"Please." She rubbed her eyes, drawing her covers closer. Then she scanned more of the room, the waiting cuff, the panels, and the machinery. "I know we need to talk. You have lots of questions. But you must see that I need something decent to eat first. Yes?"

"Of course," Kendro stood, stretching his aching muscles. "I'd be happy to have something brought to you. And yes, we must talk. There is much we need to know. Perhaps you, as well."

"I am alive. I know that. I am thankful for that."

Brie entered, trying to hide a yawn. "How are you?" she asked, aiming her words towards the translator. She'd brought a tray of the lightest foods she could think to order.

Lady Katesh attempted a smile, the corner of her lips curling softly. "Some clean clothes. Can you acquire some?"

"No problem, you look like my size." Doctor Brie left the room, returning a few minutes later.

Kendro decided then to speak. "That was your doctor you just ordered about like a servant."

When Lady Katesh stepped from the room, Kendro took a second look. Although the clothes Brie had delivered her were plain, they floated around The Lady's figure in a highly intoxicating way. Kendro shook his head at this thought. *Family!* The King reminded himself.

Refreshed, fed, attired, "Let us go," she said, picking up the translator.

Kendro took a step towards her, gripping an elbow, guiding her away from Medical. "You've a lot to take in. I'll go slowly."

Lady Katesh moved gracefully. Anyone who came across her in the hallway politely moved out of the way, staring as she passed.

While walking through the more interesting sights of the ship, Kendro explained to The Lady Katesh what the Aonise knew about their last two thousand years. In the end, she stopped, placing a hand on his arm. "It's too much. I'm sorry."

He'd allowed her to ask pertinent questions about the leadership of the four Houses within his own interrogation. Kendro saw this as a good sign.

"Don't be sorry." Kendro took her hand, feeling warmth resonating from within her, but nothing more. No Croex at all. "Anyone would struggle."

She pulled away. "May we find more to eat now?"

"Why, yes." Kendro escorted her to a private spot in the gardens where The Lady settled herself down, pulling a wrap around her shoulders. "Are you cold?"

"I'm not quite accustomed to things just yet." Lady Katesh attempted a smile. Kendro knew this time she was genuine, friendly.

Kendro ordered lunch brought for them and poured some Bea. "This should warm you up."

Lady Katesh took the offered drink, savouring the sweet liquid as it touched her lips.

Kendro observed the delicate way Lady Katesh picked at the morsels before her. "I've answered everything for you." Kendro popped a delicious root vegetable in his mouth, they were from the nurseries on board, and he had spared no expense in this private dinner. "Would you be able to talk more about yourself now?"

"You know we're related," she stated.

"Yes. In a distant way." Chewing some crisx, he swallowed, savouring its salty taste.

"My history must have been destroyed if you have never heard of me."

"I am sorry," he said, taking a drink of his warm-leafed Bea. The awful feeling in Kendro's stomach dislodged his lunch, but he choked it down. Not yet knowing what was about to be revealed, his visions did not extend to her. This worried him.

"I am the one who is sorry. If you haven't heard of me, then you wouldn't know what happened to my family. My brother."

Yes. Here it was. The truth. "Who was your brother?"

"Dalamaar Katesh," The Lady said.

Kendro put his fork down. "Dalamaar?"

"So… you have heard of him?"

It seemed too much of a coincidence. It couldn't be the same person. Lady Katesh had been inside a sophisticated suspended animation unit for two thousand years.

Lady Katesh peered at Kendro. "Something is wrong."

Kendro did not want the connection either, although instinct told him otherwise. "No, I've merely eaten too much. That is all."

"Where will I be staying?" She looked about, scowling at their surroundings, even though the gardens were beautiful.

"I've organised accommodation. Although there isn't much left."

"The Zefron. Why are you at war with them?"

"Originally, we thought they wanted our planets resources. This resulted in many battles. When our sun began dying, they became bent on our destruction."

"Have you ever talked to one?"

"We tried several communication missions. Even when captured, the Zefron committed suicide."

"How awful." Lady Katesh forced herself upright, her postured stiffening. "But, if you'll allow me, here is the why." Kendro raised an eyebrow at this. "I am going to tell you some of your history."

"Do," said Kendro, carrying on eating.

"There is a question first. Look at me. Tell me what you see?"

"What I see?" Kendro stared at her. "I don't understand?"

"Think about it." She traced a finger down the side of her mark. "What do you really see?"

Kendro regarded her briefly. "A tired, beautiful woman."

"Look deeper." Smiling, they locked eyes.

Kendro concentrated on her high cheekbones, long nose, and her steady firm gaze. He noticed the way her hair fell around her birthmark, then saw what she meant. "You aren't Aonise, are you?" he stated. Shaking his head, as his next thought sank in. *I'm not Aonise.*

"No. Well, yes, but no," she said, "you aren't, we're part Aonise, part Kieron. We are different. We are what the Zefron are after."

"Kieron? I—"

"Your history tells you what of Ari?" She rubbed the side of her temples.

Was she in pain?

"That Ari led our people to peace after years of warring."

"Did they say where he came from?"

Kendro thought for a few moments, trying to remember more of their history. "As far as I knew, he came from the desert."

"His origin is unknown because he was not from your planet." Lady Katesh took a petite sip of her drink. "He came from a place far away, distant suns and stars. At that time, you had no space travel. He was last of our kind, hunted by the Zefron for his blood."

"I don't understand," said Kendro. *Why did I not know this?*

"Although similar to the Aonise in DNA, there is one difference. Our natural blood. The Zefron hunted our species for it. Like a drug, they use it for healing their sick. When Ari escaped with the merest of followers, the Zefron pursued."

Katesh poured herself more Bea, allowing it to cool before she sipped. "Ari settled on your planet, and saved the Aonise species from killing themselves. During that time, he fell in love with Chikri. As the first King and Queen, leaders of House Niakrex, they were able to carry on his bloodline, keeping our species alive."

"Direct descendants bear *only* his blood though, *only* his DNA?" Kendro added.

"Yes, it fights off any Aonise genetic traits, holding onto pure blood. One descendent per mother, a male, kept the line intact."

Kendro sat back dumbfounded at these revelations. "What happened with you then?"

Lady Katesh turned away from him, lowering her head. "Dalamaar and I were twins. My mother, Ukiri, was a strong-willed Aonise female, and our Father, King Byer, powerful yet weakened to her. I am neither Aonise nor Kieron. My blood is not special, although it is good at faking it."

"How did you trick Doctor Brie?"

"A culmination of survival tactics gathered over the years. I'm not about to spill all my tricks, Kendro."

"So, Dalamaar wanted you dead because you were an abomination?"

A single tear dripped down Lady Katesh's cheek at the word. She found herself nodding. "Dalamaar wanted me dead because our blood wasn't pure. He couldn't become the next King."

"What happened?"

"We were rejected. He turned rogue. Bent on not only destroying me, but in eliminating the bloodline in the hopes he could rule."

Kendro frowned, his gut tightening. "I fear for us both. I must inform you I believe Dalamaar is still around."

"What?" Lady Katesh slammed her hand on the table, plates and food flying. "How?"

"I can't be sure, but Dalamaar is on board one of our ships. He's already made several attempts at my life."

Lady Katesh stood. "Then, I need to get off this ship. Put me wherever you want. I can't stay aboard."

"I'm not certain it is the same person."

"I don't care. I've spent all my life running from him. And I still haven't managed it. If Dalamaar is here, alive after all these years, I must leave."

Kendro stood, placing a calming hand on her arm. "I'll protect you."

"You can't." She buried her head in her hands. "Don't you understand?" She looked to Kendro, eyes filling with tears. "He'll get what he wants. He always does."

"How do you know that?"

"Because he managed to keep me locked up for two thousand years. Troj and I were supposed to be somewhere safe, a new home where we could start again. We left strict instructions for the fourth generation King about reviving us."

"That never happened. Have you any idea what did? Or who tried to bring you around?"

She shook her head. "No." Lady Katesh started sobbing again. Kendro sat calm, allowing her to cry.

Eventually, she looked at him. "I have to carry on. He will try to defeat me. I won't let him." She stood, wobbling. "Please, take me to my quarters. I must rest."

REPRIEVE

KENDRO SAT WITH OCTAV IN one of their meeting rooms, pondering their next move. With the *Sol'Delka* badly damaged, they had every engineer working on repairs, but even with their vast knowledge, the engineers struggled getting her systems operational.

Lace knocked at the open door, waiting, watching the two men for a moment before they invited him in.

"We've a big problem," Lace said, approaching the end of the table.

Octav pointed him towards a seat, but Lace didn't take it. "What do you mean?"

"I mean—the third ship isn't strong enough for space travel. We can't move her."

"Can't move her?" Kendro dropped his reader and it clattered on the metallic table.

"I'm sorry." Lace bowed. "No."

"Never?" Octav frowned. "Even with repairs?"

Lace thought for a moment, lowering his head.

Kendro felt no need to probe for honest feelings. Lace's shimmering birthmark gave away his aim to satisfy their hope—to speak only the truth.

Lace met the King's eyes, holding his gaze. "Never. I've had men working for several days straight. The Zefron saw to it she was ripped apart. We can't fix it."

"Keep trying," Kendro ordered. "I have the utmost faith in your team."

"Yes, Your Highness." Lace bowed, backing towards the door.

"If you'll excuse me," Octav pushed himself from the table. "Your

Highness, I will assist Lace." Kendro read his need—further talk with Lace.

"Report any findings," with the flick of a hand, "when you have some."

"She really won't move?" Octav and Lace hurried quickly for the Heiako bays. Octav hoped Lace had exaggerated for the King. And that they still had a chance.

Lace glanced back up the corridor. "We'll do everything we can. She might manage space travel for a few weeks."

Octav stopped, placing a palm against a security panel. Swift movements brought up their position, comparable to where their destination was. The points were at too wide a distance. *We'll never make it.* Then, a thought crossed his mind. "What about a jayux instead of a tricu?"

Lace raised a wrinkled eyebrow, lines furrowing deep on his forehead. "You do know what you're suggesting isn't a normal space hop, like you'd use for a fighter?"

Octav paused. He hadn't thought about it that much. The earlier tricu had been easy. But a jayux, no. He must find another way.

Lace took Octav's hand in his, bringing him out of his thoughts. "When you're connected with your fighter, so is your Routui. An energy linkup, which we just don't have on here. The sietev is our only way in."

Octav shuddered, thinking of his link up with the *Sol'Ishar*. It wasn't an easy task.

"If we get someone strong enough for the sietev to channel our combined croex, is it possible?"

Octav watched Lace's brows furrow. "Can we?"

"If we keep her travel at a minimum while we prepare, maybe? But it could be a huge risk, Ainoren."

"I don't see the choice. If we travel slower, we might make it. If we try this, we have a better chance."

"Let me run some numbers. I'll get back to you. I'll need to speak to the team on the *Sol'Delka*," Lace paused, "if permitted?"

"Yes. Just don't let Kendro know about it just yet. Yes?"

"Of course, Ainoren." Lace teetered, back, forth, hesitant to leave without knowing. "We are all right, aren't we?"

"Yes, we're fine. This getting to the planet Earth might take a little more work than I think we all envisioned."

"The Zefron aren't coming back?"

"No, they're not. We destroyed every fighter, every war-bird. If they did want to follow, it would take more than a thousand years."

Lace smiled. "Good, I don't want Sylkx in fear for his life anymore. Thank you."

Chace rolled in his bunk, banging an elbow. What normally came so easily now eluded him. Sleep was far from where his mind lay. Thoughts of the battles, the prison. Octav.

Octav? The scratching at his lower torso continued with vigour. Shoving the covers off, Chace jumped up. Maybe a shower would help.

Grabbing a clean uniform, Chace made his way to the communal showers. He stripped off, turning the dials to their fullest. Hot at its best during night hours while everyone else slept.

Allowing its sensations to ease away the piercing scratchiness around his birthmark, Chace reached for his spray soap. It stung. Looking down, a thin train of blood leaked towards his feet.

Chace stopped, turning off the shower and moved before a full-length mirror. He stared at his reflection. The lower half of his torso, normally flickering alive, was dull. Red oozing patches of his birthmark glistened back at him. *This isn't right.*

Moving to a comms panel, he keyed in for the infirmary, no answer. *Busy?*

Slipping on his trrobhas, Chace winced as they caught on his mark.

Opting to leave his shirt open, Chace left the shower room, and headed for the infirmary.

Octav turned onto his side, catching a glimpse of the time. Too early—three bells. Watching Frie as her breast rose and fell, he slipped from their bedspace. This was no good. Octav dressed, slipping on his running shoes. *The gardens.*

Stars twinkled in the darkness of space through the vast faux-glass porthole above him. He smiled, taking a deep breath of crisp air, the imitation of night, wonderful to his senses.

Lyrik. Octav stretched. *You're missed, my friend.* Warming his muscles, he twisted and turned until he was ready, and then starting at a slow jog, he built to a fast-paced run.

He ran his usual circuit, through a small wooded forest, the surrounding fields, then back. Again and again, sweat dripping from every pore. A figure stood waiting by the lake. Approaching, Octav saw the Captain. He lowered his head with a nod of acknowledgement.

"Can't sleep?" Captain Hadi frowned.

"No." Octav shook his legs, cooling muscles that burned.

"Me neither. I have the figures from Lace. Thought I'd bring them

191

over at seven bells. Didn't figure you'd arise this early." Hadi held a reader for him.

Octav took it, thumbing over the graphs. Three steady declining lines. The *Sol'Ishar*'s atrei, food, croex. They were sinking fast. He sighed. "Doesn't look good, does it?"

Hadi agreed. "No."

Octav's stare aimed at the stars. "Carry on with the repairs. Get everything, and everyone, as strong as possible. I want all personnel removed from the ship before we move her. Hopefully, it will be less of a strain when we jayux."

"I'll inform Lace." Hadi sighed. "Some of his engineers are losing hope."

"We don't need that. Do what you can to keep their faith. We must keep spirits alive. Without hope, we've nothing."

Captain Hadi took the device. "Have you had enough?" He squinted to the open field.

Octav followed his gaze. "I'm beat." Captain Hadi's smile faded. Octav added, "I do know where there is an illegal bar—if you're wanting a drink."

"Illegal?" Captain Hadi's birthmark shimmed, raising an eyebrow.

"It pays to know who, where, and what goes on, on your ship, Sheve, even the illegal stuff. They're still citizens. They need a vent, a way out."

Captain Hadi tugged at his jogging trrobhas. "Are we going in like this?"

"Perfect." Octav laughed. "Don't think they're dumb. They'll know who we are. They choose to turn the other way."

"Then let's go." Hadi grinned. "I'd like to see this underworld on board my ship."

Octav led the way down into the belly of the ship. Even with their time in space being minimal, the corridor walls were littered with graphic art.

"I've only been down this far once," said Hadi. He'd halted, staring at a crude mural of their home planet. "Of course, I know all the ins and outs of the whole design. I scaled the ship from top to bottom." He ran his hand over the inked wall, feeling each painstaking brushstroke. "This section never caught my attention, though."

"Exactly. They choose it for a reason. The chances of you coming down here were pretty slim."

Octav made his way through another corridor, this one packed with Heiako and Officers holding drinks, standing around talking. Conversations stopped at seeing Captain Hadi.

Octav wondered, *is it best to take him?* "You will be all right, won't you?"

"I am sure I can handle myself," Hadi said. "Don't worry."

"Good, some of the people in here are serious criminals."

"You've shocked me, Octav."

"Better to know your enemy, and understand them, than not know them at all. We have a mutual respect for one other."

One man stood in the pair's way. Octav stared right back at him.

Octav noted Hadi squirmed, uncomfortable. So many staring eyes. "We're here to drink, nothing more," Hadi heard Octav reply.

"You're responsible for him," the man shot a glance, once more at Hadi, "not us."

"I understand," Octav said. The man grimaced, but moving aside, allowed them to pass.

Hadi stood breathing in the exotic fragrance that wafted towards them. "What is that smell?"

"It's an herb they stew for making some of their more intoxicating drinks."

"It smells wonderful."

"Yes, I guess it does," Octav agreed.

Captain Hadi took in the view of the room. The unused hanger bay converted into a private, secluded bar. Tables, chairs, even a bar area. Hadi stood and stared. Astounding.

Kale, the barman, watching for trouble, noticed Octav walking in. Immediately, he set to pouring a glass of blue liquid.

Octav strode over, taking the drink, downing it in one.

"We've been kind of busy, Kale," Octav quipped with a smile for his drink, "or hadn't you noticed all the space battles tucked away in here?"

"We noticed." Kale laughed. "Good job. You can hold your own in a fight."

"Thanks," Octav said, placing some gems on the counter. "We'll have two of your finest shots of Grelch, please."

Kale picked up the gems. Pulling out a scanner, he slid them inside a drawer, waiting for the analysis. When the machine beeped, showing a green 100% reading, he called, "Malik." A young man sauntered over, and Kale passed him the gemreader. "For the safe."

From the corner of his eye, Octav could not ignore the two men watching this transaction. "Just be wary," Octav reminded Malik with a tip of the nearly emptied blue drink.

"Always is," Kale answered for the lad. "That will do you all night. You stopping for long?" He turned to a different bottle of liquor, pouring out two glasses this round.

"Maybe." Octav held a glass for Hadi. "If not, hold my credit."

Hadi stuck his nose inside the glass, absorbing its floral bouquet.

"Reminds me of home." He watched Octav knock his back, asking for another.

Hadi took a sip, choking. "Strong stuff. Do you drink it with an atrei back?"

"Plenty of practice, and you'll not need a back," Octav said. "The trick is don't taste it. Knock it down quick. Let the feeling warm you from the inside."

Hadi thought for a moment, staring at the liquid. Then with a quick chug, he downed it. "I must admit, it does go down nicer when my tongue isn't involved."

"Indeed it does. Kale, we'll take the whole bottle," said Octav. "Thanks,"

"Be careful, if this is his first time." Kale handed him a full one. "Don't want him hungover flying our ship tomorrow." With a laugh and a wink, Kale served another customer. Octav pointed Hadi to an empty table, about to follow him away until Kale returned.

Kale placed his hand on the counter, croex flickering alongside the sharp metallic edge. "I hoped you might come back sooner."

Octav was confused. "Why?"

"How is Chace?"

"Chace?"

"He's not answering any of my comms."

Octav looked him in the eye. "Hanya mentioned you'd had an altercation."

"I want him back, Ainoren."

"That's his choice to make," and with that, Octav followed Hadi. Taking up a seat, he poured himself a large glass wondering why Kale's wanting Chace back suddenly found a hole in the pit of his stomach.

Taking a seat, Octav shared out another glass for them both.

"I like this," Hadi said, taking a deep sniff before he knocked his second back. "First time I've really relaxed in weeks."

"Good, maybe we'll both sleep after a few." Although Sheve wasn't so sure, sleep for everyone a distant memory.

A beautiful, half-dressed Aonise female sauntered their way wearing their traditional one-sleeved satin gown, although much shorter than she should have. She smiled at Octav. "Nice of you to join us, Ainoren. Will there be any entertainment for you two tonight?"

She leaned in over Octav, her ample bosoms almost swallowing him. Captain Hadi watched with his glass halted halfway to his opened lips.

"No, thank you, Nadia. We're just here relaxing."

Hadi continued his stare as Nadia slid away, swaying her luscious behind. "You know her?"

"Not in that way." Octav shook his head. "She tries that every time I come in."

"Every time? You're really not tempted? She's the most beautiful woman I've ever seen."

"No." Placing the bottle before Hadi, Octav shook his head. "She's a paid woman. Sheve, think of Brie. Nadia's probably serviced half the men in this room tonight."

Hadi nodded. Around the room, other Aonise men called, leering at Nadia's sashaying behind as she passed. "Still, wow."

"She's also enhanced, not natural. I prefer natural."

Hadi took one last look. "Of course." He finished off his drink.

"Last one." Octav doled out another. "How are you feeling?"

"Actually…" Hadi yawned. "I'm getting tired."

"Good." Downing his drink, Octav stood. "Me, too. Shall we leave?"

"I like it in here." Captain Hadi took one more look around. "It's relaxing. Almost normal."

"That was the idea. I think they went for recreating a little bit of home."

"I agree. We all miss it."

Captain Hadi slipped back into his bedspace, curling around Katya. The booze indeed making him sleepy, within moments he snored beside her.

A few hours later, Katya shook him awake.

"What's wrong?"

"Kendro's on comms. He needs you."

"Right now?" Hadi glanced at the clock. Six bells.

"Sorry, he's waiting."

Hadi pushed the covers back, leaning in to kiss her.

"You smell!" Brie recoiled.

"Octav took me out. We had a few drinks."

"Powerful stuff." Katya grinned. "I'll see to your breakfast."

Hadi grabbed his uniform, dressing in the living room. He checked once in a mirror before leaving. His eyes had black bags underneath them, his birthmark paled. "Ughhh," he moaned.

Making his way to his office, Hadi met Kendro on the way.

"Sorry about getting you out of bed." Kendro motioned for them to continue. "I've something you must see."

"Interesting, must be very important."

"I'll show you in your office," said Kendro. "I'll want you to keep this between us for now."

Captain Hadi pointed. "Take a seat, Sire."

Kendro, however, didn't. He went straight to Hadi's computer. "This is what I've been looking at." He pulled an image of their current star

195

system. To the far right of their location, he'd drawn a red circle.

"What is this?"

"This is our destination. This is where the planet Earth is."

"You're sure?" Hadi's birthmark lit the room.

Kendro smiled, placing a hand on Hadi's arm. "I'm sure."

"You've calculated how long it'll take? To get there?"

"Figures are in, at current speeds…" Kendro hesitated, taking a breath. "Three years."

"I sense a *but…*"

"Yes. There is one of those, I'm afraid."

Captain Hadi sat, staring at the image, their new home.

"We don't have the supplies." He let out a long sigh. "We're not going to last. The sums don't add up."

Hadi knew this. He'd watched their supplies dwindling on all four ships when they still had that many. He had to be blunt. Someone had to speak the unspeakable. "I think you should bring Octav into this discussion."

"Really, why?" Hadi saw the twinkle in his King's eye. "What's he planning, Sheve?"

"Apart from worrying over you." Hadi knew the King wouldn't like it, but did they have a choice? "He's working with Lace to prepare for a jayux, Sire."

"A jayux? That's crazy. Or he is. Who would pilot it? It's not like a tricu, you know?"

"I know. It could be our only chance, if the planet Earth is too far away."

To Hadi's surprise, Kendro's birthmark remained calm. How he wished he'd the control Kendro showed, studying the image. "How far could a jayux take us?"

"Depends on the energy used." Hadi didn't want to risk a disappointment now. "It could knock months, perhaps years off."

"I'll think about it. Get me all the facts. Does Gaal know about this?"

"No, just the Ainoren and I. We've kept it between us. The repair teams have kept going."

"How much longer will it take before the *Sol'Delka* can move?"

"She can move slowly for now. At least some movement will give everyone hope."

"Then we'll get underway later today. I no longer want us in this part of the galaxy. The space junk left from the fight gives me the creeps at night."

Hadi laughed. "You aren't scared of ghosts, are you?"

"No, I feel more than haunted. I can't explain. Sorry."

"I'll organize things. We'll get the engines going at midday."

Kendro stood. "I'll see Octav later, no doubt. I'll inform him of my decision."

Hadi watched as Kendro, head held high, yet shoulders slumped, left his office. Hadi touched the small circle where the planet Earth lay. "I hope it won't take years."

NEW BEGINNINGS

A KNOCK AT HIS OFFICE door roused Sheve. Katya stood, wagging her finger. "You missed breakfast, sleepy head."

"Did I?" Sheve stretched out, cracking his neck. Not the best place to fall asleep. "What time is it?"

"Just after nine." She stepped in, placing a tray before him. "Food service with a smile."

"Thanks, I'm starving." He smiled at her, yet wondered what he'd done to deserve such a treat. He never had food in his office, terrified of spilling it over his desk.

Katya poured them both a hot drink, stirring sweetened myacin in.

"Have you eaten?" asked Sheve, tucking in as she sat on the edge of the table, watching.

"Actually," she folded her arms. "I've something that I've held off telling you."

She never crosses her arms. Sheve put his spoon down, sudden panic. *Unless?* "What is it?"

"I'm…" Katya frowned, placing a hand on her stomach. "I'm pregnant."

"How? Wh…?" he lightly touched her leg, wanting nothing more than to shout out over the comms.

"You know how." Her eyes sparkled at him, but he saw something else, too. "When, I'm not sure. I'm in the early days, but I couldn't *not* tell you."

Sheve saw his wife's fear now, deep lines creasing her brow, their happiness short lived. He remembered. Alexa. And her brave sacrifice helping the King's son survive. "Will the drugs have kicked in?" His stomach knotting with terror, could they lose another? "Will the baby be safe?"

"The drugs are working." Katya's face softened, leaning into kiss him. "The baby will be all right."

Sheer joy erupted from within him. "Really?" Only when she confirmed with a nod, did he pull her closer, holding on tight. "You're going to take it easy. No running about now. At least, until we get the first Maicrox out of the way."

"I'll take it easy. I promise."

Kendro entered Taliri's secret room, finding Mika working with Taliri on a comm's console. "You're showing him 3D matrox?"

Mika glanced up. "Actually, he's showing me." Kendro watched Taliri use their numerical system to add together a complex mathematics equation. His son learned fast.

"How are things?" Her gaze lingered.

"Not good." Kendro sat on their divano, sinking with the soft cushions. Pain throbbing through his forehead, he let a finger trail down the side of it, his energy easing it away. Wishing he could relax for just a moment, but it was impossible.

Mika glanced to their son as he finished the equation. "Correct." A computer generated voice said, and he moved onto the next problem. "They will get better," she said. "You'll see to that."

"I can't believe how he's growing." Kendro stared at Taliri, his birthmark flickering with pride. "Every time I see him, he's so much bigger."

"Brie says he's the equivalent of four cycles old, yes." Mika's face pleaded. "Kendro, he's eight weeks old. This growth is a tremendous strain on him. His birthmark's changing beyond anything I've seen before. He gets angry so easily."

Frustration? Kendro knew why. He noticed his wife's greying skin, sunken eyes. He knew Taliri's growth wasn't helping her either. "What can I do? How can I help?"

Taliri pushed himself up, toddling towards Kendro with outstretched arms. Kendro leaned, picking him up.

Mika sat up. "I don't think there is anything. I'm feeding him eleven times a day. Day and night."

"The croex you're both using must be replaced. You should ask Brie about borrowing the Nasci again."

Taliri reached up for Kendro's face, running a finger down his birthmark. It shimmered and glowed, lighting the room in a wonderful blue haze.

"Father." Taliri giggled. "Strong."

Kendro took a sideways glance, and then looked to Mika. "Did you hear that?"

"He called you Father." Her birthmark flickered. They both felt the shared pride.

"Yes, he did." Kendro took hold of Taliri's hand. "Clever boy."

Taliri's dark button eyes stared at Kendro. So much wonder there in those depths. In the end, the King asked his offspring, "What is it, Son?"

"Jayux soon, Father?"

"He needs feeding again." Mika stood, plucking Taliri from Kendro. "He doesn't make any sense when he's hungry."

But he did make sense. Kendro rose, brushing his trrobhas. "Yes, of course." Taliri knew they were planning a jayux. How?

Leaving the secret room, his thoughts swirled. Did Taliri know of The Lady Katesh? The battles and their damaged ship? Of Dalamaar, as well? Kendro commed immediately for Octav.

"Ainoren," Octav answered.

"Where are you?" Kendro knew now the jayux must be quicker, evident from his son's apt choice of words. 'Jayux soon, Father.'

"With Lady Katesh in the gardens."

"I'll come meet you," he said, signing off.

The Ainoren sat with Lady Katesh on a park bench in the gardens. She'd required more time from Kendro, but he'd delegated to a reluctant Octav instead. After hearing the concern in Kendro's voice, Octav squirmed even more at The Lady's questions. Her being locked away for 2000 years made Octav's life complicated—her need to know everything, right now. Was she a threat to them, the throne?

Octav was surprised at how quick Lady Katesh picked up their changes in language, now only using her reader's translation device sporadically, as she enjoyed filling Octav in on his own Aonise history. He feigned interest, his mind puzzling over Kendro's comm.

Octav caught the eye of a jogger. As he drew closer, he realised it was Chace. He wanted to run himself, missing morning practice as he escorted their special guest.

Chace drew to a stop before them, sweat drenching his shirt, showing each hard muscle beneath. He glanced down where Lady Katesh's hand had settled on Octav's leg. "Good to see you, Lady Katesh." Octav noted the playful tone coming from his elite pilot.

Lady Katesh regarded Chace's attire, scowling. "Thank you."

"Do we have time for a meeting later?" Chace held Octav's gaze. "There are some things we need to discuss."

"Yes, I'll let you know when," Octav replied, dismissing him with a wave.

Chace saluted, "Ainoren," acknowledging The Lady once before jogging on.

Octav felt surprised. The Lady Katesh moved in closer, heat from her breath tickling the side of his face. "Have you known Chace long?"

"Most of his life," Octav replied.

"Seems a nice young man." Her hand lazily caressed his thigh.

Octav couldn't work out what she wanted—him or the protection his rank could provide. But as Kendro walked towards them, Octav remembered how Kendro had demanded that he keep her close, and he pondered how frustrating it must be for a powerful woman to be so unclear in the way the world worked.

"Do you mind if I interrupt?" Kendro asked.

Lady Katesh stood, lowering her head before backing away. "I'll catch you again another time, Ainoren." She sauntered away, glancing back, confirming the pair still stood watching her. Octav could only think of Nadia from the bar.

"Be careful around her," Kendro warned as he sat.

"I can handle myself." Octav smiled. "Seen many a vixen before, you know. They think they seduce me, but they don't. I know such tactics."

Kendro laughed. "So you were playing with her, not the other way around?"

"Would you expect anything less of me?"

"No." Kendro sighed. "However, there is one thing bothering me at the moment."

Octav should have known. "You know about the plans for the jayux?" He couldn't keep anything from the King. "I didn't think it would be long before someone spilt the story."

"They're concerned with good reason. Something happened today, something I can't ignore."

"A vision?" Octav faced Kendro, watching his King's birthmark flicker with emotion. *Was he scared?*

"Taliri spoke today. Directly to me."

"You're joking."

"No. He said, 'jayux soon.'"

Octav felt his own croex rising to the surface. Kendro's need was evident as his mark continued flickering.

Kendro held his gaze. "We must move as quickly as we can."

"I don't think our teams can work any faster."

How to put this in a good way? Kendro struggled. "I've never known a child who's developed as he has. The visions we receive as children are much more focussed. We must listen to him."

"I'm worried for him and for us." Octav felt how special Taliri was, their connection through his Routui, very different from his connection to Kendro. "Perhaps we need to see the *Sol'Delka* for ourselves, check everything personally. It would boost moral, also."

"Then we'll take a trip out there," said Kendro. "Could you organize it?"

"Of course." Octav agreed. "I'll contact Captain Gaal. First thing tomorrow?"

Kendro agreed, standing. Octav watched, disheartened, as he walked away. The normal, strong, head held high posture his King held, was not there any more. Kendro's shoulders slumped, his gait lopsided.

Octav sat for a while, watching people pass. Eventually, he noticed Chace stretching, cooling down. He decided to head over. Perhaps a chat with his friend was just what he needed.

Chace saw him and paused his stretching. He grabbed a towel, wiping sweat from his brow. "Lady Katesh gone?"

"Yes, gone for a rest." Octav let out a sigh. "Thankfully." *I can rest now, too.*

"Kendro didn't need you for long either." Chace winked. "Ainoren."

"No one else is around." Octav grinned. "No need for formalities."

"Lady Katesh's taken quite a shine to you, hasn't she?" Chace dropped the towel, removing his shirt. He resumed drying himself, his back to the Ainoren. Octav saw him flinch. *Pain?*

"You went by the med bay this morning. Everything all right?" Octav watched the birthmark on Chace's back ripple as he threw on a clean shirt. Suddenly shy?

"Broke out in a rash, that's all." He met Octav's concerned stare. "Vawn gave me some cream, said I'll be fine."

Octav's stomach fluttered, showing him he wasn't so sure. But he backed away. "Good. I've got you tagged on a flight for the *Sol'Delka* first thing."

Kendro and Octav stepped onto shuttle bay two, the others who'd be disembarking for the *Sol'Delka* had arrived minutes ahead. "Chace will pilot," Octav informed the King.

Officers manning the control booth as they passed by greeted all with stern salutes. "Lady Katesh seems interested in meeting with House Sonaya," Octav continued. "Although I'm not sure about Emmi's sudden concern for our visit."

Moments later, the guest in question arrived at their departure zone. "Lady Katesh," Kendro said, approaching the position where his crew waited for him.

"I am honoured to accompany you on this mission." With respect, she bowed her head.

"I think it will be good for everyone. Shall we leave?" Kendro motioned to Chace.

"Yes, Your Highness."

They stepped into the shuttle. Octav checked that Kendro and Lady Katesh were secured before fastening himself in. He nodded to Chace allowing him to manoeuvre the shuttle out of the bay.

Lady Katesh stared out the view-window. "I've never seen anything like it before. I wish I'd seen space much sooner."

"It has an unreal quality—dark, beautiful." Kendro then whispered, "Personally, though, I must admit, I much prefer my feet on solid ground."

Octav shifted in his seat to face them, confiding, "I like both. Space is fantastic. So much exploring, places to see. Other planets, other species. Though I do like solid ground, too."

Kendro and Lady Katesh spoke other pleasantries during the short flight while they continued to enjoy the view. Chace brought the shuttle closer to Captain Gaal's ship.

From a distance, the external damage was obvious. Holes gaped into space with only the ship's shields protecting engineers and citizens alike. The engineers worked like ants, repairing the structure as fast as possible.

"I hadn't realised she was so badly damaged," Lady Katesh remarked. "Can she be repaired?"

"We're doing everything we can," said Octav.

As they drew closer, Octav noted their engineer's progress with a grim eye, knowing they were several weeks off finishing, despite all best efforts. Oh, he'd keep it to himself in front of The Lady, but Octav didn't think there'd be any jayuxing soon. Not as things stood. A try now and all the *Sol'Delka*'s people would be at serious risk.

Chace nosed the shuttle closer, easing it down to her landing bay.

A voice came over the comms. "Shuttle One, you are clear to board."

Chace's gloved hand used the controls deftly. "Taking her in."

The shuttle lurched. Octav glanced at Chace, sweat dripping from Chace's nose onto the console. "What's wrong?"

Chace doubled over clutching his stomach. "Take over!"

Octav took the second controls, sliding a hand into a glove, as they careened off the side of the shuttle bay. Metal on metal screeched. *The hull will hold!* They bounced through the ship's hanger doors with much less grace than Octav liked, but they didn't break apart.

Watching the screens for instructions, a new landing angle popped up. Octav knew they wouldn't make it, they were moving too fast. Quickly, he cut all power to their engines, locking them in reverse, but straightening their trajectory.

Waves of sweat dripped off Chace's back. He crammed a hand over his mouth, stifling a scream, falling from his seat. Octav didn't need the distraction—he fumbled one degree, missing their safe spot again. *Puswer!*

Lady Katesh unbuckled herself, springing to Chace's aid. Kendro helped. Together, the pair slid him away from the console. As Octav, bucking and overcorrecting, did all he could for a bumpy landing.

Katesh felt Chace's forehead. "Feverish!"

Octav eased the shuttle to a juddering—halt. No major damage. Just bumps and scrapes. *Thank Ari.*

"Something I ate," Chace moaned.

"Ainoren?" a voice came back. Dread in the single word.

Octav clicked the comms. "Send a medic."

Octav stood, releasing the hatch doors, sidestepping where Chace lay. Initial thoughts on Chace's wellbeing overtaken by the need to get his King out safe. They'd all been rather shaken with that landing. With a click and a hiss, they pressurized to match the *Sol'Delka*'s atmo as the door slid open.

Captain Gaal and Emmi, House Leader of the Sonaya's, met them. Octav bowing his head out of respect for her, then saluted the Captain, who responded likewise.

"Your pilot is sick?" Emmi's birthmark flickered. "Was he sick when he boarded?"

"No," Octav lied. "It came on sudden."

The back bay doors opened, three men rushing in wearing hospital uniforms. One approached their position, while the others held back. "Pleased to see you once again, Ainoren." The young man smiled, holding out a hand. Octav wanted nothing more than to slap the grin from his face as he remembered who he was. "I'm Doctor Jaack, if you recall."

Octav almost wished he didn't. As Kendro and Lady Katesh exited the shuttle, Octav shook the doctor's hand. "Of course, I remember. Chace is inside. Hurry!"

"Hello, Chace." Jaack quickly felt Chace's forehead. "I'm the Senior Doctor here."

"Nice to meet you, Doc." Chace groaned.

Jaack dipped into his bag, removing a small bracelet device. He locked it onto Chace's wrist. "When did you start feeling bad?"

"About twenty minutes ago."

"Where is the pain?"

"My stomach—chest. Feels like someone hit me with a lance."

The device beeped, spinning and whirring as it read. The doctor watched as it scanned Chace's vitals.

"Let's see what…" Jaack said, looking over a palm-sized pad. Reading the results, eyes narrowing.

Concern? Just tell me! Octav thought.

When Jaack finally looked to Octav, he said, "We can treat him. That's the good news. The bad news is that he's been severely poisoned." He addressed Chace, "Anything you ate that was different?"

"No, nothing. Normal ships rations."

Octav placed a hand on Chace's shoulder. As the Ainoren stared at the doctor, it hit. Realising the truth, he told them both, "You looked after me in the bar—after Lyrik passed. We ordered different foods. I didn't want mine. We swapped, remember?" And then, Octav gasped. "The poison wasn't meant for him."

Jaack located an infusion guin. "Wheels within wheels. This is serious." Jaack's eyes locked with Octav's. He sighed, loading the fastest anti-bio he had into the guin. "You saved the Ainoren's life."

He moved the guin towards Chace's neck, injecting right into the vein. "You must inform the King," he advised Octav. Assuring Chace, "This will ease the pain. We'll get you off the ship to the infirmary. I'll need something more specific to fight the poison, though. You're very lucky your blood group is different than Octav's is. If he's right, if it was a specifically designed to kill him—luckily, in your body it didn't function the same. You've just been poisoned, slowly, but thoroughly."

"It would've killed me?" Octav helped Chace to stand, supporting his weight.

"Most definitely, and within days. As it was, it was a slow poisoning for Chace." Jaack turned, calling the other medics to him.

With Doctor Jaack out of range, Octav whispered. "This was weeks ago. Why didn't you tell me?"

"I thought it was a rash, something simple after the planet Earth sickness. Vawn said it would clear."

"You should have gone to Brie. She's—"

"Don't be angry," Chace's knees buckled as he interrupted.

Octav felt the heat that was emanating from Chace's skin. These assassination attempts needed to stop. "Not mad, concerned. You're my friend and top officer." Stepping off the shuttle, two Aonise nurses stood with a reswae. *This has to be Dalamaar.*

"I'm coming with you." Octav held one side of the reswae as Chace climbed on.

Chace pushed Octav's hand away. "You need to help Kendro sort out the repairs. I'll be fine. However, when we get back to our ship, I will find who did this, and they'll pay."

"I'll take the greatest care with him," said Doctor Jaack.

"Make sure you do," Octav replied. "I'll come check soon. Anything changes—comm me direct." Octav took the Doctor's device, keying in his personal code. Doctor Jaack, the reader in hand, motioning for the nurses, began pushing Chace away.

Octav turned to one of the remaining officers. Noting his ranking bars, he asked, "You are?"

"Commander Sard." He saluted. "Captain Gaal's assigned me, when your party split." He motioned to the retreating reswae, nurses, and Doctor. "I can take you to the Captain now, if you'd like."

Octav thought for a brief moment. "No, take me to see the head of the Heiako here."

"What?" The young officer spat a curse. A hand quickly covered his mouth. "I'm sorry, Ainoren."

"Do you know who the Heiako leader here is?" Octav already knew the answer.

"I don't, I'm sorry."

"Then take me to one of the Heiako bays. I'll find who I need to see."

"Just like that? You expect them to allow you into their inner Scrie."

"I don't expect anything. However, I do have something you obviously don't."

Sard frowned. "And that is?"

"Respect." Octav laughed. "Now, please take me, or do I find it myself? Either way, I don't mind."

The officer stood back. "I can't let you out of my sight." He pointed to the door stiffly.

"Well, then let's go, I don't have all day." Octav set off at a great pace.

The commander followed, almost falling over his own feet. "Our ships were identical, but we've changed a few things."

"How do you mean?" Octav felt a sudden unease twinge inside his stomach. "You've changed what?"

"Well, Captain Gaal isn't as easy-going on the Heiako as Kendro is. I'm not sure you're going to like seeing what you'll see."

Octav stopped, palm to a control panel. *What fresh hell is this?* "You'd better fill me in before I see it. Don't lie, or it'll be an unpleasant experience for you."

Commander Sard gulped, his birthmark flickered pale teal. "I—I don't know where to start."

"At the beginning is as good a place as any."

"We've not been abl—getting food and medical supplies, ah—to the King's specifications—delivered as fast as you'd expect. I know this without seeing it," Sard temporalized. "Reports come in daily. I do my best in acting on them. Look, there are lots of people suffering down here."

"Your best. Why are you responsible for it?"

"I was assigned. A—after the battle with the Zefron," Sard replied.

"You're an officer of this ship. There were other orders issued for you. Why weren't you given them?"

"I—I don't kn—ow," Sard stuttered. "I'm sorry, Ainoren."

Octav stared at the young man before him. His eyes spoke the truth. "I'm an Ainoren second, Commander. First, foremost, I am loyal to my King. Where does your loyalty lie?"

"To my King." Commander Sard didn't hesitate answering. "Ainoren."

"Good." Sard's loyalties were true. "Then we'll sort out what is the truth in your report to Kendro. What we discover or hear does not resonate back to Gaal. Understand?"

"Of course." He tugged at his uniform, nervous.

Octav walked towards a lift, pushing for the front Heiako bays.

The commander stopped him. "We've shifted—um, things, you'll need to—" he explained, red-faced, "—towards the back of the ship. These bays here have been used for storage."

"Storage of what?" Octav palmed for access as the lift came to a stop. "I'm not privy to that information, Sir."

Octav pushed for the Heiako bays. "Well, I guess we'll start there."

"W—e won't have access."

Octav stepped into the lift raising an eyebrow. "Yes, we will." He held his left palm up. "See this?" Octav's intricate birthmark snaked and twirled around his fingers. Harnessing his croex, the mark came alive with sparks of green light. "This will get me anywhere."

"Yes, Sir," said Commander Sard stepping onto the lift.

Emmi sat primly, uneasily waiting for her King to take a seat.

"I can only apologise for the way we landed, Emmi. Unexpected illness." Kendro started, pacing near her.

They'd retired to a specially prepared meeting room. The flicker of Emmi's mark glistened off the walls, a radiant grass green. "You can't help your pilot becoming sick," Emmi replied, smoothing her dress beneath her. "I've asked to be kept informed, but I'm sure Doctor Jaack will help him." Her traditional white and green gown shivered along with her nerves, but even the most basic breathing technique wasn't helping. "Is Lady Katesh all right?"

"She's resting, she'll be fine."

Kendro had taken a seat next to Emmi, watching as her hands shook. "I can turn up the heat, if you require."

Emmi forced herself... *Breathe!* But, she continued shaking. "I'm fine, Your Highness, thank you."

Kendro about to reach for the jug of grail, Emmi stood. "Allow me." She poured them both steaming cups, while Kendro watched every move. *Please stop staring,* she pleaded within. She knew her nerves were obvious to see.

"I would insist you come back to the *Sol'Ishar* with me, but you'd decline." Kendro locked eyes with her. Emmi thought there was a hint of a smile.

She stirred her cup, her birthmark lighting the room around them, but still, she couldn't meet her King's gaze. "Yes, Your Highness." Emmi's shaking hand was now more evident, as her cup rattled.

"You have good enough reasons to stay."

Emmi needed to be honest with him, but didn't know where to start. Kendro's stare all the more evident now, he told her, "Octav informed me. I trust him. However, insubordination like this, I will not allow."

Would he believe her if she told him everything? She met Kendro's gaze. "I'm sorry, Your Highness." She fought back tears.

Am I that scary? Emmi heard his thought as though he'd spoken aloud. She steadied her cup with the other hand. Kendro told her, "I have much that need sharing with you, Emmi, but now isn't the time. You do understand that?"

"Yes, Your Highness."

He reached out. "We are alone," he said, taking the cup from her, "please, Emmi, call me Kendro."

"I have my reasons for being here," Emmi felt a little more at ease. Her hands stopped shaking. "As soon as I am free, I will join you on the *Sol'Ishar*."

"Thank you. Octav informed me you were having some trouble with the binding."

He didn't, he promised! Emmi lowered her head, her stomach knotting. "Yes."

"Why didn't you let me know sooner?"

"You had enough to worry over, Your... High—Kendro."

This time, Kendro actually took hold of her hand in his, she recoiled, but Kendro held tight. "I apologise for not being as alert as I should be." He allowed his croex to flow through into her. "I should have known you were struggling."

"It's all rig—"

"No, it isn't." He linked his fingers into hers. Their birthmarks seemingly entwined. Emmi watched as their colours mixed. Shades of green and blue as she'd never seen before, but she did not want the interaction.

"If I am not in tune with each House correctly," Kendro said, "then there could be disastrous consequences for all of us."

"Thank you." Emmi stopped struggling against him, allowing his croex across their bond. "It's been painful ever since the ceremony. It's supposed to stop, isn't it?"

"Yes. But you're the youngest House Leader in an age. I wasn't sure how it would take. Or if you'd even survive."

"If there was no pain," she tapped the side of her head, "it would be fine."

Kendro held his free hand for her. "If you'll allow me."

"But what about?"

"I'm your King, Emmi."

Emmi obliged, holding out her free hand, hoping that he wouldn't see or hear things meant to keep him safe. "I'm sorry if it hurts," she said.

Kendro's birthmark paled, as their connection became a full scrie, his eyes glazing over. "I see what's wrong." He pulled back from her.

"What is it? What do you see?"

"Something I think we need to talk over wi—" Lady Katesh knocked as Kendro finished off. "—th the good Lady Katesh."

TREASON

THE LIFT OPENED AS TWO Aonise soldiers whirled, greeting Octav and Sard in the corridor with weapons drawn. Octav reacted immediately, throwing up a shield. Sard jumped sideways as one blast aimed to take his head off.

First Chace, then Jaack. Now these malloths. Octav harnessed his croex from deep within. He hurled their weapons from their grips with a flick of a hand.

"Ainoren, forgive me." One man looked to the other first, and then, gave a halfhearted salute.

With the corridor ablaze in green fire, Octav pulled back his croex. "And you are?"

"Petty Officer Benz, Sir. This is Greer."

"I'm here to survey these bays, which apparently are full of cargo, not people."

Officer Benz glanced nervously to Greer. "You don't have authorisation, Sir."

"Insolent—" Octav reacted instinctively, grabbing Benz by the throat. Greer backed. "Don't have authorisation? You're standing in designated citizen quarters. It was not meant for cargo. I've a good mind to jettison you, and it, without inspection."

"You can't, Sir." Greer risked saying. "We don't have access."

Octav felt Benz stiffen, struggling under his grasp, the air inside his lungs used. "You need specific codes to get in!"

Letting go of Benz, Octav laughed as Benz gasped for air. *Pathetic malloth!*

Octav surveyed this door they stood guarding. "Specific codes, huh? I'll show you a code." From deep within himself, Octav called forth his croex, excitement building at the idea of demolishing something.

Commander Sard stepped back, his tiny birthmark shimmered yellow the once.

Fully charged, Octav pressed his hand against the door panel. With a sharp blast of light, the controls blew apart. The door opened.

To the two officers, Octav growled, saying, "I'll make my decision whether to dump it into space once I've seen it. If you even think of contacting Captain Gaal, I'll flush you out with the cargo. Got it?"

Both lower-ranked officers turned away. "Yes, Ainoren," they replied in unison.

Octav glared at Sard, then at his men. "Commander, care to see what is so important to your Captain?"

"Yes. Yes, I do." Sard stepped through the door with Octav. The two officers equally curious followed, Benz rubbing at his neck.

"Ainoren," Officer Greer said, "it will've triggered an alarm. If Captain Gaal contacts us, what do we say?"

"There's a malfunction, everything's normal."

"Right." Officer Benz watched, frightened, in awe as they moved further into the bay.

"How has Captain Gaal been treating the refugees?" Octav walked in-between two giant crates, running a hand down the side of one, feeling for a weakness in its design.

Commander Sard sidestepped beside him, "Honestly?" Sard checked the others crates first before speaking. "Negatively. He didn't want any more Aonise to house, or feed."

Octav found a spot, feeling the metallic structure move with the pressure from his croex. "I wonder why?" Exerting minimal croex output in comparison to blasting the door controls, Octav pried open the lid of the crate, waving a hand over the contents. "It seems he has more than an abundance of food."

Commander Sard stared at the sacks of dried bale rice and oatisan, and then turned to the guards. "I had no idea extra food stores were on board."

"I don't think anyone knows," Octav said, digging his hands inside the crate. "Bar maybe House Sonaya. They intended to keep this stock for themselves."

"Immoral," Sard kicked the crate, face turning red. "How could they hold out? When our people are in such great need?"

"That, Captain Gaal will be answering for himself. I don't believe all the—" he waved at the other crates, "are full of food. Let's check some more."

By the time Octav and Sard had opened up several more crates, Officer Benz returned looking for them. "Captain Gaal didn't believe me when I said everything was all right. He's sending someone to check." Benz stared at the contents of one of the crates. "What the Ari is all this?"

"Exactly," Octav replied. "I must have a chat with Captain Gaal."

There was more amiss somewhere, Octav knew it. He passed Officer Benz as he moved away from the crate. "Can you two watch this? Or do I need to leave Commander Sard?"

"No. We'll be fine." Benz nodded at the other officer. "Won't we, Greer?"

"Ainoren," Greer oogled all the abundance lying before him. "May we distribute some of this? It would make a huge difference, especially with the families on the lower decks."

Octav stepped away from the crate he'd been examining. "Not a problem. In fact, I think that's a good idea. I must insist though whoever takes the food also takes some down for the Heiako bays."

Looking to Benz and the co-officer, Sard nodded. "I'll make sure we do that."

"I'll return, see how things stand in a few hours." To Commander Sard, Octav added, "Do you want to be present when I deal with your Captain?"

"Yes." Sard's birthmark shimmered. "I want answers for these questions myself."

Octav walked out of the treasure-room with Commander Sard in tow.

Emmi didn't know where to look as Lady Katesh took a seat beside her. Emmi poured some tea for The Lady; her mind on all Kendro had just spilled.

"Smells wonderful." Lady Katesh took her tea. "Apologies for needing to rest. I'm not as used to space travel as you." Lady Katesh smiled at Kendro. "I feel much better. Thank you."

Emmi's confusion reflected in her shimmering birthmark—all she had talked about with Kendro, and now, this new wrinkle in their lives.

Kendro stood, having a glimpse into both women's thoughts. Cryptically, he bowed to Emmi, and said, "I have seen a truth here. I will visit Chace while you two talk."

Emmi watched The Lady's face as the King left. *What was this one thinking?* Lady Katesh sat quietly beside her, taking a hand in hers. Emmi felt the warmth from her skin, but nothing more. The coolness of her visitor caused her to withdraw her attempted link. "I don't understand," Emmi said.

The Lady let out a sigh. "Please. Call me Verona. You were supposed to guard the Powex, were you not? Do you realize my companion suffered for the lax awakening?"

Emmi gasped, ripping her hand from Lady Katesh, to cover her mouth. The truth hit home. *She's here, now!* "How? When?" she managed to blurt.

"Octav and Captain Hadi discovered my capsule… in the wreckage of the *Sol'Tar*, they brought me aboard. You did not know?" her voice wavered, unsure.

"I had men from my own ship out searching straight away, but we feared the Powex lost."

"I am safe. Kendro awakened me properly. But that wasn't the case for my mate, Troj."

Emmi knew the truth, but also knew how much this truth would hurt Lady Katesh. Alas, she needed to know. "Many years ago, your Powex was stolen from my ancestors. The lore for over forty generations back is that someone had tried to open it. They believed this, in any case. No one knows if myth was mixed with truth from so long ago."

Emmi glanced to the door, knowing Kendro had left so she could break this news to her. *Why, though?* Emmi would have liked his support. "I'm so sorry."

Tears brimmed over Lady Katesh's cheeks. "Troj is in stasis, until we reach this next place, this—planet Earth. There, I would like a traditional burial for him."

"Of course." Emmi paused. Her mind whirled. So many questions, where to start? "I…"

"Kendro was right. You do need the truth of our past."

Emmi tried to focus, but struggled. *Must this go on now?* "What is the truth?"

"You've felt different from all other Aonise, haven't you?"

She had felt different. Emmi saw something more beneath The Lady's simple question, but found it hard to admit to this relative stranger. She took in a deep breath. Feeling herself shiver, nervous, scared, the green flicker of her birthmark struck the bare walls of the room. "Y—yes."

Taking a risk, The Lady gestured for Emmi's hand once more. Emmi hesitated, smoothing her dress beneath her once more.

Plucking up the courage to take The Lady's offered hand, Katesh held one of Emmi's fingers to her own brow. She lightly traced the pale green birthmark along her own face. *What's this?* Emmi felt the bumps and lumps from the mark. What Emmi saw to be real was obviously not. *How can this be? She's a fake! I've risked all for this?*

"Emmi, I have different DNA from normal Aonise. I have no 'mark.' I'm your original ancestor."

213

"You're not—I'm not Aonise?" Again, Emmi pulled her hand away.

"Troj, yes, he was full-blooded Aonise," The Lady assured. "You're bloodline now is more Aonise than it isn't, but you do still have some of my DNA. Kendro now understands what that meant, and still means, for you as a House Leader."

Perspiration ran in delicate rivulets down the centre of Emmi's chest. "What?"

"A full binding to your people would never be normal for you."

Emmi pushed her chair back. "I knew this." She began pacing the room. "I just didn't know why. Are you both sure? Why didn't he stay? What does it mean for me? For my House?"

Lady Katesh's shoulders slumped. She ignored most of the questions that were tumbling from the House Leader. "Pain. Yes, there will be that. The rest, only time will tell. Did your mother never speak of it?"

Emmi's croex rushed to the surface. She needed release for her anger. But in the confines of this room, it was impossible. The green of her birthmark grew even paler. "My mother and father were killed. Several years back. I'd only been to First School."

"I'm sorry for that. It should have been your mother's job to inform you of your lineage."

"The Heiako?" Emmi faced The Lady Katesh, seeing such pain in her eyes just before she looked away. *Yes. So much pain for both of us now.*

"There have been a lot of changes in the last two thousand years. And the Heiako are my doing. Dilution of the Aonise gene pool."

Emmi couldn't meet her gaze. This could be the undoing of all Aonise!

Octav's fists clenched, struggling with his anger as he and Commander Sard entered the bridge. This wasn't going to be easy to broach this in front of Captain Gaal, who he'd found speaking with Kendro, Lady Katesh, and Emmi. The need to pulverise the *Sol'Delka*'s Captain was very strong. *Traitor.* Yet, so many would hear the angry words Octav had. *I can't.*

"Ainoren." Gaal smiled at him. "How is Chace?"

"I don't know." Octav held the Captain's gaze, feeling his own croex rising to the surface. *Control.* "I haven't been able to visit him. We need your office, Captain. Now." Octav's birthmark lit up the room. Concern crossed both Emmi and The Lady Katesh's faces. They shared a look, then backed a step away, knowing instinctively this might soon become physical.

Kendro raised an eyebrow towards Octav. "Is everything all right?"

"No," Octav spat. This would not stay hidden from their people!

Office be damned. "Ask Gaal why he's hiding and holding out on food stocks?"

Gaal's birthmark flushed as he took a step back from the Ainoren's charge. "You have no proof of such scurrilous accusations!" Raising a hand in protest, he told the King, "This is all lies."

"I don't believe it!" Science Officer Jenile gasped aloud.

Emmi's eyes widened at Jenile as she stared at Gaal. "He can't have?"

Kendro inserted himself before Octav and the flailing Captain. "What is this?" Kendro faced Gaal, demanding, "Holding out?"

Octav approached Science Officer Jenil's console, her red-face focused down at her console was no cover for her outburst. The entire bridge had heard. Almost pushing her aside, Octav quickly brought up several views of the forward bays. "Look for yourself! There's your proof." The camos showed the truth—food stocks being removed from their storage hold by several of Sard's men.

"What are they doing?" In three strides, Captain Gaal slammed his fist too close to officer Jenil's hand. She jumped back against her own will. "They have no right to move those cases." He turned to his Security Officer, barking, "Arrest them!"

Octav could take no more of this insubordination, blocking the path of the Head Security Officer. "You'll do no such thing." He glared at Captain Gaal, wanting to strike him now more than ever. "Those men have my permission to distribute those provisions."

"Preposterous! This is my ship!" Gaal's face had turned a mobien red. "It isn't theirs to take."

"Enough!" Like a hand, Kendro's blue croex shot forth pushing the shouting, barney Captain against the bulkhead. Silence fell. The astonishment on the crews' faces lit the room with varying coloured lights. "No food will be stored anywhere that isn't logged," Kendro thundered. "What else are you hiding?"

"Nothing—" Captain Gaal struggled for air, his head lowering against the next blow he feared was inevitable. "Your Highness, I didn't know," he begged. "I swear to you."

Kendro allowed Gaal to catch his breath, turning to Octav. "You may deal with him as you see fit. I will not look at him anymore."

Calmly, Octav ordered, "Sard." The Commander snapped automatically to attention. "You will see that all the food is logged today! What needs to be distributed will be. As of this moment, Captain Gaal is suspended from duty, pending investigation. You have command of the ship."

"Your Highness, please." Captain Gaal's birthmark flashed yellow. "You can't do this—" He turned to Emmi, begging, "—please!"

Face blank, Emmi lowered her head. Out of respect, she said, "I'll hear no more, Captain. Our Ainoren is entitled to take control of any ship."

"Ainoren! Please! Don't. I beg you." To the bridge at large, he implored, "You haven't heard my si—"

"I have plenty of time for learning all sides. Report to the holding cells, or must you be forcibly dragged there?"

Captain Gaal gave Emmi one last, pleading glance. But no one on the bridge would acknowledge him. Octav glared at Emmi, wondering. Did she know any of this?

Disgraced, Gaal's shoulders slumped, shaking his head. "I'll go of my own accord."

With a curt nod, Octav indicated dismissal. The Head of Security stepped up for the wretched task of removing his Captain from the bridge.

"Report to me if he doesn't cooperate in any way," Kendro ordered.

"Yes, Your Highness," he said, and saluted, escorting Captain Gaal out.

Kendro faced Emmi. "We'll meet in the boardroom again. In an hour?"

Lady Katesh sighed now that the drama was over. "Would you have somewhere Emmi and I could talk?" she asked.

"Yes. I'll take us somewhere." Emmi smiled, turning to the King.

"I'll learn what's happening on board this ship." Emmi could only nod as Kendro assured her, "I will know the whole truth."

Emmi lowered her head once more, an echo of her disgraced Captain's. "Of course, Your Highness." She turned, her birthmark fluttered as she also left.

"What is going on over here?" Kendro fumed, meeting Octav's stare. "I never saw this coming. Gaal? He's one of my finest."

Octav cast an eye around at the rest of Captain Gaal's crew. He had no idea who to trust anymore. That meant he would need to send Hanya or Veco over permanently to liaise with this crew.

Commander Sard spoke, "We'll get on top of it. There are loyal men here. None will be forgotten."

"Commander," Kendro asked, pointing to the camo where the crew busily shifted the liberated rations. "Can these men be trusted?"

"I've worked with them many times." Sard regarded all the men on the bridge as well. "I trust we all will do what is right."

Octav watched the crew nod in unison to Sard's words. "I'll expect them to bring you up to speed. When you have all the details, call me direct. We'll be visiting Chace in the infirmary. For now, the bridge is yours, Commander. Treat her well."

Commander Sard moved to the Captain's chair. Placing a hand on its back, he bowed his head, "Your Highness. I'll report within the hour, Sire."

Octav remained as Kendro also left the bridge. For a moment, his eyes fell to the Commander's insignia. He would need new bars. "I look forward to working with you."

"Thank you, Ainoren." Captain Sard beamed. "I'm honoured to work with you, too."

Octav saluted, as did the whole crew on the bridge. He smiled, certain Sard would make an excellent Captain. One day. "Emmi, of course, will formally promote you when the time comes. I'll let you get to work. Pressing matters require our attention."

"Yes, Ainoren."

DISCOVERY

OCTAV PAUSED ALONG A CORRIDOR, feeling turned about for a moment as he headed towards the infirmary. It took some tries until he found an undamaged lift with access to the lower decks.

He stepped out when it slowed, and slid open its doors. A woman appeared ahead who seemed not too busy. He would ask for directions to the right corridor. "Excuse me," Octav approached, feeling no need for caution. "Could you tell me where the infirmary is?"

Turning to Octav, her bright red eyes looked him up and down. "You're way off, hunny," she said, sauntering closer. Octav, again, noticed the one thing all women seemed eager to show him—a curvaceous sway to her supple frame.

Octav glanced over her in return, her birthmark small, yet in full view under her skimpy, transparent clothes. "That's why I am asking. Do you know where it is?"

"Of course." She fluttered eyelashes, birthmark flickering yellow. "I'll show you if you like, Ainoren. Anything you'd like, actually."

"You know who I am?" he asked. She hooked an arm in his, looking up through long lashes.

"Of course, my Ainoren, I've been waiting out here for ages. Captain Gaal sent me."

Ah. "Captain Gaal's no longer in charge of the ship."

Her eyes dulled. Her smile was now a bit less bright. At least she hadn't pushed him away hearing the news. "Never liked him much anyway."

"You're not an officer. Why would he send you to wait for me?" Octav asked. She dropped her hand now, and simply began circling him.

"Because, I have expert talent." Her eyes glowed yellow, stepping closer again. "Very special talents." She reached out, her croex touched with a sparking probe, no hesitant connection there.

Anticipating her, Octav stepped to one side. Taking hold of her arm, he snapped it roughly behind her back. "I don't take to being touched," he said in her ear. "What's the real reason he wanted you to seduce me?"

"You'll have to ask him," she hissed, in pain—he read that on her mark as it jumped light around the bulkhead. "See those?" With her free hand, she pointed up to a camo. "All I know is that it had to be here. Because of the camos."

"What else do you know?"

"Just what I was asked to do."

"Blackmail. I need to have words with Gaal." With one quick shove, Octav pushed past her. "Nice guy. I'll find the infirmary on my own."

"It's two blocks back." She slinked closer behind at his departing stride. "They moved it, so we could have the forward bay for housing."

Octav, shooing her away, not in the mood for this distraction, growled, "Don't follow me."

Some time later, Octav found the infirmary. It took a moment for him, but soon, he spotted Kendro and Lady Katesh at Chace's bedside. When laughter drifted his way, he wondered what their exchange could be about, but after his encounter, felt glad seeing them all smiling.

Chace's face beamed with that laughter. Although his skin was still pale, his birthmark sparkled topaz blue. *Will he be all right? Please, Ari.*

Octav approached the bedspace, knowing he'd need to work at ignoring Chace's earlier rejection. There were leadership concerns to contend with now. He leaned over the end of the bed, trying his best to look relaxed, when inside he was cringing. "You're doing better," he offered with a grin.

"Thanks, I feel a bit better." Chace glanced at Kendro, then the Ainoren. "Thought I was dead for sure."

"You were extremely lucky, Chace." Kendro grasped Octav's arm, a sparkle of croex as their skin connected. "This can't happen again." The King's touch confirmed his warning. "You must be vigilant where you choose to eat."

Octav tried smiling at Chace. "Lucky, yeah?" Inside, he knew something didn't feel right. Chace smelled different. Sickness.

Doctor Jaack approached with Chace's stat reader. His smile at them, lifting hopes.

"Thanks for taking good care of him, Doc." Octav watched the Doctor, with raised eyebrows, hoping all was right. *The results. Just tell me!*

"He's a model patient." Jaack gave a brief wink at Chace. "We'll take some blood, if you'll let me."

"Of course." Octav eased off the bedspace, concern filling his mind. As he stepped back he caught Kendro's curious glare. *What is going on between Jaack and Chace?*

Jaack pulled the curtain, separating them. The trio edged away, allowing Jaack a moment to examine Chace alone. Octav's stomach knotted.

"Something wrong?" asked Lady Katesh as Octav stood with them for a moment.

"No," Octav hesitated, glancing back to the curtain. "Nothing."

"I'm escorting Lady Katesh to a private dinner." Kendro broke into Octav's concern. "Join us, if you'd like."

Octav needed to stay, his stomach churned with the thoughts of Jaack and Chace on the other side of that curtain. "There are a couple of things. Need discussing. With Chace." He bumbled. "Perhaps I'll be along soon."

Kendro lowered his head in understanding. Octav knew he'd read all too clearly what was transpiring. Walking Lady Katesh away on his arm was the kindest thing for the King to do. Repercussions would come later.

Octav turned back to those drawn curtains. Wanting to do what he felt right, listening in where he knew he shouldn't.

"Glad you're feeling better," Doctor Jaack's voice seemed a bit too playful.

"Thanks to you—" Chace paused. "I—"

Octav's heart raced. Why? He'd never heard hesitation in Chace's voice before. He edged closer towards trying his best, aiming at peeking through the curtain's slit.

Then he saw, Jaack with a device scanning Chace's bare chest. Chace's birthmark, now black. What the—

Octav stepped through into the cubical, Jaack jumped, fumbling the device, removing his hand from Chace's chest. *He fumbled, embarrassed?* "Please—you—you'll have to wait outside."

"Wha—" Octav's croak surprised them all in its demand. "What's wrong with him?"

Chace's face flushed, trying to cover his mark, but failing. He addressed the doctor, "Give us a moment. Please?"

Jaack lowered his head, mumbling about other patients to see, and left them alone.

"What's going on?" asked Octav, fearing the truth.

"Even with the medicine," Chace pointed at his lower abdomen, "the poison's left irreparable damage."

Octav stared at his friend where hardened muscles used to be etched with the intricate details of his birthmark, now his mark was blackened, dead. It should have been glistening, responding actively with Chace's mood. It wasn't. Octav felt his croex rush forward, illuminating the room green.

Why? He slammed his fist on his thigh. *Why Chace?* Wishing he could shatter something anything into splinters, leaving his knuckles bloody seemed the only recourse for satiating this anger.

Chace reached for him. "I'd take poison for you any day." Touching his shoulder lightly, "Octav?" But as their croex mixed, he backed off. "Don't be like this," he begged. "Please."

Octav couldn't look at him. "That poison was meant for me." His fists wanted more, smashing away this truth. "I should be lying there. Not you." But there was nothing big enough to pound. *Breathe, Puswer!*

"Like I said," Chace repeated, "I'd take a hit for you anytime. I'm glad I did. So what, I lose some of my croex, and can't fight properly one-on-one."

"You're my second. It has major consequences." Octav noticed Chace's bare stomach again. He blushed now, realizing that he'd thought of Jaack's hand on Chace.

Stepping close, he queried, "Is there nothing they can do?" Octav leaned over the bedspace, closer to Chace's birthmark. The sickly sweet smell of illness cloaking Chace hit Octav's nostrils, but he didn't turn away.

Octav's croex surged. Reaching out, he touched Chace's shoulder feeling the clammy skin. Fingers following the curve of his birthmark down his chest. Chace let out a gasp, their eyes locked for a moment, and Octav saw passion.

He gulped, backing away into the curtain. Yanking it out of the way, he thought only of fleeing.

As the device in his hand bleeped, Doctor Jaack rushed in. He looked from Chace to Octav, reading all the signs. "His blood pressure and heart rate are erratic. He's suffering a setback. You. Out of the way."

"Octav, Don't go!"

Octav pushed past the doctor, out of the space. He needed air, lots of it.

Octav raced through the decks of the ship without care or thought of those around him. He bumped into several officers, caroming off them all on his way down corridors. "Ainoren." One man tried engaging Octav, but he kept going, his mind whirling with emotions he didn't understand.

Finally exhausted, he stopped. He took a moment, and at last, observed where he was—the very belly of the ship. He leaned against a bulkhead, catching his breath. A voice behind asked, "Are you all right, friend?" The query coming from a doorway he'd nearly passed.

"I'm fine." Straightening himself, Octav looked into a set of bright Aonise eyes. Heiako bay? No.

"Looks like you could do with a drink?" said another. "Hop on over here. I'll pour you some of the best." He gestured behind his shoulder.

The twinkling bar light enticed him. "I could do with one." Yet, he thought against it. If Kendro found out, the King's wrath wouldn't be calmed this time.

The gentleman before him seemed patient, a very intricate birthmark shimmering back at Octav. A Seer? Down here?

Octav stepped in, defeated. Nothing would change things now anyway. Noting only one table and a set of chairs, wide space dominated the room's centre with a gurgling still leaning against the far wall.

"Take a breather." The older Aonise poured Octav a drink. "Sit for a moment."

Octav moved to the lone table, lowering himself. He considered the dark drink he'd been handed, swirling it around in the glass. *Is it safe?*

"We're not going to poison you, Ainoren." The Seer-man spoke. Taking the glass, he drank off some of it.

"Explain yourself!" Octav fired, a knot tightened at the base of his neck. "What do you know about my assassination attempt?"

"Less of the accusations, Ainoren. My name is Alams. This," he waved to his right, "is my brother, Rae. We've information for you."

Staring at the man sitting before him, who still held his glass, Octav noted the serious detail to his face. Alam's sleeved arm bore his striking birthmark snaking across every finger and thumb. He wasn't just staring at any seer. He was looking at Kendro's mystery First Generation Seer.

He stuttered, "I—nfo— what information?"

"Drink, we'll explain." Alams swirled the glass, sliding it back across the table towards Octav.

Its potent kick burned the back of his throat, as Octav took the glass, sipping. But the swallow slid down, warming the empty feeling inside his gut. "Sharp." Octav turned the glass in his hands, staring into what was left of the murky fluid. "Thanks."

Rae was moving, letting Alams sit opposite Octav. While Alams poured another, Rae positioned himself with his arm resting on the back of his brother's chair.

Octav waited for them, watching their reaction to his drinking. He felt vulnerable here, safe, yes, but suddenly scared. "Please, tell me what you know?"

Rae's birthmark flickered red, calling forth his croex. "You're angry?"

Octav ran a finger over his trrobhas trying to stem his own mark from reacting. Alams watched him carefully. "You both know I am. So why ask?"

"Because you're anger is misdirected."

"You know Wez is on board, yes?" Alams said, also calling forth his croex.

Octav swallowed, so much croex bubbled around him. If these brothers wanted him out of the way for any reason, it wouldn't take much. For the first time in his life, Octav knew he was out of his depth.

The blue and red croex mixed towards the centre of the room. *Were they really going to do this?* Octav shivered.

Alams noticed this, and smiled. "I'm glad you see what's before you. We really do mean you no harm." Alams held out a hand. "Please, join with us. I'd like to show you something of your near future. Rae is the only one who can direct me. We need a full bond for this."

"Full—my future—" As tempted as he was, Octav hesitated. "Is that even possible?" A full Scrie wasn't something he enjoyed, especially with everything that had most recently transpired. These two men—would both see, and feel, everything he did.

Alams held his hand closer to Octav's, his croex flickered across touching Octav's skin, igniting his insides. Purity. They really did mean no harm.

With his fears abated, Octav allowed his croex to trickle forward. The smallest of connection meant the most, and he handed himself over to the two brothers, fully.

Rae moved to kneel at the side of Octav all three colours meeting— blue, red, and green. A wonderful display. The room around them electrified. A thought flashed through Octav. *We'll be seen.*

The room is shielded. No one will know we're doing this. Alams' voice came direct to Octav's mind.

As the room around Octav spun, mixed coloured sparkles caressed the edge of his actual sight. Where he sat faded away to a different place. Sard stood to Octav's right with a man he'd seen only the once, and never met, Trax.

"Your poison didn't work, it was switched." Sard spoke freely. "Octav's pilot is the one who is sick."

"Chace, why would it make Chace sick?" Confusion crossed Trax's face. "It was specifically designed for the Ainoren. No one else."

"That's something you need to ask of your scientist, Jaack. He the one who's failed us."

As Octav heard Sard mention Jaack's name in the same context as the poison, the anger inside him rushed forth. Impossible as it seemed, he wanted to smash Sard's face against the nearest wall to get him to confess everything.

223

Rae placed a hand on Octav's shoulder, their croex connection strong, but the physical one much needed. *Anger will do you no good. Listen.* And again, the voices came.

"Everything went to plan. Octav thinks Gaal's the traitor."

"You delivered well on your promise. Dalamaar will be pleased."

"And the next phase?"

"Already underway, this distraction will prove most useful."

Sard's the traitor I'm looking for? Dalamaar coerced them both? Octav's anger reverberated again through the trio's connection. About to break the scrie, Rae squeezed Octav's shoulder.

The vision faded as the room Octav sat in came back into view. Rae removed his hand from Octav's shoulder as Alams withdrew his croex.

Octav slammed his chair back, standing. "I'm going to kill them both!"

"Rae!" Alams gestured to the door. Rae nodded. There was nothing blocking Octav's path.

"You're not leaving this room yet, Ainoren."

Octav's anger turned pure rage, physically shaking. "Don't try to stop me."

"I will, you know it. Sit." Alams pointed back to the chair. "You need to think about this."

"What's there to think about? The doctor treating—"

Alams risked grabbing Octav's arm, which only served to further anger him. Octav shook him off, but then heard, "—the man you once loved. Is a traitor, yes?"

Loved? Octav stopped, anger dissipating. The room dimmed at the Ainoren's realization.

Alams tapped at the bottle his brother had set down a while ago. "Drink as much as you like, my friend. We'll leave you with your thoughts for a while. You are safe here."

Octav stirred, considering his words—this man was an all-powerful entity. His kindness went deeper than most. "Thank you for your sincerity."

The old Seer placed a hand on Octav's shoulder. "I have one last piece of advice." Meeting Octav's gaze, his eyes softened. "Be truthful to yourself, for once. Those around you love you for who you are, not what you are." Turning, limping towards the door and with those words, he joined his brother. Together, they left the room to Octav.

Thoughts whirled in Octav's head. Jaack, the creator of the poison, had to be the one to cure it. Pounding Jaack to a pulp was what Octav wanted to do to save Chace. But he'd have to let the treacherous malloth live.

The birthmark on Octav's fingers twinkled brightly against the still.

Standing, he moved to leave. Alams stepped aside.

Octav murmured, "Thanks for the truth."

"You are most welcome, Ainoren." He lowered his head just once. "I will be seeing you again. Of that I am sure."

"And Kendro?"

"Do not bother the King with my presence. My gift was to you."

Octav understood. Walking away, he would try his hardest to keep Kendro from finding out Alams' secret.

Head held high, shoulders straight, Octav marched back to the infirmary, sure of his steps.

Striding past Jaack, who barely managed to jump in front of him, Octav headed to Chace's side. "You're not wanted," said the doctor.

Octav stopped. Not expecting this at all, he daren't look at Jaack. Not being able to satisfy his anger pained him deeply. "What?"

"Exactly what I've said. He doesn't want to see you. He's very upset."

"I need to see him." Octav paused. *I must control this.*

Jaack called to his orderlies, three hurried to his side. The four now blocked Octav from stepping any further into the infirmary.

"Doctor, you will let me past." Octav harnessed his croex, illuminating the room in green flashes.

The three traded glances, backing away, but Jaack held his ground, risking a step even closer, "No need to threaten, Ainoren," he placed a hand on Octav's chest. Pausing only as he felt the croex from inside Octav, he stared into his green eyes. "It won't help your situation. I suggest you come back in the morning when you've both rested."

"What do you know?" Octav growled.

"Believe me, I know. But I'm speaking to you as his doctor here. If you care, and want to see Chace," he indicated, dismissing the other three with a wave, "I have a place where you can rest. Come with me."

Octav glanced to where Chace lay, and then, followed the doctor to a far room, knowing the man couldn't be trusted at all.

"You can sleep in here."

Octav stared at the bedspace, exhaustion flooding his body, legs weak. "Thanks," he muttered.

The doctor palmed a cabinet, and a door clicked open. Looking through the contents, he pulled out a bottle. "I'll pour you some of this. Drink it before you settle down. It will help you sleep." He eyed Octav, and measured out a smaller dose, handing it over.

Octav knew it wasn't a good idea. But he knocked it back, handing the doctor the empty glass.

"I'll check on you through the night." Jaack closed the door behind him.

Octav pulled out a cloth, spitting the liquid into it before crawling onto the bedspace, settling. He drifted into a fitful sleep.

Octav woke from a sharp sting, feeling totally disorientated. *Chace?* His croex surged as he focussed on a blurry face before him.

"Blood test," Doctor Jaack said, holding an infusion guin with a vial of blood in it.

"There's much testing we need," Jaack placed it down, alongside several others.

Why didn't I wake? What's wrong with me?

Octav yawned, still exhausted.

"How do you feel?"

"I'm fine." Octav clenched his fists. His birthmark bathed the sheet around him in green. He pushed himself up. "Chace?"

"He's managed some breakfast. He's stable. He should be up for traveling later today."

"Will he see me now?"

Jaack stared out of the room towards Chace's bedspace. "I believe he will."

Octav stretched, feeling light-headed. He stood.

"Just—" Jaack grabbed hold of Octav's arm, and then, backed off.

"Just what?" At Jaack's touch, in just that second, Octav felt his blood boiling once again.

"Well…" Jaack couldn't meet Octav's glare. "Be gentle with him."

Octav stepped towards him. The doctor backed up against a wall, his guin at his chest. "Gentle with what? What are you implying?"

Jaack held up a hand. "Nothing. Nothing at all."

Octav whirled out of the room, needing to talk to Chace now more than ever. Yet, approaching the bedspace, a shiver ran through him as memories came flooding back. *Jaack loved Chace… He'd known him, been with him.*

The curtains loomed before him. Octav's vision heaved—the one person Octav wanted more than anything just a few feet away. *I can do this.* He slipped in-between and stared right into his pilot's eyes.

Chace swallowed, finishing a drink, looking up. His fingers slipped from his cup almost dropping it. "Ainoren," he said, placing the cup on his thigh, "I'll be good to fly us out later today, I'm sure."

"Someone else will fly us out," Octav said. "May I?" He patted the edge of the bedspace.

"Of course." Chace edged over, making room, and a face at the effort.

Octav perched, staring straight at Chace, who couldn't return eye contact for more than a few seconds. "Look at me."

The longer Octav stared, the more Chace fidgeted—his eyes darting left, right.

Eventually, Octav asked, "How long have we known each other?"

"Eighteen years," Chace replied, finally meeting his gaze.

"Then, what was that last night?"

"I—I," Chace stuttered, "I don't know—I—I was ill."

Octav swallowed, the taste in his mouth, burnt amber, sickening him. He edged further up the bedspace, so he could take Chace's cup from him. "Sick. Really?" Drinking some of the hot fluid, he watched Chace's reactions as he hoped what he had felt had been mutual.

Chace's glance now had nowhere to go but back into the pillows. Octav knew his stare was making him squirm. "I—" He pulled his legs up to his chest. So vulnerable.

Octav worried he might be pushing Chace too hard. *Should I go?* But, he couldn't. He needed answers.

"The only good that poison did was to bring down our barriers." Octav flared, his croex turned the surrounding curtains a glowing green. His focus pooling it into his hand, lifting his palm upright as it grew in intensity—a living flame. "Barriers which we'd built. We'd maintained for—years."

Octav reached for Chace's arm, hovering above it, the flames licking at Chace's bare skin. "Are you sick now?"

"Yes." Chace whimpered. "Please, don't touch me."

Octav pulled back. "It's not just touching you I want," dropping his croex levels. "I want—more."

"Octav," Chace sighed, lowering his legs flat against the bedspace, "you're Ainoren of the fleet. A member of the Royal House."

Octav stared at the floor, "I don't care," feeling his whole world crashing down around him. *After all this?*

"I do." Chace extended a hand, and stopped. Octav saw the hesitation. "I'm asking Kendro. He'll transfer me to another detail."

"No." Octav clenched his fists, knuckles turning white. "You've been at my side for too long. I won't lose you to this…"

"This—this what?" A frown settled on Chace's face. "There is nothing. There will be nothing. There can't be."

"You don't feel anything for me?" Octav saw no emotion from Chace, his face blank.

How could I have been so wrong?

Without breaking eye contact, Octav stood straightening his uniform. He left. Not looking back.

Kendro waited with Lady Katesh for Chace, their departure from the *Sol'Delka* long overdue. *Where is the man?* Octav had yet to arrive, and this worried the King. The pair turned back to the bay, hearing Doctor Jaack wheel Chace in with Captain Sard walking beside them, talking.

"How are you feeling?" Kendro asked, as they approached.

Chace lowered his head. "Better, Your Highness, thank you. I'm sorry I can't fly us back"

Kendro smiled at The Lady, proud of Chace—ever the doting pilot. "Do not worry yourself. We need you well."

"The Ainoren does know you're leaving." Captain Sard glanced first down to Chace, then around, wondering at Octav's tardiness. "Yes?"

At that, Octav stepped onto the shuttle bay. As he met the group, he was studious about avoiding Chace's concerned gaze. He addressed Kendro alone, "Apologies."

"Everything all right?" Kendro asked.

"All's fine." Smiling towards Lady Katesh, he offered her an arm. "Shall we—"

The Lady stepped toward him, "Yes, although the hospitality here was good," she offered Sard a nod, "I think I prefer our own ship." She latched onto Octav's arm, boarding the shuttle after their King.

Doctor Jaack wheeled Chace inside, helping him into a chair, making sure the straps were tightened. He leaned in close. "Don't be a stranger," he whispered. But the King heard everything, inside and aloud. Chace nearly lost what control he'd displayed hearing Jaack's next words— "If you need anything, comm me, all right?"

Kendro watched Octav's facial mark flare. *These two need to sort this out, sooner rather than later.* The festering wound would not heal until they did.

No wonder Octav is acting the fool, the King thought.

FRIENDSHIP

AWAITING THE SHUTTLE'S ARRIVAL, BRIE and Hadi discussed Jaack's findings. When the doors opened, Octav greeted the couple with a stiff salute. Hadi reciprocated. "It's good to have you back, Ainoren."

"Thank you." Octav acknowledged Brie with a brief, tight smile. "I'll comm you later with my discoveries, Captain. Let me know when you're available."

Captain Hadi noticed the look and replied, "Of course."

They could both see Octav longed to make quick escape from the returning party.

Brie touched Hadi's arm. "Is he all right?"

"Don't think so," Hadi replied, watching as Octav hurried from the shuttle.

Brie waited for the King and Lady Katesh to exit the shuttle before she entered to collect Chace. Hadi followed her inside.

Chace lay with his head in his hands, sobbing. Brie felt shocked to think of Chace not caring that their pilot was there witness to these tears. She rushed to him. "Is it pain? What happened?"

"Nothing," Chace sobbed, "nothing."

"I'll take it from here." Glancing to Hadi, who hesitated, she waited until he turned about, and left her to her work.

"Nothing happened?" Brie knelt before Chace, placing a hand on his knee. "Come on, I'm your doctor, please."

"I can't. Just help me to my quarters." She saw Chace couldn't meet her concerned gaze. "I need rest."

Doctor Brie moved into action, offering him a hand. "Can you walk?" She helped Chace stand on wobbly legs.

"Will I be fit for training tomorrow?"

229

Brie watched him wobble more on his feet. "I'm not too sure. Maybe."

"I'll take it easy, Doc. Don't worry."

"I will worry." That was very true. She'd never dealt with a case this severe. *Did he even realise?* "That poison was serious, Chace." This time their eyes locked for a brief moment. He knew. "Please. Be more careful."

"I promise, Doc, just glad I was ther—"

Brie shuddered. She knew Kendro would not have survived the loss, had Octav's meal held the poison that now ravaged Chace. Quickly changing the subject, she reassured him. "If you'd feel better, I'll monitor you through the night."

Chace grinned, straightening his back, holding his head high. He accepted. "That would be great, thanks, Doc."

Brie agreed with a smile, although she hated working through the night. "I've had strict instructions from Jaack to look after you."

"Jaack?" Chace refused her hand, and took a step alone. "You mean Doctor Hands?" He grinned.

Brie took his lead, allowing him to navigate out of the shuttle bay. "I don't know about that, but I agree something isn't right. I'll look into it."

Octav stomped straight for his quarters, opening the door with a slap at the wall panel.

Frie threw her arms around him. "You're back, I was so worried." Octav pushed her off, not getting in a word, as she carried on mumbling. "Hadi said that poison was meant for you. What the hell were you thinking, eating in a strange place? You know you can't do that. You have to take better care of yourself. What would people think of—wandering around the ship, taking liberties like that—are you even listening to me?"

"Less of the lecture please, Frie."

"Lecture!" She followed him, wrapping her arms around her shoulders. "You fool!" Her birthmark flickered wildly.

Why did I come home?

"No." She all but stamped a foot at him, her blood surging red to her cheeks. "You need a lecture. It's about time you realized how much your life is at risk."

Not now! "Frie!" He settled on the divano, defeated, teeth grinding. "Please. I don't need to hear this."

"Fine," Frie threw her hands up, yanking at her own hair, her usual temper tantrum. "I'll come back when you're willing to listen." She stormed away, leaving the room's door slid open, a testament to all not yet finished between the two.

Octav sighed, resting his head on the back of the divano. *I will not get up and fix that.* A moment later, he did, though, and returned to flop on the divano.

There was a knock at the door. *Of course.*

"Forget the combination?" he shouted. *Stupid woman.* He palmed the panel so it would open for her.

The door slid aside, Chace staring back at him. Defiant.

"What do you want?" Octav folded his arms not wanting this confrontation, his nerves as tattered as his mind.

"What I want—" Chace had decided on the shuttle to risk it. To risk it all. He placed his hand on Octav's chest, forcing him backwards. Octav tried to stop him, but found himself incapable. Unable to move against Chace, he shivered. Trapped, struggling for breath as Chace said the two words Octav had wanted to hear earlier. "—is you."

Chace stared for a moment, birthmark flickering slightly. Nerves? Octav felt—elated? Uncomfortable, yes. He watched Chace lick his lips, edging closer, until both could feel their breath against each other's skin.

Octav fought back briefly, and then, relaxed, responding to Chace's lips. Soft. Wrestling Chace around so he was against the wall, Octav's inhibitions vanished. Passion raged, stronger than anything he'd experienced.

"Wh—" Frie said, from behind them, "— is this?"

Octav glanced back into his wife's angry face, red flashed and shimmered. As if on fire, Octav stepped away from Chace. "Go."

Chace scampered unsteadily to the still ajar door, head down.

"Don't you dare leave," Frie spat Chace's way. "Wait outside."

Octav waited for a reaction, a slap, anything. His head, in sudden shame, lowered at his behaviour. "Frie," he began. "I'm sorry."

"When I married you—" Frie's voice wavered, as she palmed their door closed. Her face red, anger flickering in her eyes, she stepped towards Octav, placing both hands on his shoulders. "I knew you were different." She pointed at the divano, and ordered, "Sit."

I'm such a fool. Octav complied, heart pounding. *What's she going to do? This could ruin everything!*

"When we made love that first time, I knew I'd never make you happy." She sat, crossing her legs. "You had already given yourself to someone. Obvious, but I respected your decisions. Ever the military man." She watched his every move. "I do have one question, though."

Octav knew what was coming.

"Has it been going on for all these years?" Her words stabbed at him, leaving him as breathless as Chace's kiss had just done.

"No." Octav shook his head. "I love you, but—I—" He struggled to find the right words, not wanting to hurt her more. "Until Chace was sick—I had forgotten all of it. I nev—"

"Thought of Chace like that?" Frie's birthmark flickered. "Come on! Don't take me for a fool." Frie fidgeted with her dress, the hem slipping, revealing her thigh mark flickering just as much as her detailed facial one. "I just thought it was another woman. A man, now that's different."

She waited for his response. Nothing. "You have nothing at all to say?"

"I didn't want to hurt you. I didn't want myself feeling like that. I thought we'd stopped it."

She took hold of his hand, a sparkle of croex flickering. "The only person you hurt is yourself." Their entwining croex was a myriad of colours. "I should have demanded the truth from you years ago."

"I don't know if I'd have acknowledged it." Octav stared at their connection, feeling the love she had for him. "Jaack helped put these walls up."

"Jaack?"

"One of the top scientists in his field. He helped block the memory with a certain hypnosis."

With a sigh, Frie nodded. "And now, it's all back?"

"Yes," Octav couldn't meet her gaze. "What are you going to do?"

"Our people need the Ainoren they love." Dropping his hand, she stood. "I'll stay with Roma. We'll make the decision about our marriage, after we reach the planet Earth."

"Frie," he whispered, desperate for life to stay the same. "I'm scared."

"Scared is good." Frie moved towards the door. "It means you're feeling something, not just going through the motions."

With that, she palmed the door open, leaving him alone.

Octav, eyes shut, only heard the door slide closed. Tears flowed, but he didn't turn. Resting his head in his hand, finally tears came to him. But for whom?

"Do you want me to go, too?" Chace asked, from behind Octav.

Octav's breath released. *Ari, what fresh hell are you offering?* He wiped his eyes. *Or is this my glimpse of something else?*

"No," he mumbled wearily. "There's some Reingo in the cabinet, grab a couple of glasses."

Chace did as asked. Sitting next to Octav, he poured them both a large drink. "What did she say?" he probed. "Will she tell everyone?"

Downing the whole glass of Reingo, Octav replied, "She's staying with Roma for a while. She understands politics. And more, our privacy."

Chace swallowed. "She's not coming back?" Tentatively, he reached across, placing a hand on Octav's leg all the while never breaking eye contact.

Holding his gaze, Octav felt Chace's hand slide higher, powerless to stop him. Chace drew closer, those perfect eyes a window into the younger man's thoughts. Never seeing his birthmark so close, Octav noted its perfect detail. It graced his cheek around his eye and ear. "Octav," with a finger, Chace stroked the side of his face. "I want to be with you more than anything."

Octav could see the twinkling of his own emerald green mark in Chace's eyes. There was no hiding it now.

Chace eased back. "I know I'm not going to be nervous around my best friend." Standing, he held out a hand. "Come on."

"Where—"

"The gardens. Neither of us will sleep."

"Are you fit enough to be walking around?"

"Have you seen this body?" Chase laughed, lifting his shirt, exposing his taut stomach and his blackened birthmark for a brief moment.

Octav licked his lips, blood coursing through his veins, trying his best to restrain himself again. "You know I have."

"Well, then, come on," Chace held his hand out further.

Captain Hadi sat on the bridge, watching as the stars flittered past. Although moving slower than he hoped, they were making some progress. It would have to be enough for now.

The door hissed. Turning, seeing Kendro, Hadi frowned. The King needed rest, as did he. "Your Highness," he said. "It's late. Something wrong?"

"A list of everyone who needs transferring from the *Sol'Delka*." Kendro held out a reader. "I'd like to attempt the jayux within the next few weeks. We can't wait any longer."

"Did Emmi protest—when you asked?" Hadi flicked through the list of names, recognising some, but not others.

"She wanted the truth, which I gave her. I need all important personnel here."

"Did she agree?" Hadi knew that decision for her would have been a tough one.

"Yes," Kendro took a seat near Hadi, "surprisingly enough."

"Good." He handed off the reader to be dealt with by Reel. "We'll start organizing the transfers as soon as Octav gives the all clear. The food stashes he discovered we could also share in."

"Captain Gaal is being investigated for the problems there. I presume you know his commander, Captain Sard?"

"Yes," Hadi replied, thumbing over more reports as they came in across his console, "albeit, not very well."

233

"Do you think Sard can guide the ship through the jayux?"

"I believe so. I could go across, give him some personal instruction, if you like?"

"Yes —perhaps we have time. If you think he'll benefit, organize a trip."

"No problem. I'll ask Octav to join me."

Kendro gazed into space. "He's distracted of late. Have you noticed?"

Who hasn't, Sire? "He's not sleeping, like all of us. I wouldn't say he was distracted."

"You think he's all right?"

"Yes, I'm sure he feels guilty about Chace though. They've worked together. They're friends."

"I know. It is unlike him letting anything slip by. I'll put it down to losing Lyrik."

"Maybe, I'll talk with him later. We meet a few times a week, blame it on insomnia."

"I've never suffered with it." Kendro smiled. "Thankfully. Octav always has, though."

"Just that type of thinker," said Hadi. "Some people just can't settle."

Captain Hadi stood, moving away from his chair. Commander Vax had stepped onto the bridge. She smiled at them both. "Evening, Sirs."

"You have the bridge, Commander."

"Sleep well, Captain."

"Walk me to the gardens this evening. I could do with a stroll, as could you, Captain," Kendro said as they entered the corridor. At the lift, he pressed for the lower decks.

Hadi obliged, not wanting to leave his King alone.

"How is Katya?" Kendro asked, as the lift descended.

"She's good, thank you."

"More than good, I believe." He smiled.

As they walked to the gardens, Captain Hadi laughed. "Sorry, Kendro, I forget sometimes what you feel. Yes, more than good. She is pregnant again."

"Is everything well?"

"Yes, we think so. Thank you. Do you have any other things for me to fetch from the *Sol'Delka*?"

"I think we've covered everything." Kendro halted mid-stride. "Lady Katesh seemed to get on very well with Emmi and her sister. I think when Emmi transfers here, they'll soon become friends."

"Do you mind me speaking truthfully?" the Captain asked.

"No, you can always say what you feel."

"I don't like her. Something about her just doesn't feel right."

"You are entitled to your own feelings. I understand where they come from. Lady Katesh thinks she has everyone under her control, but she doesn't. Both Octav and I are aware of her misguided thought processes. We're keeping a very close watch on her."

"Good," Hadi said. They'd arrived at the garden's main doors. "Will you be coming in?"

"No, I have my duties. Mika will need to rest." Kendro said stepping back, "I bid you good night, Captain."

"Good night, Your Highness," Hadi said, walking through the garden doors.

He took his time and wandered down to the lake, sitting at a bench. The air was crisp, clear, and the sky above him just as beautiful as on the bridge.

He'd not expected to find Octav here. After all, he'd seriously looked annoyed and tired when getting off the shuttle. Hadi saw Chace too, and they were training. He'd never witnessed skill at this level before, finding it highly revealing to Octav's tactics.

Something to use on him at a later date, he smirked.

Chace ran to the left, sideswiping at Octav's croex ball. Octav's strike countering, perhaps a bit too hard, hitting Chace square in the chest. Gasping for breath, croex spent in that single blow, Chace collapsed, winded.

Octav dropped his guard. "I'm sorry," he said. "You normally anticipate my every move." *Still sick?* A hand held out, Octav reddened, hopping Chace would take it.

"Dis—tracted," Chace wheezed, "we've an audience." He pointed to Captain Hadi.

Octav rolled his eyes. "Next time, just open your mouth, all right?"

Chace nodded. Octav helped him sit up, though he was in no fit state to rise yet.

Hadi raced the fair few steps towards the pair, reader in hand. "I'll comm Brie?"

"I'll be all right," Chace spluttered, "h—he's just winded me is all."

Octav glared at Hadi. "You put him off."

Hadi stood offering his hand to Chace. Chace took it, heaving himself up. "Thanks." Just about managing to rise to his feet, Chace stood as tall as he could.

Laughing, anything to jolly Chace, Octav replied, "It will teach you not to be distracted so easily."

"Thanks," Chace spat, pushing away again from Hadi's outstretched offer. "Don't give the sick, recuperating pilot any sympathy, will you?" he bantered back.

Captain Hadi and Octav both laughed.

"Jeeze," Chace said, though Octav read his feigned sorrow deep in his bones. "Remind me never to take another hit for you if this is all I get." Chace, too, started laughing, despite the pain crossing his face.

"No problem." Hadi looked uncomfortable.

Octav could see he didn't want to walk away though, and he asked, "You eaten yet?" He was hoping that Hadi had business elsewhere. Though that faded as Chace's facial mark flickered. He loved his food.

"Not a good idea," Chace reminded them. "We've under strict orders to use the ships main kitchens only."

"Come back to mine—" Hadi offered. "She'll be asleep. We're one of the only stations with cooking facilities. Nothing can poison either of you there."

"Sure, sounds good." Chace glanced at Octav. "I'd love some home-cooked food."

"I have some ale, too." Hadi grinned.

"Even better, then," Octav said, grimly, retrieving both swords and bits of clothing. "I'm in." *I just want to be alone.*

Octav walked behind Chace as they headed out of the gardens. Chace faltered.

"Need a hand?" the Captain asked, glancing to Octav, who avoided his eye.

"I'm not proud, please." As Hadi offered his shoulder to Chace, Octav's croex bubbled to the surface. Snapping his mind away, Octav tried to focus on anything but Chace being touched by Hadi.

The two men now had a moment alone. Octav sat opposite Chace, folding his arms, which said more than he knew.

"What was all that?" Chace asked. They'd reached Captain Hadi's quarters, and Hadi assisted Chace to the divano and went to the kitchen for drinks.

"What?" Octav retorted.

"You know well what. Your eyes when Sheve offered to help."

Octav mumbled, "Nothing." Hadi had returned with a few drinks.

"I've got fresh meat and vegetables. It'll soon whip into something."

Chace took the drink, though Octav waved his away. "Thanks."

"Cooking is as relaxing for me as training is for you two. I don't often have the chance," he said, then looked from one face to another. Octav flinched reading Hadi's face. *Sort it out, guys.* With that thought, their host vanished into the kitchen again.

Octav turned back to Chace, who'd downed his drink. "So, nothing, huh?"

Chace growled, "I'll not leave this alone."

"I didn't want him touching you," Octav replied.

"Other men will touch me, as they will you." Leaning forward, eyes to the door, Chace whispered, "Block that jealous streak. We've not even been together for twenty four hours."

"Together?" Octav asked, cocking his head to one side.

Chace sat back. "Let's eat, have a few drinks. Then, you can escort me home," he nearly smiled, "where we talk through this. All right?"

Captain Hadi whirled back into the room, deftly carrying three plates bursting with steaming vegetables and meat.

The three heartily tucked in. Octav relaxed with the two of them then and started to have some fun. He put his plate down as he downed the drink he'd refused earlier.

With the food devoured, the ale enjoyed, and conversation full, Octav slinked back into the divano, listening intently as Chace talked endlessly about his academy days.

The conversation quietened, and Octav realised he'd become silent.

"You all right?" Hadi asked him.

"I've enjoyed this," Octav said. *How could either of them know how much he missed Lyrik?* "Just missing—absent friends, you know?" Octav stood. "If you're ready, I'll see you back to your quarters, Chace."

Chace, standing also, nodded. "A pleasant evening, thank you, Captain."

"Please, when you're in my home, call me Sheve."

"Thanks, Sheve." Chace smiled. "Hope we haven't been any disturbance to your good lady."

Sheve glanced towards their bedroom. "I'm sure she's still sleeping." As Octav and Chace made their way to the door, Sheve added, "See you tomorrow."

Chace wobbled for a while down the corridor as Octav took the lead, two long but tired steps ahead.

Chace's steps behind him changed. Octav stopped, as he heard Chace asking, "Aren't you even going to offer help?"

Octav noted a security camo, and shaking his head, saw all eyes watching them. "Sorry."

"The camos won't mind if you help. I'm not jumping on you out here," he replied. "I have some control."

"It's not your control I'm worried over." Stepping back, Octav did offer him an arm, grudgingly. Chace took it as the two of them walked back to his quarters.

"Coming in?" Chace got the door opened, dreading even having to ask.

"I'm not—"

"Are you sure? We can just talk."

"Pretty talked out, to be fair." Obvious, Chace's heart sank, and he lowered his face. "I'm sorry," Octav tried.

Feigning a smile, Chace said, "That's all right." He stepped inside the doorway. "I can wait. We can take this as slow as you need too."

At that smile, Octav looked around the hallway.

"There are no camos here," said Chace.

Such hope in those eyes. Octav backed away, fear gripping his insides. "I'll see you in the morning."

"You're not leaving without kissing me." Chace reached out, grabbing hold of Octav's shirt, drawing Octav back to him.

PREPARATION

CAPTAIN HADI FLICKED THROUGH THE latest reports as he sat in his bridge chair.

Commander Vax's steps were quick, and her nerves were all but shouting at Hadi from the science station. He could see her distress, but chose to ignore it. She sat in the chair to his right, crossing her legs, and then, uncrossing them before she spoke. "Hanna and Veco are in position at the Sietev, Captain," she advised. "Officer Reel, would you secure communication with Captain Sard?"

"Yes, Ma'am," Reel replied, bringing up the Captain's image. "Captain Sard, stand by for instructions."

On the screen, Sard spoke out. "Yes, Captain."

Hadi stood. "Officer Reel will patch me to your ships comms. I'll address both our crews."

"We're connected," Officer Reel stated.

Hadi took a breath, standing as he addressed everyone.

"Captain Hadi speaking to all citizens. We will test the launch preparations for a jayux. Both our remaining ships were badly damaged in the fight. I need all of you to remain vigilant, Aonise as well as Heiako, on both vessels. This is a test. I need to know every structural defect, grunt, groan, or crack. Report back to your Captains within the hour. Thank you."

Officer Reel cut the ship's main comms.

Hadi glanced back to the single screen where Captain Sard's pale face stared back. "We're timed for five minutes. Good luck."

"Same to you. Thank you, Captain." Sard signed off, his voice tighter than expected.

Octav's echo then came through over the comms. "Engine room is ready, Captain."

The Captain couldn't sit back down. He paced the bridge, Vax's nerves contagious.

Commander Vax's eyes flicked to Hadi, and back to the timer on her console as it counted down.

"Captain," she said, "one minute."

"Engine's are starting up," details from Octav came. "Fifty percent."

Hadi stopped pacing, watching the monitor as the green light spread upwards.

"We are at eighty percent," Octav's disembodied voice reported.

Captain Hadi turned to Science Officer Lynj. "How's Captain Sard's ship?"

"They're at fifty percent, Captain. Several reports have already come through for structural concerns."

"Keep pushing her," he whispered at the *Sol'Delka* through the view port. *Hold her together, Sard.*

The pulse given off from the main engines lit up their structural repairs. Tiny sparks of light emanating from where they shouldn't. Hadi watched on with horror as a complete section from a shuttle bay blew apart. He slammed at the comms.

"Abandon the test," he ordered. "Sard! Power the engines down! Now!"

"Powering down now, Captain." Sard appeared back on the screen with apologies written all over his visage.

"Get me damage reports within the hour."

Captain Sard lowered his eyes. "Yes, Captain."

"*Sol'Ishar* holding two minutes in. Full Capax," Lynj reported. "Also powering down. Structural damage at a minimum. Ninety-seven percent, our final reading, Sir."

Captain Hadi, turning to Commander Vax, barked, "You have the bridge. I'll be in the engine room."

Almost sprinting away, Captain Hadi met Kendro in the corridor.

"Sorry," the King said, without hearing Hadi's report. "I know I should wait, nothing like seeing things for yourself."

"I understand." They spoke on the run. *This isn't going as planned. There should be more we can do.* "Sard's ship isn't fit for pulling off a jayux yet. I'm just hoping powering up hasn't caused irreparable damage."

"It had to be done." Kendro consoled, "She'll be fine. We needed to find out how far she can be pushed, before we tried this for real."

"Agreed," Hadi said as they entered Engineering. Both men paused to react as Zyler and his crew jumped to attention, saluting.

That done, Hadi spoke, "At ease." He looked around for Octav.

"The Ainoren's inside the engine," Zyler said. "A brief malfunction when we powered down."

Hadi stepped towards Zyler, almost ready to grab hold of the man. "And why did you let the Ainoren go in to fix it?"

Zyler glanced to the King. "He volunteered, Sir."

"Let me talk to him," Captain Hadi ordered.

Zyler reached towards a console, clicking a few instruments. It blinked to life as a view of Octav popped up, staring up into the comms camo. "On spot five, Captain."

"Ainoren," Kendro clutched at his chest. *Was the King in pain?* "What do you think you are doing?"

"I'm making myself useful, Sire. I'll be out in a couple of minutes."

Captain Hadi wasn't too happy, turning to Zyler, his birthmark flickered a warning. "Don't always let the Ainoren be useful. Understand?"

"Yes, Sir," Zyler said, his glance to the comms a quick one.

They watched on the small monitor until Octav had finished, and backed out of the chamber. A few moments later, he stood before them, brushing dust and trax webs from his trrobhas.

"Status reports from our ship are good," he said, handing one of Zyler's officers a reel of wire. "However, early indications show some damage to the internal energy generators here and on the *Sol'Delka*."

"A lot of damage?" asked Kendro.

"Luckily, no." Octav pulled up a view on the same console, angling it so they all could witness. "These are some of the areas we need to address before we try again." He pointed, and Zyler nodded, catching his intention immediately. The blown-up section of the bulkhead gaped like a festering wound on the other ship. Damage control had sealed off all adjoining compartments. "This is the worst area."

Kendro asked, locking eyes with Zyler, "Integrity, if we do a new test?"

"I've had Lace already talking with the *Sol'Delka*'s engineers. If we refortify this area, then she has a real chance at the jayux. But I'm not willing to test again. I think we've got one chance, that's it."

"Are you sure?" Zyler and Hadi spoke as one.

"Positive. All their other systems coped well enough."

"Good news," Kendro smiled at Octav, "about time."

"I agree. But about harnessing for the jayux?"

"Yes, Ainoren."

"There's severe unrest on Captain Sard's ship. Frankly, it's nearing all-out panic. When we next power up, maybe I should take the sietev?"

They all traded glances.

Kendro's face dropped. "I —"

Never going to happen. Hadi could see it.

241

"Why?" Octav demanded. "You must know it will serve setting everyone's nerves. I believe in our engineers. Surely you must?"

"It isn't that." Kendro said. "It's—"

"Well?"

Hadi replied for Kendro. "We simply can't be sure the *Sol'Delka* will survive."

Octav dared stepping away from Zyler's work area, reminding the King in his lowest of voices, "We've defied everything up to now. Can your visions ever be incorrect?"

"Up to now." Kendro's meaning was clear. "No. You remain here. I don't want any mistakes. I can't lose you."

Octav reached out touching Kendro's arm. "You won't. But Sire, I need to be there."

Kendro turned to Captain Hadi who could see him wrestling with the decision, his birthmark flickering.

"The Ainoren has my permission to leave the ship."

Hadi strode ahead with Octav lagging behind, the Ainoren's shuffles loud in the empty corridor. Turning, Hadi stroked his uniform, feeling nervous to broach this before Octav left for the *Sol'Delka*. "So, how are things?" Meeting Octav's gaze as they walked, Hadi hoped Octav would speak truthfully, yet knowing rank might not allow him the grace.

"Good, thanks."

"Octav," Captain Hadi frowned. "I think we've become close friends these last few months. Don't you?"

"Well. Yes." Octav's mark lit up, he agreed.

"Then, I'll ask again, how are things?"

Octav's brow furrow, confused. So, Hadi risked everything. "Okay, I'll say it. Frie's living with Roma. Every time Katya's checked on her, Frie's been there. I don't understand?"

Octav stopped walking.

"Are you having marriage problems?" Hadi probed.

"Roma is in much pain, she still grieves. Frie wanted to be with her. Besides, before all this," Octav waved a hand overhead, "I was hardly ever there. She's not used to having me around. Ship life. It's horrible on marriages, no? Guess I get on her nerves more than I should."

"I can't pretend to understand wives anymore than the next man. I just wanted you to know if you need someone, you can talk to me. That's all."

Octav needed someone to talk to—an officer other than Chace. Organizing the trial jayux with Veco and Hanya had taken all of the Ainoren's resources and time. Hadi knew that in the last week even they'd only seen each other twice in passing. "Thanks," Octav replied.

"Or if you don't think you can talk to me," Hadi continued, "maybe you'd talk to Katya?"

Octav thought for a moment. "Would she not find that conflicted?"

Hadi watched Octav's demeanour at even asking him this question, shoulders low, his swagger all but gone. He sighed. This wasn't going to be so easy. He placed a tentative hand on Octav's arm. Octav didn't flinch at the contact. He didn't chastise either. "She's a doctor, first and foremost. She knows many things that I don't."

Captain Hadi could see the conflict in Octav's mind. It was broadcast in the shifting lights of his birthmark. That made Hadi offer, "I'll ask her to stop by. She won't tell me when, or even if you do talk."

Upon entering his quarters, Kendro smiled as the beautiful aroma of his favourite dish greeted him. He walked straight to the kitchen area where Mika had just served plates of steaming Micret.

"Where's Taliri?" the King asked.

"Sleeping. Brie's been to check on him today. Everything is fine."

"Happy Triaton." Kendro wrapped his arms around her, bringing her close for a kiss. Mika snuggled into his growing beard.

"I like it," she said. "Will you keep it?"

Kendro rubbed his chin. "Maybe, I don't know yet. I guess it depends on how the planet Earth people might see me. The beard hides our birthmark somewhat. So—maybe. Yes—I'll keep it for a little while."

"Good." She pointed. "I tried to make it like back home. But there is just something missing. Sorry."

Kendro sat down. "Jogi didn't help at all?" He picked up a fork, and then, continued, "Ummm, don't worry. I noticed the moment I stepped in. It looks wonderful."

"There needs to be some things that don't change," Mika said, taking her seat opposite.

"I agree." He smiled. "This is bliss." Kendro reached under the table with his feet and playfully, she let him wrestle hers to the floor. "I love you."

"I love you too." Mika giggled, trying to avoid his gaze. "How did today go?"

"We have some hope of getting the *Sol'Delka* through the jayux."

"Will you test her again soon?"

"Maybe in a couple of weeks. As I said, we know the parts we need to be concentrating on, so it won't be as difficult now. All other system fixes can be pushed back."

"I spoke to Frie earlier." Mika took a drink. "Everyone seems positive. You've asked her to take the main Sietev, why?"

"Hanya and Veco. As powerful as they are, they were not capable enough. Octav's asked to be on the *Sol'Delka*, as much as it pains me to let him. I agree with his decision. He's needed there. Frie is our next most powerful." Kendro refused to meet her gaze this time.

"Is she in danger?"

We all are. But Kendro refrained from the truth. "No, if she can manage Octav, she can deal with this."

"Taliri's drawn more pictures today." She stabbed a morsel on her plate, but didn't eat. "Maybe you should see them."

Kendro popped a forkful into his mouth, suddenly feeling sick. He chewed, swallowed, and pushed his plate away, his favourite dish spoiled. "In the morning,"

"He's quite anxious. It took me a while to settle him tonight."

"We're all anxious." Kendro reached over, taking her hand. "We should relax for one evening."

"Only if you promise one of your infamous massages." Mika's eyes sparkled.

Kendro laughed with her. "Deal."

Octav sloped back to his quarters. Without Frie there, it seemed empty, cold.

He pushed the door open and walked, uncaring, though his living space, stripping off as he did, heading for a shower. Once he stood in the refreshing energy pulse, he enjoyed the sensation many on board had to share, seemingly cleansing his body as well as his mind.

A knock at the door roused him from dreaming. He slipped a towel around his lower half before answering. *What now!*

"Doctor?" He stared into Brie's calm face. "That was quick."

Brie's attention nil, as her eyes lingered over his bare skin. Octav felt heat rise to his face.

Continuing to look confused, Brie herself blushed. Octav added, "Sheve didn't mention you stopping by? For a talk?"

"Oh," she finally met his gaze, "I've not seen him today, sorry. You're free? Yes?"

Strange. Octav moved to let her in, realising too late that half his uniform lay strewn across the floor. "I'll grab something." He returned a moment later to find her making herself a warm drink of Bea.

"Would you like some?"

"Yes, thanks."

Brie poured him a cup, holding it out for him, staring too much.

A niggling pain struck Octav's forehead. He could do without this now, but her presence demanded some respect. "What brings you here?"

Brie turned away, as if she didn't want to be there. "I've a concerned comm from Jaack."

Octav stepped to his divano. Ah. The good Doctor. "Jaack?" Octav sat. "I haven't spoken to him since we left Sard's ship a few weeks ago."

"Well," drinking some of her Bea before adding, "I've come from Chace's quarters."

The pain in Octav's head worsened. "What is it?"

"He's asked me to come tell you—because he didn't think he could. Chace's—he'd hate me for saying, but his condition is getting worse." She paused. "Doctor Jaack thinks he could be dying."

"No." Octav dropped his cup, shattering it, the drink running into his discarded uniform. "No way."

Brie moved across to sit beside him. She placed a hand on his, trying to steady the sudden shakes tugging at Octav's whole body. "I'm sorry."

Octav's eyes flashed green. "Sorry, why?"

"Chace—told me a few things."

All he could muster was a sound of disbelief. He pushed her hand away.

"I'm not here to judge you in anyway. I'm here because Chace asked me. To be the one who tells you—"

Octav stood. "I…"

Brie said, "Go to him. He needs you right now."

Octav stood, hovering near the divano. He had to go.

"Is there any hope?" Tears brimmed, but he fought them, fearing the worst. He was almost to the door when Brie spoke.

"Just be yourself." She reached out, touching his arm. That brief connection settled Octav for a moment. "That's all he wants. And Jaack's coming on the next shuttle. But I can't promise you anything."

Octav ran for the door, leaving Brie to clean up the shattered glass.

THE TRUTH

ALL ATTEMPTS TO COMM CHACE brought no answer. Octav tried at each comms station he passed. Now at Chace's door, his shaky hand found it locked. *What else?* Octav focused, steadying himself, knowing he wasn't thinking clearly. *What? What can I possibly say? Or do?*

Then, he decided. He focused on the security panel. Harnessing his croex, within the space of a breath, he overrode its locking mechanism, and let himself in.

Chace nowhere to be seen in the dark living space, Octav crept towards the bedroom. With a creak, he gently pushed the door, now able to see Chace curled inside moving blankets. *Is he crying?*

Octav hesitated, but on hearing a sob, nothing could stop him. With two strides, he reached the bedspace, lifting the blanket, and slipped in next to Chace.

He wrapped his arms around Chace's quivering body.

"I don't want you here." Chace sobbed, trying to push him away. "You can't stay."

"If you didn't want me here, why tell Doctor Brie everything?" Octav sighed, stroking Chace's face. "Come." He pulled closer. *I'll risk it.*

"You're staying?" His look told Octav he was unsure.

"I'm staying," he replied. Octav silenced him with a kiss.

Kendro woke to a tugging sensation. Opening his eyes, the small face of his son looked deep into his.

"You have grown, haven't you?" Kendro squinted—this visit, a great opportunity to see his son's birthmark. Beautiful.

Taliri in stretched pyjamas, too tight on his growing frame, tugged at

246

the King's arm again. Kendro slid out of his bedspace, following his son into the supposed safe room.

"How'd you even get out?" Kendro queried.

Taliri looked up at him with sparkling blue eyes that flashed and twirled in the dark.

"You can harness your croex already?" Kendro rubbed his eyes, feeling tired still. "Amazing."

Father, I am young in body, not in mind. Taliri's voice sounded triumphant in Kendro's mind.

Kendro nearly laughed. *I should have known. You understand everything I say, too?*

I'm learning. I don't like speaking, just yet.

We thought your body was developing too fast for your mind, but it's on equal levels?

Taliri didn't answer. He wandered to a play-desk, picking up a reader and handing it to his father.

Kendro flicked through several pictures, all advanced, nearly schematic, if made with a child's finger.

"This is one of our engines." Kendro's hand rested in a light touch on his son's head. "How do you even know what it looks like?"

Taliri picked out one particular picture, zooming in and out at varying points on the image, looking up to his father with pride. It bore several equations scrawled about. At the top a printed name—Demak.

Please get this to him. The information is vital. That is your right word, Father? Vital?

Kendro had no idea what these equations meant. "And you understand this?"

Taliri's small shoulders shrugged. *I see them. I know they're important.*

Kendro glanced at some of the other images. He thought Octav might need to see them. He bent down to his son. As Mika had said, Taliri was anxious. Now, his father could see why.

Taliri yawned.

"You should be asleep," Kendro said, picking him up.

Father, the doctor says I am getting old. Is old bad?

"No, you're perfect." Kendro placed Taliri down onto his bedspace. "Sleep, little one. Let me worry about your future. Fast as it seems to be approaching." Kendro pulled a blanket up over him, tucking his son in tight, hoping this time that he wouldn't escape.

I had to, Father. I'm just trying to help.

Kendro leaned over, kissing his forehead. "I know, son. Get some rest."

Kendro then left a message on Mika's reader. "Be extra careful. Taliri can let himself out of the safe room." *Mischievous young man.*

Kendro made his way down to the fighter pilots' quarters. He was certain Octav would be there. Most soldiers would still be asleep in their beds, the bare minimum of staff working.

Kendro buzzed Chace's door, waiting, gently tapping on the bulkhead. Patience not his thing at present, he forced himself to stop, resting his hands at his sides. He wanted to show Octav Taliri's new plans for the engines.

Octav opened the door in a pair of trrobhas, nothing else. He saw Kendro and froze. "I—"

Kendro frowned, considering what Octav's presence in this causal state meant to the pair. "Octav."

Octav let out a deep sigh. "He's dying." The emotion he fought flickered once across his birthmark.

Kendro maintained composure as the intensity of Octav's feeling's flooded through their bond, all thoughts of the engine's plans leaving him.

"It's all my fault." Octav just managed the words, which Kendro found disturbing.

"I'm sorry." Kendro slid himself inside the room. Leading Octav to a chair, he sat down with him.

"I— shouldn't be here."

Kendro glanced once to the open door, Chace's laboured breathing echoed through. "We will talk, but not now."

Shock registered on Octav's face, so Kendro added with more sympathy. "I've known since the day you both met. Even beyond Lyrik."

Octav looked away. "I'm an embarrassment to the Royal House. You should have me thrown out." Green flashes lit his mark, but his face darkened.

"Tell me what's going on?" Kendro asked aloud, hoping he could help turn Octav's mind from the troubles they would soon have to face.

"Brie tried explaining it, but I don't understand it all." Octav's demeanour said everything. His shoulders slumped as his mark stopped flickering. "Can you do something?" Octav nearly demanded of his King. "Anything?"

"Octav." Kendro's heart went out to him. His next words wouldn't comfort. "I'm sorry."

Octav let out a moan, resting his head in his hands.

"I'm drained. It'll take me years to regain my full strength. You know that." Kendro reached out, lifting Octav's chin so their eyes could meet. "If I could do something, I would. You'll have to believe in Brie's ability."

As they sat in silence, Kendro allowed some of his croex out into Octav, who accepted the generous offer. Their sudden closeness was strange, but comforting for them both. "You need to rest."

"Jaack is coming over on a shuttle." Octav lifted his face, almost begging his King. "Will you meet him with us, please? You'll understand what he says more than I."

"Of course."

Octav rubbed his weary face. "You're not angry?"

"You're family," Kendro soothed. "A brother to me. I could never be angry. Others will be. You know that, too."

Octav nodded. "I never intended to bring this to the House."

"I know," Kendro replied. "We'll face it together." Kendro gazed towards the bedroom. "May I see him?"

"He's asleep. Took hours." He hesitated, standing. "But, yes, of course."

Kendro followed Octav into the bedroom, the light from the living room illuminating Chace's shrunken frame. Kendro sat by him. Bringing forth his croex, the room took on an eerie blue glow. Kendro placed his hand on Chace's chest. Chace didn't move, nor wake. This unsettled the King more than he thought it would, usually his connection did so much. Such loss lately.

No sooner had Kendro's croex touched Chace than the King wanted to withdraw, but he didn't. He could do no healing here, that he already knew, even if Chace had been strong enough. Kendro knew his presence made a difference, though. Chace's breathing slowed. *Calm yourself. We're doing everything we can.*

Chace began to come around hours later, twisting to face Octav. "You stayed…" As he stared into his eyes, he risked confessing, "I thought I was dreaming."

"No dream," Octav replied, letting a finger trail down the side of Chace's cheek. "I'm here. Now go back to sleep. You need to rest."

"The King—"

"Yes. But first, rest."

While Chace had slept fitfully, Octav hadn't. *Why now? I've wasted so much time.* He stroked Chace's back.

Octav slipped out to get a drink. Whilst pacing the living space, he grabbed his shirt. Returning to climb back into bed, Chace stirred, rolling over in his slumber. Octav felt more comfortable with Chace than Frie, he had to concede this to himself, yet still, his mind raced along with the feelings he had. Octav curled around him, holding tight. He drifted asleep for a short time.

"Are you all right?" Chace's sleepy voice asked. Octav glanced to the clock to find it was just before lunch.

Octav wanted to answer, to say 'no' but didn't dare.

"Maybe I should have been poisoned a long time ago." Chace tried joking.

"Please." Octav pushed him. "Don't ever say that."

"Do you know how many nights I've spe—" Chace coughed, "—nt alone wishing I could be with you like this?"

Wanting to believe him, Octav frowned, looking away, feeling he didn't deserve it. "No." He tried to change the subject. "We had a visitor while you slept."

Chace pushed the covers back, feeling hotter to Octav's touch. "It really was Kendro, wasn't it?"

"Yes." Octav palmed the reader at the side of the bed, adjusting cool air to blow across them. He shivered. Octav couldn't look back at Chace. Everything would change now. He knew that.

Chace reached for him, touching his face, running a finger down his mark. "Octav, I'm sorry. I'm—"

"Sorry for what? It seems everyone knew about us, before there even was an 'us.'"

Chace coughed again. Octav reached feeling his forehead. "You're burning up. I'll get you a cold drink."

"I don't want you being my nurse." Chace grabbed hold of Octav's trrobhas. "I'm not that sick."

"No." Octav tried to tug away, but Chace held fast. "I'll do it anyway. You'll be sick of the sight of me by the end of the day."

Chace's face changed, running his hand down Octav's chest, they both watched as Octav's birthmark flickered, changing colour and shape.

"I never knew it would do that with anyone." Octav looked down, watching as his body came alive with Chace's continued touch. "Frie knew we weren't properly mated. She could never make me respond like this."

Chace withdrew his hand. "What are you saying?"

Octav knelt before him, taking both hands in his, wishing the truth didn't have to come out. "Do you remember our first real mission together?"

Pushing back into the pillows, Chace yawned. "It was a long time ago."

"So, you don't remember?" Octav leaned into the bedspace, staring, needing a reaction.

"Of course, I remember." Chace slapped at his arm. "I'm joking. I never knew you were so serious."

Octav, hoping he really did remember, asked, "What happened, then?"

"I'd been assigned to your detail for less than a week."

Octav watched as Chace's facial mark flickered slightly. Octav added, "You were sent on recon towards the Zefron home planet."

Creases settled across Chace's damp brow. "I made some bad decisions on that mission."

Octav attempted to stroke that memory away.

This should follow the previous sentence. "But, you also made some right ones. We wouldn't have gotten away from the Zefron without you."

Chace bristled, and almost demanding, "Where are you going with this?"

"Your detail celebrated that evening." Octav knew it was coming now. All or nothing. "I was about to walk past. You called me over. Poured me a beer."

Joy flooded through Octav, the memory overwhelming him.

Chace laughed. "The other guys said I was crazy, and that the Ainoren never joined them after a mission." He pushed a straggle of hair out his eyes. "But you did that day."

"That was the first time. The only time, because of what happened."

"We got drunk. Remember? You helped me back to my quarters. That was all, wasn't it?"

Chace stared at him. Octav knew he waited for any tell. His straight face never gave anything away. For that, he was sorry, but proud. "No. No, it wasn't."

Chace took hold of his hand, knotted his fingers into his. When Octav pulled back, he held tight. "Was it so bad?"

"You made me laugh so much it hurt," Octav admitted, "you were really drunk. So was I. In your bedroom, we fell onto your bed." Octav remembered, feeling those emotions anew. "When I watched you, my stomach churned. I'd never felt so much passion. So, I kissed you."

"You kissed me?" Chace's mouth opened, and unconsciously, he licked his lips.

Octav gazed into Chace's eyes. *Why did I push this all away?* "It was the most amazing kiss I'd ever had."

"Did we do anything else?"

Octav steadied their hands, sucking in a breath.

"Yes, we did." Octav stared right into Chace's face. "But I felt so foolish."

Chace took a deep breath, closing his eyes, as memories flooded his mind. Drunk, maybe a little, then he felt that raging passion.

Chace felt Octav's breath against his fingertips. His warmth filling him with hope, he opened his eyes. "I remember." As though a veil lifted, it all came to him. Chace rested a hand on Octav's knee, more to steady his shaking than anything else.

With nimble fingers, Octav unbuttoned his shirt. Chace helped

Octav out of it, exposing the green flickering birthmark.

"You—" Octav's throat tightened, drawing forth his croex so that the truth would finally be out in the open. "You left me this—"

Watching as the flickering mark moved, it parted to show Chace the curled insignia of a mated Aonise. His insignia. Frie must have known this, unless Octav hid it. Skilled beyond anything he'd known.

Chace was not sure what to think or feel. "You shielded it so no one else knew, not even me. I'd been drunk, but I wasn't that drunk." Chace folded his arms. "I blocked it because of the pain, thinking I could never have you. Second in command to the King—more than my wildest dreams. Then, in the hospital?"

"A brief lack of concentration—"

"You never reciprocated the bond," Chace said.

"That's not entirely true." He swallowed, not wanting to reveal all just yet. "I had you called to the medical deck the next day. You remember Jaack—W—well, he helped me block your memory."

Chace's brow furrowed, increasing the tiny lines around his eyes.

"It wasn't a full bond." Octav averted his eyes. "I'd only partially woven the connections."

Chace tugged his shirt off, Octav reached out, touching him. "Here, see." A partial mark became visible. The twisting insignia, almost perfect.

"Oh, Ari—" Chace took hold of Octav's hand. "I can't believe you did that. Well, almost did!"

Octav's eyes twinkled green. Chace almost let go. Their hands sparkled with Octav's croex.

"Let's finish what I started"

"What about Frie?"

"She knows we're not properly joined. I couldn't be. I should have known that. I cheated her."

"No," Chace said. "You gave her what she wanted. A way into the Royal House."

"I guess," he replied.

"I want more than anything to finish what you started eighteen years ago. But—" Chace felt Octav's heart miss a beat.

Chace let go of his hand. "What if bonding puts you at risk? I don't know anything about this poison; it might travel across the bond."

"I feel so useless," Octav stated. "Like I've never done anything right in my whole life."

Chace stood, struggling. Octav offered his hand. "No. You've saved thousands of lives. Don't think you're useless."

"I can't save the one that means the most. You."

"I don't need the full bond to feel what you feel. I know it."

"The shuttle will be here soon." He moved away from Chace, head low, defeated. "I'll get us some breakfast."

"Stop running away." Chace laid a hand on his arm, feeling the warmth beneath. "When things get tough, you bolt out for the nearest exit."

"I'm sorry. Habits are hard—"

"Get us some food. I'll make a drink. Then, you need to get everything else off your chest. All right?"

Octav walked out of the mess hall back to Chace's quarters carrying a tray of fresh food. He let himself in, heading for the bedroom.

Then, he saw Doctor Brie leaning over Chace, while Captain Hadi watched. Brie's gaze met his wide eyes. "I'm just checking in," she said. "Don't panic."

Octav set the tray down. "Captain," he acknowledged, asking Brie, "How is he?"

"I've been monitoring his vitals," she pointed to a bracelet around his ankle. "There were some irregularities over the last few hours." *Oh, Ari, the thought. They both must know.*

"He's all right?"

"Everything's normal now, yes. We'll let him eat. Should I send someone to fetch him to the infirmary?"

"No. I'll take him." Hadi scowled at this, but Octav's final words, "We'll be fine," came out before he thought for them.

Turning, Hadi watched Chace gaze at Octav. *Was he upset?*

Hadi said to Chace, "Need anything else, just comm me, all right?"

Chace nodded. "I will do," then reaching for the plate of food, just out of his grasp, "Thank you both for stopping in."

Doctor Brie packed her few things away. Hadi gave Octav a strange glance as they were about to leave. *He really was upset.*

Octav passed Chace his plate. "Eat. You'll need your strength."

Chace took off the wrapper, pulling off a bit of meat. "Are you going to fuss like this all the time?"

"No, I did wait until they left, after all. I have others I need to fuss over. I take my position seriously, you know that."

Chace grinned. "And I was just getting used to you being around. Now you're going to leave me?"

Octav's face fell until he saw Chace's smirk.

"I'll be right back." Octav all but ran after Hadi.

Hadi and Brie were not in the corridor, instead Octav almost ran over Jaack, instead. *He's here already?*

"Ainoren, a word." Jaack looked on edge, sweat beading on his upper lip.

Octav backed away. "About what?"

"I wanted to ask you to—" Jaack hopped, one foot to the other, "— explain your behaviour with Chace. After all, we did to stop it happening. You went ahead anyway." Jaack's fists balled together, knuckles turning white.

Octav saw a flicker of anger within Jaack's birthmark. He flustered. "What we do is none of your business. You're just a civilian."

"Excuse me?"

Jaack's glare unsettled Octav more than he thought it would, his eyes boring into his skull. "What I do in my spare time is my business, not yours."

"This will rip apart anything we have going for our species, don't you see that?" Jaack threw his hands in the air. "It's like you don't even care."

"I do care." Octav reached for him, grasping a shoulder. "I've cared more for the throne and our people than anything else in my life."

Jaack spun around, his mark flashing. "I'm not talking about the throne."

Octav lowered his head. "Then, what?" He didn't understand.

Jaack shook his grip off, rubbing his arm.

A door opened at the end of the corridor, two soldiers exited, moving towards them. Jaack took a step back waiting for them to leave.

The lift pinged. Opened, they cast Octav a glance before the door closed.

With no way to get out of this confrontation, Octav threw out the only thing he could. "You loved him, right? Am I never allowed to feel that?"

Jaack stared at him. Blank.

"Wouldn't you do anything for him?"

Red croex flared and bounced off the walls around them. "You know I would."

"Then, you'll understand why I won't change my mind this time."

Pain etched deep in Jaack's features, lips tightening. "Are you telling me you love him?"

"Yes," Octav didn't hesitate, "I love him."

"What about Frie?"

"I love her, too," Octav paused, thinking, and then added, "in my own way."

"You can't do this, you'll break his heart."

Octav frowned. "I am not leaving him this time."

TEST RESULTS

KENDRO MET WITH DOCTOR JAACK and Octav on the way to the infirmary. "It's good to see you again, Doctor Jaack." Kendro smiled.

"I wish it were under much better circumstances, Your Highness." His glance to Octav revealed nothing. Kendro saw how Octav fumed, both on the outside, and on the inside.

"Thank you for meeting me. I know we have lots to discuss. Let's get to the infirmary so Brie and I might work quicker."

"Of course," Octav replied, pointing down the corridor. "Follow me."

"How is he?" Jaack had refrained from asking until the lift began descending.

"For the most part, he looks and acts normal."

"The pain?"

"Severe," said Octav, curling his lip. "At the moment, he's bearing it, but I don't think he'll be able to bear it much longer."

Jaack thought on this before saying, "I've brought several pain relief methods for when it becomes too much. Insist he uses them."

"I'm his Ainoren, I'll order him." Octav tried to smile, but inside, it genuinely hurt him imagining Chace in pain.

"You will do anything necessary—" Doctor Jaack glanced towards Kendro, unsure of what the King knew. "—I understand."

Octav noticed the concern, nodding to Kendro. "You can say anything. There is nothing unknown between us."

Jaack relaxed hearing this, and ventured, "Would you be able to walk away? If it were in Chace's best interest?"

"If that is what I have to do," said Octav, struggling with a yes.

"I have a theory." Jaack smiled. Holding a hand up, he added, "Only

255

a theory."

At this, the King stepped in. "Be careful with your theories, Doctor."

"It's all right." Octav sighed. "I want to hear it. Any theory is a starting point."

"If you insist."

"I believe because you are partially bonded," the lift reaching the lower floors, but Doctor Jaack held the doors closed for this next bit of news, "the poison designed specifically for your DNA has found something to cling to within Chace's system." Kendro shook his head at this treachery. "His own system—well, where yours meets his—it has started crossing the barrier. To work on destroying his cells."

"So, you're saying I have to remove the bond?" Octav's voice shook.

"This is where I'm in the dark," said Jaack. "If you remove the bond—"

Kendro sighed. "—you might never be able to get it back."

"What if we were bonded properly?" Octav asked, reaching for any way out of this.

"Then the poison might leave his system for yours."

My death. "I understand." Octav lowered his head in thought. "Have you spoken with Doctor Brie about this?"

"I asked her about attaching a monitor last evening, when I first spoke to her. Was I correct?" He looked to Kendro now.

Kendro nodded.

"So, I'll have some results to look over." He released the lift doors. "I would suggest—" he turned to Kendro, "that you keep Octav busy for a few hours, Sire."

"What? You can't ask him to keep me away." Octav's back straightened, his eyes sparkled green.

This is going to be very difficult for him. Kendro knew he might have to step in here.

"Chace is my patient." Jaack added, "Don't get me wrong—this is for both of you." The Doctor addressed Kendro now. "I'm afraid I must insist."

Kendro reached out, stopping Octav from following the Doctor though the open lift doors.

"You're serious."

"No. Come with me. I have another job for you."

Kendro escorted a weary Octav towards a flight bay. Octav stopped at the door. "You want me to leave the ship now, don't you?"

"I need you to take these drawings to the *Sol'Delka*. Get them to Lace's friend, Demak." Kendro held a reader out for Octav.

"Kendro," Octav stared at the reader. The image made no sense to him. "This is killing me."

"You and Chace will not be making any hasty decisions while you're separated. I believe this is the best course of action for keeping you both alive. You were to leave anyway to pilot through the jayux."

"Yes, but—" Octav's eyes flicked back to the corridor, about to bolt.

Kendro pointed at the reader, distraction. "Taliri drew these."

Octav turned back. "Taliri?"

"Yes." Taking the reader and flipping through the images, Kendro quickly picked one drawing out, and passing it back to Octav. "This is what we need. We must get the *Sol'Delka* through the Jayux."

"I don't want to leave him."

"I know." Kendro sighed palming the door open. "You've never felt this before. You don't know how to deal with it. Let those that love you help you through it. Trust in me."

"All my instincts are fighting you."

Octav entered the bay, quickly looking around for a different exit. There was none. He noticed the crew going about their daily tasks. Shuttles gleamed. There really was no choice for him, and Kendro knew it.

Kendro eased him back with a hand. "If I have to, I will order you to leave this ship."

Lowering his head, Octav stepped back again. When he looked into Kendro's face, his eyes flashed green. "You might have to!"

Kendro's birthmark flickered blue light across the wall as he stared hard at Octav. "We'll keep you informed. Trust me."

"Don't let him die without me..." Octav pleaded. "Promise me?"

Kendro couldn't promise anything. "I'll try."

Kendro entered the infirmary, seeking out Jaack, fire burning inside his mind. "You had better be right about this."

Jaack shrugged. "The point I tried to make is—none of this may go as planned. At least while Octav is off the ship, we have a better chance getting Chace to cooperate."

They made their way through the doors into the infirmary. Kendro looked towards one of the private rooms where Brie waited for them.

Brie and Jaack shook hands. "Good to finally meet you."

Chace lay before them, naked and sedated.

"What happened?"

Brie placed her hand on Chace's sleeping shoulder. "We informed him of your plan. He didn't like it. Wanted to go after Octav. We had no choice but to sedate him."

"I hoped you wouldn't have to," Jaack said.

"How's Octav?" Brie directed to Kendro.

Kendro stared at her. His birthmark flickered slightly, turning the white walls blue. "He's following his King's orders." He asked Jaack, "What is your plan?"

"We need to monitor him from the time Octav leaves the ship. See if it makes a difference." Jaack paused, and then added carefully, "I believe it will. I think the poison will slow down Octav's—"

"We all know, Doctor. Don't be coy," Brie said.

"Well, with his closeness to Chace gone, the poison might settle enough to remove it."

"I hope so." Kendro's gaze drifted to Chace's figure. "I've never seen any Aonise lose their connection to their life force before." He reached down, touching the dead birthmark. There was no life at all in it.

"If we stop the process," Brie said, "will it regenerate?"

"This is a first," Kendro said. "I don't know. I hope so. An Aonise without their mark would be devastating. We don't know any longterm effects." He turned to Captain Hadi. "Who is investigating the kitchens?"

"Veco's on it. So far, he's not been successful tracking down the poison's origination point. He has had a few leads though, and is almost positive he's identified a suspect."

"Good, keep pushing those leads, I want this traitor." Kendro watched Jaack's eyes widen. *Why?* "We can't have this getting out. Their attempt failed. I'm hoping they'll believe it wasn't a viable poison."

Lady Katesh made her way through the ships corridors as if she'd been on board her whole life. She'd studied the ships design from within her quarters for quite some time before risking going out without her chaperone.

At the back of her mind, something tugged deep within the ship's hold. She scoffed at herself. She was no seer. *Feelings, what were they?* But she couldn't ignore the fact she felt pulled down to investigate.

Entering the lower corridor, she noticed no other Aonise or Heiako around. This made it much easier. A door before her depicted nothing interesting. A generic 'Seti-1476.'

Approaching with caution nonetheless, Katesh placed her palm to the panel. A red flashing light followed.

"Puswer," she cursed.

A door at the opposite end of the corridor opened. A man entered, walking quickly towards her. Katesh could do nothing. Straightening her back, she waited for him to walk past. Instead, he met her eyes with an unwavering confidence.

He smiled and stopped before her. "My lady."

"Do I know you?" She felt the door panel at her lower back. *Shouldn't have come down here.*

"We've not had the pleasure of meeting yet." The man lowered his head. "My name is Trax."

"What do you want?"

"I've been ordered to take you to your brother."

Lady Katesh's legs almost buckled. She forced herself to stand upright. "Dalamaar really is alive, and on board?"

"Yes, ma'am." He pointed back down the corridor. "Please, with me."

Octav sat waiting while the shuttle's engines stopped. They were safe on Captain Sard's ship. He'd thought long and hard about his last moments with Chace. His hand instinctively on his chest, resting where Chace's mark lay etched.

Octav disembarked, greeting Captain Sard, who waited on the deck.

"Good to have you aboard, Ainoren." Sard saluted with a grin.

Octav returned his salute, but wasn't impressed with his over-friendliness. "Let's see how you're shaping up after the tests." He pulled out the reader, bringing up the drawings. "I don't think these will mean much to you. I've been ordered to take them to Demak."

"I studied engineering extensively." Sard paused, studying the pages. "They're new parameters." A frown in his expression concerned Octav, and knowing the depths of his betrayal and connections to Dalamaar, all Octav wanted was to bring them all down. "Seems way out there. Is it even possible?"

"I don't know. I can work out the basics myself, nothing more."

"All right, we'll find Demak, and try to see if this is possible. I think he's in the mess hall. It's about lunch time now."

Octav patted his stomach. "I think lunch would be a nice bonus."

"Shall we?" Sard signalled the door.

On the way, Sard informed Octav of the changes he'd made as they walked further into the ship. "Several adjustments. The Heiako now have more room, food, and medical supplies. I'm glad you came to visit us those few weeks ago."

"I'm glad, too." Octav smiled, he would never have known Sard was the real traitor otherwise. Looking around though, things had really improved.

"Everyone has a new found passion for working together."

"Good, all down to you."

"It's been a team effort. Emmi's helped a lot. She rallied most of the smaller Aonise sects. We have been doing well, though." Captain Sard paused. "How is Officer Monro?" he asked gently, watching Octav's strong demeanour change.

"He's in the best hands. If the King contacts you, please find me."

"I will. You have free reign of the ship. I can't stay with you and your duties. I'll assign a guard, if you need one."

"No," Octav laughed, "no need. I can look after myself."

"It isn't a problem…" Captain Sard placated.

"Kendro asked you to assign me someone, didn't he?" Octav watched as Sard's facial birthmark flickered, Octav sighed.

"Sorry," Sard looked away, "but, yes."

"Then, be my guest. Just don't count on me becoming their best friend."

Sard laughed. "I'll ask that he join us in the mess hall."

Even in their short walk to the mess hall, Octav noticed how much things had truly improved. The corridors were cleaner, doors to quarters were propped open, and citizens milled around, talking rather than skulking, or hiding.

The main mess hall inspired Octav the most. It sparkled with good hygiene practices, everyone eating together—no prejudice for Heiako to Houses. "Well done, Captain," he praised.

Captain Sard beamed with pride. "Thank you. That does mean a lot. Demak is over to the right. I'll get our food and bring it over if you like."

"No offence, I'll get my own," Octav said.

"Of course, Sir." Sard showed Octav the way to the kitchen queue. Behind strode Eco, Octav's new shadow, at a discrete distance.

"Everything all right, Captain?" Demak asked, as the two officers approached him from the opposite side of the hallway.

"We're just here to chat," Octav said. "I've brought over some new configurations for the engines. Eat first, I'll show you later."

"I beg your pardon, Ainoren," Demak said, "But if you're here specifically, they're important." He shoved his meal to the side and leaned in. "Show me now, please."

Octav reached into his pocket, extracting Kendro's reader, he handed it over.

Demak studied it for a while. His birthmark flickered once as his fingers tapped and slid to reveal each image. Eventually, he asked, "Who drew these?"

"I don't know," Octav lied. "Why?"

"There is only one person who could understand these engines as well as this, and he died building them." Demak paused. "Ainoren, I

260

might be Heiako, and I value discretion more than anything," he placed the reader on the table between them, a single finger tapping the diagrams, "but this guy, I have to meet."

"It isn't going to happen," Octav replied.

Demak frowned. "Well, maybe one day."

Sard looked over one of the drawings. Octav could see he understood nothing. "Do you think there is something in them?"

Octav watched Demak, whose birthmark gave nothing away. Yet, there was a glint in his eye. He met the Ainoren's stare. "Yes, there is, despite my reservations." He took the reader back from Sard, this time his birthmark flickered. Excitement. "In fact, I should get working on them right away." He finally stood, tapping a finger on the reader, "This is what we needed. At the next jayux, we will be good to go. I'm sure of it, Ainoren. I'm off to main engines." Lunch was forgotten. "You can join me there if you want, Sir."

Octav nodded. "Shortly," and with a laugh, he let Demak leave.

Sard said, "I thought there was something in them that would get him excited."

"Lace spoke very highly of him," Octav said.

"You probably haven't mixed with too many Heiako until recently, have you?"

"No, not that I have nothing against anyone."

"I understand," the Captain said. "Some of the brightest minds our species has ever known were Heiako. As Demak said, Jurr built the first space-capable engine, and died doing so. There hasn't been anyone coming close to that brilliance in the engineering field for decades."

"You do know your engineering." Octav smiled. "All I know is how to fly. I can only fix them under supervision."

Sard laughed. "And fly very well, you do, Ainoren."

"Thanks. Let's eat up, then I can go see why Demak's so excited."

Officer Eco wolfed down his food to their right. Sard motioned to him. "Take it easy, we're not rushing you."

Octav cast him a cursory glance before continuing with his meal.

Doctors Brie and Jaack worked together in her small lab. Chace's image on a view screen next to another that displayed all his vital statistics. The gentle slow beeping in the background indicated Chace's heart rate. As the beeping increased, Brie turned her attention from the Rastrom before her to a window separating them from Chace.

"I think he's waking." Brie watched as Chace's form turned in his bed.

"I'll go, and talk to him," Jaack replied. "At least we now have some

261

results to explain."

"I'm glad you were right about Octav leaving the ship." Brie sensed Jaack's excitement, but also something else. Not completely sure she liked the man, but she couldn't fault his skills.

"Believe me, so am I."

Brie watched Jaack enter Chace's private chamber, a calm smile on his face. *What in Ari's name worries me so much about him?*

Jaack's calm voice came over the comms. Brie moved to her panel about to turn it off when she heard. "You're a monster. Why can't you leave us alone?"

Brie instantly turned to the screen, looking closer at Chace. Although struggling to sit up in the bed, his face said everything. Birthmark flickered wildly with the little croex he had left.

"I'm trying my best to help you and Octav."

"Don't you call him by his name."

What is going on?

Brie moved closer to the window. "After all these years, you've never gotten over our break up, did you?" Chace's shaky voice came through as Jaack sat on the edge of his bed. Chace slid further back trying his best to get away.

Chace and Jaack were together? The more Brie watched, the more it made sense. Octav's hostility towards Jaack, and the way Chace reacted every time he entered a room.

No. Then the biggest part of this puzzle hit her. Moving quickly back to her panel, she comm'd for Kendro.

When Kendro's image came on her screen, she saw his instant worry. "Sire, I believe I know who our assassin is."

"Who?" Kendro's eyes flashed blue.

"I have no proof."

"Katya, please." Kendro lowered his head. "Just tell me."

Looking once more to Chace and Jaack as they continued their conversation, she revealed her information. "Chace and Jaack—have a history—together. I believe Jaack is responsible for the poison."

"It must have been a long time ago." Kendro tapped into his console, and a number came up on the screen. "This is Veco's comm, I'd like you to speak with him as the investigating officer. I'll talk with Octav."

"Yes, Sir. Should I do anything else?"

Kendro frowned. "No, not yet. Just be careful around him. Please."

Brie agreed, signing off. She commed for Veco, who explained everything about Jaack and Dalamaar. Their conversation, only brief, left Brie with a heavy settling in her stomach. She leaned over, vomiting. This Maicrox passing so quickly, Brie rubbed her stomach, feeling hope alive within. *Our baby.*

Chace struggled with his emotions as Jaack tucked a pillow behind his back. "Explain why?" He stared the doctor down. "Why did you sedate me?"

"We needed you calm, and getting worked up over Octav leaving wasn't helping."

"He's really gone?"

"Let me explain." Jaack perched on the end of the bedspace. "He had to leave. It was the only way."

"You want him gone, so you can try to win me back."

"I can't lie to you. That's all I've ever wanted. But I didn't want this." Jaack waved a hand over the bed. "Please, let me do my job."

Jaack fidgeted with his reader, and began. "If we introduce a separate virus, it could draw out the poison, and we might be able to try removing the bond, completely."

Chace listened, although he didn't fully grasp everything apart from the devastating fact. "We're never going to be able to be together?" Chace's voice wavered. *This couldn't be happening!*

"We're working on it, for now. But, no, not at the moment."

Chace sank back into the bedspace. "If nothing works. If you can't cure me." Chace grabbed Jaack's arm, his strength still there. When Jaack twitched, he let go. "Then you'll let me make that decision? Won't you?"

Jaack rubbed his arm where Chace's hand had touched, shaking his head.

"It is my life." Chace felt tears brimming, but he fought to stop them.

"You're my patient. My first job is to get you better."

"What if you can't?" Chace felt a tear slip out. "Really?"

"Let me worry about it. For now, well… the next few days will take it out of you," Jaack warned.

"What's the plan?"

"At the moment, nothing. Brie is quite the genius in a lab though. We've isolated the poison more thoroughly than I did earlier—"

Chace knew the real issue. "It's the bond, isn't it?"

"Yes."

"I'll do anything you ask." Chace let out a breath, knowing the futility of even asking. "Can I at least talk to Octav?"

"If I can arrange it, promise me you both can stay calm?"

"I promise," Chace said, lowering his head, the pain unbearable now. Never in his life had he felt so powerless.

Lady Katesh followed Trax through many of the ships corridors. She didn't pay attention to where, knowing her fate already decided.

Dalamaar would surely kill her. This was it, she'd done it all for nothing. Lost all that time with Troj, and their child. Tears welled up, but she brushed them back. She would not let him see her cry. Not now.

Trax stopped, opening a door before her. "Go in," he said, "he's expecting you."

Katesh sucked in a deep breath and stepped into the room. With his back to her, Dalamaar stood surveying a screen of a thousand images. *It really is him? How?*

"You're hacked into the camos' main frame?"

Dalamaar turned, lips tightening into a forced grin. "Verona, how good it is to have you finally awakened."

Katesh kept her composure. He hadn't changed at all. A little heavier around the edges, his once jet black hair now with streaks of white. His birthmark though, never faltered, and glittered his face with various hues of gold. Her brother could melt the heart of anyone else, but her. "You've brought me here for one reason only." She sighed. "You plan to kill the King."

"My plan was set in motion by Ari himself. The King is so weak. Anyone who met him for battle would defeat him."

"And there, that is your problem." Katesh walked towards the large projection. With deft fingers, she brought two images up into larger view. Kendro in a meeting room with Houses, Sonaya, and Flikait. Hadi on the bridge working his crew.

"These men will not follow you."

"Pah, of course they will, when they realise who their true leader is."

"No. They won't."

Dalamaar threw his hand up in the air, the view screen vanishing, turning into a blank wall.

Katesh hoped she'd done enough. "Brother, the King's heir is already on the way."

Dalamaar paced the room. She saw he wasn't surprised at this information. So why was he going for Kendro now? "You cannot kill Kendro. You must take Mika down first."

"I wanted him to know his end was coming." Dalamaar stopped pacing before her, taking her hands in his. "I wanted my sister back, so that we may rule together."

Katesh almost laughed. "You know that's not possible."

"We've left Letháo, so anything is possible."

Maybe, but you're still so undisciplined. Katesh stepped with him over towards a divano. There she tugged him down. "Tell me how you're still alive?" With a wink, she grinned. "Then, let me tell you my plans."

JAYUX

IN THE LAB, BRIE FLITTERED from one side to the other, processing vials, logging details. Jaack returned, standing at one end with his hand on his hip as he watched her.

"He seemed to take it pretty well," she directed at him.

"You were listening, that's all right." He edged closer. Brie felt suddenly threatened, and she took a step back.

"Although—" Jaack placed a hand on the counter, "he's usually not so shy."

Brie laughed, but guilt plagued her, the conversation with Veco confirming everything. Jaack was working with Dalamaar, and this terrified her. "I'm not used to seeing him so subdued. It's not like him." She pointed, first to her microscope, and then, the console, hoping this would distract Jaack while she waited for Veco. "Take a look. I think we're getting somewhere."

Jaack stuck his face over the scope's eyepiece. "On board, we see the military side of our patients for so long. In Octav's instance, he's not just the Ainoren. He's the King's Second—a public, proud confident man. As their doctors, we see a personal side no one else does." He glanced up from the scope. "You're new to attending Military and Royal needs, aren't you?"

"Yes." Brie nodded, meeting his gaze. "Did no one attend them before me?"

"I treated Octav and Chace, once, a long time ago. The Royal House hasn't needed anyone specific, nor had anyone been requested. I've been in service to Emmi and House Sonaya for seventeen years."

"It looks like its working. The poison's retreating, slowing down. I just want to be sure we have it all before we let them know."

"Amazing, yes?" She indicated the console again, thankful for the trust Kendro had in her to keep quiet. Yet, she was unsure what her King would do with this man as a traitor.

Jaack moved aside as she went back to the scope. "It's easy to see why the King singled you out," he said.

Brie, confused at this, asked, "What? Because I'd happened to be on duty at the time?"

"No, you ask Kendro next time you see him." Jaack laughed. "I am sure he will tell you the truth."

"Shall we tell him?" Brie pointed back at the screen.

"Let's leave it a while longer. See how the DNA looks in a few hours." Jaack watched as cells squirmed and moved before them, decreasing in size.

"I understand." Brie hoped they were right this time.

Octav walked into the engineering room with his assigned shadow, Officer Eco, in tow.

Demak had Taliri's diagrams enlarged and pinned on a white wall. Several men and women scurried around as they worked. One of the officers noticed Octav first. "Ainoren on deck," everyone stopped, greeting Octav with stiff salutes.

"Please," Octav saluted back, their respect noted, "at ease."

Octav then located Demak two hundred feet below, knee deep in the wires and conduits in the engine's main computers.

"It looks complicated," Octav shouted sticking his head down the hatch opening.

"Yes." Demak gave Octav's uniform the once over. "Fancy getting your hands dirty, Ainoren?"

Octav turned to Officer Eco. "Don't follow me. I'll be up soon." With that, he vanished down the hatch.

Rung by rung, Octav felt his way down, careful not to look farther down than his next foot on the next rung. Even if heights never bothered him, he preferred not to expand that view. A few moments later, Octav stood next to Demak. "Tell me what you need, I'll help."

Demak instructed Octav for more than a few hours. Together, they rerouted most of the internal computer systems.

Officer Eco stuck his head inside just as Octav climbed out. "Ainoren, are you finished?" Eco held out a hand for him.

"I guess." Octav smiled, taking the younger officers hand. "We'll see when we turn it back on."

Demak followed Octav up, heading for the main console. "Time to test her out." Demak pushed the comms, speaking directly to Captain

Sard, then turning to Octav. "Would you do the honours?"

"I'd like that." Octav stepped forward. "Thank you."

Demak moved aside. Several other engineers closed in around, waiting to see if the engines would respond well worth these new calibrations.

This has to work! Octav frowned, placing his palm to the console. He keyed in several commands, waiting.

Nothing happened.

With a pop, and a whir, the floor started vibrating.

"Engine's are powering up," Demak said. "Give them a moment."

The engine's hummed as the ship's croex came to life. Octav cast a glance back to the engine's main computer hatch. Sparks flew out, bouncing around the room. The engineers around him scattered.

"Keep calm," Octav ordered. Octav reduced power, waiting for the computer to catch all their changes, and then, he pushed her once more, asking for full power.

Demak's eyes lit with pleasure as the engines responded to Octav's touch, flickering to life. Octav's birthmark lit the room around him.

"Engines are at one hundred percent," Octav reported, turning to Demak.

Eco smiled. "We're going to make it?"

Octav and Demak shook hands, a touch of laughter in his voice as he said, "Job well done."

"Time for a drink." Demak turned to his crew, whose joy and laughter now filled the room. "Would you like to join us, Ainoren?"

"That would be great," Octav replied. "Well done to everyone. We all did it." He met each of their smiles with a curt nod. "I think we've earned it."

Just as they were leaving, Sard came back through on the comms. "Ainoren, report to the bridge please. I have some news from Doctor Jaack."

Chace?

Octav straightened his smile fading. "I'll have to join you later, Demak." He almost ran from the engine room.

"I'll give you some privacy." Sard ushered Octav into his own office. "The channel is secure."

Octav sat at the Captain's desk, pushing a shaking hand at the main console switch. An image of Doctor Jaack popped on the screen before him.

"Good evening, Ainoren." Jaack's face flushed concern evident as he lowered his head.

"Just tell me, Doctor."

"Initial results are good. With you being so far away, the poison has stopped spreading. Brie has altered the original antidote I created. We're about to administer it."

Octav tried his best to fight the urge to shout, just get to it! Instead, he found himself almost whispering, "What aren't you saying?"

"All right."

Confound it, man! What was he getting at?

"There are some risks—" Jaack's face softened, "—as with any treatment."

"I understand. How is he, really?"

"Asking for you, of course." Jaack smiled. "We can arrange for you to talk, if you'd like to."

"Do you think it will help him?"

Jaack paused. "You want my honest answer?"

Octav noted Jaack's face twitch. Jaack had a *tell*. Traitorous malloth.

"Yes." Octav fidgeted in his chair, keeping his fists tight against the arm rests. He watched Jaack intently, wanting nothing more than to throw him and Sard into space.

Not yet! They both needed to serve their purpose, to get to the planet Earth, and to see Chace back to full health.

"No," finally, Jaack meeting Octav's stare through the monitor, adding, "I don't."

More than anything, Octav wanted to speak to Chace, to hear his voice, even if it were fleeting. The words stung as he spoke. "Tell him you can't contact me."

"Of course." Jaack raised an eyebrow. "As soon as we have anything else for you, I'll comm."

Octav felt his croex rising. He stopped it from showing on his face. *Ari, please help him.*

Kendro stood on the *Sol'Ishar*'s bridge with Captain Hadi. He felt all his citizens' apprehension. Houses to Heiako. He knew all their inner thoughts.

"This is it?"

He'd seen within. All over, the *Sol'Ishar*'s citizens manned their posts.

A voice whispered in his mind—*what if we don't make it?*

He'd witnessed Mika sitting with Taliri in their secure room.

Another voice, stronger than the others. *My mum's on the Sol'Delka. Please, Ari...*

Roma and Frie trying to distract themselves by playing a Chinoo game. *Ari, help us all.*

268

"Everyone's ready," said Hadi. "Both ships are as prepared as they can be."

"Has Octav contacted you?"

"With Sard, awaiting final instructions."

"Sard? The Sietev?"

Hadi knew he should have mentioned it. "Demak wouldn't have it any other way. He's merging with the ship."

Kendro stepped back, surprised at this, but he trusted his men. "When you're ready then, Captain." Taking a seat at the Captain's left, Kendro buckled himself in. Tight. "You may give the order."

"Officer Reel, secure a connection to Captain Sard and the Ainoren, please."

Reel brought up a screen. Captain Sard and Octav became visible, sitting on their respective bridges. "All secure, Captain," Reel intoned.

"Sard. Ainoren. Are you ready?"

"We are ready, Captain." Octav tugged at his belt meeting Hadi's approval.

Kendro knew all too well the bridge and engineering were places gravity failed now and then. He turned to make sure every crewmember wore the correct equipment. Octav glanced to Kendro over Hadi's shoulder—saying nothing. But Kendro knew his thoughts. Felt his fear.

"Begin launch procedures," Hadi ordered.

"Affirmative, Captain," replied Frie and Demak from their respective Sietev positions.

From inside the *Sol'Ishar*, the engines sparked to life, the humming buzz associated with them spreading throughout the ship. Kendro knew the Heiako huddled together for comfort and support in their bays.

Officers' families had gathered in larger numbers so not to leave wives and children alone. Comfort was everywhere, as was their hope. Kendro felt it within, and sent it back out to touch them all.

Hadi met Lynj's expression as she looked up from her console. "Engines—one hundred percent, Captain."

Captain Hadi held fast, awaiting confirmation.

"Our engines are also at one hundred percent," Octav reported.

Sard spoke at Octav's side, "See you on the other side, Captain."

Seeking affirmation, Hadi turned to Kendro, but it was ultimately a Captain's decision and Hadi knew it. "On my mark—" he said, "and— Jayux."

The ship's engines fired with a jolt. Kendro felt the force as the *Sol'Ishar* propelled forward with an intensity he'd never experienced. Groaning beneath them, Kendro could only hope they would survive.

On their view-screen, space before them, shifted and bent, the blackness, phased, turning white.

"Amazing," Kendro managed, inertia stealing any other sounds from his throat. Hadi glanced to him, and then back to the viewer.

Space whirred past them. The blackness turned every colour as stars, suns, and entire systems melted into one blurry mess.

The ship shook with the tremendous pressure. Hadi glanced to his crew, who weren't fazed. He tightened his buckle, feeling unsecure.

Kendro witnessed Hadi's birthmark fading. Neither of them had seen anything so terrifying.

Sparks of croex, not unlike their own, shimmied past the view screen. In those few seconds, they'd traversed across space into the unknown.

Shaking, Kendro gritted his teeth, looking around was the most he could do. His shoulders plastered back into his seat. The crew flicked their anti-tronin boots and gloves on, so that they'd stick solid to their stations. They tapped computer systems, checking reports as they came in, all in slow motion. Hadi blinked at Kendro.

And the ship—stopped.

Dead.

Throwing everyone forward.

Hadi slammed up against the buckle that held him, straining, in place. "Location," he ordered.

Lynj pulled an image on screen, finding nearby star systems that related to their charts. "We're far outside the planet Earth's solar system. Captain, but we're close. Maybe four parsec."

Hadi unleashed himself from his harness and leapt to his feet. "Status?" he commanded, yanking on his own gav-vest to manoeuvre. Pointing at Reel, "Get Sard on comms. Now!" Hadi looked back to Kendro. *Please be safe, please.* Kendro heard and felt Hadi's worry.

Reel tapped his console, frantic. "Can't raise them."

The entire crew watched the screen before them as Captain Sard's ship blasted through space in a trailing explosion of metal fragments and hull panels.

No. Ari, no!

Alarms sounded.

Sparks ripped through Sard's ship, igniting anything flammable.

"Status!" Sard shouted as his crew frantically tried to bring systems under control.

Demak screamed over the comms. "The Sietev contains too much croex, Captain. We need to eject her Routui."

Sard fumbled eyes wide at the Ainoren. Octav instantly took it as indecision. *No. Dammit. Not now.* Acting fast. "Eject the *Sol'Delka*'s

270

Routui, now!" he barked.

Octav stepped forward, ordering Demak, "Pull out, now!" Sard could do nothing but move aside.

Octav inputted command after command quicker than anyone else could have, believing in Demak on his end down below.

"We've lost starboard decks. Seven through eighteen." Jenile gasped.

"Close all vents," Octav commanded. "All systems?" He questioned to Grey, "Shields?" Her paled birthmark attempted a flicker as nimble fingers ran across her console.

"Shields will hold with partial power, Ainoren."

"Divert what we have to Decks Six and Nineteen. Seal it, dammit. Do it now!"

Octav looked over to Sard, standing lost and frightened. "Captain, take the comms and try reaching Hadi."

Sard snapped to attention. "Yes, Ainoren." He moved decisively now to the comms. Vega stepped aside.

"Communications aren't responding, Ainoren." Sard lowered his head, shamed.

Doctor Mai's shaky voice echoed around the bridge. "Captain Sard, injuries all over the ship. We are over capacity."

"This is Ainoren Broki, Doctor Mai. Follow protocol. Categorize patients for any major incident. We will get help as soon as we can."

"Ainoren, a distress comm?" Captain Sard queried. "I've got coordinates loaded."

"No need. But normally, yes. Hadi will have already mobilized all available resources our way. Concentrate on getting communications open. We need to talk to them."

"Yes, Ainoren."

An explosion shook them all as their Routui launched.

Demak's comm came again from below. "Ainoren, the Routui's gone."

"Thank you, Demak. Help anywhere your expertise is needed. Keep me informed."

Slight happiness circled the bridge in Demak's next statement. "Those modifications were intense. But for the most part, they got us here."

Captain Hadi issued a hundred rescue shuttles into action, hoping that the damages to their ship were less than it seemed.

"*Sol'Delka*'s scans show severe damage through several decks," Officer Lynj stated.

"Work on opening communications as fast as you can."

Kendro stood, walking towards their viewer, placing a palm to it as if he might reach those on the crippled vessel. "Please eject. Please eject."

The crew watched, mouths open, as the blazing ship jettisoned its Routui into space with enough pressure that it seemed to be a shooting star streaking up and over and between the two ships.

Kendro saw what was coming as Hadi shouted, "Shields at full!"

The Routui headed straight for them. "Brace for impact," Kendro said as it drifted closer.

The Routui exploded beyond their ships shields, sending a shockwave back towards them. Bracing himself, Kendro waited. As it hit, he stumbled backwards falling over the science console.

"Are you all right?" Lynj helped her King back to his feet.

He didn't speak, watching the screen intensely.

Lynj returned to her console. "Our shuttles survived the blast, Captain. They'll be docking soon."

Octav watched several shuttles draw closer now. The blast had shaken them, but didn't cause any more damage than had already been sustained. He breathed a sigh of relief. *Hurry though.*

"Ainoren," Officer Jenile smiled towards him, "we have a communication link with one of the shuttles."

"Patch them through."

"Captain Sard, this is Commander Vax. Please respond."

"Sard, here, Commander." He gave a knowing look to Octav, adding, "Ainoren Broki here has a question."

"You do have medical personal on board?"

"Of course, Ainoren. Doctors Brie, Jaack, and several teams are with me. May we board?"

"Our hatches aren't responding." The Ainoren looked to Jenile, who shook her head.

Octav hoped it would all work out, addressing back. "Negative, Commander. Our hanger bay hatches are still compacted. No entry through there. You'll have to embark via the pods hatches. A tight fit for med supplies, but that's all we have now. Who's your pilot?"

"Hanya and Veco, Ainoren. Pod docking is no problem. We'll be on board soon."

Octav eyed Captain Sard, his brow furrowed, concern obvious. "Bounce me a signal through their comms."

"Possible." Sard quickly moved to the comms, pointing his younger officer in the right direction. "One minute, Ainoren." The two of them worked together until Sard gave Octav a nod.

Captain Hadi's voice crackled over the comms. "Sard, please

respond?"

"Captain Hadi, this is the Ainoren."

"Thank Ari." Hadi sighed. "Where's Captain Sard?"

"Sard's taken over establishing comms. We're working with the damaged hatches," Octav replied.

Hadi asked tentatively, "What's the status of the ship?"

"Severely damaged. Major failures throughout several vital systems."

"Just tell me," Kendro's weary voice almost whispered.

"She—" the Ainoren regarded all the faces around him, "—isn't going to make it. We need to evacuate. Now."

Sard met Octav's gaze, pain in his eyes. "No, she can't be."

"Captain, it wasn't anything you did." Octav tried to reassure, feeling Sard's failure growing deeper. "She just wasn't strong enough."

Sard clenched his fists. "I wasn't strong enough."

Octav shook his head no, traitor or not, this man took his captaincy seriously. "We've been through the impossible. Your reactions have been commendable." He stepped aside. "Captain, you have the bridge. I'm going down to help Demak with the shields. Captain Hadi will start evacuation procedures as soon as he can. I fear we don't have much time. We must keep them up for as long as we can."

"She's going down?"

"Yes, prepare for the worst, Captain. Announce it to your crew. They deserve hearing it from you."

Captain Sard took his seat once more. "Thank you, Ainoren."

Octav left the bridge, knowing there was much work below. He paused, speaking only to Vax at a comms panel. "Is Lace also on board one of the shuttles?"

"Yes. Shuttle sixty."

"Have him report straight to engineering."

Octav palmed the panel for the nearest lift, waited, but it didn't recall. With a sigh, he headed to a stairwell, opening the hatch. Without looking down, he climbed inside. Rung by rung, he descended towards engineering. Thankfully, the stairwell was undamaged, but the descent, slow.

Above the hissing of their struggling power room, Octav shouted, "Demak!"

"Here," a holler came back. "Stack four, Ainoren."

Octav stepped over cables and twisted pieces of metal, finding Demark by his voice. Deep inside the bowls of a re-routed power cell, Demak worked at pulling wire after wire.

"What are you doing?" Octav yelled.

"Rerouting more power stored in these base cells."

Octav moved to traverse down the hole.

"Stay where you are Ainoren," Demak called back. "This is too dangerous!"

Helpless, Octav shouted over the hissing and crackling. "What can I do?"

"Follow my progress on the main console. If this is going to work, you must mirror the changes to the adjusted system."

Octav shouted back, "Got it!" Standing at the main engineer's console, he couldn't hear Demak, but he mirrored every change made within the systems for what seemed like hours. Demak was beyond fast, Octav couldn't even comprehend the changes being implemented.

"Brilliant, isn't he?" a voice behind him. Octav turned. Lace stood beside him. "I'll take over if you like?"

Moving away, Octav watched as Lace matched Demak's changes with complete precision. "Is there anything else I can do?"

"No, we'll be fine here." Lace motioned the doorway with a nod.

"All right, I'll coordinate with Captain Hadi." Octav took the prompt leaving the engineering station. A crackle came from his reader as Sard spoke. "Ainoren, we have full communications. You are live with the *Sol'Ishar.*"

"Octav, can you hear me?" Captain Hadi spoke clearly.

"Loud and clear, Captain," Octav responded. "How are we looking?"

"We have all available rescuers in this. We're not using escape pods, unless we have to."

"Good call. It would use too much power."

"Exactly." Octav continued back to the bridge, reaching a stairwell he'd used earlier. He looked up, the climb daunting, not much easier than coming down.

"Ainoren," Hadi almost whispered. "I'm with Chace."

Octav fumbled the first rung. "Is he all right?"

Chace's voice came back. "Worried?"

Leaning against the wall, instead of climbing, Octav took a breath. "Is this channel private?"

"Yes, Ainoren," Captain Hadi said. "I'll leave you two to talk."

The silence in the corridor deafened Octav.

"Octav," Chace stammered. "I—if they're evacuating the ship. We're back to square one."

"I thought the new drug was working?"

"No." Silent pause again. "The pain's the same."

"I'll stay here as long as I can." Octav screwed a fist tight, croex surfacing, illuminating the tight space he was wedged in. "I'll move into the Heiako quarters at the base of the ship, if it helps."

More silence.

"I just want you back." Chace's whisper mirrored Octav's thoughts. "I need you back."

"I—" Octav clutched at his chest, feeling pain across their bond. "You're in too much pain. Why haven't you told them?"

"They keep drugging me. I can't feel our bond when they do."

"Chace," Octav warned. "Please take the drugs. I'll be there sooner than you think."

"Promise me."

"I promise, soon," Octav lied. Knowing it would be much longer than he wanted, hating the idea even more so.

"Soon?"

Octav hesitated with an answer as Kendro's voice came back over his near reply. "Octav, a nurse had to slip him a needle. His heart rate's shot through the roof."

"Puswer."

"Stay safe, Octav. We all need you back here, my friend."

Octav took a deep breath pushing up from the floor. "I will. Look after him for me."

Octav signed off as Sard's comm came through ship-wide. "This is your Captain. Please make way to your designated evacuation points."

Octav sighed. "Chaos ensues."

Octav hadn't needed to go to the infirmary, but felt useful doing something. As Ainoren, his presence anywhere gave comfort to their people. Brie smiled as he walked in, making her way over.

"I'm glad you came aboard. I feel lost amongst this ship. Everything's different."

"How's it looking?"

"Everyone's prioritized. All surgeries completed. We're just catching up with broken bones and minors now."

"Anything I can help with?"

"We've some injured prisoners." She picked up a bag, "If you'll accompany me to the brig, we can see to them."

"I'll lead the way." Octav waved her to the door, taking her bag.

They walked through several smoky corridors before climbing a gangway down to a lower deck.

Stepping into the brig, Brie stifled her shock. The room, dishevelled, tables upside down, mirrors shattered. She was met with several injured Aonise. Assessing the situation, she stepped to see the former Captain Gaal, with blood pouring from a deep head wound.

"Ainoren?" Gaal asked as the pair approached him. "You've brought

275

a Doctor?"

"I'm Doctor Brie. Let me see that head."

Raising his eyes at her, his mark flickered his annoyance. "Feel free." He pointed to the large gash.

Brie pulled out a wrist scanner, attached it, and then took a closer look at the gaping gash over Gaal's left eye. The scanner beeped. Octav watched her work, closing the wound neatly.

"You've a bad concussion. No permanent damage. But you also have a severely dislocated arm. It will need popping back into its socket."

"Not now," he moaned. "Patch me up. I must assist with the evacuation."

"You're still suspended," Octav said.

"I might be suspended, but I know protocol more than anyone else does. If this ship is going down, we need order, not chaos."

Captain Sard's voice came through on the comms. "Ainoren, shields on Deck Six are failing. We're moving personnel as quickly as possible. They're starting to panic. Can you assist?"

"Give us a moment. We'll assist where we can."

Octav turned back to Gaal. "I couldn't agree more." Instinct told him still not to trust Gaal or Sard, investigation pending or not. But, needs must.

"Let's get your arm set before you do anything else," Brie commanded. "Your health is my priority."

"Getting everyone off my ship safely is mine," Gaal retorted, glaring at Octav.

Octav held his stare. Defiant, yet so protective. "I'll allow it. You may assist. But know this," he said, needing to keep his new admiration to himself, "this isn't your ship anymore."

Brie reached, pulled hard, then pushed on his arm, and Gaal screamed. He then just as suddenly smiled. Almost pain-free. "Allow me to redeem myself. Please?"

"This is for the pain," Brie hit him with an injection, and proceeded to wrap a sling around the old Captain's neck, manoeuvring his arm into it.

Octav asked her, "It won't impair him in any way, will it?"

"No," she shook her head, looking around the room. "If you wish to go, I'll be fine here."

"Are you sure?"

"I'll get Security to see me safe."

"This brig should be one of the first sections we move," Gaal stated.

Octav turned to the Security Officers standing by the door. "When she's finished, escort her to your evac point. Don't let her go back to the med bay."

276

The security guards saluted, and Octav motioned for Gaal to stand. "We're needed. Care to join me on Deck Six? The outer shields are failing."

Eyes darkening, Gaal replied, "That's a Heiako bay."

"They need assistance. And you did offer your help. You'll come with me."

TRAPPED

CAPTAIN HADI STOOD WITH KENDRO on the *Sol'Ishar*'s bridge. Several of the hundred shuttles disembarked from the *Sol'Delka*, the first to leave with evacuees.

"It's a slow process," Hadi said, bringing up a 3D image for Kendro. "I don't even know where we'll put them."

"Anywhere we can, Captain."

"We're overcrowded as it is!" Hadi stated the obvious, hoping his King could alleviate his fears.

"I know." Kendro placed a hand on Hadi's shoulder. "What else is there? Leave them?"

"No," he moaned. *Thank Ari for Octav's work below decks, without it…*

Kendro heard it all. "Well, then. We'll squeeze them in. And we will survive."

Hadi's birthmark flickered as he placed a hand to his chest. "And our friends Chace and Octav? How are they?"

Kendro frowned. "They're scared, but Octav's enlisted Gaal. It seems to be the right decision. Vibes are coming over, satiated."

"Can Gaal be trusted?"

"If Octav believes him," Kendro dismissed the image, "there must be something in it."

"What does Sard say?"

"The Heiako bays need calm, they need the Ainoren."

Hadi stepped closer to their main viewer, staring at the screen. Kendro didn't pry, but wondered what he was thinking. Instead, he waited.

"If we run out of time, I have one idea." Hadi faced his crew.

Kendro's frown showed Hadi his worry. Hadi spoke to the King

278

anyway. "Well," moving back to his console, tapping in a few commands, "the original ships were designed to—"

Kendro saw the issue. "Don't both ships require engine capacity to manoeuvre?"

"Yes, I think I can pilot her in the correct position. It would be much easier to evacuate the forward decks if we could dock them together."

"It's your call," Kendro conceded.

Captain Hadi swallowed. The decision weighed on him.

With a click, a different 3D image popped up of their two ships. With Hadi issuing more conning commands, they moved closer to each other, and within seconds, the two images connected.

"I believe in you." Kendro touched his arm. "I don't think you'd suggest it, if you couldn't do it."

"I'll clear it with the Ainoren."

"No need. Coordinate with Sard."

The comms beeped loudly. Officer Lynj spoke out. "Captain, I have the infirmary wishing to talk to the King regarding pilot Chace."

Captain Hadi nodded. "Take it in my office. I'll speak to Sard."

Kendro moved towards the office, stepping inside. He sat at Hadi's desk. With a swipe of his hand, he opened the comms visuals to the infirmary.

"What's happening?"

"Your Highness." Nurse Ouise couldn't meet the King's gaze. "He woke a few minutes ago. His vitals are dropping fast. I can't get hold of Brie or Jaack, should I sedate again?"

Kendro thought of Octav stuck on the other ship, his heart sank. "I'll be right there." Signing off, he left the office.

Hadi walked straight over. "Is it bad?"

"Don't inform Octav."

"Sire," Hadi pleaded, "he should know if something's wrong."

"Not yet," Kendro replied firmly.

At the King's decision, Captain Hadi nodded. *But what if it's the end?*

Out into the corridor, Kendro met with concerned stares from all crewmembers. He dismissed them and continued on, pausing, taking a deep breath, then turned away from the infirmary. Instead, he walked with purpose straight for his own quarters. One chance.

Their door hissed open, Kendro whirled in shouting, "Mika."

Mika appeared, running to him. "Oh, Ari, why is this happening to us?"

"We must be strong. For everyone." Kendro wrapped his arms around her, taking comfort in her warmth. "I believe Ari has a plan."

"Your visions about the Zefron were right?"

"They were right about one ship surviving." He sighed. "They were wrong about how many of us lived. We'll survive well enough, my love."

"Please bring Octav back. I can't bear him being on that ship."

A hiss behind them made them both turn.

Six-cycles-old Taliri stood rubbing his eyes in the doorway. Mika raised her hand to scold him back into his room, but Kendro reached out, stopping her. "I've come for him."

"You can't, I won't let you."

Taliri stepped from his secret room. "I understand why, Mother." He held his pale hand out towards his father. Kendro took it in his, hoisting him onto his hip.

"You can't take him out there. Everyone will know!"

"They won't know a thing." Kendro shifted Taliri's weight until it was comfortable. "They'll just see me with a child. If anyone asks—he's sick."

"But—" Mika fussed Taliri's long hair from his eyes, smoothing it over his elaborate birthmark.

"We'll be back, Mother, I promise."

Kendro went for the door, palming it open again. Taliri waved goodbye as Mika let out a small sob.

Kendro carried Taliri towards their personal lift, shifting him from one hip to the other. "I can't believe how big you are."

"Are you disappointed in me?"

What? Kendro shocked, stopped walking. "No, I just wish tha—"

"I could have a childhood."

"Well, yes."

Taliri reached out, and touched his fathers face. "If Ari wishes it, it will be."

So young, yet so wise. Kendro's thoughts whirled. He came to the lift, waiting, and then, stepped inside, all the while not knowing what to say to his son. *We must spend more time together.*

"The infirmary?" Taliri asked.

"Yes," said Kendro. "There's a very sick man who needs our help."

"Chace—I know. We can help him together, Father."

Not one Aonise roamed the corridors they traversed. They were all busy in preparation for the incoming evacuees.

Kendro slowed as they reached the infirmary.

Taliri squirmed in his grip. "I will walk in."

Taliri straightened himself, looking as tall as could be, yet his blue eyes wavered. So small. Kendro tempted to hold his hand again, but refrained, knowing his son would want to do this alone. "Just do—"

"—speak." Taliri's birthmark flickered, pale blue.

Kendro smiled, walking them in, pride filling his core.

Nurse Ouise rushed over on seeing the King. She noticed Taliri and took a step back. "Is he hurt?"

"No. One of the bridge's crewmembers." Kendro patted the top of Taliri's head. "There's much going on up there, so I have him with me. Can you show us to Chace?"

"Of course." Ouise turned away. "Follow me."

Kendro and Taliri followed. At Chace's room, Kendro added. "We're fine from here. You may leave us."

"Do you want me to look after the boy?"

"No, thank you." Kendro opened the door, allowing Taliri inside first. He followed. The King locked the door, moving to close each blind.

Propped up with several pillows, Chace stared at Taliri as the boy edged towards his bedspace. He met Kendro's eyes with a flicker of his mark. "No!"

Kendro placed a finger to his lips, shush. With a quick lift, Kendro popped Taliri onto the bed, and he sank into the soft quilt before sliding himself closer to Chace.

"I'm Taliri." He held out a delicately birthmarked hand.

Chace hesitated, staring at the boy, and looked to Kendro for approval. Kendro was not surprised. His own eyes flashed with a quick burst of croex. Sparks flew as he wiped out the camos inside the room. Next, Kendro removed Chace's ankle monitor, smashing it beneath a boot.

"It's all right," Kendro assured. "He means well."

"But?" Chace took Taliri's hand in his. As soon as their skin connected, Taliri's croex surfaced. His bright blue eyes darkened, his birthmark lighting the room with several colours.

Chace swallowed. "You can't..."

Father. Taliri motioned for Kendro. *Will you explain what I must do?*

Kendro took a seat at Chace's opposite side. "Look at me, Chace."

Chace faced Kendro. "Don't fear." He touched Chace's bare arm, feeling his clammy, rough birthmark. Without this, he knew Chace would die. "I'm being honest. We're here to break your bond with Octav."

"You can't." Chace tried to pull away from Taliri. "I won't let you!" But the boy's croex was phenomenal.

"Trust us," said Kendro.

Chace's heart beat faster, his breathing erratic.

"Chace—take a deep breath," Kendro stated, firmly vocalizing what Taliri murmured within his mind. "Trust in your King."

"Octav doesn't know you're doing this." Chace still panicked. "He'll think something's happened."

"There's no other way." Kendro nodded towards Taliri. "He can't know, or we wouldn't be successful here."

Chace's breathing slowed. The blood flow to his birthmark had almost stopped. "I—I—"

Taliri's croex filled the room with static. Chace witnessed the building croex inside him and around the room. His face paled all the more in realisation.

Keep his attention from me.

Kendro reached out, tugging Chace's face so their eyes locked. "Trust me."

"I do. I trust you." Tears streamed, and Chace's hands shook. "I'm sorry."

Taliri steadied the shake, his croex seeping into Chace's hand from his own, curling and entwining around the dead birthmark.

Now.

Octav and Gaal assisted the soldiers stationed between Decks Six and Seven, herding the Heiako through to safer areas as quickly as they could. It was hard to keep everyone moving quickly without the panic. As good-natured a species as they were, everyone's tempers were fraying now.

"These shields aren't going to hold out," Gaal shouted above the noise of a hundred scrabbling men, women, and children.

Octav raised his left hand, hurling a blast of croex into the air. All eyes turned. Scared. Octav stared into the face of a young boy, who'd stifled a scream. Octav winked the once, and shouted for all to hear. "We can only move you out if you are calm. Remember your heritage. Who we are! Three at a time through the corridors! Rescue shuttles on their way."

The silent room stopped panicking, the soldiers allowing them to move through slowly into the next bay once again.

Octav slipped inside, instructing Gaal. "I'll do what I can with the controls."

Gaal didn't have time for protest. Octav watched him disappear as he made his own way to a mains console. Reaching it, Octav realised the extensive damage the jayux had made. Removing the front clips, he pulled out and secured an unbroken screen. Above his head, sparks ignited as the power found another alternative, a dangerous route. He was now able to input new codes, along with different paths for the stored power to help with their systems. He grimly set to work.

"Watch out!" Gaal shouted, appearing at the door.

Octav just had a chance to look up as a piece of metal sheered away from one of the ships support beams. Without Gaal's warning, Octav would not have seen it, let alone jumped to his left, as it slammed into the console. A cloud of dust covered him, pain exploding from his leg. The beam had him pinned.

Moving wasn't an option, he couldn't.

Gaal struggled against the fleeing citizens as dust and rubble stretched before him, and he could no longer make out the Ainoren.

"Keep moving!" Gaal pushed the scared citizens on.

At Gaal's command, soldiers urged them on, the lines moving once again. Without waiting for an answer, Gaal shouted, "I'm going in for the Ainoren." He tapped one of the soldier's arms, pointing into the dust cloud towards Octav's last position.

Kendro watched in awe as Taliri's croex centred on Chace's hand, spreading through his body.

This will hurt us all, Father.

Kendro braced himself. "Steady, now," he said aloud, knowing nothing would prepare Chace for this ordeal.

Taliri reached forward into Chace's chest. There he snatched hold of his Routui. Chace cried out. Kendro held on all the tighter through Chace's pain.

"Keep focussed," Kendro spoke clearly. "Breathe. You can get through this."

The strands connecting Taliri to Chace were knotted, and feeding off each other. Where blue met blue, sparks electrified. Kendro could now see the physical bond between Octav and Chace, green entwined with blue, but only in parts. Taliri selected each strand carefully, lifting one away like pulling building blocks from a messy toddler's game. Slow and deliberate.

One.

By.

Agonizing.

One.

Chace gritted his teeth.

Octav coughed, squinting through the dust. He tested, one hand before him, bumping and stopping against something hard. The beam. He pushed. But it wasn't moving.

He coughed more as his chest tightened. Pain blasted through him like nothing he'd ever experienced before. He screamed.

"Octav!" Gaal shouted, narrowing in on his position.

Octav tried focusing, hearing mostly his own wheezing. No commands now, only a brief, "Here."

283

Gaal's face appeared over him in amongst the rubble. Then, a hand came through a gap, touching Octav's arm. "You hurt? Or just trapped?"

"Pain. Leg's broken," he let out a gasp, "and stuck, can't move."

Gaal pushed on the beam, and as he tried to lift it, Octav screamed out again.

"What?" Gaal said.

Octav sucked in the dust the shifting had caused. Immediately irritating, he coughed. "Keep trying."

As Kendro watched, Taliri carefully separated each entwined strand with a delicacy he didn't think even he possessed. Chace's essence was extracted from Octav's.

With each pull, Chace flinched, and all Kendro could do was hold on. The ache they all felt crossed their connection. The trio worked in pain.

"I can't move it," Gaal finally screamed at Octav. "I'm going for help!"

Octav felt the pain in his chest worsening. His leg was well, and truly, stuck. He knew in his heart as his birthmark flashed green, lighting up the beam around him in a sick hue—there was nothing Gaal could do.

Ripping at his shirt, Octav strained his neck, peering down. *What is this?* Chace's signature mark had faded. "No!" he cried out.

Octav could see Gaal searching for anything that might help prise the beam away. He stopped rummaging. Octav followed his line of sight to a piece of metal piping. With a heave, Gaal lifted it, then grappling it into position.

"I've got to try." Gaal panted. "There's a space below you. Slide yourself to it."

One last stab caught Octav off guard. Clutching his chest, he tried fighting for Chace. But suddenly, as grief hit him, he fell back, hard, off his elbows that had propped him up though this ordeal.

Chace's bond had broken. Octav felt every piece of himself seem to flicker then drain away. Until, with a bellow, the blast of croex Octav threw out used more force than anyone could have anticipated.

Gaal bellowed out as the green hit him. Rocketing him backwards alongside the beam, they both slammed into a wall. The shield in the bay fluctuated—bright sparks of croex pulsed in a rainbow of colours, and then vanished.

Moments later, an emergency siren brought Octav around. Sharp blaring was piercing his ears. He looked up. Debris still covered everything. "Gaal!" Octav called.

No answer.

His legs reminded Octav something was broken. But seeing a crumpled body ahead of him, he pushed up, his elbows nearly failing to keep him upright. Agonizing stabs ripped through him with each pull, but Octav managed to crawl forward.

Gaal lay unconscious.

Octav shook him. "Captain!"

No response. Octav tapped his comms. Nothing but static came through. "Gaal, you've got to come to. I can't get you out of here on my own."

The pain in Octav's chest ached more than he could bear. He curled next to Gaal.

Nothing left to live for. Ready to die when the shields failed. Chace was gone.

BROKEN

KENDRO COULD FEEL CHACE AND Octav slipping away from him. He willed his son to finish quickly, relief flooding his mind when Taliri let Chace's Routui go.

I hope it's enough.

The young pilot collapsed back into the pillows. The sparks around the room vanished, along with the pain the King felt himself.

It is done, Father. They are no longer bonded.

Kendro let out a sigh of relief. "I must get word to Octav that Chace still lives."

"T—tell him—" Chace stuttered, as slight colour returned to his facial mark, "—I love him, please."

"Chace, you must rest." Kendro placed a hand on Chace's arm, feeling through their connection what Taliri had accomplished. "The poison within your system should die now. But we don't know for sure…" Kendro reached for Taliri's hand, feeling his son's weariness. "I'll send your message. Now, I must get Taliri back."

Kendro paused for one moment, observing with the most solemn of expressions. Chace closed his eyes, then let sleep take him some place he deserved to go.

Taliri hopped off the bedspace, wobbling. Kendro picked him up. "Don't worry, my son, you can sleep, too," the King whispered, kissing his forehead.

On the way out, Kendro spoke to Ouise. "Leave him to rest. I'll get the boy back to his mother." Quickly, they left the med bay heading towards a lift.

Taliri squirmed in his grip. *You must go to the bridge. Father.*

Kendro stopped walking, allowing Taliri to the floor. "Bu—"

286

I can make my own way home.

Kendro watched as his son walk away, head held high, leaving him no choice, but to go on, alone.

Kendro commed for Captain Hadi at the nearest main station. Hadi's image popped on screen. "How is Chace?" he asked immediately, eyes wide.

"He's recovering. I must get word to Octav."

"I'm sorry, Your Highness." Hadi frowned, his birthmark flickering. "There's been another explosion. Octav was with Gaal. We can't raise either of them on comms."

No! Not after our success with Chace!

"We're trying everything we can to get hold of him," Hadi reported. "Though Gaal's vitals through his prison monitor aren't looking good."

Kendro clenched his fists together. Taliri's 'you must go' had been right. His eyes flashed blue as anger took hold. "Try harder!"

Captain Hadi didn't dare argue. "Yes, Your Highness." He moved to Officer Lynj's console where she stepped out of the way, allowing him room to comm Captain Sard.

Feeling his resolve crumbling, Kendro turned to stare down the corridor. It wasn't often he snapped like this. Using the comms smaller panel, he pulled up an image of the *Sol'Delka*, which stared right back at him, pieces drifting away as she continued breaking asunder. A myriad of pods, landed then shot off, others returning for more of his people. *This can't be happening!*

"Sire, if we can get someone back onto Deck Six, we should be able to pick up their signals." Lynj spoke from behind Hadi.

"Patch it through as soon as you can. I'm on my way," Kendro ordered, not able to watch their second vessel's demise any longer. His people were suffering on board. He could feel every pull as another life faded from his Routui. Too many deaths.

Reaching out with his mind, Kendro sought Octav's life essence. His Ainoren clung to life by a thread. "Fight, Octav. I can't lose you, too." Kendro all but collapsed against the nearest wall, the weight of everything so hard to bear.

Gritting his teeth, he tried his hardest to push for the bridge, but instead, he made for the nearest unoccupied meeting room.

Once inside, he sat, allowing himself the time to gather his strength. He wanted no one to see him like this. His withered soul ached. *How can I keep on going? Through all this!*

A moment later, and Hadi's voice came through on comms. "Your Highness, we've got a link, there is no response yet. I'm patching it through to your location now."

Kendro managed to croak out, "Thank you," then a loud static hiss echoed around the room.

"Octav," Kendro spoke, "I know you can hear me. Chace is alive."

No response.

Kendro raised his voice. "Ainoren Broki, I know you can hear me. Chace is alive."

The shields protecting Deck Six from imploding failed momentarily in a tiny section of an outer bulkhead. A hiss of oxygen lost through this fissure alerted Octav. He grasped at his chest, struggling to breathe. The pain lessened with each laboured breath, as the shields and atmosphere repressurised. But there was no fight left within him. *It's over.*

A voice in the distance shouted, but he couldn't make out the words.

Until he heard the word *alive!*

Octav tried to focus. Only the severe pain of slapping his broken leg brought him around with a gasp.

Kendro's voice boomed in his ear. "Ainoren Broki, I know you can hear me. Chace is alive."

Octav pushed himself onto his elbows. He would get them out, no matter the pain. With one hand, he tugged Gaal's shirt, and with the other, he heaved the two of them towards the main doors.

Twenty paces.

The pain in his lower leg shot through Octav with every tiny move that he made. But Chace was alive. He would not give up.

Ten paces.

The ships shields flickered once more. This time the hiss lasted much longer. Lack of oxygen and the build up of acid in Octav's system burned through his muscles. He couldn't pull Gaal any longer. Octav's adrenaline pumped through his veins so fast he thought they would burst.

He felt his life ebbing, drawing on his final reserves of croex, but he forced himself on.

Four paces.

The doors opened. Several Aonise in full suits appeared, one rushing over and placed a mask over Octav's face, and one over Gaal's, limp as he was. Kendro talked in his mind, but Octav couldn't understand any of it. *Am I finished?*

Octav sucked in a deep breath, oxygen bursting through his lungs, giving him life and hope.

Taliri stood at an intersecting corridor in his greying, sleep suit, watching the swarm of activity as citizens rushed to respective destinations. He looked ahead towards the lift that would take him home, but instead, turned right. His small legs took him somewhere else, the need to be anywhere but home, strong.

Mum will worry. But I'll be back soon.

Following a corridor, Taliri took a different lift down into the belly of the ship. He paused only once to check his bearings on a comms panel up on each bulkhead, nearly too high to read. A passerby noticed the small boy, and hefted him up for a closer look. "Here you go, son, that help?" Tiny fingers flew over the touchscreen with ease. When he knew where he was, Taliri zoomed in on the image before him. A storage room.

"Thank you, Sir." He bowed, knowing others would make such a courtesy, if he had been the one to offer his own help.

It wouldn't be too much further, so with a small wave, Taliri pressed on, further away from the safety of his family.

Moments later, a single door stood before him. There was no access panel, but he placed his palm to the cool metal. The door clicked ajar. Taliri pushed for it to open, closing it behind him.

Once inside, Taliri's mark illuminated the room. The blue glow was just enough to allow him to see.

There was nothing inside, other than a small box. Taliri approached carefully. It was no larger than he was, nor wider than the width of his slight shoulders. Placing his hand on it, Taliri felt vibrations from within. He spoke. "You're alive?"

A female voice resonated inside his mind. *I await final instruction, Your Highness.*

What is this? Taliri asked.

You are not, King?

Not yet!

Then leave. I await instruction, but not from you. This was her brusque reply.

Taliri felt her words stab at him. He turned around knowing he needed to leave as commanded, yet his feet wouldn't allow him.

Leave now, Taliri. We're not to meet yet. You're too young. Her voice, calmer, filled him with hope. *Come back soon.*

His feet moved then and he stepped away. *I will return to you.*

Taliri left the room, heading back towards the lift, which would take him home.

As the lift carried him higher, his thoughts filled with dread. Placing his palm to the controls, he stopped it.

He wanted to comm his father, but didn't. He waited a moment, keying in commands. The lift started once more, and then a moment later, he reached his destination—below the Royal chambers.

Taliri opened the door, peering out. No one occupied the corridor. He was alone. Yet, he knew he wasn't. No sooner had he stepped out of the lift, someone moved at the opposite end of long space.

Taliri placed a palm to the panel. He gave the command 'do not return,' allowing the lift to move off.

Small as I am. He walked slowly forward, breathing in deep. *I can do this.*

He stood waiting in the corridor as the shadow moved towards him. Appearing before him, a man, dressed in a long cloak with a hood. He lowered his head, slipping the hood back to reveal one of the most intricate birthmark's Taliri had seen. Taliri thought for a moment. He knew this man. But how, he wasn't sure. Taliri's croex flickered to the surface, preparing for the worst.

"Do not be alarmed," the man said.

Why are you're hiding beneath my mother's chambers?

The man's green birthmark flickered. "You do not speak?"

No, Taliri lied. *Who are you? What do you want?*

"I wanted to see your mother to confirm. But I see a very different truth." The man smiled.

Taliri knew he saw much more than he let on. A Seer.

You know who I am?

Lowering his head, bending to one knee, the man looked straight into Taliri's face. "Yes, Your Highness."

Who are you?

"I am yours to command." His gaze constant, the man was so sure of himself. "My name, irrelevant, but your father calls me Wez."

Taliri held out a hand, croex sparking, awaiting a connection. As Wez lifted his, they made contact. Green met blue and became something entirely new.

I see who you are. Your intentions?

"I'm true to the Royal House."

Taliri felt it. Wez's honesty shone through. *There are those who doubt you?*

Wez nodded. "And you?"

I have seen the truth. We must keep in touch. But for now, leave.

Captain Hadi stood on the bridge, thoughts of hope, love, their future, all while surveying his view screen. Could they finally be close to resting?

Watching his crew, he read their demeanour. The Zefron had been relentless. Each face reflected those struggles, personally and emotionally, pushing all to their limits.

Sard appeared on a side screen before him. "We have Octav and Gaal within the safe zone."

"Thank Ari."

"I'll be sending them over on the next shuttle with Doctor Brie."

"Injuries?"

"Octav has severe internal bleeding. A broken leg. Captain Gaal is much worse. We have him in a support unit. It was some secondary explosion. I don't know what caused it."

Behind his shoulder, Hadi heard the nervous reaction to these reports from his crew.

"Brie has high hopes that with the proper care they will both survive," Sard added.

"Thank you, Captain," Hadi replied cutting the comms. There was still some hope.

Vax placed a hand on his shoulder. "They're coming home."

Hadi breathed out a sigh of relief. Ari was finally on their side.

To their left, Officer Lynj monitored all of the ships vital signals. She studied Hadi and Vax, so wrapped up in their relief, she couldn't bear disturbing them.

Hadi felt her stare, heard her monitor bleeping. Facing her, he demanded, "Report."

Officer Lynj swallowed before answering. "I believe its First Contact, Captain."

Hadi whirled back around, facing the viewer before them. His crew left their posts to take a closer look.

There, indeed, before them all spanned a new solar system. One bright sun glowed at its centre.

"We made it," Hadi let out a breath, thoughts flickering to only Katya and their unborn child. "We've made it."

His crew let out cries of joy, clapping, and they all turned towards him.

Lynj gently placed a hand on his shoulder. "Please, let everyone know. They're all waiting for this news."

Hadi turned to Reel, who brought up ships wide comms in a second from the nearest post.

Hadi swallowed, preparing. "Citizens of the last surviving Aonise vessel, we have reached the planet Earth."

Kendro finally wandered the corridors that led back toward the bridge, more than exhausted, but thankful that things seemed to be turning in their favour. He felt everyone's relief through his Routui. It gave him the strength to push on, despite wanting to curl up and hide from all those that loved him.

Kendro didn't notice three hooded figures up ahead, until he was almost upon them. Immediately, he sensed trouble, stopping in his tracks. *What now?*

The men didn't move from their awkward positions. Kendro looked around, feeling inside his pocket for his reader. It wasn't there. The King had no time for this. Should he turn, and backtrack? But, no, ruffians like these wouldn't hesitate to follow. He knew they would catch him.

Kendro reached inside for defensive croex, but it was so low, he could do nothing to defend himself.

As the men moved closer, they each removed their hood. One to the left, Lieutenant Euro, the one on the right Kendro knew as Trax, the seer.

The man in the middle wasn't anyone Kendro recognised, but the fact the man's harnessed croex was flashing golden shadows all around him meant more than trouble.

Their eyes locked and Kendro knew—

—knew this might be the end, his end.

Dalamaar!

"It is good to finally meet you, Kendro." Dalamaar stopped, facing him, allowing Kendro to see his fully harnessed powers.

A shiver ran down Kendro's spine. Images of Mika and Taliri flashed through his mind.

"Why are you here?" Kendro asked, trying with all his might to be able to pull some croex from within. Still nothing.

Dalamaar's perfect smile greeted Kendro joined by a laugh. "I thought it was time you met the next King."

"You'll never be King."

Dalamaar's croex lashed out, grabbing Kendro by the throat. "If your wife wasn't pregnant, I would crush you now.

Kendro struggled for breath, feeling the life he had slipping away. *It can't end like this. We are here. This planet, Earth, should be the happy end to our tale!*

Dalamaar stepped closer, face-to-face with Kendro who sank to the floor, and the intruder confided, "I know my limits. Your skills are needed to negotiate us safe passage on whatever this planet Earth turns out to be." Slackening off his strong hold, Dalamaar allowed Kendro to breathe. "Then, I will be coming for your son—and the throne."

Kendro managed enough croex to push Dalamaar away, gasping for breath. "You can't, you're not powerful enough," the King spat towards him. "You and your sister are an abomination. The failing of our species, not its salvation!"

Dalamaar turned his back on the King. "No, Kendro. You are not powerful enough. I am going to kill your wife and son. And I will be the next Aonise King."

THE END

MAIN CHARACTERS

Note: Please be aware not all characters are listed.

House Niakrex

Kendro M'akshaw – House Leader, King of all Aonise
Mika M'akshaw – Devoted Queen
Octav Broki – Ainoren and Second in Command to Kendro
Frie Broki – Mate of Octav, no children
Lyrik Horr – Special Opps reports to Octav
Roma Horr – Mate of Lyrik, 3 sons

House Magalite

Polr Howd – House Leader
Jea Howd – Mate of Polr, 2 daughters
Ins Shal – Jea's sister, no children
Raki Shal – Mate of Ins
Maz Ritck – Second in Command, no children
Frac Ritck – Mate of Maz

House Flikait

Madrall Criaic– House Leader
Sorea Criaic– Mate of Madrall, a son and daughter
Fylix Teno – Single, 1 son
Ij'la Fla – Mate to Kivt
Kivt Fla – Madrall's brother, mate to Ij'la
Retray Mak – Second in Command, a second generation seer, wife and two sons

House Sonaya

Emmi Dres – House Leader
Chiki Dres – Sister of Emmi, a total problem child
Anrel Forst – Potential mate of Emmi, also second in Command
Grie Stron – Mate of Donos
Donos Stron – 2 daughters, 1 son
Sylv Forst – Younger brother to Anrel

FLEET SHIPS AND OTHER CHARACTERS

The *Sol'Ishar*

Captain Sheve Hadi – Mate of Katya
Doctor Katya Brie - Main Ships Doctor
Doctor Vawn
Commander Vax
Science Officer Lynj
Chief Engineer Zyler

Fighter Pilots/Special Opps

Veco
Chace
Hanya

The *Sol'Delka*

Captain Mkl Gaal
Commander Sard
Doctor Jaack
Wez – Kendro's First Generation Seer

The *Sol'Tar*

Captain Della
Commander Mas

The *Sol'Rayn*

Captain Brayer

Heiako

Petty Officer Cryz – 1 daughter
Lace Grec – Engineer
Sylkx Grec – Son of Lace
Kale – Barman and partner to Chace
Hax – Young Engineer
Demak – Oldest and most important Engineer

The Bad Guys

Dalamaar Katesh
Trax – Dalamaar's right hand man
Yuko – Assassin

AONISE LANGUAGE

Ainoren – Admiral/General
Atrei – water
Ari – Their God
Ascendere – Assension, passing on
Bea – A leafy tea drink
Bedspace – Bed
Calmarix Shruz – Who are you?
Croex – power/energy
Capax – capacity
Crulang – Medicinal smelling herb
Dregnot – Med equipment
Garbael – meat dish
Gibri – Torture tool
Guin – drug administration device
Holosnap – Hologram
Helix beam – Tractor beam
Jayux - Large Jump
Jeno – baby – my love
Malloth – maggot – derogatory term
Malinga – arthritis of the spine
Maicrox – First Trimester – pregnancy
Micret – Kendro's favourite dinner
Nelliss – Tractor Beam
Nasci – Anti-natal energy device
Octo – Left
Pentax – Right
Powex – Safety chamber
Puswer – Swear word
Rakia – Meds
Rastrom – Med equipment
Reingo – Alcoholic drink
Reswae – floating bed
Rieatte – meaning 'Bond of three'
Routui – magical core, heart.
Sietev – First post – main computer, merging
Suzrai – Bright yellow suns ray
Scrie – Centre
Triaon – Sister/friend
Tricu – small jump
Tripax – Large machine, like Crane
Triaton – Anniversary

Trrobhas – Trousers
Trax webs – Like a spider web
Trexon – Dopamine levels. Doctor's terms for Aonise power levels
Wielse – Small creature from their world
Yenjo – Aonise alcohol
Xions – Electric eye pieces

ACKNOWLEDGEMENTS

I would like to mention the following people, who each deserve recognition and more than a hug or two.

For my partners in crime - Steven Kogan and Jamie Bengzon. They each added to TSK and its vast world something of themselves—from Stephen's penned episodes in the TV series to the fantastic character animations that Jaime is working on for an animated short film.

To the very good friends who have kept me going through my many ups and downs, Melvin Johnson and Chris Murphy. You really are the best. To Jerry Quinn and the Ubergroup for being uber-awesome and to the beta readers in my cycle.

Huge, huge thanks to my team TZBF, for their extra hard work. Especially, Stephen Kittel, Ani King, and Jason Smith.

And finally, to EJ Runyon and Rogena Mitchell-Jones, who helped me where no one else could.

Without each of you, my world would have been a dark and sad place. Thank you, each of you, for the joy you bring to me and to my life. This book is the result of all of your continued support. Now I'm really looking forward to the next one!

ABOUT THE AUTHOR

DAWN CHAPMAN has been creating sci fi and fantasy stories for thirty years. Until 2005 when her life and attention turned to scripts, and she started work on The Secret King, a 13 episode Sci Fi TV series, with great passion for this medium.

In 2012, Dawn returned to her first love of prose. She's been working with coach EJ Runyon who's encouraged her away from fast paced script writing, to revel in the world of TSK and Lethảo as an epic prose space journey.

She's had success with a web series, co-written with Melvin Johnson, produced by Nandar Entertainment, and a short film Irobe, also co-written. This year her experience of working with Producers/Directors from the US and AUS has expanded. From Drama, Sci Fi to Action, Dawn's built a portfolio of writing, consulting, and publishing

45647464R00184

Made in the USA
Charleston, SC
30 August 2015